# A Taste of Danger...

Kiss me!" Rose clapped her fingers over her mouth. She hadn't meant to blurt it out like that. "That is, Sir Blade," she said, "Would ye do me the honor o' grantin' me a kiss?"

"Nae." The word was cold, hard, final. "I won't be used in such a manner."

She gulped. "I meant no offense," she whispered. "'Tis only that I've never had a kiss, not a proper one."

Blade's voice was a low growl. " Do ye expect a disgraced felon to give ye a *proper* kiss?"

His words dizzied her. But Rose wasn't afraid. He wouldn't hurt her. She *knew* he wouldn't. "Aye."

The hands that seized her jaw weren't gentle. They were demanding. His harsh stubble scraped across her cheek without a care for her delicate skin. And his mouth... His mouth consumed her like liquid fire.

She should have detested his touch. 'Twas rough and brutal and shocking. She should have fought her way free, wiped his cruel kiss from her mouth.

But she didn't want to.

Book design and illustration by Richard Campbell

Glynnis Campbell – Publisher
P. O. Box 341144
Arleta, California 91331
ISBN-10: 1938114043
ISBN-13: 978-1-938114-04-5
Contact:glynnis@glynnis.net

*May your life be about the journey and not the destination!*

# Passion's Exile

# Glynnis Campbell

*Glynnis Campbell* (signature)

**Glynnis Campbell - Publisher**

10/14

# PASSION'S EXILE
Glynnis Campbell


Other books by Glynnis Campbell:

KNIGHTS DE WARE TRILOGY
My Champion
My Warrior
My Hero

WARRIOR MAIDS OF RIVENLOCH
Lady Danger (writing as Sarah McKerrigan)
Captive Heart (writing as Sarah McKerrigan)
Knight's Prize (writing as Sarah McKerrigan)

Danger's Kiss (writing as Sarah McKerrigan)

Captured by Desire (writing as Kira Morgan)
Seduced by Destiny (writing as Kira Morgan)

For my brother Brenn,
who sometimes deems himself unworthy,
but is always welcome home.

Thank you for Sancho and Pancho,
Trolly and Wishvicky,
Sewers Beer, pine-needle forts,
and wacky radio dramas,
and remember, I am co-captain of the team.

Did you say it?  Did you say it?
(Maniacal laughter)

## Acknowledgments

Thanks to
Olivia Hussey and Viggo Mortensen
and the kids from
The Highly Gifted Magnet
of North Hollywood,
in particular,
Thomas Hanff, Bryan Haut,
and Daniel Souleles,
who were endlessly amusing and inspiring
and are herein immortalized.

# *Chapter 1*

AVERLAIGH MANOR
NEAR DUNBLANE, SCOTLAND
SPRING 1391

Rosamund tickled the downy feathers of her falcon's throat, cooing softly to the bird. Wink's talons gripped her leather glove, and the falcon cocked its head, studying her mistress's curving lips with its one good eye.

"Such a bonnie lass," Rose purred, bobbing her arm to make Wink spread her splendid wings.

The falcon might be maimed, but to Rose, Wink was the most beautiful bird in her mother's mews. Rose's gaze roamed over the others—hooded gyrfalcons and tiercels and merlins caught in the wild, now leashed to their perches—and she furrowed her brow at the subtle reminder of her own imminent capture.

"'Twon't be so bad, Wink," she said, trying to convince herself as well as the bird. She swept her long sable hair back over her shoulder and smoothed the falcon's wings into place. "I'm sure Sir Gawter will provide a fine, warm mews for ye." And, she silently added—her brow creasing with displeasure—a fine, warm bed for *her*.

She'd met Sir Gawter of Greymoor a fortnight ago. He'd been a homecoming surprise from Lady Agatha, Rose's mother.

Because Rose had been sent away from Averlaigh at the age of seven to be fostered at faraway Fernie House for the last eleven years, she hardly remembered her mother. She definitely didn't recall having a betrothed. The news had come as a nasty shock—for her *and* for Wink.

The falcon had taken instant exception when Sir Gawter tried to kiss Rose's cheek in greeting, screeching and swooping at the man's head.

True, Rose *had* been slow to call off her bird. But 'twas only because she'd been so astonished by the kiss. Naturally, she was punished for the insult, forbidden to fly her bird.

It hadn't stopped her, of course. She'd simply removed the bells from Wink's jesses and been more secretive about her daily escapes into the countryside to exercise her pet.

But ever since, Rose had counted the weeks to her impending marriage with growing dread, as if she awaited her execution.

'Twasn't that Sir Gawter was abhorrent. He was young and tall and rather comely. He had lively blue eyes, a boyish dimple, and a fringe of golden curls. He was gallant, well-spoken, and clever. He could wield a sword and play the lute with equal agility. And he extended favors and flattery with a generous hand.

But Rose felt nothing when she was around him, other than a vague and nagging sense of doom.

Rose blew gently upon the bird's breast, riffling her feathers. "I wish I were a falcon," she sighed. *"Ye've no use for a silly husband, have ye? All ye need are the open sky and the wind under your wings."*

She glanced again around the moldering mews—at the gaps between the battered timbers and the feathers thickly littering the ground. Rose's stepfather had done nothing to keep the place up, and now that he lay dying, the decrepit pile of stones would become Sir Gawter's when they wed.

Rose couldn't imagine why he'd want it. The manor was in ruins. Riding up to Averlaigh for the first time since she was a small child, she'd experienced a pang of disappointment.

Compared to her home at Fernie House, which—though not lavishly appointed—was at least tidy and well-kept, Averlaigh looked like a withering old crone. The plaster walls of the great room were chipped and stained with char. Mice crept through the moldy rushes in the hall's corners and pattered across Rose's chamber floor at night. An odor of faint decay hung in the air within the stone walls, and outside, the once resplendent gardens were overgrown with thistles.

Rose's mother, however, seemed to have suffered no such wear. The manor might crumble apart, but Lady Agatha was careful to keep her own appearance untouched by age.

Like Rose, her complexion was the color of fresh cream, her eyes an enigmatic blend of gold and brown and green, her hair glossy black. Lady Agatha took great pains to rouge her cheeks and lips, to perfume her skin, and to keep her sumptuous garments in perfect repair.

Rose couldn't be bothered with such nonsense. She could hardly sit still to have her hair plaited, and she had no patience for the endless lacing it took to get her into her layered gowns of silk and brocade. The moment she awoke, splashed water on her face, and tossed on a kirtle, she was ready to fetch Wink for a walk through the hills or saddle a palfrey for a morning gallop.

Indeed, this morn she'd cast aside the gown of amber damask embroidered with threads of gold that the maid had laid out for her, choosing instead a sturdy kirtle of blue frieze. There was no need to fret if the hem grew soiled from the mews or the garden or the heather-cloaked knolls.

"Well, bonnie Wink, let's see what Apollo can find for your supper today."

Wink tipped her head and fluffed up her feathers, as if she understood.

Because Wink couldn't hunt for herself, she needed to rely upon skilled gyrfalcons like Apollo to bring down prey for her. But that was Wink's only concession to her impaired vision. The little falcon, as willful and impetuous as Rose herself, careened fearlessly through the sky, unconcerned with the consequences of such blind and reckless flight.

Within a short time, Apollo managed to catch a sparrow for Wink and a young rabbit for himself. Rose let the birds gorge, and by the time she returned Apollo to the mews, 'twas almost time for her own supper.

She tarried on her way to the great hall, in no hurry to sup with her betrothed. Seeing Sir Gawter only reminded her that very soon he intended to share not only meals, but a bed, children, and the rest of their lives together.

With Wink upon her glove, she ambled past the dog kennels, pausing to scratch the ears of the oldest flea-bitten hound, and pulled a thistle as she crossed the courtyard. She peered up at the ragged blue pennon fluttering from the half-collapsed tower and nodded to a maid drawing water from the well. She kicked a stray pebble through the grass until it rolled against the stone wall of the garden.

A horse whickered softly from the stables nearby. Rose slid her gaze toward the lowering sun and the long-shadowed hills in the west. There was just enough time left to visit the horses and settle Wink in her bedchamber before supper.

The groom was gone, but Rose knew which palfreys were tame and which would bite. As she crept into the hay-sweet warmth of the stable, slivers of sunlight pierced through the cracks between the timbers in long golden spears, illuminating airborne dust and bits of straw. The dun-colored gelding stamped his hoof, and the russet mare chomped noisily on a mouthful of hay.

A curious rustling of straw at the back of the stable made Rose's ears perk up. She stopped in her tracks. Silence.

Then it came again. She frowned. Rats, most likely.

But as she took one silent step forward, the rustling took on a rhythmic pattern. This time she thought she heard whispers. People.

Intrigue.

Her eyes widened. Rose knew that stables were a favored place for trysting. By the sound, 'twas indeed what transpired.

She caught her lip between her teeth. She should leave. She knew that. She should turn around and creep back out the way she came in. 'Twas probably just the groom and one of his mistresses. 'Twas sinful to spy. Sinful.

But—curse her impulsive nature—once something piqued her curiosity, Rose couldn't turn away.

Quietly, she secured Wink to a wooden post. Then she let her naughty feet propel her stealthily forward until, from behind the pillar of the last stall, she caught a glimpse of naked flesh.

They didn't see her. The couple was lost in their passion, writhing on the bed of hay, their limbs tangled, their bodies bucking in violent counterpoint, their gasping mouths fouling the air with vile and interesting words the like Rose had never heard.

She stood gaping in fascination and revulsion. The man's bare buttocks flexed and shuddered as he pumped mercilessly against the woman's body. And yet the woman made no complaint. Instead, her ankles hooked around his waist, and her fingers clawed at his back, as if she were a spider consuming a fly. They smacked together faster and faster, their oaths turning into incoherent moans, until finally the woman shrieked, the man groaned, and they collapsed back on the straw, spent.

If Rose hadn't been so transfixed, she might have escaped unnoticed. But the man chose that moment to lift his head, and when he turned toward Rose, shock forced a slow, ragged gasp from her throat. 'Twas Sir Gawter. And beneath him, panting from her exertions, was her own mother.

Their eyes met, and for a moment no one spoke. Rose felt paralyzed, as if she'd stumbled into a nightmare where the world was cast completely awry.

"Shite," Lady Agatha finally muttered. Then she giggled weakly, laying her head back on the hay.

Gawter didn't find the situation so amusing. "What are ye doin' here?" he snarled, his normally gentle face contorted with rage.

"I...I..." Rose gagged on her words. She longed to run, to flee out the stable door and keep on running, to run until the sun

5

disappeared and the night came and the darkness blotted out all memory.

"Leave her be, Gawter," her mother said.

"I asked ye a question," he insisted.

Rose tried to look away, but her gaze seemed fixed on them. Gawter concealed his now shrunken member with a fistful of straw, but Rose knew she'd never forget the pathetic sight. And her mother lolled unabashedly on the hay, her nipples pinched and red, the black hair between her legs damp with sweat.

Rose shivered in revulsion. Gawter angrily clenched his teeth and made as if to stand, but her mother stayed him.

"I'll speak to her," she purred, smoothing the hair back from his forehead. "Get dressed, love, before the whole manor comes to see what wild beast has made such a fierce howl in the stables."

Gawter pinned Rose with a gaze like an iron spike, but he did as Lady Agatha advised, shoving his arms into his shirt and cote-hardie, stabbing his legs into his trews. Meanwhile, Agatha watched Rose with amused interest.

Rose staggered out of his way when he stepped forward, thinking he intended to pass. Instead he grabbed her by the neck and shoved her back against the wall of the stable. The back of her head thudded against the wood, splintering her sight, and his fingers tightened around her throat, crushing her windpipe.

She scrabbled at his hands, to no avail. Through a stunned haze, she heard Wink's piercing cry and the ineffectual flapping of the bird's wings against her tether.

"This changes nothin'," Gawter bit out. "Nothin'! Do ye hear? Ye'll still be my wife. Breathe a word o' this to anyone, and I'll kill ye."

Dazed breathless, she shut her eyes tightly against his horrible visage—his face flushed purple with exertion and fury, his eyes narrowed to beady slits, spittle gathering at the corner of his cruel mouth.

"Mark my words. I'll kill ye," he hissed.

He let her go then, and she collapsed forward, choking, falling to her knees on the stable floor. She didn't watch him leave, but Wink screeched at him as he passed.

"Poor bairn," Lady Agatha cooed when he had gone, her voice like honey laced with hemlock. "Ye've had a nasty startle, haven't ye? Come to your mother."

Rose clasped her bruised throat. Come to her? She couldn't even *look* at her.

"Come along, sweet." Agatha patted the straw beside her in invitation.

Rose wheezed, steadying herself against the urge to vomit. Was the woman mad? She slowly shook her head.

"Rosamund!" her mother snapped, shuffling into her discarded garments. "Don't be a shrew!"

Rose's head swam in chaotic circles of outrage and disbelief. She needed to stop her ears against her mother's strident voice. She should never have come into the stable. She should never have come back to Averlaigh at all.

Agatha picked at bits of straw clinging to her velvet sleeve. "I'm sorry," she quipped testily, "if ye were surprised by what ye saw. But Gawter is right. It changes nothin'."

Rose didn't mean to speak. She meant to remain silent until she could gather her wits to scramble to her feet and flee. But, as usual, her tongue had a will of its own.

"It changes nothin'?" she rasped. "God's blood! How can ye believe that? Ye lay with him, Mother. Ye swived him, for God's sake!"

"Faugh!" her mother warned. "Heed Gawter well. He means what he says. If ye speak o' this, those words will be your last."

Rose stared at her mother, incredulous.

Agatha came to her feet and regally smoothed her skirts. "I think, my dear Rosamund, your foster mother has neglected to teach ye the ways o' the world. Very well then. 'Tis up to me. Come." She held out a hand toward Rose.

Rose shuddered.

Agatha sighed, then crouched beside her, catching Rose's chin in a firm grip. Rose reeled from the musky smell of sex upon her. "So lovely." Agatha smiled bleakly. "I was once as lovely as ye." She ran her thumb along Rose's lower lip, and Rose jerked her head away. "But even ye—sweet and young and fresh as ye are—can't hope to satisfy the insatiable appetites o' such a man."

Rose narrowed her eyes in disgust.

"'Tisn't *ye*, dear daughter. 'Tis the way o' men. The ravenous beasts cannot be content with just one lover." She tilted her head. "Ye haven't lost your heart to him, have ye?"

"Nae," Rose said between clenched teeth. "Ne'er."

Agatha smiled. "That's my little lady. Then there's no harm in it, is there? He'll wed ye and bed ye, and ye'll have the bairns..." She strangled on the word, then recovered with a fleeting smile. "The bairns I can no longer bear."

Rose clamped her lips shut, fearing she might retch at any moment.

"But ye understand why ye mustn't tell, don't ye?" Agatha spoke to her as if she were still a child of six. The last of the sunlight faded from the fissures in the stable walls, limning Agatha's face with ominous shadows. "We'd lose Averlaigh, wouldn't we? And we can't have that."

If she expected a docile response from Rose, she was disappointed. 'Twas all Rose could do to bite back a scream of fury.

"Run along now, poppet," Agatha bade her, patting the top of Rose's head before she could duck away. "And remember, 'tis our secret."

Somehow Rose found the will to rise, collect her falcon, and walk out of the stable. But 'twas at a nightmare's sluggish pace that she crossed the courtyard and climbed the steps to her chamber. She closed the door behind her and slumped back against it, her body limp, her senses numb.

Wink's impatient fluttering roused Rose from her stupor, and the twisted truth of what she'd witnessed suddenly curdled like poison in her belly. With a sickly groan, she staggered across the room and dove for the basin. There she retched and retched, till nothing was left but the bitter taste of betrayal.

"Oh, Wink," she whispered weakly. Lifting the jug of water with trembling fingers, she rinsed her mouth and spat into the bowl. Then she wiped the cold sweat from her brow. "God's wounds, what will we do?"

She sank onto her bed, loosening Wink's jesses and letting the bird hop up on her perch. Once she'd seen the pitiful condition of the mews, Rose had insisted upon keeping Wink in her own chamber, and in such close quarters, the falcon had become her closest ally. Even now, the bird, as if understanding Rose's distress, started scuttling anxiously back and forth along the wooden perch.

Rose, too, paced across the threadbare carpet, her mind whirling with images of her mother's depravity. Nae, she'd never accept Lady Agatha's solution, never submit to life with an incestuous adulterer. The thought of what they'd done...

"We have to go," she muttered, biting at her thumb. "We have to leave Averlaigh."

She fingered her battered throat. There was no question in her mind. Sir Gawter was dangerous. He'd meant what he'd said—he'd kill her if she revealed his sin.

"On the morrow," she decided, "before anyone wakes." Now that she'd made the decision, her heart raced like that of a loosed falcon. But where would she go?

She could think of only one refuge. "Fernie House. We'll go back to Fernie House."

Wink bobbed in agreement from her perch. Rose flung open the oak chest at the foot of her bed and began tossing linen chemises and satin slippers and velvet kirtles atop the mattress.

'Twas a desperate flight, a perilous one. All manner of outlaws and wild beasts frequented the roads. And she had no idea what she'd do once she reached Fernie House.

But what choice did she have?

"We'll watch out for each other, won't we, Wink?"

Still, as she stuffed her garments into a large satchel and slipped her eating knife into the small sheath at her hip, she began to doubt the wisdom of such a reckless escape.

Fernie House was near St. Andrews, at least a four days' ride. And this time, she wouldn't be traveling with guards. 'Twas an enormous risk for any fugitive, even greater for a lass alone. Worst of all, once Sir Gawter noticed her missing, he'd send his men to hunt her down.

Who could she trust? Who would accompany her? She'd only been at Averlaigh for a fortnight. She knew no one.

She dropped onto the edge of her bed again, chewing at her nail. There had to be a way... People traveled to St. Andrews all the time.

Some vague memory teased at the edges of her mind. She'd heard something recently, something about a pilgrimage...

She sprang to her feet, startling Wink.

At chapel last Sabbath, the father had announced a pilgrimage traveling from Stirling to St. Andrews. Stirling was only a half-day's ride from Averlaigh. If she joined that pilgrimage...

A lass might travel in safety in the company of pilgrims.

The priest had said they were to gather at an inn for the journey. What was the name of it? The Black Boar? Nae, The Black Hound.

The pilgrims were leaving the morn of Saint Anselm's Day. Rose quickly calculated the day on her fingers. Her heart plunged. Tomorrow was Saint Anselm's.

But she refused to be daunted. It could be done. She'd have to pilfer a horse and steal away at nightfall. She'd have to pray the road was well-marked and free of thieves and wolves. And she'd have to ride like the wind to reach Stirling before daybreak. 'Twas a bold plan, full of risk. But she could do it.

"Besides, Wink," she said somberly, unlacing her soiled blue kirtle, "I suspect we'll be safer tonight in the woods than within these walls."

She was mistaken.

Sir Gawter was already having her watched.

Rose never noticed the spies' vigilant eyes as, hours later—clothed in a fresh linen underdress, her best surcoat of scarlet velvet, and her brown woolen cloak—she quietly led her mother's palfrey from the stable, mounted up, and set out from Averlaigh.

She'd ridden several miles along the road toward Stirling when she sensed she was being followed. She dared not turn and look. But by Wink's unrest, she could tell someone was there. Who, she wasn't sure. It might be Gawter's men or common thieves or drunken ravishers. But one thing was certain—no person on honest business rode with such stealth in the middle of the night.

Rose clucked to the palfrey and whispered, "A wee bit faster, love." She nudged the horse to a brisk walk.

A furtive glimpse under cover of her hood a moment later told her that the riders—two of them—had quickened their pace as well.

At present, they were a hundred yards back, but that could change at any moment. What could she do? She was still miles from the haven of Stirling.

She spared her pursuers one more glance, and in that instant, her worst fears were realized. Even at this distance and in the meager light of the waxing moon, she could see that the men wore Sir Gawter's colors.

She stared straight ahead, her heart in her throat. If they were Gawter's knights, they'd be riding warhorses—strong, powerful animals that could easily outrun the palfrey. 'Twas useless trying to lose them.

She considered turning around and bargaining with them, doling out a generous portion of the coin she'd brought with her to ensure her freedom and their silence. But Sir Gawter had far more wealth to barter with than she, and if they'd come to slay her as she feared, they'd simply steal her silver when she lay dead and bleeding on the road.

Shivering, she peered ahead to the place where the curve of the road dipped and disappeared beyond a thick stand of trees. 'Twas a good furlong away, but if she could make it as far as that bend...

Rose tucked her falcon into her cloak so the bird wouldn't startle. What she planned was mortally perilous, but she had little choice. Wrapping her hands tightly in the reins, she whispered a prayer and silently counted, *one...two...* Wink ruffled her feathers abruptly, almost startling Rose from her mount, but 'twas too late to delay. *Three!*

She dug her heels sharply into the horse's flanks. But instead of bolting forward, the animal reared in protest.

"Come on, come on!" she commanded, struggling to stay atop the unruly beast and hauling sideways on the reins. Finally, the horse turned and surged ahead, galloping down the road, while Rose leaned forward over the horse's pumping neck.

"Faster!" She kicked at the palfrey. "Faster!"

The horse's hooves thundered on the hard-packed dirt, and Rose's hair whipped against her cheek as her hood fell back. The scenery jerked by, and shadows raced past her head like veils in a frenzied dance.

She dared not look back. She knew they were coming. And though she rode with the speed of a coursing river, the bend in the road still stretched far before her, an eternity away, while the menacing storm behind loomed closer and closer.

What she proposed was hopeless. She knew that now. But 'twas too late to withdraw, and she had no intention of surrendering. Now the curve seemed to rush toward her at breakneck speed, and she searched desperately for an opening in the dense woods. But the moonlight was shining on the wrong side of the road, and the trees flew by so rapidly, 'twas nearly impossible to find a break in the forest.

When she turned at the bend, she saw she had no options, for beyond the curve, the road extended in a straight line away from the haven of the forest. 'Twas now or not at all.

She hauled back hard on the reins. The palfrey whinnied in complaint, skidding in the dirt. Its hindquarters dipped low, and it took all of Rose's strength not to tumble backward over the croup. She slid down, unmindful of the way Wink's panicked talons dug into the tender flesh of her arm as she flung her hand to release the bird into the air and toward the safety of the woods. With trembling fingers, she unpinned the cloak from her shoulders and whirled it over the palfrey's withers.

The cloak pin tumbled to the ground. Rose dropped low, still clinging to the reins. She patted the ground desperately for the pin, unable to find it, fearful the horse might spook and charge off at any moment, dragging her down the road.

She glanced frantically back over her shoulder. In another instant, the riders would turn the corner and run her down. She had to escape. Now! Where was the cursed pin?

At last her fingers closed around it, earning her a painful prick. She snatched up the piece and, with hopelessly clumsy fingers, finally managed to stab it through the wool of the cloak, securing the garment about the horse's neck. Then she gave the palfrey a hearty slap to send it barreling down the road.

Which it refused to do. Instead, the contrary nag snorted in complaint, standing its ground.

"Bloody hell!" Her heart in her mouth, Rose drew the small eating dagger from her belt and jabbed at the horse's hindquarters. With a startled snort, it bolted, charging off at a gallop.

Then Rose ducked into the cover of the woods to wait.

She didn't wait long. She held her breath as the pursuit roared closer and closer. Finally the riders passed in a maelstrom of rocks and dirt, thankfully gulled by Rose's cloak, which still flapped atop the fleeing horse like a passenger. How long the riderless palfrey would keep running, she didn't know, nor could she guess how soon Gawter's men would discover her ruse. She had to move away from the road at once.

Wink had perched in a nearby oak. Rose retrieved her, and the two of them fled through the dark forest.

Rose ran for what felt like miles, until she grew breathless and could no longer see the thoroughfare. Her lungs burned, and she pressed her palm to the sharp ache in her side.

"I think...we'll be safe now," she gasped, perusing the woods surrounding them.

Unfortunately, there was little to differentiate one tree from another. If she found her way to Stirling, 'twould be by God's grace. If she made it by morning, 'twould be a miracle. Surrendering the horse had not only banished her from the main road to Stirling—it had cost her precious time.

She gazed up at the small patch of the heavens visible above the treetops, at the stars twinkling like gems. She hoped she remembered how to find...

"That way is north." She pointed toward the northern star. "Stirlin' lies to the south." She moved her arm in a half-circle to the right. "That way."

Naturally, her finger pointed toward the densest, deepest, darkest part of the wood. She swallowed hard, vividly imagining the fierce wolves that were probably licking their chops even now.

Then she frowned. There was no point in fueling the fire of her fears. Besides, hungry animals weren't her only problem. She'd sent most of her belongings down the road on the satchel affixed to the palfrey. All that remained with Rose were her falcon, a purse full of coin, and the single surcoat on her back. She couldn't afford to get lost in the woods, not with so few provisions.

"Come along, Wink," she said with forced optimism. "'Twill be an adventure. We'll find the way. Ye keep watch for wild beasts." She glanced up once more toward the night sky to get her bearings. "And I'll keep prayin' to Saint Christopher to get us safely to The Black Hound."

# Chapter 2

This eve, the night before Saint Anselm's, marked two years since he'd left Mirkhaugh, but for the man known only as Blade, it felt like a lifetime. Anselm was a fitting saint to commemorate the beginning of his own exile, he thought, as he pissed out his third pint of ale against an oak tree in back of The Black Hound.

The cursed longing for Mirkhaugh was strong in him tonight. Whether 'twas being so near the manor of his birth, the significance of the date, or just the extra tankard of ale he'd drunk, he couldn't say. But he felt the beckoning tug of home like a chain wresting a hound to heel.

A dying star streaked across the indigo sky, and he shivered, less from the unseasonably cool breeze than the doubt plaguing his spirit. Change was clearly in the air.

Perhaps Wilham was right. His trusted brother-in-arms had told him 'twas time for Blade the Wanderer to die, and for Sir Pierce the Knight to be reborn, to return home. Two years, he'd said, was long enough for the people of Mirkhaugh to forget, long enough for them to forgive.

Maybe he *could* go back, Blade thought, staring at the stars twinkling in the dark sky.

But then the bloody image that was never far from his mind invaded his hopes, and he closed his eyes against a wave of pain.

It didn't matter what anyone else thought. *He* couldn't forget what he'd done. He couldn't forgive himself. And until he did, he couldn't return.

The inn door swung out suddenly, and the subsequent rustle in the bushes startled Blade, prompting him to close his braies and quickly tie up the points. The Black Hound was crowded, and there was no telling who else might wander outside to make use of the bushes.

Before he could clear his throat in warning, he overheard a harsh whisper.

"'Tis settled then. We'll travel with the pilgrims."

Blade hesitated. Someone whispered back, words too soft to decipher, then the first replied.

"O' course 'twill work. Nobody would think to look for us on a pilgrimage."

The second whispered inaudibly again.

"People go missin' all the time," hissed the first. "No one will know what we've done. In a year they'll stop lookin' for him."

Blade frowned, wondering what mischief was afoot.

"I swear to ye," the first continued, "by the time we reach St. Andrews..." The voice took on an ominous tone. "Archibald o' Laichloan will be dead. Dead and forgotten."

Archibald of Laichloan? Blade knew that name. Laichloan was a stone's toss from Mirkhaugh, a sizable chunk of land with many tenants, ruled by a rich nobleman, Laird John. Archibald was John's son, a lad of perhaps thirteen or fourteen years and the heir to Laichloan.

Was some villain threatening to kill the lad? God's bones, if Laird John lost his only son...

"Naught will go awry," the first whisperer said. "Ye'll see."

The second murmured in reply.

"We won't be caught. St. Andrews is a crowded place." There was a pause. "Ye fret too much."

Before Blade could confront the scoundrels, they scurried off in the dark, slipping back into the inn like a pair of crafty mice.

He couldn't pretend he hadn't heard them. True, he was no longer the laird's neighbor. He hadn't seen John in two years. But he couldn't let harm come to the man's son. He had to do something.

So he told himself. What he didn't add was that he'd welcome any excuse to delay his return to Mirkhaugh. Hunting down assassins sounded like reasonable justification for staying on the move. Besides, he thought—reverting to his mercenary habits—Laird John would probably offer a sizable reward for the return of his heir.

He entered the inn, thinking the culprits would be easy to spot. But in the clamor and confusion of the crowd, 'twas a hopeless task. He scowled, cursing under his breath. Damn his eyes, he didn't know who he was looking for, didn't know their size or sex or age. Their whispers had been indistinct, and the night had been too dark to discern their features. All he knew was that there were two of them and that they had dire plans for the son of Laichloan.

"Ach, there ye are! I got us a table." Wilham gave him a wink, pressing a tankard of ale into his hands. Then he wrapped a companionable arm around Blade's shoulder, nudging him toward a corner of the room.

The last thing he needed was another pint, Blade thought as they squeezed through the crushing throng. But that didn't stop him from wanting one, and 'twouldn't stop him from drinking one.

"Not bad for a halfpenny, eh?" Wilham gave the wobbly table a shake.

Wilham spoke in jest, of course. He'd had to pay far more than a halfpenny for the luxury of a table in these cramped quarters and the lodging he'd procured for the night. But though their mercenary livelihood necessitated that they travel light, subsisting on what they could carry on their backs, their swords earned them more than a comfortable living. They'd earned enough coin in the last year alone to live in affluence the rest of their days.

Even at that, the table was little bigger than a merlin's perch. Still, it served to hold a tankard and two elbows, both of which Wilham planted on the ale-sticky surface as soon as they were seated.

"Well?" Wilham prompted, his brown eyes twinkling expectantly.

Blade intentionally ignored him, melting back into the shadows to scan the crowd for dubious-looking characters.

"W-e-l-l?" Wilham drawled impatiently.

"Well, what?" Blade grumbled distractedly.

"Ye know what." Wilham sighed. When he got no answer, he muttered his frustration into his cup of ale.

Blade frowned. "Did ye see anyone come in just now...a pair o'..." How could he describe them? Whisperers? "Anyone in a hurry, anyone suspicious?"

"In here?" Wilham shrugged. "Everyone is in a hurry, mostly for their next ale. Why?"

He explained what he'd heard outside—the whispers, the threat, the name of Laichloan. But instead of lighting up at the prospect of intrigue and peril as he usually did, Wilham was uncharacteristically quiet. He sipped at his ale and fixed his gaze thoughtfully upon the scarred surface of the table.

"Did ye hear me?" Blade asked.

"So," Wilham said, scoring the oak further with the edge of his thumbnail, "ye're off on another adventure then. Ye don't intend to go home."

Blade swallowed hard. Wilham was right, of course. He stared at his brooding companion, then let his gaze drift out over the milling crowd. How could he explain? How could he tell Wilham that until he was free of his guilt, he never intended to return?

He chewed at his lip, searching for the right words. "I...can't."

Wilham nodded, knowing, and looked up from his drink. Foam flecked the stubble above his lip, and his sorrel hair fell in boyish tangles over his forehead.

Blade felt like a churl. Sometimes Wilham seemed so young, even though the two were the same age. Perhaps 'twas the man's goodness that kept him youthful. His soul, unlike Blade's, was unstained by sin. Wilham was always there with a merry smile and a friendly jest, no matter how foul Blade's mood. It still amazed him that Wilham had stayed beside him all these months. Anyone else would have deserted him long ago.

And now what had Blade done? He'd wounded his only friend. He glimpsed rare sorrow in Wilham's eyes, and it wrenched at his conscience to so callously fail his one champion.

He bit the inside of his cheek and glared into his foamy ale, ticking a ragged thumbnail against the side of his tankard. There were a hundred excuses he could make for avoiding Mirkhaugh. But 'twas useless lying to Wilham. Wilham could see through his deceit. And 'twasn't in his heart to deceive his old friend.

"Damn it all, Wil," Blade finally grumbled, "'tis too soon."

Wilham was disappointed. Blade could see that. But—good man that Wilham was—he'd never admit it.

Blade furrowed his brow, angry with himself. "Ye go," he decided. "Ye go back. Ye have family at Mirkhaugh—brothers who grow as fast as weeds, sisters who hardly remember ye..." He smirked ruefully. "Lasses who long for your bed."

Wilham obliged him with a chuckle. Then he straightened, wiping the suds and the smile from his mouth, and gripped Blade's forearm. "I won't go back. Not without ye."

His fierce loyalty caught suddenly at Blade's chest and lodged in his throat, bringing him perilously close to tears. He clenched his jaw and wrapped a bracing fist around his tankard as the space of silence thickened between them.

"Besides," Wilham said at last, relaxing his face into its usual irrepressible smile and jostling Blade's arm before he let go, "don't we have the matter of a murder to solve?" He clapped Blade on the shoulder. "What good is your sharp blade without my sharp mind, eh?" he said, tapping a finger to his own temple.

Blade wasn't about to argue with him. They'd traveled too long together, one step ahead of danger, foxing their way out of tight spaces by their swords and by their wits, for him to make light of Wilham's cunning.

"Laichloan," Wilham considered, stroking his chin. "That should bring us a tidy sum. On the other hand, I seem to remember Laichloan's daughters were a handful o' spoiled imps. The lad may be just as rotten. Are you sure there wouldn't be a bigger reward *helpin'* these assassins?"

Blade flashed him a chiding glare.

Wilham snickered, then scrutinized the occupants of The Black Hound at length, finally tossing up his hands. "Well, they all look guilty to me. I say we round up the lot o' them!"

But Blade was only half listening. His mind was mulling over what he'd heard earlier. Pilgrimage, the conspirators had said. They were going on a pilgrimage to St. Andrews, which was where they planned to kill Archibald. Blade narrowed his eyes at the parchment swinging from a nail below the lantern on the far wall. Setting his tankard down, he pushed up from the table.

"Hey, where are ye goin'?" Wilham asked. "Ye haven't finished your..."

Blade didn't answer. His gaze was centered on the notice. He elbowed his way through the mass of people and snatched the parchment from the wall.

'Twas an announcement for a pilgrimage, the day of Saint Anselm's, beginning at The Black Hound and proceeding under the guidance of Father Peter to the holy shrine at St. Andrews. Blade scanned the note again. There could be no mistake. This must be the pilgrimage the assassins intended to undertake.

Returning to Wilham, he tossed the parchment onto the table in front of his friend. Wilham choked guiltily on Blade's ale, having wasted no time in partaking of the abandoned tankard.

"What's this?" Wilham burped, squinting at the notice.

"We leave on the morrow."

"Father Peter..." Wilham read. "Pilgrimage to St. Andrews..." Then his eyes widened, and he muttered an oath. "Ye're not serious?"

"I am."

"A pilgrimage?" he squeaked. He sank his head onto his hands. "Why?"

"The best way to catch the assassins is by infiltratin' their ranks."

Wilham pulled a face that looked like he'd tasted rotten meat. "But a pilgrimage. Stuck for days with religious zealots and pious, whey-faced maids." He shuddered.

The corner of Blade's mouth drifted up. "Ye're always tellin' me I could use a measure o' redemption."

"Aye? Well, if I suffer this for ye," Wilham bargained, stabbing a finger at Blade, "ye'll owe me a fortnight in the most expensive stews of Edinburgh."

"Done."

'Twas idle banter. Wilham, for all his swaggering, had too tender a nature to frequent brothels. He loved one woman at a time, and her with all his heart.

Out of temper, Wilham spitefully drained the rest of Blade's ale, crossly banging the tankard down on the table. "I suppose we'll have to be on some sort o' penitent mission," he grumbled. "No knight with half a wit would go on pilgrimage unless 'twere as punishment."

An hour later, when they retired upstairs, noisy revelers still packed the inn. Blade lay awake on the straw pallet, remembering small slivers of time when he, too, laughed and drank and made merry until the sun came up, when he slept on a feather bed instead of the hard ground, when he wore rich velvet instead of worn leather, when his life was untroubled by hardship and exile.

Those days were gone. Now, more often than not, he fell asleep in the cold to the sound of owls and crickets, with Wilham snoring at his feet.

Even now, Wilham snorted from the foot of the pallet. Blade punched his straw bolster into a more satisfactory shape, checked to ensure his sword was in reach, then forced his eyes shut. They would embark on a dangerous mission on the morrow, and he wanted to be well-rested.

Of course, as fate would have it, his night was filled not with rest but with troubling dreams. He writhed and tossed in slumber, struggling to escape the hellish visions, but they haunted him without mercy.

Even in sleep, the unforgettable smell of battle—iron and sweat and blood—assaulted his nostrils. He felt again the shocking sting in his back, the wrench of his shoulder as he turned with his weapon. Every time he had the dream, he tried to change it, tried to stay his arm, to halt the blow. Every time he failed. His sword plunged forward, finding its target and sinking deep. And then came the piteous scream.

It echoed with savage cruelty in his mind's ear. And when he woke with a start in the dark, jerking upright, he swore he still heard vestiges of the heart-rending sound. Icy sweat poured from him, his chest heaved with phantom exertion, and despair racked his soul.

He buried his face in his hands, then ran shaking fingers through his damp hair. God's eyes, would he never be free of his sin? Was there no salvation for him?

'Twas only a few hours till dawn. He knew he'd get no more sleep. He scrubbed at his eyes and rose from the bed, dressing quietly, despite the knowledge that after so much ale, even a siege cannon wouldn't wake Wilham.

There was something he had to do, something Wilham had reminded him of, to add believability to his presence on the pilgrimage. Strangely, the idea brought some measure of peace to his soul. Maybe this was more than just another lucrative undertaking for him. Maybe, following in the footsteps of other lost pilgrims, he'd find redemption.

Then he gave his head a shake. Such thoughts were foolish. There was no redemption for what he'd done.

He hefted his great helm from beside the bed. 'Twas tarnished with age and dented with blows from a hundred battles, but it had served him well. All he had to do now was find an armorer who, for a few silver coins, might be persuaded to fire up his forge at this ungodly hour.

By the time he returned to The Black Hound hours later, the sun had begun to stab through the branches of ash and elm, warming the inn's plaster walls and rousing the tenants. Nodding to the open-mouthed tavern wench as he swept past, Blade trudged up the stairs and shouldered open the door of his chamber.

His eyes widened when he saw Wilham standing in the midst of the room—sawing with his dagger at a hank of hair stretched above his head, a pile of brown curls at his feet. "What the devil?"

"There ye are!" Wilham scolded, tossing his last lock to the floor and squinting at his reflection in the small polished steel mirror. "Where have ye been? I've had to crop this myself," he complained, riffling through what little remained of his hair, "and I'm sure I've made a mess of it." He growled and sheathed his dagger. "There. Do I look penitent enough?"

Blade was still staring, speechless, when Wilham turned and saw him for the first time.

"Zounds!" Wilham yelped. "What have ye done, man?"

Blade finally found his tongue. "What have *I* done? What have *ye* done?"

Wilham drew himself up proudly. "I've disgraced myself as a knight," he declared. "I'm not certain how yet. I'll think o' somethin'. But *ye*..."

Wilham circled to look at him from all angles, whistling under his breath. Heavy shackles encircled Blade's wrists, and between them hung a thick chain of iron links. Blade ground his teeth in annoyance, already regretting his impaired ability to clout Wilham.

Finally Wilham stopped before him, his fists planted on his hips. "Chains forged from your own armor. Classic." He shook his head. "Always doin' me one better. And ye've no doubt got a fantastic tale o' dishonor to go with this?"

Blade gave him a rueful smirk and tossed him the newly cast key to the shackles. "I'm certain ye'll come up with one."

'Twouldn't prove too challenging, he was sure. The truth was enough to warrant the shame he now bore for all to see.

Rose wondered if she looked as haggard as she felt. Even Wink drooped on her glove, her feathers askew, her good eye squinting against the increasing light of day. Rose had trudged all night through the dark wood, jumping at every rustle in the leaves, shuddering at every glowing set of eyes she encountered. Each time a hooting owl or a howling wolf broke the eerie silence, her entreaties to Saint Christopher increased in volume and vehemence. And somehow, whether 'twas due to prayer or sheer determination, she made it through the forest unscathed.

Bone-weary, Rose smiled when the sun finally rose before them on the shoulders of the thatched cottages at the outskirts of Stirling, like the star over Bethlehem, showing them the way. As anxious as she was to find The Black Hound, she still had the presence of mind to take a moment before she emerged from the wood and onto the main road to beat the dust from her skirts, wipe the sweat from her brow, and pass her fingers through her snarled tresses to give them some semblance of order. Perhaps if she looked presentable enough, no one would question her sudden appearance from out of nowhere.

Wink could have found The Black Hound with her one eye. The imposing whitewashed, black-timbered establishment— nestled against the northern edge of the town—boasted an enormous sign depicting the snarling, sharp-toothed beast that gave the inn its name.

Standing upon the threshold, Rose absently stroked the falcon to settle the both of them. She made one final scrub at a stubborn streak of dark mud on her scarlet surcoat, and with her velvet sleeve, polished the carbuncle pendant hanging about her neck. Then she took a deep breath, pushed open the door, and was swept into a world of chaos.

People crowded the dim room, scurrying here and there, elbowing past one another, lugging goods, satchels, and bits of breakfast while they chattered like birds at daybreak. The odor of ale was strong, but the smell of baked bread, rose water, and tallow mellowed the aroma of the room, creating a panoply of scents as varied as the individuals who bore them.

A few wore somber attire and expressions, as she'd expected of pilgrims, but the bulk of the blabbering mob looked as if they prepared for an entertainment of some sort. Two stocky, dark-bearded fellows tossed dice noisily onto a table, and a trio of fresh-faced lads munched on brown bread. Rich laughter from a voluptuous woman seated at one of the tables rolled over the top of the droning speech of an ascetic who seemed to be lecturing a timid brown straw of a lad.

"Will ye be joinin' us, m'lady?" The jovial, rumbling voice addressing Rose belonged to a man who looked like something made at a cooper's stall. His robes and his tonsure marked him as a priest, but the belt closing his cassock strained about his round belly like a hoop around a barrel.

"I... I..." She nodded. "Aye."

"Brilliant. I'm Father Peter. I'll be leadin' the pilgrimage." He rocked back on his heels, and for an instant, Rose feared the rotund man might tip over. "And ye are?"

"Rosamund, Lady Rosamund o'..." Too late, she realized she should have used a false name. "O' Doune." 'Twas the first town she thought of, and she wondered how much penance she'd owe for lying to a priest.

"Lady Rosamund," he said, louder than she would have liked. "And who is your bonnie friend?"

"Ah. My falcon, Wink." She added firmly, "She goes everywhere with me."

"Wink, is it?" He hooked his thumbs in his belt. Rose was amazed there was *room* for thumbs. "An apt name."

He nodded and motioned Rose forward. "Come join the rest o' the company then," he said merrily. "Make your own introductions. Have a bit o' somethin' to break your fast. We'll be on our way within the hour."

Rose *was* hungry, and the smell of bread made her mouth water. She had no idea how much the pilgrimage would cost, all told, but she was willing to spend a good deal of her coin this morn on something—anything—to stop the growling in her belly.

"Food first," she murmured to Wink, "friendship later."

For three pence, she feasted on ale and a fresh-baked loaf of heavy brown bread with butter as she studied the faces of the pilgrims.

They were a motley bunch. More than a few of them—the gaunt gentleman with the sly eyes, the pair of burly men playing at dice, the dismal young man who looked aged beyond his years—seemed dangerous.

But better she should travel in league with this lot, as rough as they were, than have to fend off outlaws on her own. Besides, Father Peter seemed a decent enough fellow. Surely he'd see them safely to their destination.

A woman suddenly shrieked beside Rose, leaping back, tossing her dark blonde curls, and clutching a hand dramatically to her overripe bosom, which bulged above a richly brocaded surcoat. "Ye aren't bringin' that...that beast, are ye?"

Rose's hackles went up. "'Tisn't a beast," she said, lifting her chin defensively. "'Tis a falcon."

The woman trembled with fear as she glanced distractedly around the room. Then she abruptly frowned, annoyed by the fact that no one was paying much heed to her apparent distress. "Hmph!" she muttered. "Where's a knight in shinin' armor when ye need one?" Her worry vanished instantly, and she held forth her hand in friendship. "Brigit's my name," she said, a twinkle in her green eyes. "Your bird doesn't bite, does it?"

"Nae. Unless she's threatened." Rose extended her own hand. "I'm Lady Rosamund o'..." She supposed it made no difference on a pilgrimage who was titled and who was not. "Call me Rose."

"Pleased to meet ye, Rose." Brigit winked. "This your first pilgrimage?"

Rose nodded. "And ye?"

"Hardly." Brigit smirked, then flashed open her cloak. Next to the guild pin which marked her as a brewster were a half dozen pilgrim badges. "This'll be the year," she said, wagging her finger. "I'm goin' to catch me a husband, I am. Six years o' widowhood is long enough."

She must have spotted a prospect just then, for her attention immediately deserted Rose. Brigit adjusted her tightly laced kirtle, boosting up her bosom until Rose feared it might topple out, saucily tossed her blonde tresses over her shoulder, and minced toward the far end of the room.

As she left, a fair-haired, broad-shouldered giant ambled up. His sea blue eyes and weathered skin betrayed his Viking ancestry. "That's a fine bird ye've got there." He gestured with his tankard of beer. "That a peregrine?"

"Aye."

"Well, she's a beauty, even if she's missin' that eye." He narrowed his azure gaze. "Tell me, how do ye manage to feed her?"

Rose's heart skipped a beat. How indeed? What a fool she'd been. On the journey from Fernie to Averlaigh, she'd had Apollo the gyrfalcon with her. Who would hunt for Wink now?

She was spared having to answer when a squat bear of a man arrived to thump the Viking on the chest. "Fulk!"

"Drogo!" the giant replied, clapping the intruder on the back. "Are you goin' to St. Andrews as well?"

Drogo grumbled something into his black beard, something that included the words "wife" and "nagging" and "reprieve." Then he brightened. "But why have *ye* come, eh, Fulk?"

Fulk, for all his manly size, looked slightly embarrassed. "I'm gettin' married come summer." He rubbed self-consciously at one of his large-muscled arms. "She won't have me till I've repented o' my sins."

"Sins?" Drogo barked. "What sins?"

Fulk glanced at Rose. "I'm a butcher," he explained. "She says I must go on pilgrimage to redeem my soul for all the beasts I've killed."

There was a moment of silence, and then Drogo burst into long, rollicking laughter, causing Fulk a good deal of irritation.

"Women!" Drogo exclaimed after his laughter ended. Then, remembering Rose, he awkwardly cleared his throat.

Fulk smiled and shook his golden head, then made introductions. "My lady, I'm Fulk, and this is Drogo. He's an old friend and cook at Ingleloch House."

She nodded. "I'm Rose."

"Handsome bird," Drogo remarked. Rose stifled an urge to snatch Wink to her breast, fearing the man might be sizing the falcon up for his cooking pot.

A trio of young lads came forward, jostling each other with teasing elbows. The curly-headed one spoke first.

"We were wonderin', m'lady, is that a lanner or a merlin?"

She opened her mouth to reply, but the lanky, dark-haired youth spoke. "Or maybe a kestrel? I think 'tis a kestrel."

"'Tisn't a kestrel, Daniel," said the tallest lad, rolling his eyes. "Kestrels have no such markin's. I say 'tis a lanner."

Daniel scowled.

"Nae, 'tis a merlin," the first boy said. "See the streaks?"

The tall lad towered even more authoritatively over his fellows. "And just what would ye know about falcons, Bryan? Your father keeps hounds."

Bryan sputtered in anger, and Daniel raised a condescending brow. "*My* father has falcons," he boasted, "mostly gyrfalcons and even a saker from the East."

"Please, my lady," the tall youth said, "explain to my companions that your bird is a lanner."

"Thomas..." Bryan warned, punching his arm. Thomas punched him back, discreetly.

Rose's head was spinning. The three lads waited for her answer. "Actually," she told them, "'tis a peregrine."

The youths looked shocked, then crestfallen, then began battling amongst themselves again.

"I told ye 'twasn't a merlin."

"Well, 'twasn't a lanner, was it?"

"A peregrine. That would have been my second guess."

"Thank ye, my lady," Thomas said with a nod before they ambled off in a flurry of whispered insults and friendly clouts.

"Scholars from Glasgow," Fulk explained when they'd gone. "They live to bicker."

"Fulk," Drogo said, "let's see if we can stomach a bit o' the breakfast they serve here, eh?"

Fulk nodded, and they set off after the innkeeper.

So far the pilgrims seemed benign. Fulk was a kindly giant, despite being a butcher. Drogo, the cook, would keep them from starving. The three scholars, though youthfully rude, appeared harmless enough. Brigit was too embroiled in her own affairs to care much for those of Rose. And Father Peter was congenial toward everyone.

Rose ran the back of her finger along Wink's throat, soothing the falcon after so much attention, and studied the rest of her fellow travelers.

The gaunt man in gray was a palmer. His cloak was studded with numerous pilgrim badges, among them the palm leaf of Jerusalem. His walking staff was darkened with wear. Men such as he made a comfortable living traveling on pilgrimage on behalf of wealthy nobles who didn't wish to be inconvenienced by the journey. He conversed with an old apple-cheeked woman who eyed him rather like a knight sizing up a warhorse.

A meek youth of surely no more than thirteen years, as thin as a claymore, huddled at a tiny table, nibbling on a crust of bread. 'Twas difficult to discern his history, as 'twas that of the solitary man swilling ale in the dark corner and the buxom woman with pouting scarlet lips and thick locks of chestnut hair.

The loud pair of leather-skinned men whose beards were dotted with foam must be laborers of some sort, and by the look of the elderly gentleman whose waist, throat, and fingers gleamed with gilded treasure, he was either a successful merchant or a goldsmith.

A pair of young nuns stood shyly in one corner, their fair faces glowing like candles in the darkness of the inn. By their matching wide eyes and frail features, they had to be sisters. Despite their timidity, 'twasn't long before the scholars began haranguing them for advice on finding pious wives.

Rose let her gaze drift over the white wimples and gray habits of the nuns and pondered for the first time what life in a convent might be like. Now that she'd fled her betrothed, one of the options left her was joining a holy order. Most women her age shuddered at the thought. Internment in a convent was a common threat issued to wayward daughters. But Rose had heard favorable things about the church. In the service of the Lord, a woman might enjoy a great deal of freedom and, 'twas rumored, aspire to great power.

And what of the disadvantages? As far as she could see, there were only two—celibacy and boredom. After the abomination she'd witnessed in the stable, celibacy seemed desirable. As for boredom...

She was still reflecting upon her future, absently stroking Wink, when her eye caught a flicker of silver from the darkest shadow in the deepest corner of the room.

She hadn't noticed the man before. His black cloak and dark leather chausses made him seem part of the smoke-seasoned timbers of the inn. Even now she couldn't see him well. His eyes were hidden by the hood of his cloak, which revealed only the lower half of his face—a grim mouth and a square, black-stubbled jaw—and yet somehow she felt he watched her.

A forbidding thrill shivered along her spine. She turned aside, raising her hand to her face so she could peer at the stranger in secret from behind her fingers.

His boots extended beneath the table in a lazy, almost insolent manner, and except for occasionally running a single finger along the rim of his cup, he scarcely moved. But when he lifted his arm to drink, she saw it again—the glint of metal.

Her heart bolted into her throat. He wore shackles. He was a criminal then. She'd heard about men like him, dangerous men who chose to go on pilgrimage as punishment for their crimes. She gulped. What might his villainy be? Theft? Adultery? Murder?

Maybe going on a pilgrimage hadn't been such a wise decision after all.

But before she could change her mind, Father Peter clapped his hands together, calling for silence and summoning the pilgrims to draw near.

She rose from the table, and when she dared look again, she saw the man in shackles had come to his feet and thrown back his hood.

Her breath caught. He stood tall over most of the other pilgrims. The width of his shoulders and the breadth of his chest marked him as a man of uncommon strength. Candlelight illuminated the angled planes of his face, accentuating the hollow of his cheek and the depth of his brow. Dark hair slashed down in long, unruly locks over his forehead, shadowing his softly glimmering eyes.

Rose swallowed a rough knot of fear as she glanced at the irons shackling his wrists, wondering if the length of heavy chain slung between the thick cuffs would hold.

Father Peter spoke, issuing instructions for the pilgrimage, but she didn't hear a word. All her attention was focused on the dark figure that seemed to reign over the room.

He must have sensed her scrutiny, for in the next moment, he slowly turned his head until he stared at her as intently as she watched him. His brow furrowed, and his mouth hardened as he studied her in a bold, leisurely manner from head to toe. His gaze commanded her own, for try as she might, she couldn't tear her eyes away from him.

Yet 'twas more than fear that held her. Something in his glittering eyes excited her, challenged her, aroused her. He was absolutely beautiful, sinfully so, she realized, more striking than any man she'd ever seen. But there was something terrible in his beauty, some dark secret that lodged within the handsome confines of his form.

His eyes narrowed upon her for a long moment, as if they delved into her soul. Her heart raced, her breath grew shallow, her knees weakened. Overwhelmed by a mysterious, powerful shock she couldn't name, she gripped the table to steady herself. When he finally looked away, so intrusive and lasting was the impact of his gaze that Rose felt as if she'd been violated.

# Chapter 3

Blade scowled in the direction of the priest, his heart pounding far too forcefully. That woman, the one with the half-blind falcon, had unsettled him. And he was unaccustomed to being unsettled.

"Look penitent," Wilham hissed beside him.

Blade made the attempt, but soon the curious furrow crept back between his brows.

He'd spied the lass the instant she'd walked through the door, arriving on a stream of sunlight like an angel alighting from heaven. Her rare beauty had astonished him, and he wasn't a man easily astonished. She was as small and slim as a child, yet she possessed enough womanly curves to be the mistress of a king. Her snug white underdress, exposed in the slits of a sideless surcoat the color of ripe cherries, revealed a delectable form that sent his heart racing and his thoughts spiraling along all manner of sins.

Her features were as delicate as a fawn's, yet strong and pure in color. Her skin was pale and smooth, like cream, her lips the hue of summer wine. Fine black brows arched over impossibly enormous eyes of a curious color he couldn't distinguish. And tumbling down past the swell of her hip, unbound sleek black tresses as shiny as satin reflected the flickering firelight.

But 'twas more than her beauty that snared his eye.

She didn't belong here. 'Twas plain in the nervous darting of her glance. She was as out of place amidst the milling pilgrims as a lily in a field of thistles.

Where were her things? he wondered. Noblewomen always insisted on packing chests of clothing, necessities they claimed they couldn't live without, even if they ventured but a day's ride from their home. Despite the rich velvet of her surcoat and the quality of the fine silver chain and small polished carbuncle that dripped tantalizingly upon her bosom, this woman appeared to possess nothing but the garments she wore and the falcon. How could she have planned to journey to St. Andrews without provisions?

Wilham elbowed him. "At least *feign* to listen," he muttered.

Blade lifted his head and attempted to focus on the fat priest jabbering on about rules and lodging and the sanctity of pilgrimage, but soon his mind wandered again. He lifted a hand, wincing at the clank of the chains, and scratched at his brow so he might peek at the woman between his fingers.

God's breath, she was dazzling. Her attention was upon the Holy Father now, but by the rapid rise and fall of her bosom, 'twas clear she was ill-at-ease. He slowly perused her again from top to bottom, lifting a brow at the state of her attire. Her gown might be made of costly velvet, but there was a small tear at the inside of one sleeve, the hem was muddy, and the lower quarter of her skirt was littered with bits of dry grass. What mischief had the lass been up to?

Everyone around him murmured, "Amen." He belatedly echoed the sentiment. Then the mob began gathering their possessions and shambling toward the door.

"Seven miles a day," Wilham said, shaking his head. "'Tis a snail's pace."

Blade slung his pack over his shoulder and tried to purge the entrancing angel from his thoughts, scrutinizing the pilgrims one by one as they filed past. There were two scheming culprits in their ranks, and he didn't have much time to find them.

"'Twould take us two days on horseback," Wilham complained, shouldering his own burden.

Blade grunted, not really listening. Who could the perpetrators be? Who looked capable of such villainy? The lass in red glanced fleetingly over at him again. Could she be an assassin? 'Twas unthinkable. She had the sweet countenance of a cherub. Still, he was wise enough to know a bonnie face oft hid a black heart.

"Well," Wilham sighed, "at least we'll be comfortable enough tonight—dinin' on spun sugar and sleepin' with hot-blooded nuns."

Blade absently nodded, then drew his brows together. Never mind the angel with the ebony hair, he chided himself. That brawny man with the week's growth of beard and the threadbare cloak had a ruthless edge to his stare. Was he a killer?

Wilham cuffed him. "I knew ye weren't listenin'."

"What?"

"Come along, Blade. I'll fill ye in."

They fell in behind the last pilgrim.

"By the way, I've brought your sword," Wilham said smugly.

Blade gave him a sharp glare. "I won't use it."

"'Twas a foolish vow," Wilham muttered. "Ye'll regret makin' it."

Blade disagreed. The surrender of his sword, like the shackles about his wrists, lent credence to his disguise. And in a strange way, unburdened of the blood-stained weapon that had weighed upon his soul for two years, he indeed felt the faint hope of redemption.

'Twas a glorious spring morn. If he'd been less intent on his mission and less distracted by the scarlet temptress moving along the path well ahead of him, Blade might have enjoyed the pleasant march. The sun was bright, the sky cloudless, the air filled with birdsong. But his ear was attuned only to the quiet conversation around him, listening for any clue as to the identity of the killers.

A few of the pilgrims seemed above suspicion. He highly doubted that Father Peter, the organizer of the pilgrimage, had so dire a plot in mind. The priest was the most verbose of the travelers, though the man's girth left him huffing breathlessly as he waddled along the path, stabbing at the ground with his staff. The priest took enormous pride—almost sinful pride—in the many pilgrimages he'd made in his life. There was no end to his bluster. It seemed he'd been to every shrine in Christendom, and for each he had a story—a very long story—to relate.

Halfway through a wheezing oration about the incredible flagellants the father had encountered abroad, Wilham nudged Blade, muttering, "For a parish priest, he spends little time in his parish."

Blade nodded. The fact that Father Peter was in essence a wayfarer cast a shadow of suspicion on his character. But 'twas difficult to believe the prattling priest could keep any secret— and more to the point, a secret involving murder—for more than an hour. They'd only started their journey, and already Blade knew more than he ever wished to know about the man.

Following closely at Father Peter's heels were the two young nuns. They complemented the priest well, for they talked hardly at all. They never questioned the Father's gushing proclamations, but gazed at him in wide-eyed wonder, as if he spoke the Gospel every time he opened his mouth.

Staring at the nuns' round, rosy-cheeked faces framed by linen wimples only a shade lighter than their skin—their blue eyes so alike, their small mouths made for murmured prayers— 'twas difficult to envision them as assassins. Indeed, the mere mention of violence would likely send the fragile creatures into an overwrought faint.

Directly behind the pious sisters walked the fascinating woman with the falcon. Her straight ebony hair caught the breeze, streaming out like a dark pennon against the bright green of the spring saplings all around them. Her gait was almost regal, and she bore the falcon proudly upon her gloved wrist. Blade wondered how soon she'd tire of carrying the thing.

Peregrines were light, but as any knight bearing a shield knew, even a light thing grew heavy over time.

The bird was a pretty thing, despite its maimed eye, but he wondered why the woman would keep such a pet. It couldn't hunt for itself and must be more trouble than 'twas worth. He doubted she'd even given a thought as to how to feed it on the journey.

Something was definitely wrong. She hardly looked prepared for a trek of this magnitude. 'Twas as if, in the impulsive way of females, the lady had awakened in the morning, snapped up her falcon, and decided to walk to St. Andrews, with never a notion as to how she'd get there or what to pack.

Blade almost pitied her. He too had left the comforts of a manor for the wilds of the woods. 'Twasn't easy to adapt. She'd probably given no thought whatsoever to what she'd eat, where she'd sleep, or how she'd get dressed without the aid of a maidservant.

Then again, he thought, maybe that was her aim. Maybe she was a true pilgrim who intended to humble herself by journeying without her usual luxuries to seek understanding and salvation.

The path ahead looped sharply so that the line of pilgrims folded back almost upon itself, and Blade, walking at the end, watched the lady pass in profile. She *was* captivating. She carried her head level, letting her eyes dip gracefully to guide her as she stepped forward. Her hands were delicate and fair, as if she did little more with them than wave or pray. Her beguiling chin came almost to a point, and her dark curtain of hair framed her face and brushed her waist like a cloak made of satin. Her skin looked as soft as a dove's breast, and the enticing swell of her bosom stole the very breath from his mouth.

Then she caught him staring, and her grace disappeared. She tripped. The falcon's wings flapped wildly for an instant, and the lass stumbled forward into the nuns ahead of her.

"Bloody he-..." he heard her mutter, and then, "Sorry."

When her glance fell upon him again, he sobered. The lass was as skittish as a kitten in a stable full of warhorses. Why? What did she have to hide?

Rose cursed inwardly at her clumsiness. She had to stop dwelling on that brooding outlaw in the shackles. Surely she only imagined he was watching her.

She'd intentionally placed herself near the fore of the line, where persons of more piety and less menace seemed to congregate. Yet she could feel the felon's merciless, penetrating gaze even at this distance.

God's eyes, what did he want?

Perhaps he was a thief. Perhaps he'd seen her jeweled pendant and her valuable falcon and, guessing she carried silver, meant to steal it from her.

Yet he'd apparently chosen to travel on the pilgrimage, shackled and shamed, of his own will. Didn't that mean he'd repented of his crime?

Rose glanced up again, surreptitiously. Faith, the man was audacious. He was *still* watching her. She felt her cheeks grow warm.

She wondered again what his crime could be. Theft? Murder? Rape? Her mind suddenly filled with a terrifying image of the dark criminal in shackles looming over her, ravishing her. She squeezed her eyes shut against the shocking vision.

But they opened again of their own volition, and her gaze flickered inexorably back to him. Still the knave stared—his brow furrowed deeply, his mouth grim, the soft clank of his chains sinister among the cheery chirps of sparrows on the wing.

She snapped her head about sharply to focus instead on the plump priest at the head of the line. She wouldn't look at the outlaw again. She refused.

Her heart fluttered beneath her pendant, and though 'twas absurd, she knew 'twas more than fear quickening her pulse. Something about the dangerous black-cloaked figure made her feel the same exhilaration she did when she rode faster than was safe on her palfrey or strayed too far from home. 'Twas that sort of forbidden excitement that she found in his gaze, a clandestine thrill that hastened her heartbeat and snatched her breath away.

But now she steeled herself against the lure of deeper peril. She was in enough trouble already. Though she'd ridden fast and far, pursuit was not long behind. Gawter's men would know they'd been gulled and by now would have reported back to her betrothed. They'd tell Gawter she'd ridden east, and he'd guess she was on her way to Fernie House.

Perhaps Gawter would abandon the chase, perhaps not. With her out of the way, he might simply wait for the Laird of Averlaigh to die and take the mother to wife instead of the daughter. Surely he knew that Rose bore him no affection and wouldn't contest the wedding. On the other hand, if he wished to hold on to Averlaigh permanently, he needed an heir, and Lady Agatha was too old to give him one. For that, he needed Rose.

Averlaigh had been the incentive for the betrothal all along. She knew that now. Sir Gawter possessed wealth, but no property. Lady Agatha possessed property, but no wealth. While the Laird of Averlaigh hung onto life, Rose's mother wasn't free to remarry, but with Rose as a sacrifice, the barren Agatha and rich Gawter could both gain what fortune they lacked and enjoy a surreptitious liaison into the bargain under Rose's nose. As for Rose, she'd supply the heir required to keep hold of Averlaigh.

Rose shivered at their treachery.

The pilgrims had traveled for a few hours when Father Peter declared 'twas time for a rest. He called the company to a halt beneath a grove of elms bordering a flower-studded glen.

The old apple-cheeked woman took the priest's words to heart. She collapsed beside a rotting stump and in moments was snoring away like a well-fed hound. Most of the others dug in their satchels for bits of bread and cheese they'd brought along or hefted skins of quenching beer.

Rose licked her dry lips and swallowed thirstily. She'd been forced to abandon all her provisions when she'd leaped from the horse. It hadn't occurred to her to purchase spare provender at the inn. She supposed she'd been so preoccupied with evading death at the hands of Gawter's men that she hadn't considered she might well die of starvation on the road.

At least they'd stay at a manor this eve, where they were likely to be fed generously. There she'd eat a small supper and cache a bit of food for the next day's travel. Meanwhile, rather than stand about with her tongue sticking to the roof of her mouth, she decided to stroll across the daisy-strewn meadow to let Wink stretch her wings.

Behind her, the soothing murmur of voices diminished as she crossed the grass. In the midst of the glen, Rose loosed Wink's leash from her jesses. The instant the falcon was released, she took to the sky. Rose lowered her hand, massaging the muscles of her arm, which ached with the burden of carrying the bird for so long. She smiled as Wink circled overhead. How free the falcon flew, unbound by worry and the weight of the world.

For a long while the bird turned lazily in the sky, skimming past the emerald tops of the trees, her tawny wings fluttering in the gentle breeze.

Rose envied the falcon's freedom. Ever since learning of her betrothal, Rose had felt trapped, like a leaf caught in a swift current, tossed at a whim, steered by destiny. The thought that she had no control over her own future filled her with dread.

Wink dove suddenly and soared past, rising high again in the sky, and Rose shielded her eyes with her arm to watch the bird's antics. The falcon might not see well enough to hunt, but she'd never lost her love of speed.

After a while, in the distance, Rose heard Father Peter summoning the pilgrims to continue their journey. With a light sigh, she held her gloved hand aloft, beckoning Wink. The trusty falcon obediently glided down, alighting on her wrist, and while Rose secured her jesses, Wink plumped her feathers as if boasting of her flight.

How the man stole upon her unawares, Rose didn't know, but the instant she wheeled around, the dark, chained felon filled her vision like some giant raven swooping down to carry her off. Her heart slammed against her ribs, and a rough gasp was ripped from her throat.

A dozen fears coursed through her brain: she was alone; she was cornered; he meant her harm; no one would help her. And yet she stood frozen to the spot, as if by some perverse enchantment. Though every instinct told her to run—run now, run fast—her feet wouldn't budge.

Instead, as if she moved through honey, she slowly lifted her gaze past the ominous shackles and the heavy chain linking them, up between his powerful arms to his massive chest, past the dark scrub of his strong chin, settling on his wide mouth. He didn't speak, and the continuing silence frayed her nerves until she could bear it no longer.

"What is it?" she whispered, her nostrils flaring. "What do ye want?"

Surer than a falcon on the hunt, he grabbed her free wrist. She yanked back, but his grip was firm. She glanced down. His great scarred knuckles seemed to devour her trembling hand. The iron of his shackles was cold upon her wrist, and she swallowed hard as the links of the chain softly clanked against her sleeve.

Against her will, her gaze was wrenched back up to his face. He frowned, and she noted the color of his eyes. Gray. Unrelenting gray. Cold, hard, sinister gray. The color of consuming fog and impending death. A scream gathered in her throat, and she drank in a lung full of air to give it voice.

"Hush," he quietly warned her.

She should have ignored his threat. After all, a host of pilgrims stood nearby. A dozen defenders would have come to her rescue had she cried out. But something flickered in his gaze, some suggestion of controlled composure that calmed her enough to prevent the gathering scream.

He dropped his gaze to her bare hand, then turned it until 'twas palm up. She watched, breathless, and it occurred to her that he might snap her wrist with a single clench of his fist, strangle her with the length of chain, or draw a dagger to slay her, and no one would reach her in time to prevent him.

"Open your hand," he bade her.

As if he'd uttered a spell, she slowly unfurled her fingers. With his other hand, he dropped something carefully into her palm, something small and round and warm. Furrowing her brow, she peered down. 'Twas a single blue robin's egg.

She blinked up at him, confused. Was it a trick of the light, or did she detect slivers of azure amidst the gray of his eyes, a warm spark in the cool ash? 'Twas extinguished almost as quickly as 'twas born, and he released her hand with equal haste.

"For the bird," he explained.

She glanced in wonder at the gift. Of course. Food for her falcon.

Before she could gather her wits to thank him, he nodded in silent farewell. In a sweep of dark wool, worn leather, and rough iron, he turned to rejoin the group.

Once Rose set the egg on the grass, Wink made quick work of it. But 'twas a long while down the road before Rose's heart ceased its erratic beating.

Wilham gave a low whistle when Blade fell in beside him. "Well. *She's* magnificent," he whispered.

"Aye," Blade blandly agreed, his eye fixed on the trail.

"Make a man a fine prize, eh?" Wilham prodded.

"Aye."

"Lovely as a spring day?" Wilham mused.

Blade shrugged. "Pity about the eye, though."

Wilham stopped in his tracks with a disgruntled frown, and Blade walked past him, the hint of a smile twisting his mouth.

For all Wilham's virtues, he could be an incessant nag, worse than a doting mother, constantly goading Blade to abandon the road, to take a wife, to purchase himself a parcel of land and settle down. Blade didn't want to hear another word about the lass with the falcon. Not after the way the woman had knocked his brains all askew.

He shouldn't have spoken with her. He'd probably frightened her. In a rare moment of distraction, he'd forgotten that he was no longer Sir Pierce of Mirkhaugh, but Blade the mercenary. For an instant, there had been no tragedy, no dishonor, no past.

But the lady wasn't blind. She could see his damning shackles. She was witness to his shame. Naturally she'd assume he meant her harm.

Approaching her had been doubly foolish considering his mission. Familiarity tainted objectivity. He couldn't afford to befriend any of the travelers, knowing he planned to expose two of them as assassins.

He hadn't meant a thing by the gesture. 'Twas only that he'd seen the lass had brought no food with her, and while it might do *her* no harm to go hungry till their next meal, the falcon would suffer without proper sustenance. Live prey was hard to come by, but eggs were easy to find. They weren't as palatable to a peregrine as fresh kill, but they'd serve. And so when he'd discovered a robin warming a nest in the crook of a tree, he'd shooed the bird aside and pilfered one of her clutch.

He meant to hand the egg to the lass with a good scolding, chiding her for bringing along a pet for which she couldn't care. But once he felt her delicate hand within his fist, once he glimpsed the guarded look in her eyes—eyes the color of polished cobbles at the bottom of a stream, olive and russet and emerald mingled—once he beheld the trembling of her rosy lips, he could only speak gently to her.

He silently damned himself for inspiring such revulsion when he only meant her well, but he supposed such was his curse. After all, good intentions had caused the burden of pain he now bore.

How many miles they trudged, he didn't know. He paid little heed to the woods around him. Wilham and he had traveled so extensively across the countryside, it sometimes seemed he'd committed every tree to memory. There was little in the landscape to surprise him.

'Twas strange, however, to travel with so many companions and to stop so frequently. Mounted on fresh horses, Wilham and he could ride fifty miles in a day. What was two days' ride would take them ten on pilgrimage. He supposed the leisurely pace would ultimately prove a blessing, for he could use the time to unmask Archibald of Laichloan's enemies. But it didn't ease Blade's mounting suspicion, born at The Black Hound, that change was in the wind, that somehow this journey, this pilgrimage, would alter him forever.

By the time the pilgrims paused again, Blade was certain the lass must be thirsty enough to drink the holy water out of the vial the priest wore around his neck. She hadn't brought a wineskin or even a cup as far as he could see, and no one seemed aware or willing to remedy that. It entered his mind to offer her some of his own beer, but she'd doubtless refuse him. A gentlewoman would hardly drink from a vessel that had touched an outlaw's lips.

Fortunately, the country cottage where they stopped featured an ale-stake protruding from the thatched roof, a sign that fresh brew was available. Blade noted that the lass dug out a few pennies from her purse at once, giving them to the elderly woman, who'd offered to purchase ale for them. At least she'd brought coin.

He leaned back against the shaded wall of the cottage, waiting his turn. Slaking the thirst of a score of pilgrims would take a while. He could wait.

In the meantime, he harkened to the conversations around him, listening for some clue, some slip of the tongue that would betray the identity of the plotters.

The man named Jacob, the goldsmith, paraded past the other pilgrims, no doubt so they could admire the sunlight flashing off his gold jewelry. The voluptuous dark-haired woman walked beside him. Blade didn't know her name, but 'twas obvious the two knew each other. She exchanged sly glances with the goldsmith and giggled at his every word as he expounded upon the details of his craft.

The two tanners, Ivo and Odo, squatted beneath an oak and spoke in barely coherent growls, their conversation consisting of crude comments about an alehouse near Falkirk at which one might procure more than just drink from the alewife.

The three scholars were engaged in another debate, this one regarding the merits of mounted men-at-arms over dismounted archers on the battlefield. Blade could have instantly settled their argument for them—he'd been in enough battles to know— but they'd only find another subject upon which to disagree.

Simon the palmer, clasping a wooden cross in his pale hand, murmured prayers with his head bowed. But when Drogo, the cook, happened near, Simon ceased his prayers and invited him closer to look at the sliver of the bone of Saint Regulus he carried in his satchel.

Blade smirked. He wondered if the bone had belonged to some unfortunate nameless beggar found by the roadside or someone's butchered pig.

Wilham had wandered off to find a tree, but Blade knew he'd be back soon. During their travels, his comrade had developed a discriminating taste for ale and could correctly identify the proportion of barley, wheat, and oats in almost any brew, which apparently proved so amusing to the alewives that they'd often give him an extra cup at no charge. Blade, of course, had his own ideas about the alewives' generosity—'twas Wilham's bonnie face and not his discerning palate that earned him the ale.

Blade sighed, crossed his arms over his chest, and rested his head against the plaster wall, closing his eyes. He could hear the pilgrims' gossip much more clearly now. Fulk, the butcher, talked about a recent visit to Edinburgh. The goldsmith, Jacob, chuckled importantly, flirtatiously chiding the woman he now referred to as Lettie. Bryan, the most boisterous of the scholars, addressed the timid lad, asking for his name, and Blade could even hear his soft reply—Guillot.

Then someone touched Blade's sleeve, and he sprang off the wall. His chains clanked as, in one swift motion, he unfolded his arms and instinctively reached for his absent sword.

His intended victim flinched, hissing, "Holy Mother o'...! Shite! I mean..."

'Twas her, the lass with the falcon, and he'd done it again—startled her, this time into an oath at odds with her sweet lips. Her hazel eyes were wide, and the cup of ale she held aloft partially spilled over her hand, though she fought to hold it steady.

He let out his breath and lifted his hands in a gesture of apology.

"Well," she said, her rapid pulse visible in the hollow of her throat, "I'd no idea ye were so easily startled. Forgive me."

"My fault," he grumbled, not entirely sure whether her tone was sincere or sarcastic. He glanced about at the pilgrims. Fortunately, the incident hadn't attracted as much attention as he imagined. The others carried on with their chat, scarcely noticing he'd nearly leaped out of his skin.

"I thought... I've brought..." she began, pressing the cup of ale toward him, then blurted, "This is for ye."

He stared at it stupidly.

"To thank ye." She lifted her brows. "For the egg?"

He frowned. She owed him nothing. What he'd done, he'd done out of concern for her pet, no more.

"Unless ye've sworn off ale," she added.

"Aye. Nae." He winced. What was wrong with him? Irritated by his own rapidly diminishing wit, he took the ale from her and downed it all at once, wiping the foam from his lip with the back of his sleeve.

She raised a single slender brow in astonishment. "Shall I fetch another?"

Blade shifted his stance. She shouldn't be conversing with him. A young noblewoman had no business speaking to a shackled mercenary.

"Sir?"

He blinked and looked down at her again. Lord, she was a beautiful creature. What had she asked him? Did he want another?

"Nae. 'Tis enough."

"I'll gladly bring another if..."

He pressed the cup back into her hands, disconcerted by her attention and eager to be rid of her. "There's no need. I expected no payment." He saw the old woman emerge from the alehouse, carrying two cups. "Go," he bid her. "Your own ale awaits."

The lass lowered the cup and, with it, her defenses. "'Twill wait a bit longer," she said, surprising him. In a great show of courage for one so small, she straightened her back and looked him in the eye. "I've an offer to make ye."

He swallowed. A dozen highly improper offers dashed through his mind, most of them involving the delectable lass flat on her back. He waited with bated breath, but wisely held his tongue.

"For each day ye fetch an egg for my falcon," she offered, "I'll buy ye an ale."

He hesitated. 'Twas unwise to enter into any such dealings with the lass. He knew that. 'Twasn't that he was unwilling to fetch food for her bird. He had as soft a heart as any man when it came to the welfare of helpless animals. But such a bargain represented a commitment. It meant that they must see each other, speak to each other, daily. He couldn't afford to form an alliance with her, no matter how small. Her presence was far too distracting.

There was no question. He couldn't agree to the bargain. Someone else could fetch eggs for her. She was a bonnie thing. With those dewy eyes and that sweet mouth, she could get any one of the men of the company to do the deed, ale or no ale.

Certainly he, Blade the mercenary, wasn't the man to agree to such an alliance. 'Twas foolish. And irresponsible. And dangerous.

"Aye, fine."

What devil put the words in his mouth, he didn't know. But as soon as they left his tongue, the gratitude lighting her eyes sparked an ember deep inside him that he'd almost forgotten, one that had lain dormant for months.

Her touch upon his arm was fleeting but potent. "Ye won't regret your kindness, sir."

Blade doubted that. He already regretted it. He watched her whirl away in a swish of scarlet skirts and ebony tresses and cursed himself for a fool.

Wilham strolled out of the woods, sniffing the air as he passed by the other pilgrims, waving the aroma of ale toward him with his hand, then confided to Blade, "Oat with a kiss o' barley." He flipped a penny into the air with his thumb, catching it again in his hand. "Shall we?"

When Blade didn't answer, Wilham stopped and inclined his head. "What is it? What's happened?"

Blade stared bleakly at the ground.

"Blade?"

He raised his eyes to glare at Wilham.

"Holy Mother, Blade, what did I miss?"

Blade clenched his jaw, then released it. "Nothin'," he said. "Nothin'. Go buy yourself a pint." He nodded toward the alehouse door. "Buy me one as well." When Wilham had gone, he added in a mutter, "I'll pour it o'er my witless head."

# Chapter 4

A re ye daft, lass? Consortin' with his like. The man's a felon!"

Rose heard a Highland lilt in the spry old woman's voice as she whispered in horror, hauling Rose aside rather familiarly by the elbow.

Rose's heart raced. But she wasn't afraid. She was excited. She stole a glance backward. The felon's friend, the cheery man with the dancing eyes and cropped hair, stood beside him now, making him look even more dark and dangerous in contrast. "He's not so ferocious."

The woman snorted. "I ken men, lassie. That one? Pure trouble. Handsome as the devil and mean as a bear."

"A bear?" Rose's mouth quirked up at that. How odd that the woman should mention bears. Long ago, when she'd first arrived at Fernie House, a bear-baiter had come to St. Andrews. All the children of the village had gathered about the great iron cage to peer at the fierce beast inside, though none dared venture too close.

But fearless Rose had glimpsed the weariness in the bear's eyes and the scars of too many battles, and she'd felt sorry for the poor creature. Pity had outweighed caution. While her maid's back was turned and as the other children looked on in awe, she'd approached the cage and stuck her hand between the grate, stroking the bear's coarse fur. For one brief moment, she'd sensed the animal relax, felt the warmth of its hide.

Then, naturally, her maid had shrieked in horror, surprising the bear, and amidst its startled roar and the screams of the children, she'd barely snatched Rose from the bear's swiping paw. Afterward, Rose had been scolded roundly by her maid and whipped soundly by her foster father. But she never forgot the excitement she'd experienced, petting the savage animal.

'Twas how she felt now. A part of her shivered with fright at what she'd dared. But another part was exhilarated. She'd reached out, touched the beast, and come back safe.

"I wonder what his name is," Rose mused, her gaze drifting back to the man leaning against the alehouse wall, shadowed and pensive and silently menacing.

"Ach! There's a tale," the woman volunteered, wiping ale froth from her pursed mouth. "I heard his companion call him by name."

"And?"

The woman arched a grizzled brow. "Blade," she confided, shuddering. "Blade! What ilk of a brute has a name like that?"

Rose's eyes were drawn to the dark felon again. Blade. A dangerous name for a dangerous man. Alone again, he stared somberly at the ground. She wondered where his thoughts drifted.

"God's hooks, dinna look at him!" the woman hissed.

Rose ignored her. Blade. Such a cold, hard, unyielding name, like the flint in his eyes, like the strength in his hand. And yet, as with the bear, she sensed there was something tender beneath his hoary hide, if only she could reach out and touch it.

"Ye may thank Matildis for guardin' your virtue, lassie." She extended a pudgy hand. "That's my name. Call me Tildy."

"I'm Rose."

The woman's fingers were rough, her grip strong, her hand worn from honest labor. The guild pin she wore on her ample breast marked her as a wool merchant, and her finely embroidered cote-hardie and bejeweled belt distinguished her as a successful one. She was short, squat, round. Her face was as rosy and wrinkled as a rotting apple, and her eyes sparked like pine boughs on the fire, full of life and wit and wisdom.

"Well, wee *Rose*, ye'd best heed my words," she warned, "lest some knave come along to pluck ye ere ye've *bloomed*." She snorted at her own cleverness and gestured toward Rose's cup. "Here, lassie, drink up. Ye've got a thirsty look about ye."

Thirsty? Aye, that she was. For ale and for adventure.

But by the time the sun hung low and the pilgrims' shadows stretched before them as long and thin as lances, Rose could scarcely plant one foot in front of the other. Her arm ached from transporting the falcon. Her lips were chafed and sore, and she could hardly keep her eyes open. How she longed to lay her head down upon a mossy bank somewhere, to get the sleep she so desperately needed. Her arm began to sink, and her eyelids flagged.

She snapped awake instantly at the sudden drumming of horse hooves. Riders rapidly approached from behind them. Her pulse rushed through her ears, and dread sent a paralyzing shock along her spine.

Bloody hell! What if 'twas Gawter's men?

"Make way!" Father Peter called out. "Riders! Make way!"

The pilgrims shuffled off to the side of the road, and Rose fell back, hoping to disappear in the deep shade of a sycamore. She turned away from the road, concealing Wink as best she could in the crook of her arm. Her heart throbbed almost painfully as she waited for the men to pass.

But they didn't pass, not at first. Instead, they stopped to exchange words with Father Peter. At one point, they drew so close that Rose could hear the squeak of tack and the horses' huffing. One of the riders chuckled. His mount stamped upon the sod. The tension stretched inside her like a silken thread strained to its limit.

And then, finally, they rode on. Rose, sick with worry, weak with relief, hazarded a glance at them as they left. They weren't

Gawter's men. She shut her eyes tight and expelled a shuddering sigh.

But just as she brought her falcon out and turned back toward the path, she felt *his* keen glare. Blade. Her breath froze in her throat. His eyes narrowed perceptively, and she faltered beneath his wordless accusation, blushing with guilt. Then his penetrating gaze left her to study the departing riders. She bit the inside of her cheek, suddenly certain Blade knew what she'd done and would reveal her crime at any moment, calling after the men to come collect her and escort her back to Averlaigh.

But whatever suspicions he had, he kept them to himself. Sending her a puzzled frown, he lumbered back onto the road and rejoined the march.

'Twas a long while before she breathed easily, but at least she no longer struggled to stay awake on the path. Though her eyes stung with fatigue and her limbs hung like lead weights, she was too anxious to drowse.

Only when the sky darkened from periwinkle to deep azure in the fading light of the afternoon, only when they broke through the fringe of trees marking the place where the forest ended and the gentle slope of Clackmannan began, did Rose realize where they'd come.

Rising before her against the dimming canopy was a grand manor that might have looked welcoming to Rose in her weary state, but for the familiar yellow banner streaming out from its square tower. Her heart sank. They'd come to de Murs, the home of addled old Sir Fergus, with whom Wink had had...the unfortunate accident...just a fortnight ago.

"Lucifer's ballocks," Rose whispered to the falcon. "Not de Murs."

It hadn't been Wink's fault.

They'd stopped at this exact spot on their journey from Fernie House to Averlaigh a fortnight ago. 'Twas only for a few hours, to rest their horses and ease their hunger. Sir Fergus had been a generous, if feeble-witted, host. But while his renowned cook was preparing a supper feast for them, Rose and Wink had retired to his guest chamber. While Rose was napping, Wink managed to pry open the cage of prize finches Sir Fergus kept in the room and had enjoyed her own feast. What ensued was an ugly scene Rose didn't care to recall.

They couldn't possibly stay here. Sir Fergus was sure to recognize her. Or at least her bird. And yet there was nowhere else to go.

With each step up the arduous path toward the manor, Rose's pace slowed and her thoughts raced.

Maybe she could abandon the pilgrims and slip away unnoticed. She could hide in the stables or the mews and rejoin the company in the morning.

But nae, there was *one* who would surely note her absence. Blade had been eyeing her all day like a hawk watching a mouse.

Rose silently cursed. What a coil she was in. Of all the houses in Scotland, why had they come to de Murs? Even now, from one of the high windows, a servant waved at them in welcome. If only she had her cloak or something—anything—to cover her face... Even so, the by-now-infamous feathered, one-eyed murderer would surely give her away.

If she were discovered now, if all her running had been for nothing, and she had to return to Averlaigh, to her pathetic mother and the depraved man she was supposed to marry...

Rose felt ill.

Ill.

That was it! Aye, she felt ill, quite ill, too ill to dine with the others. Too ill, in fact, to even meet their host.

Carefully furrowing her brow, she tried thinking ill thoughts. 'Twas little challenge. Having traveled all night and all day with scarcely a bite to eat, forced to consort with outlaws and scoundrels, pursued by men who wished to slay her, she was already half sick with apprehension. She let out a weak moan. The nuns turned to see what was amiss.

Rose pressed her fingers to her temple.

"Does your head ail ye?" one of the sisters inquired.

"Aye." Rose emitted a shaky sigh. "It troubles me from time to time."

"Maybe ye should go directly to bed when we reach the manor," the other sister suggested.

Rose nearly smiled at how neat and simple it had been. But just for good measure, she kept up her pretense, lurching along the road, clutching her head, and moaning occasionally.

At one point, she wondered if perhaps she should be less conspicuous. After all, she didn't wish Sir Fergus to fetch her a physician who might reveal her fakery.

But 'twas too late. Unbeknownst to her, she'd already drawn the eye of the one with enough cunning to expose her.

Blade's senses grew alert the moment he saw the lady weave off the path. He thought at first 'twas mere fatigue. Her strength had been waning for the last hour. He'd seen it in the declining angle of her arm and the slowing of her step. He'd begun to wonder if she'd make it up the shallow hill to de Murs manor.

But now she'd started groaning as if gripped by pain.

"Old Sir Fergus," Wilham murmured obliviously, nodding toward the fluttering pennon. "Do ye think he'll remember us?"

"I doubt it," Blade replied, watching as one of the nuns spoke with the lady. "The man's mind is like a sieve."

"I recall from our last visit, however," Wilham said, "that the old man keeps a fine cook. We'll eat well anyway."

Blade grunted. The lady staggered along the path. Was she ill? Injured? Or simply weak with hunger?

She was cradling her head in her hand when Wilham finally took notice. "What's wrong with *her*?" he whispered.

"She hasn't eaten since morn."

Wilham lifted a surprised brow, then flashed him a sly grin. "I knew ye'd been watchin' her."

"I've been watchin' everyone."

Blade wished he had time to knock the smug smile off his friend's face, but they were at the house now, and de Murs' steward greeted them.

The man's hearty welcome had scarcely spilled from his lips when one of the nuns hastened forward to whisper something in his ear.  He nodded and clapped his hands for a maid, who immediately escorted the young lass and her falcon off inside the manor.

Blade sighed impatiently, foiled by how easily she'd slipped from his vigil.  His suspicions regarding her had grown since their encounter with the knights on the road.  She'd been rattled when the men reined up, though the three seemed harmless enough.  They'd told Father Peter they were on a mission to purchase arms at the Dunfermline fair.  Why should they cause the lass such alarm?

Unless...she feared they would recognize her.

"What's her name?" he asked Wilham suddenly as they entered the manor with the rest of the pilgrims.  "Do ye know?"

"Who?  Our falconer?"

He nodded.  Wilham shrugged.

"Where did she come from?" he pressed, but Wilham didn't know that either.

All at once, Wilham's eyes widened.  "Ye don't think *she's* the assassin?"

"'Tis possible."

"Ye're jestin'."

"I hope I'm wrong," he said.  Blade didn't like to think that such a seeming innocent was capable of such villainy, of so bloodthirsty a crime, any more than Wilham did.  And yet, of all the pilgrims, the lovely and delicate wisp of a woman was so far the most suspicious.

"Impossible," Wilham said as they stepped into the cavernous great room of Sir Fergus's manor.  "That blushin' flower is as sinless as a saint, or I'll eat my trews."

Blade hoped Wilham was right.  But the fact that she'd joined the pilgrimage unprepared, that she'd concealed herself from the riders, that she'd hurried upstairs before Sir Fergus could lay eyes on her, didn't bode well for her innocence.

As it turned out, Sir Fergus remembered neither Wilham nor Blade, though Blade had championed de Murs less than a year ago against the man's greedy cousin who'd tried to lay claim to the manor. The old knight's mind was as weak as his sword arm, but Blade had been amply paid for his defense of de Murs' lands at the time, and the table Sir Fergus spread now for the pilgrims displayed that generosity as well.

Unlike its owner, the manor was kept in good order. What the knight was lacking in wits, his servants made up for in hospitality. After Sir Fergus issued a faint welcome to the pilgrims, several pitchers of water were brought so the guests could wash the dust from their hands and faces. Then they were led to the enormous trestle table in the midst of the hall, where flagons of golden perry awaited to quench their thirst.

Sconces brightened the great hall, whose heavy-beamed ceiling arched upward to double height and whose stone floor was laid with fresh rushes. The massive hearth at the end of the hall flickered with cheery flame, and the wooden screens concealing the buttery were painted with twining vines. Twin stairways spiraled up opposite sides of the hall, leading to half a dozen upper chambers.

Blade perused the doors along the upper story as they sat down to supper. The lass hid behind one of them, secure for the moment, but he wondered if, when they awoke on the morrow, she'd still be there.

The food *was* excellent, as Wilham had remembered—roast pike in brasey sauce, mussel and leek caudle, freshly baked bannocks, spring peas with onions, a salad of spring cresses, and a fine Bordeaux to wash it all down.

Blade ate with difficulty. Shackles were not conducive to proper table manners, and the clank of metal against his flagon every time he took a drink made him wince in irritation.

Still, he was glad of his decision to embark upon the pilgrimage with chains of disgrace upon him. It meant he could observe the travelers without interruption, for most of them left him in peace, fearing to speak to a dishonored knight. Most of

Passion's Exile

them except the lass, he amended, who was too unworldly to realize she shouldn't consort with his kind.

"Blade." Wilham nudged him, then gestured meaningfully with his brows toward the spot where the three scholars sat. The lads were engaged with the nuns in what seemed to Blade to be a harmless discussion.

"Fate?" Bryan groused. "Faugh! I can't wait for Fate to steer my course."

"Nor I," Thomas agreed. "I'd make my own fortune."

Daniel nodded. "'Tis why we go to St. Andrews."

"All great things—knowledge, wealth, power," Bryan decreed, "come not to those who dally..."

"But to those who pursue them relentlessly," Thomas finished.

"And bearin' that in mind, 'twould seem," Daniel concluded, "that the most virtuous o' wives may be found in such a place as St. Andrews."

"Where pilgrims and seekers o' truth gather," Bryan chimed in.

"And where men of enlightenment might be welcomed," added Thomas.

"Do ye not agree, Sister Mary?" asked Daniel.

Sister Mary looked as glassy-eyed as a deer.

"Perhaps," Sister Ivy deflected softly. "But matters o' marriage are oftentimes best left in the hands o' God."

Sister Mary came out of her stupor, blinking in wonder. "The hands o' God?"

"Aye," Sister Ivy said. "Just as *our* destinies, sweet sister, have been so decreed."

The scholars looked displeased with her answer. Before long, however, a new debate picked up their spirits, one involving the question of which God created first, the hen or the egg.

"Did ye hear them?" Wilham whispered, nudging Blade. "They spoke o' makin' their fortune in St. Andrews." He leaned in close, gesturing with a chunk of bannock. "What greater

57

fortune could there be than ransomin' the son of a wealthy laird?"

"The plotters I heard didn't speak o' ransom, Wilham. They spoke o' murder."  He finished off the last gulp of wine. "Besides, those three couldn't agree on the most efficient way to kill a flea."  He pointed at Wilham's fish.  "Are ye goin' to finish that?"

"I couldn't eat another bite."

While Wilham watched in slack-jawed astonishment, Blade stabbed the pike with his eating dagger and moved it surreptitiously onto the linen napkin in his lap, where a mound of peas and a wedge of bannock already nestled.

What moved him to such selflessness, he wasn't certain, but while the kitchen lads continued to present platter after platter of savory dishes to the table, all he'd been able to think about was the half-starved waif upstairs.  As far as he'd seen, no one had knocked at any of the doors to offer the lass sustenance.

If he knew Sir Fergus, the old knight had forgotten all about his upstairs guest.  And apparently, in the exuberance of sating their own appetites on the delicious fare, so had all the other pilgrims. Even Wilham.

"Midnight nibble?" Wilham asked, eyeing his cache.

Blade shrugged.  Let Wilham believe that, if he liked. 'Twas easier than explaining the strange protectiveness he felt for a woman who might well be a murderer.

Supper seemed to drag on.  Blade drummed his fingers restlessly upon the table and listened with little interest to the conversations around him.

Fulk soothed Drogo's ego, whispering to him that despite the impressiveness of the meal, Drogo still reigned as the finest cook in all of Scotland.

The tanners, Ivo and Odo, toasted loudly, draining their flagons again and again.  Blade wondered if they knew how much stronger Bordeaux was than the beer to which they were accustomed.

Brigit the brewster giggled at something the goldsmith said, leaning close to give him an unobstructed view of her ample bosom, which earned him a sharp kick from Lettie, across the table from him.

The silent soldier sat staring into his wine, garnering several shy glances from the lad, Guillot, beside him.

And seated beside their host, Simon the palmer and Father Peter orated about past pilgrimages until Sir Fergus's head drooped and his thin gray beard began to dip into his trencher.

Sweetmeats were brought last to the table, and Blade, having little taste for sweets, dumped the lot of his serving into his napkin. He nudged Wilham. After a disgruntled frown, Wilham surrendered his portion as well.

Then Father Peter announced that, because Sir Fergus had so generously provided food and lodging for all the pilgrims that passed this way—which announcement roused the poor old knight from his slumber—the pilgrims should repay him with a bit of entertainment, namely the telling of stories. He further charged that on each of the evenings of pilgrimage, two travelers should relate a story, so that by the time they reached St. Andrews, nearly everyone would have told one tale.

Blade fought the urge to roll his eyes. A man of few words, he didn't relish telling stories. Fortunately, Father Peter was quick to volunteer himself for the first tale.

'Twas a parable Blade had heard before, The Divided Horsecloth, so as the priest began to relate in dramatic fashion the misadventures of the merchant who yielded too much of his wealth to his son, Blade let his gaze wander along the upper chambers of the hall.

She was probably in that first room at the top of the stairs. The central chambers were larger rooms and likely reserved for the pilgrims. The last room belonged to Sir Fergus himself. The first chamber was much smaller, though well-appointed, with tapestries and carpets and even Sir Fergus's pair of pet finches. 'Twas where Wilham and he had stayed as guests when they'd defended the manor.

The priest finished up his tale, citing the moral as a warning to those who are about to marry off their sons, that they shouldn't strip themselves so bare as to rely upon the charity of others in the end.

Blade dutifully applauded with the others, and the priest, beaming at the praise, lingered over it until he was forced to pass the task onto the next storyteller. The curly-headed scholar, Bryan, wasted no time in volunteering.

"An envious man and a covetous man were friends—as much as such men may be," Bryan began.

Wilham elbowed Blade, whispering, "I like this one."

"Saint Martin himself found them travelin' upon the road and decided to reward their evil souls," Bryan continued. "So he said, 'I'll bless each o' ye with a gift. The man who reveals to me his desire shall be granted it, but the man who refrains from speech shall be granted twice what is bestowed upon his fellow.'"

Wilham grinned, and Blade nodded. He could already see the story would end badly, and he ignobly wondered how long the telling would take.

He folded the napkin over the food he'd scavenged, lifting his eyes again to the upstairs chamber. By the time all this nonsense was over, the lass would surely be asleep. After all, she'd looked half-dead on the road. He frowned down at the useless bundle in his lap, silently cursing as the tale droned on and on.

"And so the envious man said to Saint Martin," the scholar finally concluded with great elan, "'I can't bear that my fellow might have double my bounty, therefore, I pray ye, pluck out one o' my eyes that my fellow may lose both o' his.'"

The pilgrims reacted variously, some gasping, some chortling, some nodding wisely, but a good third of them didn't understand the tale. Of course, when Bryan tried to explain it to those who were lost, an argument commenced between him and his fellow scholars as to the distinction between envy and covetousness, and 'twas a long while before anyone, besides their host—who sat snoring with his chin upon his hand—grew weary enough to seek slumber.

Rose's stomach growled again. She winced, pressing the flat of her palm against her hollow belly to stifle its rumblings.

The chamber was lavishly furnished, from the Turkish carpets gracing the floor to the Arras tapestries hung on the walls. Three copper lanterns housed beeswax candles, and in a fit of extravagance, she'd lit all three. The bed was massive, carved of oak, and a cherry wood chest squatted beside the window, which featured both mullioned glass and wooden shutters. Rose settled gingerly onto the plump feather pallet, fingering the bedhangings of sapphire velvet.

Wink, with grim irony, perched atop the ornate steel cage that had once housed Sir Fergus's finches but now hung empty and incriminating.

The chamber's appointments, as sumptuous as they were, did nothing to assuage Rose's hunger. After so little breakfast and such a long march, her dizzy head was no longer a pretense.

Yet almost worse than her hunger was her boredom. Despite her fatigue, she was far too anxious to sleep. In the hours since she'd arrived, she'd inspected every tapestry in great detail, paced across the carpet until she feared she'd worn a furrow in it, and nosed irreverently through the chest, looking for treasures, finding only linen sheets. She'd stared from the window while the sun took cover behind the hills, but no clouds had gathered to bloom in rosy profusion at its setting, and at twilight, neither bird nor squirrel nor deer had stirred amidst the endless expanse of grass.

Now, as she rose to peer once more from the window, the stars stood motionless in the stagnant heaven. The landscape, as fixed as the scenes in the wall tapestries, glowed with a dull, gray, unchanging haze.

She closed the shutters and sank onto the bed again with a sigh, staring at the thick oak door that separated her from the rest of the pilgrims. She wondered what they were doing.

"Certainly they've eaten well," she told Wink. Sir Fergus's cook was famed far and wide.

But surely the company had finished their meal by now, and they probably reveled in some sort of entertainment. Maybe Father Peter delivered a sermon. Or those two tanners, Ivo and Odo, served up a bawdy song as coarse as their hides. Perchance the three scholars expounded upon some fine point of philosophy. Or Guillot, the quiet mouse, amazed everyone with a resounding singing voice.

Rose grinned, enjoying her guessing game.

"I'll wager Jacob the goldsmith knows a carole, and he's dancin' with Lettie and Brigit," she told Wink, who shifted slowly from one foot to the other.

"Drogo the cook is likely recitin' a dark legend about dragons," she decided, "and Fulk, for all his size, probably has a light touch with a viol."

Wink bobbed her head.

"The nuns are probably good for little except reflectin' softly on the virtues o' the Holy Mother. And Simon the palmer is sure to deliver some dry history. Perhaps Tildy plays the bagpipes."

She chuckled. Wink fluffed out her feathers and let them settle. Rose wondered silently about the sad soldier, whose occupation she'd overheard from Brigit. She envisioned him playing tragic madrigals upon a harp.

Rose glared hard at the door now, itching to see through it. Most of all, she wondered what talents that dark outlaw, Blade, possessed. Shackled as he was, he could play neither pipe nor harp, nor would he be able to dance. He seemed to part with words begrudgingly, as if he must pay for each one he uttered, so she imagined he had little skill with weaving a story. But the more she thought about it, the deeper her curiosity grew, and finally, after what seemed to her an excruciating amount of patience, she could endure no more.

She gave Wink a warning glance. "Ye be still."

Then she rose from the bed and tiptoed to the door, pressing her ear flush against the oak. The wood was too thick for her to hear anything. There wasn't even a decent space to peer through at the hinge of the door.

She toyed with her necklace, idly winding a finger into the chain. Surely no harm could come of easing the door open just a crack. The chamber afforded a clear view of the great hall below, and no one would notice her peeking out from the door.

Very slowly, she lifted the latch. Her heart thumping, she pried at the door until it creaked open the merest bit.

She expected to see the arched beams of the ceiling and the great hall below, pilgrims gathering around a huge feast, laughing and singing and dancing. But all she heard was silence. All she saw was black.

Looming before her was the outlaw. His chest caught her at eye-level, blocking her view, and his shadowed face was indiscernible but for the soft flickering reflections in his eyes. At her startled gasp, he raised a warning finger to his lips, which only alarmed her further. But by then 'twas too late to close the door.

Not that she didn't try. But when she shoved forward against the thing, he blocked it with his body, then forced his way inside.

She should have screamed for help. He was an outlaw, after all. God knew what he intended—thievery, assault, murder. But something about his nerveless manner, and moreover, something about the tantalizing aroma of food wafting into the room, stopped her.

Still, she retreated to a safe distance as he entered. He leaned back against the door till it closed. Rose swallowed heavily. They were alone.

"What do ye want?" she whispered, one fist coiled tightly in the bedhangings.

He held one palm up in a gesture of peace, then swept back his cloak and offered her a linen bundle. "Hungry?"

She stared at the package, unconsciously licking her lower lip. But her wariness proved more compelling than her hunger.

"What is it?" she asked.

An almost indiscernible smile hovered about his mouth. "Does it matter?"

She lifted her chin proudly as if it did indeed matter, but couldn't help gazing longingly at the bundle.

He unfolded the napkin to reveal what he'd brought. "Fish, peas, bannock. The cook has talent."

"I know," she replied without thought, realizing her mistake when he suddenly narrowed his eyes. "I've heard," she amended.

"Ye must be hungry," he coaxed.

Her gaze fixed upon the food. "Are those...sweetmeats?"

"Aye."

Rose loved sweetmeats.

"I'll just leave them here," he murmured, walking slowly toward the cherry wood chest, like a hunter wary of spooking a deer.

Rose realized she was being ridiculous. The man meant her no harm. If he did, he certainly wouldn't attempt anything here, where one shriek from her would send a dozen servants rushing to see what was amiss. Besides, he'd fetched an egg for her falcon out of simple kindness, the same kindness that prompted him to bring her food now.

He bent to place the bundle on the chest.

She loosened her grip on the bedhangings. "Here," she said, stepping toward him with her arms extended. "I'm not the ungrateful shrew I seem."

He carefully placed the laden napkin into her hands. His knuckles were rough and battle-scarred, and as they slid raggedly against her palms, a shiver of delicious fear raced through her. What a different life he must lead, she thought, from her sheltered existence at Fernie House. He was a knight, after all, who risked his life daily.

He snorted. "Eat." He seemed in no hurry to leave, despite how his presence affected her appetite. He meandered about the chamber, perusing the tapestries, leisurely running a hand over the carved wood of the bedpost, almost as if he possessed all he touched.

Rose glanced down at the food. It smelled wonderful. Her stomach grumbled in anticipation.

"Go on," he bade her, brazenly lifting a hand to scratch familiarly at Wink's breast.

Bristling at the liberty with which he stroked her falcon, Rose nonetheless managed to hold her tongue. She settled onto the edge of the bed and began to pick at her supper. Despite her raging hunger, 'twas difficult to eat while the dark and dangerous stranger prowled nearby. She hardly tasted the food. Her attentions were riveted on the mysterious, disgraced knight who went by the name of Blade.

He peered out of one of the shutters to the night beyond and asked casually, "How do ye know Sir Fergus?"

She choked on a sweetmeat. How had he guessed? "I...I don't."

His steely eyes turned to fasten on her. 'Twas clear he saw through her lie.

She delicately cleared her throat. "That is, not well."

"But ye're acquainted with him."

She reluctantly nodded.

"How?" The moonlight streamed in through the parted shutters, silvering his dark hair and sketching harsh shadows across his face. He might have shown her kindness, but he looked as dangerous as a stalking wolf.

She gulped, loath to reply.

He draped an arm over the top of the shutter and nodded toward the food. "Enjoyin' your supper?"

Rose blushed. His point was obvious. He'd brought her food. The least she owed him was an answer. A *truthful* answer.

She sighed and stared at the scattering of sweetmeats still gracing the napkin. "I visited here a fortnight past."

"And?"

Her gaze flitted about the room, everywhere but at him. "And...there was an incident."

"An incident? What kind of incident?"

She stalled, wiping her mouth with the corner of the napkin, then finally mumbled, "My falcon ate Sir Fergus's pet finches."

His elbow dropped abruptly off the shutter, and the sudden rattle of chains made her look up. She was surprised by the momentarily unguarded alarm in his face.

"'Twas an accident," she said defensively. "'Twasn't Wink's fault. How would a falcon know the difference between a pet and prey?"

She wasn't certain, but when he nodded, it looked as if his lips were twitching with amusement.

And now that she'd revealed her acquaintance with Sir Fergus, she realized what a profound mistake she'd made.

The felon might well expose her. With this new knowledge, he trod too perilously close to the truth of her escape. She'd been a fool to tell him anything.

Summoning up what arrogance she could manage under his piercing regard, she sat arrow-straight. "Ye must take your leave now, sir. If ye'll remember, 'twas ye who said we shouldn't be seen speakin' together."

"We've not been seen," he assured her.

She pressed fingers to her temple. "I said I was ill."

There was definitely an upward curve now to the corner of his lip. "I've seen better playactin' at Michaelmas."

She blushed furiously. "I *am* ill."

He lifted a dubious brow at the near empty napkin. "Ye seem to have a healthy enough appetite."

She crumpled the napkin over the unfinished fare and shoved it toward him. "I've lost it again."

He only glanced at the bundle. "Save the rest for later." He gave her a cocky nod, then swept past her, close enough so that his cloak brushed the bottom of her surcoat.

She snapped her skirt out of his way. Childish fury surged through her veins. She'd tried to deceive him, and he'd caught her in that deception. She fired a scathing glare at his back as he left.

When he turned unexpectedly at the door, he caught her enraged gaze. But he seemed largely unimpressed, which only angered her further.

"Ye needn't distress yourself," he murmured. "Sir Fergus can scarcely remember events of a day ago, much less those of a fortnight past."

She blinked.

"Sleep well," he told her. Then he gently closed the door.

She flounced down on the bed, spilling half the sweetmeats onto the carpet. Mumbling a curse, she managed to quickly gather the sugared fruit back onto the napkin, blowing it off for good measure, and set it aside.

Damn that wicked knight. He'd unearthed part of her secret. How long would it take him to discover the rest?

She wrested out of her surcoat, flopped onto her back in her linen chemise, and stared up at the knot of bedhangings centered above the bed. Was he right about Sir Fergus? Had the old man forgotten her?

If so, departing in the morning would be simple. But if he happened to remember her or Wink—or, more significantly, if someone *stirred* his memory—'twould be difficult indeed to escape without Sir Fergus alerting her kin at Averlaigh.

Could she trust Blade to keep silent?

With a fretful sigh, she turned on her side, exhausted. Before her heart beat thrice, she fell asleep. And before she'd drawn three breaths, she began to dream.

She dreamt she was being pursued by a midnight rider again, galloping along the dark road, faster and faster. This time he caught up with her, snatched her from the saddle, dragging her onto his own mount, confining her there as they rode mile after mile. When day dawned in the dream, she swung around to look at her abductor, fearful 'twas Sir Gawter, her betrothed. But instead, her captor was Blade. With a grim smile, he bade her open her hand. She did as he commanded, and he placed upon her open palm, not a robin's egg, but a kiss.

Rose awoke to the sound of Wink shuffling along the steel rungs of the cage. In the pale sunlight, the threads of her dream slowly unraveled into oblivion till all that was left was the memory of her handsome captor and the gentleness of his touch.

# Chapter 5

Blade bit off a piece of the oatcake they were served for breakfast, then stuffed the rest into his pack. The lass had come down for neither the service in the chapel nor the morning meal, despite his reassurances she'd not be recognized. He sincerely hoped she wasn't still abed. Father Peter seemed to hold to a strict schedule. He might well leave loiterers behind, particularly those who saw fit to avoid Mass.

He told himself that his concern wasn't for her in particular, but for young Archibald of Laichloan. After all, if the group splintered, the lad's assassins would be more difficult to track.

He paced across the hall yet again, restlessly flexing his fists, glancing up at the still closed door. Then Father Peter began announcing their departure.

"What's the trouble, Blade?" Wilham whispered, falling in beside him. "Are ye that anxious to go?"

"We're not all accounted for," he muttered around the bite of oatcake.

Wilham scanned the residents of the hall. "The lass."

Blade sent a glance toward the upstairs chamber.

"I never would have believed it," Wilham said, shaking his head in a pretense of wonder, his voice thick with sarcasm. "She's slipped off, hasn't the little shrew, to do her dirty business? By God, she *is* the murderer."

But just then, to Blade's relief and Wilham's amusement, the door swung open, and out peered the lass, looking warily both ways along the hallway. When she saw the way was clear, she retreated momentarily, then stepped onto the landing.

Blade almost choked on his oatcake when she reappeared.

The lass had been resourceful, he had to admit. She descended the steps, her head and face veiled by a modest swath of white linen. No one but he recognized that her concealing wimple was made of a supper napkin.

She managed to elude Sir Fergus's attentions. The pilgrims said their farewells and cleared the hall, and the lass discreetly collected her falcon. But as she passed by, Blade couldn't resist commenting under his breath. "Lovely veil."

She blushed in a most becoming manner, and he found himself hoping that, despite his suspicions, the lass with the falcon wasn't the assassin he sought.

Wilham elbowed him, breaking into his thoughts. "I think ye'd better train an eye on the goldsmith and that Lettie woman," he confided.

"Why?"

"While ye were off last night, deliverin' that midnight feast—"

Blade snagged Wilham's arm, stopping him in his tracks. "Ye knew about that?"

Wilham raised a brow. "Oh, don't be so shocked," he said. "Ye know as well as I do, 'tis my occupation to watch your back."

Blade released him with a disgruntled sigh.

"Anyway, while ye were..." He cleared his throat. "Out, I saw the goldsmith leave his bed and go out the door. I followed, watchin' him from the doorway. He waited outside the ladies' chamber for a long while, and eventually a woman emerged."

"Lettie?"

"Aye. Where they went, I don't know. But I know he didn't return to bed until after ye'd come back."

Blade frowned thoughtfully, looking over the heads of the pilgrims toward the goldsmith who, predictably, walked beside Lettie. 'Twas possible they were the culprits. Lettie, in particular, looked capable of slipping poison into a young lad's drink without skipping a breath. Blade would keep watch on them both today.

As they traveled through the wood, 'twasn't long before Blade's eye chanced upon a small nest lodged in the fork of an oak tree not far off the path. It contained two tiny eggs and a larger one he knew belonged to a cuckoo. Performing two good deeds with one act, he slipped the invasive cuckoo egg carefully into the pouch he wore at his hip, to keep it warm until 'twas time for the falcon to feed.

The morning blossomed into the kind of spring day to make a Scotsman boast. Puffy white clouds floated like thistledown across a jewel bright sky. Squirrels spiraled up the trunks of ancient oaks, and sparrows twittered and flitted about, their beaks laden with bits of dry grass and twigs. Newly-hatched butterflies embroidered the grass, alighting on daisies and bluebells and dandelions scattered on the emerald sward. The air was balmy and fragrant, full of new life. Even the scuffling of twenty pairs of shoes and the incessant drone of conversation created a lulling lay as the travelers strolled like minstrels through the countryside.

By mid-afternoon, they stopped to rest. The Gray Swan, a squat, crumbling tavern tucked away in a dark grove of oaks, far from any town, nevertheless made the pilgrims welcome. Blade wasn't familiar with this particular establishment, but he knew their type well. Hardly a day passed that some traveler wouldn't journey along such a road, whether a group of pilgrims, a fair-bound merchant, or a knight's retinue. The Gray Swan fared well on the purses of wanderers. 'Twas also a perfect site for secret assignations and gatherings of a less wholesome nature.

Indeed, Blade's mind was so attuned to possible intrigue and danger that when he felt someone tug suddenly at his sleeve, he started and almost instinctively raised his fists.

Fortunately, he stayed his hands in time, but his fierce scowl made the woman gasp, and her falcon flapped wildly on her arm.

"Sorry." He raised his hands in apology. "Sorry." His heart banged against his ribs. Bloody hell—had he almost struck her? There were times when a knight's instincts were a curse. Then he twisted his mouth bitterly. One of those times he remembered all too well. 'Twas a time that haunted him every waking moment. He lowered his hands and growled, "Ye should ne'er steal up on a man-at-arms."

He glimpsed the momentary sting in her eyes, but what he said, he said for her own good. He'd not withdraw his warning.

To his amazement, she didn't dissolve into tears and run away. Instead, when her falcon calmed, she drew herself up to her full height, which still left her only shoulder-high to him, and disdainfully held out her closed fist.

He frowned, puzzled.

"Take it," she snapped.

He warily held out a shackled hand, and she dropped a penny on his palm.

"For your ale," she explained, flushing prettily with ire. "I expect ye to live up to your end o' the bargain. My falcon grows hungry." Then she whipped around in a swirl of scarlet skirts to stalk off.

He caught her by the elbow. She gasped, and he could see her pulse racing in her throat. He should let her go. He knew that. He was a knight, not an outlaw. Or at least he *had* been. 'Twas brutal to accost a frail angel in such a manner.

Still, he detained her. He wrapped his fingers around her upper arm, holding her there, and, enclosing the penny in his other hand, reached into the pouch at his hip. Her brows lifted when he produced the cuckoo's egg, and she had the grace to look chagrined when he placed it in her hand.

"Thank ye...sir," she muttered, clearly abashed.

He felt a moment of grim satisfaction as she hurried off to feed the bird.

Despite the gloomy outward appearance of The Gray Swan, once they went inside, the tavern maids were cheery, and the ale was cheap. But a few dubious characters whispered in shadowed corners. Blade never kept his hand far from his dagger. The tavern was an ideal place to plot devilry.

Wilham obviously agreed. The ubiquitous sparkle of his eyes vanished, replaced by watchful sobriety. While the rest of the pilgrims drank greedily, he and Blade sipped at their cups, keeping their minds clear, their wits sharp.

The first pilgrim to leave the tavern was Jacob the goldsmith. Blade wasn't the only one watching him. Two nefarious-looking oafs took keen interest in his going, perhaps with an eye for his gold.

"Shall I follow him?" Wilham asked.

"Not yet."

Blade watched the oafs. They were in no hurry to follow the goldsmith either. Perhaps he'd misjudged their intent. But in another moment, Lettie rose from her bench and sauntered toward the door.

"Now?" Wilham asked eagerly.

"I'll go. Ye keep an eye on those two nefarious-lookin' oafs." He nodded toward the men.

Disappointed, Wilham slumped at the table, and Blade slipped out the tavern door in time to see Lettie vanish beyond the trees. She was easy to track—she didn't trouble to hide her passage or silence her footfalls—and after exchanging a few badly done owl calls with someone, 'twasn't long before she met up, as he suspected, with Jacob. Blade hid in the bushes, close enough to see them, but not to hear their whispers.

Soon, however, he discovered the purpose of their secret meeting. They plotted not assassination, but adultery. Lettie kissed the goldsmith, then chuckled in rich seduction, turning and bending forward at the waist to flip up her skirts while Jacob fumbled with the points of his braies.

Blade squeezed his eyes shut. He wished to see no more. 'Twas bad enough that he couldn't stop his ears against their grunts and squeals nor leave without alerting them of his presence.

It didn't take long. Blade was able to conceal himself well enough that, when they were done, they passed by one at a time—for appearance's sake, of course—without seeing him. He waited several moments, then emerged from the brush and started back along the trail, disgusted at the waste of his time.

The trees crowded this part of the wood, forming a leafy canopy overhead that cast deep shadow on the ground below. Blade was struck by misgiving about the place and its unnatural dark, as if the forest was accustomed to harboring evil and might turn on him at any time. More than just the sin of adultery took place here, he was certain.

Something rustled the thick blanket of dead leaves off to his right, and he froze, his hand gripping the haft of his dagger. A squirrel suddenly bounded from the pile, its tail twitching as it scampered into the bushes. Blade let go of his weapon.

He heard another shiver of leaves—a wren this time, flitting among the branches.

But a larger movement drew his eye, and he slipped behind a fat sycamore trunk to observe. Through the maze of saplings, he spied Guillot. The timid youth, with his woven satchel slung over one bony shoulder, was groping along the bole of an oak. A finch flew past the lad's head, and the boy ducked in panic. His gaze darted nervously around the forest, and fear drained the color from his face.

As Blade watched, the lad reached into the hollow bole, wincing distastefully at whatever skittering creatures lurked there, then withdrew his arm. Into the hollow went the satchel. Then the boy picked up a stone and scratched an X into the trunk above the bole. When he was done, he dropped the rock, wiped his hands on his breeches, hastily scanning the woods, then scurried toward the spot where Blade waited.

Blade stepped out from his hiding place to intercept the lad. But when he caught the youth by the shoulders, the poor lad instantly went as limp as a dead dove. Indeed, Blade didn't so much restrain the lad as hold him upright. If Guillot was part of a murder plot, Blade thought, he must be someone else's instrument, for the boy's heart was clearly too weak for intrigue.

"Please do not kill me." His voice was as thin as thread, colored by a faint French accent, and tears welled in his wide eyes. "Do not kill me. You can have it. You can have it all."

"Shh. I won't kill ye. I just want to know what mischief ye're up to."

"I meant to give it back. I swear I did. Only do not...do not tell him. Do not tell him it was me." Then he began sniffling like a child, and 'twas all Blade could do to calm the pitiful lad.

"What did ye take?" he asked gently. "What did ye leave in that tree?"

"S-s-silver, my master's silver." He clutched at Blade's shirt, pleading with him. "I wouldn't have taken it, but I had no coin of my own."

He frowned. "Ye wish me to have pity on a thief?"

The boy clamped his lips together, stifling his sobs. "I'm no thief. I know that now. That's why I left the silver there. I mean to send word to him where it is hidden."

"So, a *remorseful* thief."

The boy sank his head onto his chest in shame.

Blade sighed and glanced at the oak where he'd cached the silver. There must be more to the story. "This man is your master?"

He swallowed hard and nodded.

"And ye are his..."

"His apprentice, a locksmith."

He narrowed his eyes, suspicious. "Why would ye have need o' his silver? A master provides for his apprentices."

Guillot's chin trembled, and tears welled anew. He whispered something, but Blade couldn't hear it.

"What? Speak up."

But the lad buried his face in his hands to hide his weeping. Blade reached into his pouch, whipping out a cloth to dry the boy's tears, but to his surprise, the gesture made Guillot recoil in terror, throwing his arms in front of his face.

"'Tis only a cloth," he murmured, showing the youth. Then Blade glanced at the boy's upraised wrists. They were purple with recent bruises. More mottling he hadn't noticed before ringed the lad's throat in shades of sickly yellow and green.

He swallowed hard. 'Twasn't the first time he'd seen signs of abuse. Images of Julian, his brother's wife, flashed through his mind unbidden—a blackened eye, a bruised cheek, a burned hand. His fury rose like a roused wolf, the way it always had with Julian. But he was older now, and wiser, and instead of lashing out against the injustice, he leashed the beast and let the anger growl inside him.

"Your master beats ye," he murmured with far more calm than he felt.

His blunt statement surprised the lad. He lowered his arms and self-consciously tugged his sleeves down over the bruises.

"And ye ran away," Blade guessed.

Despite his shaking limbs and spindly frame, Guillot's words were firm. "I will not return. No one can make me return."

Blade's eyes smoldered like banked coals. "No one will."

If Rose had known the forest would be as busy as St. Andrews on market day, she would never have considered sneaking into the trees to answer nature's call. Luckily, when the foot traffic began, she'd already taken care of her business.

First, Jacob passed by her hiding spot, then Lettie. A moment later, the timid French lad traipsed past in the opposite direction. Finally, *he'd* come skulking by. Blade. The dark outlaw.

Fortunately, no one seemed to see her standing frozen behind the clump of bushes. Blade was preoccupied with spying on the apprentice, who was preoccupied with stuffing a sack into the hollow of a tree. When the lad walked past again, Blade had nabbed him. What ensued was a fascinating exchange between the two.

Apparently, Rose wasn't the only one using the pilgrimage as a means of escape to St. Andrews.

"I have to give the silver back," Guillot told Blade. "I cannot go home to Calais with the stain of thievery on my soul. But I will not return to my master."

Rose agreed. She wouldn't return to her abuser either. But she thought the lad deserved to keep the coin as payment for the beatings.

"Ye can't leave the silver here," Blade said.

"I mean to send a missive to him, telling him where it is hidden."

"It may not be here when he arrives," Blade said plainly. "And if 'tis gone, not only will he bemoan the loss o' his silver, but he'll also know when and where ye passed this way."

"He might follow me," Guillot realized, his eyes darting fearfully. "He might find me." He pressed a bony fist into his palm. "What shall I do?"

"Take it with ye until we reach St. Andrews. There ye can find a priest to see it safely returned."

The boy nodded.

Then Blade glanced about the dark woods, and a brief shudder betrayed his emotions. "Ye'd best retrieve your sack now. There's no tellin' what manner o' men lurk in these woods."

No sooner had he spoken than three such men emerged from behind a huge joined pair of gnarled oaks in the deep shadows. Quick as lightning, Blade curved an arm around the apprentice, pulling the lad behind him to protect him from the filthy fiends who approached.

Rose stifled a gasp. The men—if they could be called that—seemed made out of the leaves and dirt of the woods. Mud coated their faces and stained their garments, and oak leaves stuck out from their sleeves and hats. The only things not besmirched with camouflaging dirt were the vicious daggers they held before them.

"Aye." The first man's voice was coarse, like a rusty hinge. "Ye'd best retrieve yer sack now, young lad."

"So's we can take it back to its rightful owner," the second sneered.

The third man, who not only looked like a tree, but had the same gargantuan proportions, mindlessly grinned. "Right, so's we can take it back."

Before they even finished giggling, Blade drew a dagger.

Rose's heart lurched. She'd never seen a real fight, only tournaments, where the blades were blunted, knights were rarely injured, and men exchanged insults with harmless glee.

This battle would be real. Blood would be spilled. Blade was not only outnumbered, but shackled. No matter how good a fight he put up, the three thieves would surely defeat him.

She had to do something.

She sprang forward. At least, that was her intent. Actually, since her skirts snagged on the bushes, 'twas more of a lunge and then a topple. By the time she managed to disentangle herself and scramble upright, cursing all the while, the fight was already well engaged.

Rose was astonished by Blade's skill, his speed, his ferocity. Despite his shackles, he slashed with the dagger in bold arcs, forcing the thieves away. He yelled at Guillot to get back, and the boy wasted no time scurrying off, Rose hoped, to get help.

Blade's dagger sliced forward, nicking the second thief's arm, and the man howled in pain.

"Go get the silver," the first robber whined to his wounded companion. "We'll hold him off."

"Nae!" Rose shouted. She astonished them all, for none had noted her presence till now. Without considering the consequences and before they could gather their wits, she tore off for the tree where the silver was cached.

Behind her, Blade suddenly bellowed, "Nae! To me!"

But the thieves were apparently more interested in the silver than his challenge. When she stole a glance over her shoulder, all three were lumbering after her.

She skidded on the leaves in front of the tree, and she was sure the robbers would simply push her out of the way, reach in, steal the treasure, and disappear.

She hadn't counted on Blade's speed. He roared up on their heels before they could grab anything, and his dagger whistled about their heads, taking the first thief's hat and leaving a bloody gash alongside his ear.

The second thief, angered now, thrust his knife forward. Blade dodged out of its path just before it would've skewered him and dealt the man a bruising blow to the arm with his left fist.

Meanwhile, the giant retreated. Though 'twas hard to see the bent of his dim-witted thoughts, he appeared to plan some mischief.

"Run!" Blade commanded, glancing at Rose.

But she set her mouth in a stubborn line and shook her head. She wasn't some timorous maid to flee and hide. She intended to help him.

The first man recovered and seized the second man's dagger.

"Come on! Come on!" the man snarled, whirling both daggers in his fists, egging Blade to strike so he could dodge in and inflict damage from two places at once.

The robber probably never expected to be struck in the back of the head by a flying rock. Rose beamed in triumph. She'd hit her target and successfully stopped his forward progress. Her victory, however, was short-lived. To her dismay, not only did it *not* knock the man senseless as she'd planned—it served to further enrage him. He wheeled toward her, bubbles of angry spit dotting the corner of his mouth.

"Ye're next," he sneered.

Rose was undaunted. Anything that broke the thief's concentration had to be helpful to Blade. She searched the ground for another missile.

Blade fended off another attack, this time by both men at once, for the second had produced yet another short knife.

Rose glanced over to see the giant—his dim eyes narrowed, his tongue at the corner of his lip—poised to throw his dagger toward Blade.

"Nae!" she screamed, diving for the ogre.

Her shriek startled Blade enough to distract him, and in that moment, he earned a gash across his thigh from one of the thieves. But it also startled the giant enough to make him hesitate in his throw. She hurled herself at the muddy beast's back, knocking him against a tree. Her pitiful weight couldn't do much, but she hung tenaciously onto his immense neck while he thrashed like a hound trying to loose a kitten from its back. She clung to him for all she was worth, kicking at his legs and clawing at his face when she had the chance.

She should have known 'twas hopeless. She might possess twice the dolt's wits, but she was no match for his strength. And, unbeknownst to her, he still had the dagger.

With one powerful arm, he yanked her from his back and planted her between his two trunk-like legs. Then he hauled her back against his wide belly and set his dagger to her throat.

The steel edge felt cold and dangerous upon her neck. But the look Blade sent her when he saw what had happened was sharper and far more chilling, a glare that said she should have listened when he'd told her to run.

To her dismay, Blade, wincing with bitter regret, let out a great sigh, dropped his dagger to the ground, and raised his hands in surrender.

# Chapter 6

Blade silently cursed his wretched shackles and his lack of a sword. If not for those self-inflicted hindrances, he'd have been able to dispatch the thieves in a matter of moments.

Instead he'd been dealt a stinging wound, he'd been forced to relinquish his only weapon, and the lass...

Curse her—where had she come from, and why hadn't she done as he'd ordered? The apprentice, at least, hadn't questioned his command. What mulish stubbornness possessed the maid to make her interfere in what was clearly a man's battle?

Yet 'twasn't anger, but icy dread, that filled him as he gazed upon her.

She was a pale dove caught in the talons of a monstrous griffin, her limbs insubstantial, her throat vulnerable. Why the ogre bothered with the dagger, he didn't know. The brute could probably strangle her with one paw. The chilling thought crystallized the breath in Blade's chest.

But strangely, as the lass returned his stare, her eyes weren't filled with fear, but with frustration. She clearly realized the folly of her actions now.

As disappointed as he was, he couldn't fault the maid, not really. He would've done the same in her place. Her bravery, apparent in the stoic tilt of her chin, caught at his heart, even as it terrified him.

But there was nothing he could do now. The robbers would take the silver and probably his dagger. He only prayed to God they wouldn't take the intrepid lass's life as well.

The first thief had one final act of unspent rage left inside him. Before Blade could draw back or cast up his chains to block the blow, the man rounded on him with his knife, slicing Blade's cheek open.

The lass gasped in horror. An instant later Blade felt the burn of the slash, the welling blood. But the cut was shallow, dealt more as a punishment than to inflict damage. 'Twould leave a scar, but little more.

"Get the sack," the thief growled to his companion.

The second man began to lurch off toward the tree, but halted suddenly at the sound of distant voices. All of them stiffened. Faraway calls echoed among the trees, growing rapidly nearer.

Help. The apprentice had summoned help.

"Hurry," the first thief hissed, nervously gesturing with his bloodied dagger.

Blade glanced at the giant. The approaching men obviously made the slow-witted oaf uneasy, for he furrowed his brow like a fretting child, swaying absently from foot to foot. Unfortunately, his grip was steadily, inadvertently tightening around the lass.

The pilgrims were unaware of the precarious situation, or else they'd approach with more stealth. Blade heard them breaking through the trees already. God's wounds, if they crashed into the clearing and startled the fearful blockhead, one slip of his knife would end the lass's life.

Blade clenched his fists. He had to do something now, *before* the men arrived. 'Twas an enormous wager, but if he was right in his guess about the giant—that the poor fool idolized his companions...

Blade eyed his discarded dagger, lying among the leaves. 'Twas too far out of reach. He'd have to use something else.

The robber before him wiped a hand across his sweating lip. The man still brandished a knife, but his attention was focused elsewhere. If Blade moved quickly...

"Hurry!" the man snarled again. "Hur-"

Blade lunged forward, knocking the man's dagger loose. Before the thief could recover, Blade jerked him about, bringing his shackle chain down around the man's throat and hauling back on it.

The man let out a strangled cry as his fingers scrabbled at the chain. And, to Blade's satisfaction, the action had its desired effect.

The giant looked suddenly dismayed, as if he couldn't fathom something so dire happening to his dear friend. He let his guard slip a notch. The knife faltered in his fist.

"Let her go," Blade threatened.

"Nae, Jock! Don't listen to him!" the second thief cried, his arm sunk deep in the bole of the tree. "Hold onto her!"

But 'twas obvious where the Jock the giant's loyalties lie.

"He's hurtin' Gib. Don't hurt Gib," the giant pleaded, slowly lowering the knife.

"Nae, ye fool!" the second robber spat. "He's playin' with ye! Don't let her go!"

Blade jerked on the chain around Gib's neck, and his captive sputtered, rising on his toes in panic.

"Gib!" the giant sobbed, letting go of his prisoner, dropping his dagger, and stumbling forward.

This time, the lass wisely staggered out of harm's way.

Blade let up on the chain, releasing his quarry. With the heel of his boot, he shoved Gib as hard as he could toward the oncoming giant. They collided with a dull thud.

Just then, Wilham broke into the clearing, his eyes steely, his sword drawn. Beside him, Fulk brandished a hand-axe in one meaty arm. Campbell the soldier, spying the thief about to make off with Guillot's silver, flung a dagger with deadly aim, pinning the thief's sleeve to the tree trunk and leaving the blade shuddering in the wood. The sack of silver spilled to the ground.

Coins scattered and shivered and rolled across the leaf-fall with a sound like discarded chain mail.

Blade swept up his dagger, Campbell drew his sword, and the quartet of armed men charged toward the thieves.

The thieves knew they were outnumbered. Gib hauled on the giant's arm. "Come on, Jock!" he choked out, scrambling backward in the leaves.

The robber who was pinned to the tree began to shriek in panic.

"But Ralf's still..." Jock the giant protested.

"Aye! I'm still..." Ralf screamed, trying to rock the dagger free, while his two companions scurried off through the trees. "Nae! Nae! Don't leave me!"

Fulk the butcher walked slowly and deliberately toward the shrieking robber. The man yanked and pulled and tugged, his eyes rolling in panic, as Fulk raised his axe. Fulk never got the chance to deliver the blow, though Blade wasn't sure if he intended to lop off the man's sleeve or his hand. Just as Fulk drew close enough to strike, the robber tore his sleeve free and scrambled off after his fellows.

The thieves dissolved back into the shadowy forest like leaves melting into mulch, and the rescuers put away their weapons. Blade sheathed his dagger and made his way over to Rose.

She leaned against a tree, one hand braced behind her on the trunk, attempting to stay her gasps. Stray strands of raven hair slashed across one cheek, which was as pale as cream, and a tiny drop of blood welled at her throat where the giant's knife had nicked her.

The sight made him shudder. Fighting, there'd been no time for fear. But now that the danger was past, now that there was visible evidence of how close she'd come to being slain...

"Ye're...bleedin'." His voice cracked.

She absently touched her throat, smearing the blood. Then she looked at him and furrowed her brow. "*I'm* bleedin'? *Ye're* bleedin'."

Blade wiped at his cheek with the back of his hand. "'Tis a scratch."

Wilham chose that moment to barge forward with a wad of linen. "A scratch! Ha! So he'd say, my lady, were his head lopped from his shoulders." He handed Blade the rag, frowning. "I can't leave ye alone for a moment," he complained. "Ye keep this up, and ye'll ruin that bonnie face o' yours." Still scowling, he spared a wink for the lass, for which Blade gave him a glare of reproof. Then Wilham strode off, muttering and shaking his head, to help the others retrieve the spilled coins.

"Forgive Wilham," Blade told her. "He..."

"He cares for ye."

Her words gave him pause. She didn't know how accurate they were. Wilham was the one who saved Blade from himself. "Aye."

"*That* is far more than a scratch," she whispered as she glanced at the cut on his leg. Her nose quivered. The coppery scent of blood was likely not one to which she was accustomed.

He shrugged. "'Twill heal."

She guiltily bit her lip. "'Tis my fault."

*'Twas* her fault. If she'd only done as he bid her and stayed out of the way, he might not be wounded now.

Indeed, he might be *dead*.

"Far better the scrape on my shank," he admitted, "than a knife in my heart. I think I owe ye my life."

Ever so carefully, he lifted her chin with his thumb so he could use the wad of linen to swab at her tiny cut. Her skin was so soft, so vulnerable. He felt her swallow beneath his fingers before she spoke.

"And I owe ye mine."

Their eyes met, and her gaze, filled with wonder and gratitude and a little trepidation, cracked at his armored heart like a mace upon mail, making him feel things he knew he shouldn't, things he didn't deserve. He forced his eyes away.

"I'm a knight," he said gruffly. "'Tis my duty." He resumed dabbing at her throat more perfunctorily, steeling himself against their unsettling intimacy. "But the next time, do as I command."

She stiffened under his wounding words. "Leave ye alone to fend off robbers, shackled and swordless? How could I?"

He scowled, avoiding her gaze. "'Twas hazardous to stay. Ye should have obeyed me."

"I'm not a coward," she told him, snatching the rag from his hand a bit crossly. "And neither, I suspect, are ye. Would ye have left *me* had I commanded it? Turned and run?"

He deepened his scowl.

"I thought not," she murmured, rising up on her toes to press the cloth to his bloody cheek. He flinched. Her smooth brow wrinkled with genuine concern. "Does it hurt?"

He swallowed hard and shook his head. 'Twasn't pain that made him recoil. 'Twas amazement. He couldn't recall the last time a woman had touched him with such tenderness. Most women dared not even draw close, let alone lay a hand upon him. He was dark and dangerous and savage. Touching him was like stirring a bed of hot coals. She shouldn't do this. She shouldn't touch him. Innocent and young, she didn't know what she roused in him, how he ached for...

Her tongue slipped out to moisten her rosy bottom lip, and a wave of desire washed over him.

"The cut isn't too deep," she murmured. "'Twill leave only a faint scar."

He scarcely listened. "Why are ye speakin' to me, touchin' me?" he wondered aloud. "Why aren't ye afraid?"

She paused in her labors. The mischievous hint of a smile touched her eyes. "I suppose because I once ruffled the fur of a bear," she said cryptically. "And ye're only..." The humor faded from her gaze, replaced by something far more threatening. "A man."

He might have imagined the rough desire in her voice, but he didn't think so. Suddenly he felt the inexplicable need to frighten her, to distance her. "I'm a *dangerous* man," he told her,

86

letting his eyes, aglitter with all the hunger and desire he felt, rake her body.

Though he saw her breath catch and her eyes widen, she remained undaunted, resuming her tender ministrations. "And what makes ye so dangerous?" she asked breathlessly.

He seized her wrist and reminded her in a hiss, "I'm a dishonored knight."

She gulped, and her nostrils fluttered, but she held her chin high. Her eyes shone like brimming pools of autumn rain. "Ye've shown me no dishonor," she whispered.

Her gaze lowered to his mouth, making his heart stagger against his ribs. He thought instantly of a dozen ways to dishonor her, all of them immensely pleasurable. But he knew, despite his salacious imagination, 'twas honor that left him incapable of pursuing them.

He released her wrist.

Rose felt lightheaded, not only from the hazardous encounter of the afternoon or the dizzying sight of blood, but from the reckless rush of her wayward thoughts.

As brash and improper and forward as it seemed, she longed to heal Blade's hurts the way she had that bear long ago in St. Andrews. That he might be dangerous didn't trouble her in the least. Indeed, it excited her. Even his scent—all smoke and musk and metal—was intriguing. Her heart felt drawn to him, like a moth drawn to the moon. And the daring woman within her desired to touch the man beneath the worn leather and hard iron, the man of warm flesh.

Thankfully, Blade took the bloodied rag from her hand before she could do something impulsive and foolhardy.

"Ye should go back now," he said curtly, avoiding her eyes. "Wilham can take ye to the others."

"Nae." The word popped out of her of its own accord.

He locked gazes with her.

She swallowed. "I don't wish to return yet."

His eyes, once as cold and hard and gray as stone, softened. They were flecked with shards of blue and green, she realized, the color as mutable as the spring sky. She wondered what he saw when he looked into her eyes, if he perceived the yearning there.

"Go," he bid her firmly. "Robbers I'd gladly battle, but I've no desire to war with Father Peter or your Highland mother hen over your virtue."

Her virtue? His mind *was* on desire. The thought dizzied her, loosening her coy tongue. "Faugh, sir," she scolded flirtatiously. "I thought ye were braver than that."

His lip curved up the tiniest bit in response. "Nae," he said flatly.

She feigned shock. "Ye won't protect me from the scoldin' they're bound to give me?"

He shook his head. "'Tis doubtless well-deserved. Ye're too headstrong by half."

"Headstrong? I'm not..." She couldn't finish the lie.

He smirked, and his gaze slipped down to her mouth. Then he sobered. "Go," he prodded.

But she didn't want to go. Blade was far too beguiling. And stirring. And seductive. "I haven't rewarded ye properly yet for rescuin' me."

She saw his jaw tighten as his eyes locked again on her lips. When he finally tore his gaze away, he sniffed, almost as if she'd insulted him. "I *was* once a knight, even if I wear shackles now." He draped the rag over his wounded thigh and knotted it firmly. "Ye owe me no reward. 'Tis only part of the oath I took—to defend the helpless and to guard the virtue o' lasses like yourself."

"But I—"

"By the Saints!" boomed the familiar voice of Father Peter, destroying the intimacy of the moment. "What's happened here?"

Blade stepped back to a polite distance as the priest barreled forward. Rose would have sworn there was a glimmer of satisfaction playing about Blade's mouth as the father began lecturing her in clamorous tones.

And so the priest carried on—sometimes addressing Rose, sometimes Guillot, sometimes the company in general—all the way to The Red Lion, their lodging for the night in the firthside village of Culross. The journey was but an hour's trudge away, and yet it seemed far longer, for at every step, Father Peter reminded them of the dangers of going alone into the forest.

Once or twice, Rose ventured a glance over her shoulder for a glimpse of her dark rescuer and was rewarded by a knowing look from him that told her he believed she deserved every word of reprimand.

By the time they smelled the briny air of the Firth of Forth, the sun had lowered enough to make the water look like a shimmering swath of silver silk. The Red Lion stood along the main firthside road, and Rose was glad to find a peddler hawking his wares beside the inn. She purchased a few items with which to make the journey more comfortable—a cake of tallow soap, a length of cheap linen for washing, and a wooden comb, which she used at once to whisk the tangles from her hair.

A humble supper of thick cod pottage and oatcakes washed down with cider soon filled Rose's belly, yet she tasted little of it. Despite the watchful eye of Father Peter, who sat beside her, her gaze kept roving to the handsome outlaw dining at the far end of her table.

His face was washed clean now, his hair still damp, darkening it to the shade of coal. His cheekbone bore the thin red slash that would fade to a scar and yet do little to mar the coarse perfection of his face. Already the mark seemed to enhance his rugged countenance.

Tildy, sitting at her other side, jabbed her and leaned close. Her breath reeked of cider. "Remember, that one's trouble, lass," she murmured, "no mistake. 'Twouldn't surprise me if those robbers were friends o' his."

Rose scowled. "What do ye mean?"

Tildy nodded. "Ye popped up and spoiled their thievin'."
She hiccoughed. "If ye ask me," she whispered, "there's more
danger here in this company than in the woods." She wagged a
cautioning finger. "We women've got to keep our eyes open."

Rose dismissed Tildy's warning as drunken prattle. But the
words haunted her the rest of the night. Could it be true? Could
Blade have been an accomplice rather than a victim?

Nae, 'twas absurd. He'd returned the silver to Guillot. He'd
warned Rose away. And he'd earned a couple of nasty gashes
fighting the thieves.

Yet he'd allowed the outlaws to leave with their lives,
disappearing into the forest, none the worse for their escapade.
And there was still the matter of Blade's chains and the crime
he'd committed to earn them.

She glanced again at the shackled hand resting on the table.
Was that the hand of a thief? A traitor? A killer? Surely the
hand wielding a dagger in her defense and dabbing gently at her
cuts was incapable of such crimes.

But whether she believed it or not, Tildy had planted seeds of
doubt in her mind. She perused the faces of the pilgrims along
the trestle table with new eyes. Any one of them, she realized,
might betray her for the sizable reward her betrothed could offer.

She made a silent vow then to remain as aloof as possible
from the rest of the company. The pilgrims, for all their feigned
piety, might sell her for a piece of silver. The fewer who knew
her name and her history, the better.

Blade had saved her life today, aye. But Tildy was right.
There was no cause to trust him. For the right price, even he
might turn her over to Sir Gawter. No matter his forthright gaze,
his tender heart, his tempting mouth...

Blade stuffed the last bite of oatcake between his teeth. The
lass was staring at him again. He could feel her eyes, all drowsy
and liquid, upon him. What she wanted from him, he didn't
know. Or perhaps he *did* know and just refused to allow the
thought to surface.

On the other hand, after Father Peter's harsh rebuke, the lass might never speak to a man again...unless, as he suspected, she was one of those wayward creatures who liked to contradict advice.

He wished she'd look somewhere else. It made his heart pulse wildly when she looked at him like that, and it roused the beast in his braies he'd let slumber far too long. Both of which distracted him from important matters at hand.

There were still questions about the incidents of the afternoon that he couldn't answer. Chief among them was why the lass had been in the woods at that particular time in that particular place. She hadn't strolled in with Guillot the apprentice. It seemed almost as if she'd been spying on the lad.

She'd left her peregrine at the inn. So what had drawn her into the forest? Could it be that she planned an assignation with someone there? Or even more disturbing, had the thieves not been thieves at all, but accomplices of hers? Maybe he'd saved her not from robbers, but from her fellow conspirators. 'Twas enough to make his head throb.

"So what we know now," Wilham murmured, shoveling a spoonful of pottage into his mouth and talking around it, "is, despite the fact he's a foreigner, Guillot the apprentice couldn't be part o' the plot."

Blade nodded. He'd seen the lad's bruises, felt his fear. He knew the signs of ill-use. He was certain Guillot's story was true.

"Nor is the murderer Jacob the goldsmith. The man obviously only unsheathes his dagger for Lettie." Wilham snickered at his own jest, then swallowed down his last bite of oatcake. "It can't be Fulk or Campbell. They were only too pleased to grapple with the thieves. Did ye see how Campbell threw that dagger?" Wilham whistled. "The soldier has deadly aim."

Blade had his doubts about Campbell. The man was too silent, too reclusive. "Soldier? Or assassin?"

Wilham frowned. "Good point." He took a thoughtful sip of cider. "What about Rose?"

"Rose?"

"The falconer." Wilham shook his head. "Some spy ye are. Ye didn't even know her name, did ye?"

Blade snorted. "'Tis o' no consequence." But despite his claim, the name instantly reverberated in his head like plainsong echoing through a cathedral. Rose. 'Twas a fitting name, for she was as fair as her namesake flower. Rose. Sweet. Pure. Beautiful. Then he gave himself a mental shake. "'Tis likely a false name," he grumbled, downing the dregs of his cider.

'Twas the goldsmith's turn to tell a tale, and since the two nuns had already retired upstairs, and Jacob was well-sated with drink and adultery, he related a bawdy story that Blade guessed was closer to truth than fiction. Lettie's cheeks reddened at the telling of it, but her eyes dipped languidly, as if she relived each lascivious moment.

The others took great interest in the tale. The tanners hung on his every word. The scholars listened as if he recited a lesson of Plato. Fulk and Drogo nodded their agreement at the passages concerning fickle women. Father Peter seemed oblivious to the suggestive language of the story. Even the palmer, though his lips thinned with disapproval, harkened with glitter-eyed attention.

Blade grew quickly bored, for the tale rapidly turned to an improbable and pointless embellishing of the goldsmith's own sexual exploits. He swirled his refreshed cup of cider and took a sip. Over the rim of the cup, he glanced down the table. Rose, much to his amusement, listened with her mouth slightly agape.

Her expression amused him. Her sheltered ears had likely never heard such things. And that idea aroused an ignoble longing within him—he'd like to whisper such wicked words in her ear, to make her blush so.

When the tale was over, Father Peter, as if finally realizing the crude nature of the entertainment, tapped upon Rose's sleeve, obviously trying to convince her to go upstairs. But Rose would have none of it. And the thought of tangling with the rebellious, wanton wench sent a shiver of desire coursing unbidden through Blade's loins.

The second tale was offered up by Brigit the brewster. It, too, was rife with ribald acts, which she related with a spark of authenticity and promise in her eye that soon had every man in the room squirming like a hound in season.

This time, when Blade glanced at Rose, her lids seemed curiously weighted. Her bosom rose and fell rapidly, as if she were equally excited and appalled by what she heard. And this time, she caught him staring.

Rose's cheeks flamed. Their eyes met for only a moment, and yet in that moment, such a strong wave of desire surged through her that it seemed to wash all reason from her brain.

Suddenly, against her will, she imagined herself as the faerie in the brewster's fanciful tale, lying naked in a summer bower, awaiting the arrival of her mortal lover.

And to her horror, by the subtle smile on his face, Blade read her thoughts as clearly as his own and seemed more than willing to step into her fantasy as that mortal.

She tore her gaze away and, catching her breath, stared into her full cup of cider. She tried to block out the sound of the story, but her ear still managed to catch on the most vile words.

She couldn't escape. In the eager silence of the inn, her leaving would draw attention. Why hadn't she listened to Father Peter? She should have gone upstairs while she had the chance. Damn her insatiable curiosity! It never ceased to earn her trouble, whether 'twas poking at a wild bear, spying in her mother's stables, or squirming under the gaze of an outlaw.

Her eyes lifted to him again of their own will. This time, thank God, his attention rested elsewhere. But once her gaze alit on his dark-stubbled jaw, his strong chin, his hooded eyes, she couldn't force it away. The firelight burnished his skin to a deep bronze and cast shadows along the lean hollows of his cheeks. There was a seasoned cast to his face, lines and scars that told of past battles, past adventures, past pains. And yet the wide curve of his mouth belied that harshness, lending him a quality of compassion.

She wondered what 'twould be like to kiss him...

Laughter and applause burst out around her, and Rose was jolted back to the moment as everyone rose to retire.

She caught his eye once more before they climbed the steps to the upper floor. He saluted her with a courteous nod and a knowing smile, and she scurried up the stairs to join the others.

The next morn, the chill, damp air threatened rain as the pilgrims quietly plodded from Culross Abbey, where they'd attended Sabbath Mass. Above the mist, the skies were hung with shrouds of gray and white, draped like wet silk with their burden of moisture, while the firth below reflected their dreary mood. Rose, too, felt the somber weight of the weather. Immersed in her own thoughts, she paid little heed to the breakfast of barley bread and hard cheese the pilgrims ate as they set out along the road.

After the ribald tales of the evening before, Rose's night had been so filled with lusty dreams that she awoke blushing in the morn with the guilty impulse to make confession for her imagined sins. And those impure thoughts served to remind her of the grave decision awaiting her in little more than a week.

She needed to think earnestly about her future. Mere days from now, she'd be faced with a choice that would determine the rest of her life—whether to yield her innocence to an adulterous husband or remain a virgin in a convent for the remainder of her life. Up till now, she'd deceived herself into thinking there might be some other alternative, that by returning to Fernie House and the people who'd raised her she might somehow cajole and plead and worm her way out of her betrothal.

But such thoughts were childish. Above all, the laird and lady of Fernie had taught her honor. She'd been promised in betrothal, and she must abide by that promise or seek refuge in the church. 'Twas that simple. 'Twas not a decision to be made lightly, but at least the choice was ultimately hers.

She focused on the sisters walking before her. They seemed placid and comfortable in their chaste life, blissfully resigned to their passionless existence. Their manner was peaceful, and no trouble marred their pale brows. Life in a nunnery might be pleasant. Nuns were well-educated and well-respected. 'Twas even rumored that falconry was a favored pastime in convent. Within the church, a woman was queen of her own destiny and might aspire to great power.

Yet Rose wondered how long 'twould be before she tired of the plain gray habit and the monotonous daily prayers, the hush of women's voices and the cloying scent of incense.

A few tentative drops of rain plopped from the sky, one landing on Wink, who shook her head in annoyance. Rose soothed the bird with a soft word and a scratch at the back of her neck.

But soon the raindrops grew heavier and more frequent, vexing Wink despite Rose's best efforts to shield the falcon against her breast. Rose shivered, beginning to miss the cloak she'd been forced to leave behind. There was no help for it now, but she supposed she'd have to part with more of her silver when they reached the next town to buy a proper woolen cloak. In the meantime, the dilemma raging inside her would keep her from thinking too much about her sopping velvet gown.

What if she decided to return to Averlaigh, to her philandering betrothed? If Gawter truly wished to claim her for his wife, he'd have to forgive her for fleeing, at least publicly. After all, 'twas common for young brides to harbor misgivings about marriage. She could claim that she sought to clear her soul before her wedding by making the pilgrimage to St. Andrews, and none would argue.

She'd earn a respectable holding and a noble husband. She'd bear heirs and run a household of her own. But at what price? Her body would belong to Gawter, but her heart she'd keep under lock and key. And she'd always know that her husband didn't love her well enough to be faithful.

Her eyes clouded with sorrow and fury. 'Twas a pathetic existence.

Yet the convent might be just as unsatisfying. What if her own passions tormented her? What if she found the burden of celibacy too great to bear?

The choice was so difficult. If only there was a way to try both paths...

A part of her wanted and needed more than to serve God, and a part of her desired more than children born of a loveless marriage. She wanted that feeling she saw on the faces of some of the ladies she knew, whose eyes lit up when their men came marching home from battle. She longed to snuggle by a warm fire on a rainy day like her fostering parents, to walk hand-in-hand over the heathery hills like the dairy maid and the shepherd, to share a trencher and a bed and a lifetime with someone who cherished her like a precious jewel. Was that so much to ask?

A drop trickled down her cheek, merging with the rain already wetting her face, so that only Rose knew 'twas a rogue tear. Self-pity, however, didn't suit her, and she swiftly wiped the drop away with the back of her hand.

That hand was still aloft when something swooped down upon her like a huge dark falcon. She gasped, making Wink screech and flap wildly. Black wool suddenly surrounded her, blocking out what meager light penetrated the clouds. She fought against the suffocating cloth, battling for freedom as it ensnared her.

"Easy!" Hands braced her shoulders, stilling her struggles. "I mean ye no harm."

She turned and peered up from beneath the enveloping shroud to see Blade—his hair damp, his brow furrowed, his eyes as gray as the day.

Beside her, Tildy screeched like a crow. "No harm? What the devil do ye mean, sneakin' up and..."

"Tildy!" Rose snapped, silencing the woman, for now she understood. Blade had surrendered his cloak to her. The black wool hung heavily upon her shoulders and dragged in the mud, and the hood all but swallowed her head, but already it lent her comfort and warmth.

She lifted her eyes to him again, giving him a watery smile. How kind Blade was. Kind and thoughtful and caring. If only her betrothed were so kind, she considered, she might look forward to her marriage with something other than dread. All at once, she felt the most mortifying urge to sob. "Thank ye," she managed to squeak out before her chin began to quiver.

Blade clenched his fists. Now he'd made the lass cry. He'd only meant to ease her suffering a bit, not bring her more torment. She'd forgotten a cloak, and he simply intended to remedy that until they reached the next town, where she might procure one for herself.

As for Blade, he was accustomed to traveling in all sorts of weather. His heavy leather and woolen garments would stand him in good stead. And he refused to trudge one more step along the muddy road, snug in his woolen cloak, while the lass shivered in her sodden surcoat and flimsy linen underdress.

But all his pains had earned him nothing but her weeping.

He should leave her now. His presence obviously upset her.

Still, something in her liquid, melancholy gaze, the trembling of her mouth, the teardrops mingling with the raindrops on her cheek, held him there, drawing words from him he knew he shouldn't utter.

"What troubles ye, lass?" he murmured low.

His question distressed her even more. Her brow crumpled, and her olive eyes spilled over with tears. Silently, he cursed his all too eager tongue.

"Nothin'," she said, and he knew she was lying. Still, he dared not linger lest he be blamed for those tears. With a sigh, he turned to leave.

She caught the links of his shackles, halting him.

"Lassie!" Tildy hissed beside her, but Rose ignored the warning and coiled her pale hand in his chains.

"I don't know what ye did to deserve these," she whispered in desperate haste before reason could prevent her, "but ye've shown me nothin' but chivalry."

Her words jolted him. Chivalry? Was that what she thought? Blade was anything but chivalrous. He'd lost the right to that claim two years ago. And yet for a moment, he'd forgotten that he was no longer Sir Pierce of Mirkhaugh. For a moment, he'd dared imagine he was once again that noble knight, sworn to protect the innocent and helpless. Lady Rose had made him believe, if only for an instant, that he might be a hero.

He scowled at his own stupidity. She couldn't be more wrong. He pulled the chain from her grasp, leaving her without a word, to rejoin Wilham.

No sooner had he fallen into line than thunder cracked, and the heavens opened, letting loose their store of rain upon his bare head, drenching him.

Wilham offered to share his cloak, but Blade refused it. After all, the storm matched his sullen mood. Perhaps the driving rain would wash the madness from his mind.

# Chapter 7

As the travelers followed the shore of the firth past Inverkeithing, the waters gradually widened to become the mouth of the North Sea. The trees thinned, giving way to patches of tough seagrass and sandy soil. The sky stretched, as gray and somber as a nun's habit, toward the empty horizon of land's end. The wash of waves, bestirred by the storm, hissed over the wide bulwark of rock shielding the trail, and the brisk scent of the sea mingled with the smell of rain and wet sod.

Just as the pilgrims slogged miserably toward an inn at the cliff's edge where they might take shelter, in a great show of irony, the tempest quieted as swiftly as it had begun. The clouds cracked apart like an eggshell, revealing the yolk of the sun, and shafts of pale gold light streamed down to illuminate the green swell of the firth and breathe steam upon the shore.

Blade and Wilham were the last to stomp the mud from their boots upon the wooden steps leading to the inn. Blade shook his head like a hound, spattering a protesting Wilham with rain, then slicked his hair back and went in.

The common room was merry and inviting and, best of all, dry. Tallow candles smoked from sconces set into the walls. The air was warm with the aromas of cooking venison, strong ale, and the coarse laughter of fishermen. A cheery fire burned on the hearth, and the pilgrims wasted no time in using the nearby pegs to hang up their wet mantles.

But Blade's was not hung among them. He frowned, casting his gaze about the room as Wilham left to procure a brace of ales. There, beyond the crush of people, in a corner of the inn, Rose, still wearing his oversized cloak, blew out a candle and set her falcon to perch upon the crossbar of the extinguished sconce. At last, she took off the garment, as gingerly as if 'twere an abbot's cope, holding it carefully aloft lest it drag upon the floor. Her fussing made him smile, for the last several inches of the hem were already filthy.

But what she did next wiped the amusement from his face. She glanced marginally about the room to make certain no one saw her. Then, as he watched in breathless disbelief, she pressed the folds of his cloak to her face and closed her eyes, inhaling deeply. The sight made his heart gallop unsteadily, and he felt the breath leave his lungs.

"Here," Wilham interrupted, pressing a tankard into his numb fingers. "This should warm your bones. Young barley with a touch of oats, although... Blade?" Wilham snapped his fingers suddenly in front of Blade's eyes, making him blink. "Blade!"

"What?" he snarled.

"What's wrong with ye? Has your brain gone soft with rain water?" He followed Blade's gaze. "What are ye lookin' at?"

Blade didn't answer. He couldn't think. He didn't know what to make of the woman's actions. So he did the only thing that would steady his nerves and silence Wilham. He slugged back the whole tankard of ale in one greedy gulp and shoved the emptied cup into his friend's hands.

"God's hooks, Blade," Wilham muttered. "Show some respect for the alewife. You didn't even taste that draught."

Rose had left her corner. She now made her way through the crowd with his cloak, coming directly toward him. Irrational panic filled Blade's chest. "Buy me another," he told Wilham.

Wilham raised a brow, but left to do as he was bid. By the time the lass reached Blade, he was alone.

Her face was flushed, likely from cold and not the exhilaration that afflicted him, and the scarlet of her cheeks made her fair skin all the more striking. Her dark hair hung in damp tendrils about her face, adding to her frail quality. He hadn't noticed before, but the corners of her mouth curved up slightly, as if she were accustomed to smiling. At the moment, however, her eyes were touched by a subtle longing, a bittersweet melancholy he could neither comprehend nor remedy.

"I can't thank ye enough," she murmured, absently caressing the wool of his cloak as if 'twere a favorite pet.

He wondered if she knew what that caress did to his insides.

"'Tis nothin'," he said, nearly strangling on the words. God's blood, what was wrong with him? So the woman had sniffed at his cloak. Perchance it smelled of smoke or sweat. Surely he'd only imagined that look of sensual bliss on her face.

She awkwardly handed him the cloak, and he awkwardly took it. Their fingers met, hers warm, his cool. Then she withdrew her hand to toy nervously with the neckline of her gown.

She cleared her throat and spoke with forced casualness. "How much farther do ye suppose 'tis to Hillend?"

"Two, three miles." He narrowed his eyes. 'Twas obvious she had something on her mind besides the distance to their next lodging. And she was reluctant to say what that was.

He saw Wilham approach with his ale, and he met his gaze, surreptitiously nodding him away. Wilham understood at once and retreated to another table.

Blade took a deep breath and turned aside, dropping his head to stare nonchalantly at the rush-covered floor. "Lass," he murmured, "ye should speak your piece and be gone. I told ye before, 'tis unwise for ye to converse with my kind."

"But I need..." she gushed, then paused, deeming it best to conceal her desperation. "I wish...to speak with ye." She cast a furtive glance over her shoulder. "Alone."

He flinched, then rubbed a hand across his bristled jaw. "That is doubly unwise."

"'Tis o' the utmost importance," she said, the urgency in her voice perilously compelling.

He lifted his gaze to scan the room and saw what he least wished to see. The ever-watchful Highland woman glowered beside the falcon's perch, her arms crossed, her mouth working. He murmured, "Your guardian would disagree."

She ignored his comment. "Ye still owe my falcon her supper. Maybe some tidbit has washed ashore in the storm. Go down to the firth," she implored him in a rush, catching his sleeve. "I'll make some excuse and follow ye."

'Twas a mistake, all this clandestine activity. After all, they both knew what had happened the last time she stole off. "Lass," he muttered, "ye're invitin' trouble."

But when she looked up at him in entreaty, all beautiful and flushed and full of hope, he couldn't find it in his heart to refuse.

Cursing her poor judgment and his weak will, he muttered, "I'll wait a quarter hour, no more."

He strode off to where Wilham sat, slung his cloak over the table, took one bracing gulp of ale, and set the tankard down with a weighted sigh. "I'm goin' out."

Wilham gave him a half-grin, but wisely said nothing.

Blade wheeled away from the table and out the door, squinting against the shock of the taunting brilliant sunlight that now graced the heavens and glittered off the surface of the water below.

Behind the inn, he followed a narrow trail that cut across the cliff face, descending gradually and depositing him onto gravel at the bottom. Caves and inlets pocked the cliff, and nesting seabirds circled rocky shelves and high ledges further along the shore where Blade might find eggs for the falcon. But scaling the wall without a grappling line and in shackles was out of the question. Besides, he dared not wander too far. 'Twas one thing to meet the woman by the firth. 'Twas quite another to lose her there.

He watched gulls swoop and soar along the shoreline, dropping mussels onto the rocks, fighting over crabs, and squawking indignantly when they lost a meal.

He soon tired of watching the birds and sank back into the shadowy shelter of a cliff outcropping, his back braced against the rock, his arms crossed over his chest. He wondered morosely if the lass truly intended to meet him or only attempted to cheat him out of his spot at the hearth. Just as he was about to give up on her and slog back to the inn, a sweep of claret skirts flashed from the base of the cliff.

She didn't see him at first, and he took the liberty to watch her at his leisure as she held up her skirts to move gingerly across the wet gravel. What a lovely creature she was, so graceful, so beguiling. And—he remembered bitterly—so damnably vulnerable, as were all women.

This undertaking was baldly audacious, even for Rose. She'd lied to Tildy, telling her she intended to make use of the privy and asking her to watch Wink. Then she'd stolen out of the inn to meet in secret with a man who was practically a stranger. And now, even petting that wild bear in St. Andrews paled in comparison to what she intended to request of the dark outlaw. But desperate times required desperate measures, and this might be her last chance to weigh the destiny that awaited her.

"Sir Blade," she whispered loudly, shielding her eyes from the bright sparkling jewel of the firth. She spied no dark silhouette against the white-ruffled waves. Perhaps he'd wandered further. She dared not follow too far. "Sir Blade, where are ye?"

The devilish knave must have been watching her in silence for a full minute, for she'd almost stumbled upon his hiding place when he finally announced his presence. "Here."

Her heart leaped into her throat.

"Satan's ballo-" she exclaimed, pinching off the foul oath just in time. There he was, lounging in a pocket sunk into the cliff wall, as still as death, as quiet as shadow. She made an attempt at nonchalance. "Ye...gave me a fright."

He pushed away from the niche, moving into the bright sunlight. "Aye? Well, ye *should* be frightened."

Was it only her imagination, or did he loom larger, darker, more menacing? Perhaps 'twas only a trick of the light. Or perhaps she'd made a mistake. Perhaps she should go back to the inn and forget about her brilliant stroke of inspiration.

"What is it?" he demanded. "What do ye want?"

She chewed at the corner of her lip. Now that she stood before him, dwarfed by his massive warrior's body, intimidated by the stern gravity of his countenance, she feared she'd made a grievous error. He was as dangerous as the sea, she realized—powerful, undaunted, and unpredictable.

"Every moment ye're away," he warned her, "feeds rumor."

He was right. She'd come this far. She might as well plunge into the icy waves headfirst.

"I want to explain why I've come on pilgrimage." She didn't intend to tell him all of the truth, just the bit she required.

His mouth tightened into a hard line. He obviously didn't think the conversation warranted such privacy.

"I'm..." She swallowed. "I'm thinkin' o' joinin' a holy order."

"What!" His bark startled her.

She blinked. "I'm thinkin' o'...o' becomin' a nun."

If she weren't serious, she might have laughed at the curious expression of distaste and revulsion that passed over his features. "Why?"

This was where she planned to sidle past the truth, and for that, she couldn't look him in the eye. She cleared her throat, studied her fingers, and thought about all the reasons one might enter a convent. "I wish to devote my life to God. I wish to help the sick. Feed the poor. Read the Bible each day. Be a bride o' Christ."

He was silent so long that she was forced to look up at him. His eyes mirrored the sea, stained in mutable shades of green and blue and gray that deepened and flickered in the fickle sunlight. His gaze narrowed now as if he guessed the truth. Yet he remained silent, allowing her to slip her own neck through the noose of her lies.

"I don't plan to return to Averlaigh," she told him.

"Averlaigh," he repeated, and her heart stopped. "Odd. I heard ye'd come from Doune."

"Well, aye, or-, originally," she stammered. Damn her eyes, she hadn't meant to reveal that. "Anyway, I'm considerin' enterin' the convent in St. Andrews."

"I see." There were definite glints of both humor and irritation in his gaze now, and it vexed her. "Well, I suggest ye learn to curtail your swearin'. They don't much like swearin' in convents. And I wish ye the best in your endeavor." He made as if he would leave.

"Wait!" She placed a restraining hand on his chest. "I have a favor to ask o' ye."

He arched a brow.

She twisted her fingers together, glancing along the cliff wall, where seabirds flapped and dipped along crevices in the rock. 'Twas far more difficult than she'd expected to lend words to her wishes. "'Tis not such a great favor. 'Twill cost ye nothin'. 'Twill take but a moment o' your time, and 'tis not altogether unpleasant, I'm told. But..."

"Is this a rebus then that I must disentangle?" He crossed impatient arms over his chest, making her even more anxious. "Lass, I pray ye be frank."

By the Saints, his eyes—touched by amusement, shimmering in the water's reflection like buffed pewter—entranced her. Against her will, she lowered her gaze to his mouth, wondering if 'twas soft or firm... She gulped. Lord, what would she do if he said nae?

He mustn't. He must grant her this favor, or she'd perish of humiliation.

She took a fortifying breath and decided, "Ye must swear to tell me aye."

He squinted suddenly sober eyes against the dazzling sunlight and gazed out over the firth. "I ne'er make blind promises." He picked up a shell fragment at his feet and tossed it casually across the shore.

"'Tis but a wee favor."

"Yet ye're loath to name it." He collected another shell and tossed it to the water's edge. Two seagulls, expecting food, hopped near to peck at it.

Curse the felon, all this conversation was diminishing Rose's courage. Maybe she'd made a mistake after all. She worried the velvet of her surcoat between her finger and thumb. Blind promises, he'd said. He never made blind promises.

Suddenly she straightened. "Does a knight not swear fealty to his liege to do all that he commands?"

"Aye."

"Is that not a blind promise?"

The corner of his mouth lifted. "I never claimed I was the king's man. And at the present, I'm a mercenary. I serve no master. I owe fealty to none."

Rose pondered his words for a moment, then sighed, murmuring, "I wish *I* were a mercenary."

"Ye?" He gave a mirthless laugh. "Ye don't have the bloodthirsty look about ye."

"Nor do ye." In fact, the irreverent curve of his lips gave him a rather knavish air.

He sniffed and bent down to palm a piece of clamshell. With a flick of his wrist, he sent it skipping across the whitecaps. "'Tis a miserable existence," he muttered, watching the waves lap at the shore.

She followed his gaze, wondering how such a life could possibly be miserable. "But to owe no allegiance, to come and go where ye will, to be as free as...as a falcon..."

Blade was silent a long while. Rose closed her eyes, lulled by the gentle undulations of the water, imagining such freedom.

At long last, he let out a heavy sigh. "Very well. I'll do it. Curse me for a fool, but I'll grant your favor."

Her eyes popped open. "Ye will?"

"Aye."

"Ye swear it?"

"I swear." He did not look happy about his decision. His arms were crossed, his brow was deeply furrowed, his mouth curved in self-mockery, and he exhaled again like a defeated warrior.

She refrained from jumping up and down with glee, deciding wisely that he'd not respect such childishness. "Thank ye, Sir Blade," she said with as much dignity as she could. "Ye'll not be sorry."

"Not Sir Blade. I'm only Blade." He sniffed. "And I'm already sorry."

She smiled. She knew he didn't mean that. There was a gentleness in his heart that his shackles and black leather and scowl belied. 'Twas that gentleness that had made her choose him for the task.

He gave her a slightly sardonic nod of his head. "So what is it My Lady Nun desires?"

A wave of heat rushed over her face at his choice of words. What she desired was not at all befitting a nun. Maybe she'd been too impulsive. She scarcely knew the man. And he'd doubtless think her request completely mad. Yet he'd sworn. He'd *sworn*.

"The day grows short," he cautioned.

She knotted her fingers tightly together, lifted her chin as bravely as she could, considering the circumstances, and, though it mortified her, looked him square in the eye. Then she couldn't speak the words.

He frowned. "Lass, if ye don't find your tongue quickly, ye'll give that Highland woman a fit of apo-"

"Kiss me!" she gushed, then clapped her fingers over her mouth. She hadn't meant to blurt it out like that.

He drew back as if she'd threatened to spit in his face.

"That is," she said, "Sir Blade..." She shook her head, correcting herself. "Blade. Would ye do me the honor o' grantin' me a kiss?"

He shuddered as if she'd asked him to kill a troublesome rat. Then his eyes snapped at her, blacker than coal. "What game do ye play, lass, and why?" he growled. "First nun and then harlot?"

"Nae!" Dear God, was that how he saw her? "Nae! 'Tis not that at all." Then what was it? the demon inside her taunted. What did she want from him? "I just... I only..." Bloody hell, her thoughts tumbled together like the churning currents of the firth. She'd never expected she'd have to explain herself to him. She'd assumed that like most men, he'd leap at the chance to kiss a young lady and ask no questions. As to her intent, that was her own affair.

He expelled a disgusted sigh and started to go.

She scrambled into his path, halting him. "Ye swore. Ye swore ye'd grant my favor. Listen. I'll explain."

The glower on his face told her she hadn't much time.

She quickly licked her lips. "Ye see, I haven't entirely decided to enter the convent." She lowered her eyes. "'Tisn't an easy decision, as ye might well imagine." She glanced up. He didn't look as if he wished to imagine anything. She dropped her gaze again and took a few shallow breaths. "But if I'm to decide to give my life and soul and...and body to God, I would know what 'tis I'm surrenderin'."

He was silent. She dared not look at him.

"I'm only askin' for a kiss," she murmured, too humiliated to speak louder.

The firth lulled to a soft hiss, as if it, too, awaited his reply.

"Nae." The word was cold, hard, final.

It felt like she'd been kicked in the stomach. Her breath fluttered in her breast. Never had she imagined he'd refuse her. She wished she'd never asked him to meet her, wished she'd never spoken with him at all. Her voice came out on a wisp of air. "But ye...ye swore."

His tone was grave. "I won't be used in such a manner."

She gulped. "I meant no offense," she whispered. "'Tis only that I've never had a kiss, not a proper one."

His voice was a low growl. "Then why me? Do ye expect a disgraced felon to give ye a *proper* kiss?"

She hadn't thought of it that way, and now that she did, his presence seemed suddenly menacing, his kindness less evident. Though she was certain he didn't advance toward her, he seemed somehow to loom nearer.

"Ye'd rest the weight o' your decision," he continued, "on how well ye enjoy my kiss. Is that it?"

It sounded inane when he said it aloud, and yet 'twas unerringly accurate. She'd never kissed a man. If she entered a nunnery, she never would. How else could she make an informed choice?

"I ask ye again," he said. "Why me?"

She faced him squarely, mustering all her courage. "Because ye're kind and...and courteous...and honorable...and gentle..."

As she spoke, he began slowly, almost imperceptibly, shaking his head. "Ye don't know me at all. I wear these shackles for a reason," he purred, lifting them for her to see. Then he stepped nearer, as if he wished to frighten her, and her breath stopped. "Would ye taste a man's desire?" he whispered, letting his warm breath sear her upturned face. "'Tis neither kind nor courteous nor honorable nor gentle."

Her heart beat like the wings of a caged falcon, and his words dizzied her. But she wasn't afraid. He wouldn't hurt her. She *knew* he wouldn't. Just like she knew that bear in St. Andrews wouldn't hurt her. "Aye."

"Ye're certain?" he hissed, his whisper laced with brutish threat.

And still she trusted him. She parted her trembling lips and nodded faintly.

He was absolutely right.

The hands that seized her jaw weren't gentle. They were demanding. He pressed the length of his hard-muscled body brazenly against hers, careless of propriety. His harsh stubble scraped across her cheek without a care for her delicate skin. And his mouth... His mouth consumed her like liquid fire.

She should have detested his touch. 'Twas rough and brutal and shocking, not at all the sweet, gentle caress she expected. She should have fought her way free, wiped his cruel kiss from her mouth, and fled gratefully to the nunnery.

But she didn't want to.

His strength was intoxicating, his taste intriguing, his lust fascinating. She wilted against him, surrendering her lips, her limbs, her will to him. And 'twas heaven.

A sensual lethargy poured over her like rich oil, slowing her, weighting her eyelids, singing in her head like the buzzing of a hundred bees. Her arms traveled up of their own accord, settling upon his broad chest, and her fingers bunched in the thick cloth of his doublet. She breathed his breath—warm and heady with ale—and heard and felt his lusty growl. A curious vibration, like that of a plucked harp string, strong and resounding, wound its way through the core of her body, singing in her veins and echoing low in her belly.

Then his thumb opened her jaw wide, and he made full assault upon her mouth. His tongue thrust between her lips—hot and wet and demanding—and a thrill coursed lightning-swift through her veins at the sensation. She groaned in pleasure and shame as he violated the soft recesses of her mouth. And still she didn't want him to stop.

Blade couldn't stop himself. God, the woman tasted sweet, as delicious as ambrosia. And her body—so small, so frail, yet so warm and willing against his—was driving him mad with desire.

He'd meant to frighten the overcurious wench—for her own good. She'd have no doubt, when he was through with her, that a nunnery was exactly where she belonged.

He hadn't counted on her liking it.

Instead of recoiling in horror like any self-respecting virgin, the woman answered him, kiss for kiss, with a passion of her own. And now he began to lose himself in her desire.

'Twas when her tongue eased forward to lap tentatively at his own that the last of his control slipped away. He broke free of the kiss, but only to lift his shackled hands up and over her head, to enclose her in his arms and pull her closer.

He recaptured her lips, laying siege to her mouth until she opened for him and gave him her tongue again. A bolt of current surged through him, bringing him to instant arousal. His heart pounding, he slid his hands down her back and cupped the gentle curve of her buttocks, drawing her toward him. He pressed her against that full, aching part of him that cried out for relief, and though she gasped within his mouth at the bold contact, still she didn't withdraw.

Breathless with passion, he moved his rigid length with brazen need against the flat of her belly. There could be no mistaking what he desired, and yet she neither shrunk from nor bristled at his insolence. Instead, to his increasing amazement, she wrapped her arms about his neck and strove upward, meeting him.

Finally, with a defeated groan, he lifted her so his swollen staff pressed at the tender spot between her legs. Lord, 'twas sweet agony, despite the layers of clothing separating them. She writhed sensuously against him, and her innocent movement drove him to a more profound desire than he'd ever experienced.

For one lingering moment, Blade forgot who he was, where they were, what he'd done, and knew only this overwhelming yearning to join with the woman. She clung to him fervently— her kisses desperate, her moans insistent—compelling him to take what she offered. And he longed to take it. He longed to slake his savage hunger, to drive himself deep into her body and find shuddering release.

In another instant, he might have. He might have cast caution to the winds, tossed the bonnie maiden upon her back in the shelter of the cove, lifted her skirts, and had his way with her on the pebbled shore. But before the last shred of sense left him, a familiar voice made him freeze.

"Blade!" Wilham hissed.

Rose immediately broke free in a panic, panting rapidly, pushing against his chest.

Lust and fury warred within Blade as he pierced Wilham with a glare that would melt steel.

Wilham's face was guilty, his voice urgent, as he nodded toward Rose. "That Highland woman is comin'!"

Blade bit out a curse. Rose gasped and backed away, but trapped within his shackles, she almost fell backward over the chain. He caught her in time, and a short struggle ensued as they both tried to disentangle her. Meanwhile, the sound of furious footfalls crunching on gravel grew nearer.

"Lassie!"

Rose's eyes widened, and she frantically wiped at her mouth, as if it bore evidence of his kiss. Blade frowned with all the furor of his thwarted desire, and Wilham glared back, pointing meaningfully below his belt.

Blade glanced down. The bulge there was painfully obvious. Suffering under Rose's flustered sob, he adjusted his chausses and tugged down his doublet until his arousal was at least partially concealed. He was certain, however, that there was no hiding the lust in his eyes.

"Rose, lassie! Where the devil are ye?"

"Here!" Rose cried out, her voice strident with forced levity.

Tildy slogged forward, venom in her narrowed gaze. Blade knew there was no fooling the cunning merchant.

"Ye see, good woman?" Wilham interjected before Rose could incriminate herself. "I told ye the lass was safe. She came to seek food for her falcon. And Blade, gallant fellow that he is, wouldn't let her go near the firth where she might—"

"Dinna mistake me for an addlepate, young swain!" Tildy snapped. "I can still see the lump in yon 'gallant fellow's' trews."

Blade was certain he flushed red, but he resisted the urge to open his mouth and make matters worse.

"Come along, Rose!" Tildy barked, then added pointedly, "Ere this dark devil charms ye into deeper waters."

Rose cast one last longing look at Blade, and 'twas then he felt the weight of his misconduct. Satan's claws, what had he been thinking?

"What the devil were ye thinkin'?" Wilham demanded when the women had gone. "That's no mere milkmaid for ye to trifle with. She's a titled lady. Court her, certainly, but don't seduce the wench. Do ye know what—"

"Aye!" Blade snarled. "I know."

He said no more. There was no way to explain what had transpired. Wilham would have laughed in disbelief had he tried to explain that the kiss was the lady's idea. 'Twasn't worth the effort. Besides, 'twouldn't happen again.

"Ye know, there are a couple o' willin' wenches at the inn," Wilham grumbled, "if a man's dagger is in need of a good polishin'."

"Wil?"

"Aye?"

"Enough."

Blade's command fell on deaf ears. Wilham chided him all the way back up the cliff and all the way to the inn. He supposed 'twas a fitting penance for the sheer madness in which he'd just engaged.

As it turned out, a few of the bored residents of the inn had made a game of trapping a mouse for the falcon, and through their efforts, the bird now feasted on fresh meat. Though Rose sat nearby—her ears likely blistered from the Highland woman's scolding—she looked up neither at her bird nor upon him, but kept her gaze trained on the table before her.

A strange mixture of satisfaction and disappointment filled him.

'Twas best this way. He'd not discouraged her from the secular life as well as he'd hoped, despite his overbold embrace

113

and far too intimate kisses. Indeed, she'd seemed to enjoy his touch too well for one bound for the church. He only hoped her mortification at being caught would drive her to scorn earthly pleasures and ease her submission to a life of chastity.

And yet a secret part of him didn't hope that at all. She was far too fair a flower to wither and die in the smothering confines of a nunnery. Such a blossom should be nurtured and worshipped and allowed to bloom in all its glory. She should taste love and bear children. Wasn't that God's blessing to a woman? And this woman, in particular, with the depth of her passion and thirst and wonder, shouldn't deprive herself of the fullest measure of that gift.

He downed a healthy gulp of ale, then shook his head, scattering his wayward thoughts. Her destiny was not his affair. Unless Rose was a part of the scheme to kill Laichloan's son—something he highly doubted—then she was no longer his concern.

Wilham was right. The inn housed a few willing wenches upon whom Blade might slake his lust. And he would have, he assured himself, if they'd stayed any longer. But Father Peter was already gathering his flock to depart. So Blade tightened his breeches and shouldered his pack, carefully disregarding the scarlet skirts that swirled at the edges of his vision.

By the time they'd marched north to Hillend, the sun had sunk behind the knees of the western hills, and a coverlet of chill fog had followed them in from the firth.

The circumstances of their lodging caused the first battle of the pilgrimage. Father Peter had made arrangements through a third party with a man of substantial wealth and title to house the pilgrims within the man's demesne. Upon arrival, however, 'twas apparent the residence was far too small to accommodate such a large number. 'Twas obvious to Blade that the man— who was neither as wealthy nor as titled as he'd proclaimed— had overstated his capacity in order to earn a share of the pilgrims' wealth.

'Twas too late to secure other lodgings. So after a brief display of temper on the part of Father Peter, who was mollified by Simon the palmer, and a stubborn renegotiation of fees on the part of Jacob the goldsmith, the pilgrims managed to squeeze into the modest great room for an equally modest supper of broth thickened with eggs and breadcrumbs.

Blade kept his head buried in his trencher, unwilling to risk a glance at the lady whose lips he could too well remember upon his own. He drowned his desire—desire that was wont to rekindle—in the cup of coarse beer set before him. And only when the stories of the night were begun did he manage to think of anything other than the delectable woman in scarlet.

Lettie told the first tale. It began well enough, with three thieves competing to see who could best the others. One thief stole the eggs from under a magpie. The second thief replaced them without disturbing the bird. But while the second performed this task, the third stole the man's hose from off his legs.

After that, the story fell to pieces. Lettie kept mixing up the thieves' names, and she couldn't recall which thief stole what from whom, nor how they managed to trick one another. She ended the telling in a sheepish giggle, unable to bring it to a sensible conclusion. The pilgrims nonetheless applauded politely, and Jacob the goldsmith patronizingly patted her hand, while the scholars murmured amongst themselves, trying to unknot the tangle of the story so they could decipher how it *should* have been told.

Blade narrowed his eyes at the blushing storyteller. He wondered if Lettie's addlepated manner was real or feigned. If 'twas genuine, he doubted the woman possessed the intellect to carry off murder. Her companion guildsman, however, seemed capable of a villainous plot.

Campbell the soldier was then asked for a tale. He demurred at first, claiming he knew no stories but those of grim wars and bloody battles.

"Then tell us one o' those," Father Peter declared, "and we shall welcome it, for e'en the Gospel recounts mighty wars fought in the name o' the Lord."

Campbell, still reluctant, began his tale quietly, in a voice so low the pilgrims had to remain nearly silent to hear him. He related the story of a company of gentle knights, bound in service to a cruel laird. They served their liege with honor for many years, though his ways were often brutal.

As he spoke, Blade noticed that Campbell's fist tightened around his wooden cup, and he knew instantly 'twas no story, but a true tale.

"They besieged crumblin' keeps where no riches were to be gained, solely for the amusement o' the laird," Campbell said, his eyes glassy as he stared into his beer, "starvin' the men, slayin' lasses too weak to fight and ch-" He choked, then swallowed down bitter memory. "And children too young to understand." He paused to gather his thoughts, and no one breathed.

Blade furrowed his brow. He'd seen Campbell's pain before, in the faces of men forced by fealty to do things against their hearts, against their will.

"On a winter day they lay siege to the keep of a nobleman with four daughters as fair and pure as snow. By sunset, the outer wall was undermined, and the knights easily entered the keep. But this time, the loathsome laird desired that his men spare the nobleman and his four virtuous daughters." Campbell took a bracing drink of his beer before continuing. "He wanted his knights to..." His jaw tightened. "To deflower the maidens, with their father as witness."

Gasps of shock circled the table, but Campbell was too far into his tale to take notice.

"Three o' the knights did as they were bid," he said stonily. Blade could read the man's torment in his face as he relived the horror. "Despite the maidens' pleas and their father's appeals, they...savaged them without mercy. But the fourth..." Campbell bit at his trembling lip. "The fourth refused. He knelt upon the stones o' the keep and begged the daughters for their forgiveness o' his sinnin' companions. He threw himself upon the mercy o' his liege, askin' him to cease these godless acts." The pause was so long then that the listeners began to shift upon their benches. But none dared break the heavy silence. "The laird drew his sword forthwith and lopped the man's head from his shoulders."

More gasps ensued. Even Blade drew in a sharp breath. He'd been certain that Campbell had been that honorable soldier.

One of the impertinent scholars commented, "Well, surely the knights then rose up against their liege."

Campbell pinned him with a glare. "So ye'd think, would ye not?" he spat bitterly. "But then ye're not a knight. Ye've not sworn fealty to a nobleman. Ye know nothin' o' loyalty and honor and allegiance."

The soldier's fierce words silenced the scholar and gave Blade pause. *He* knew all about honor. Honor had destroyed his life and apparently Campbell's as well.

"They did nothin'," the soldier snarled. "The fifth... The fifth...churl, even as his companion lay bleedin' on the flagstones beside him, even as the women sobbed in horror and their father pleaded for mercy, even then...the bastard did as he was commanded and thrust himself upon the youngest maiden."

The room fell silent as the soldier stared, unseeing, at the beer-stained tabletop. Meek Guillot was the first to move. Sitting beside the soldier, he rested a hand of comfort on Campbell's forearm.

The soldier drew his arm back violently, as if the lad had branded him with fire. "Nae!" he cried. "Don't touch me."

Everyone grew uncomfortable then, for they all knew there was more than a grain of truth in his tale. Guillot withdrew his hand, his young eyes wide with hurt.

"Don't," Campbell said more evenly, "touch me."

While those around him began tentatively to reinitiate the conversation and lighten the mood, Blade reconsidered the soldier's tale. The story had no ending. Had Campbell become plagued by the burden of his sin? Was that why he'd come on pilgrimage, to seek forgiveness and redemption? Or was he still slave to his wicked master? Was he yet loyal to the deranged demands of his overlord?

Could Campbell be the murderer? He'd slain man, woman, and child without hesitation. He'd scarcely blink to kill a laird's only son if his liege so ordered.

Despite Campbell's assistance with the thieves and his painful tale, the soldier clearly had both the will and the stomach for violence, and Blade couldn't overlook the overwhelming evidence that he might be the assassin.

Rose dug her nails into the battered wood of the trestle table. The soldier's story was deeply disturbing, all the more so because she feared 'twas true. But Campbell, at least, was on the path to salvation. His crimes might be abhorrent, but they were at least in his past. There was deliverance, even for him. When they reached St. Andrews, his soul could be redeemed.

Rose, however, engaged in perfidy even now. Somewhere, miles behind her, her scorned betrothed raged at her absence. And not only were Rose's thoughts *not* with Gawter—they were centered on another.

She wished she could dismiss their seaside encounter from her mind as easily as Blade had. He'd hardly looked at her since their arrival in Hillend. But she couldn't stop thinking about him, about his kiss, his hands upon her, the taste of his tongue inside her mouth...

Even the recollection dizzied her. A fervid blush stole across her cheek as she gazed at his somber profile, and she found it almost impossible to believe the breathtaking felon had actually kissed her earlier.

The feeling had been so much more intense than Rose had anticipated. She'd been attracted to his dark good looks and his kind heart, so she'd expected his kiss to be a pleasant thing. Never had she imagined 'twould be so compelling. And now she craved more.

She longed for the crush of his demanding arms and the heady scent of him—all leather and iron and man, the savage feast of his hungering mouth and the erotic, blinding haze of his passion. She wanted his warm flesh, his sultry gaze, his delicious mouth. Even now, looking upon him, her heart quickened, her breath grew shallow, and her nether parts ached with yearning.

But if her desire was far greater than she'd foreseen, so was her dilemma. How could she resign herself to a nunnery, feeling what she now felt? How could she sacrifice a lifetime of such pleasure for the chastity of the church? 'Twas a coil that would torment her long into the night.

The trestle table was put away and mats laid out for beds upon the floor of the cramped hall. No modesty was afforded tonight, for men and ladies alike shared the single room. Father Peter did his best to divide the chamber diplomatically, but his designs were futile. Lettie couched herself near Jacob, and Brigit brazenly sidled up between the two tanners. As for Blade, none ventured near the fearsome felon, and by the time Rose set Wink on a perch and bid the bird goodnight, no other place remained for her.

"Don't ye even think of it," Tildy snipped under her breath. "*I'll* take the spot nearest that villain, and ye'll sleep 'twixt me and the nuns."

Though a rebellious retort hovered on Rose's lips, she bit it back, knowing 'twas best this way. If she planned to take the veil, then she must resist the temptations of the secular world, and 'twas best she start now. So, with a small sigh, she snuggled beneath the furs the host provided and watched the hall grow dim as, one by one, the candles were all extinguished.

The fire, of course, would burn low all night for warmth, and as Rose rested upon the rush mat, she watched the shadows of flame lick at the plaster ceiling. How had she come to this pass? she wondered—a fugitive, traveling with strangers, sleeping on the floor. As a child, she'd had everything she wanted—warm clothing, rich food, a soft bed. Now she had nothing. And her destiny was poised on a blade's edge.

For a long while she lay still, listening to the pilgrims snore all around her. Tildy's loud rasping soon filled the quiet hall, and the nun beside her murmured softly in her sleep. But Rose could find no rest.

She swept a finger pensively across her lips, wondering if some stain of Blade's kiss remained there to mark her. If so, 'twould eventually fade, she assured herself, along with the strong wave of emotion that remembering his touch evoked. At least, she hoped 'twould fade. For even if she ultimately decided to forego the church and wed Gawter, she dared not carry the memory of Blade's caress to her marriage bed.

Thinking of her betrothed left a bitter taste on her tongue. She knew instinctively Gawter would never make her feel the way Blade had. All she could recall of Gawter now were his frantic, jerking buttocks, his sweating flanks, and his pig-like grunts of passion as he mated with her mother. Rose's eyes filled with angry tears, blurring the patterns on the ceiling. 'Twas so unfair, this awful choice fate had thrust upon her. Especially when so desirable a destiny slept not six feet away.

She swallowed heavily. 'Twas completely improper, thinking of Blade in that way. First of all, she scarcely knew him, and what little she knew was that he was a mercenary, a man who changed residences, masters, and most likely lovers, on a whim. Secondly, he wasn't some puppet to perform at her whim. He was a man with his own life and his own future. Aye, he'd obliged her with a kiss, but he would have done the same for any woman in the company. 'Twas folly to make more of it.

And yet, she couldn't stop thinking about him. She eased up on her elbows and gazed over Tildy's bulk. The dark outlaw lay facing away from her, the contours of his linen shirt illuminated by firelight. She caught her lip beneath her teeth. How she longed to feel it again—that breathless, tingling, heart-racing, burning need that was simultaneously stirred and relieved by his touch.

Her pulse thrummed in her bosom. A reckless notion hastened her breath. Dared she?

She bit at the edge of her nail. Tildy slept. No one need know. And it might be her last chance to sample the pleasures of a man's body. She'd not wake him. She only wished to nestle against the strong breadth of his back, to inhale his fascinating male scent, to pet the wild beast, and to pretend for a little while that she belonged to him.

Swiftly, before too much reflection could make a coward of her, she slipped from beneath the furs and crawled past Tildy. Scarcely daring to breathe, she crept up on the slumbering felon and carefully stretched out beside him. His breathing was slow and steady and deep.

Inches still separated them, but already she felt the heat of him—vibrant, virile, powerful. Already her body responded to him, flushing with desire, tingling with need.

Closing her eyes, she imagined he was her husband—her strong, protective, faithful husband—who would slay dragons for her and have children with her and love her forever. She moved forward another inch, until her breath rippled the linen of his shirt. How safe she felt beside him, as if she needed fear nothing.

Casting aside the last of her restraint, she tipped her head to nuzzle the spot between his shoulder blades. When he didn't waken, she let her hand drift up, lightly grazing his spine with the back of her knuckles. Then, turning her hand over, she allowed her fingertips to rove tenderly across the sculpted contours of his back. Stripped now of his doublet, with only the thin layer of his linen shirt between them, Rose felt his warmth and the solid muscle that made up his warrior's body. A sudden spark sizzled through her, awakening her blood and kindling the banked fire between her legs.

With a ragged, silent sigh, she braced her hand gently upon his hip and eased herself forward until she lay full against him. She turned her cheek against the blade of his shoulder and cushioned her breasts upon his back. His firm buttocks pressed against the part of her that burned with yearning.

Exquisite pain and profound pleasure warred within her body as she reveled in unrequited desire, all of her senses engaged with only him. She writhed subtly against him, seeking what she couldn't have. Her pulse hummed in her ears, and her limbs moved of their own accord.

At last, her brazen arm—draped over his hip and curving downward across his flat belly—proved too bold.

Her wrist was trapped suddenly in a bone-crushing grip that almost made her cry aloud. An instant later, she heard Blade's low voice, like the warning growl of a hound.

"Don't ye dare."

# Chapter 8

Blade had been awake for some time. After all, he hadn't earned his reputation with a sword by dozing while trouble was afoot. But he didn't guess who his stalker was until she sidled up against his back and her delicate fragrance enwrapped him.

Even then he hadn't revealed himself, partly because his inquisitive nature demanded he first discover her intent and largely because, though he was loath to admit it, he enjoyed the sensation of the woman's soft body cradled against him.

But then she'd gone too far. A kiss was one thing. Lying beside him was another. But letting her hands rove where they didn't belong, so near to the fire that smoldered low in his belly, waiting to be roused, was deadly perilous.

"Go back to your bed," he whispered over his shoulder, removing her hand forcibly from his stomach.

After a long pause, she asked, "Why?"

He scowled, taken aback. What did she mean, why? Because she'd been caught. Because 'twasn't fitting behavior for a lady. Because the woman who'd appointed herself guardian to the lass slept a mere few feet away. There were a dozen reasons.

"'Tisn't proper," he grunted, unwilling to name them all.

"That isn't a good reason," she whispered, her breath tickling his back.

"And ye're playin' with fire," he hissed.

"I'm not afraid," she murmured.

"And..." he began, growing more aroused and angry and confused by the moment.

Then, desperate to extricate himself from this awkward position as quickly as possible, he did the vilest thing he could imagine. He seized her hand again, stuffed it down his braies, and pressed her palm against the hot, rigid proof of his desire.

"And there's this," he snarled.

It worked. She gasped, utterly flustered.

"Oh," she said. "Oh."

When he released her hand, she snatched it back at once, scrambled away without another word, and crept back to her mat.

He shut his eyes and smiled grimly. Surely Lady Rosamund would go barreling off to the convent now without a backward glance.

Part of him, however, thought he must have lost his wits. Perhaps he was like the flagellants who scarred themselves in devotion to God, for he felt irreparably branded by Rose's touch. The memory of her soft palm burned his flesh.

Another part of him ached, not only with unslaked hunger, but with a hollow sorrow. Rose's gentle caresses had soothed his battle-weary bones and recalled to him a time when his sword was unstained with blood. Her innocence awakened his chivalry. And her fearlessness... He smiled ruefully. Her fearlessness amused and amazed and captivated him.

The flames eventually dwindled on the hearth, as did the fire in his loins, and sleep came upon him. But his slumber was fraught with dreams of battle and bloodshed, so when the servants roused before the sun to stoke the fire and prepare breakfast, he welcomed the approaching morn.

Despite their close quarters, Lady Rose spared him not a glance as the travelers ate their morning meal and prepared to leave. He'd obviously made his point, and she was too abashed to meet his eye. When the pilgrims departed, he saw she'd made the wise purchase of a plain gray cloak, for which she'd soon be grateful. The mist this morn had unfurled across the glen and lay thick upon the ground.

The falcon seemed to dislike the clime. She fretted on the lady's glove, ruffling her wings and shifting her perch while Rose struggled to keep her still.

The fog dampened the sounds of the forest, muting the plodding footfalls of the travelers. But whether 'twas the falcon's restlessness or that inherent sense of trouble Blade possessed, he began to suspect they were being pursued.

"Ye hear it, too?" Wilham murmured when they'd marched a few miles.

Blade nodded.

"Horses," Wilham said, "but they're laggin'."

"Aye."

Wilham cast a surreptitious look over his shoulder. "Fog's too thick to see them. How many do ye wager? Two? Three?"

"Hard to tell."

They walked on. No one else seemed to notice the faint hoofbeats behind them. Then the falcon emitted a disgruntled screech.

"What's wrong with that bird?" Wilham asked after a bit.

Blade shook his head.

Wilham scratched his cheek. "Maybe the falcon senses our pursuers as well."

"'Tis more likely the falcon bristles at her *mistress's* unease," Blade said.

"Ye think the lass hears the riders?"

Blade narrowed his eyes at the gray-cloaked figure, blurred by the mist, on the path ahead of him. As he watched, she whispered to her falcon and cast a nervous glance back along the road.

"Oh, aye," he told Wilham as a dark suspicion gripped him. "She hears them."

He remembered the first group of riders and how the lass had hid from them. 'Twas almost as if she'd expected pursuit. And now, when more horsemen approached, she grew as skittish as a kitten in a kennel.

Suddenly he realized an interesting possibility. Rose might be a fugitive herself. She may have spoken the truth about joining a holy order, but perhaps she was seeking sanctuary there for some crime. Perhaps someone hunted her, and she was fleeing the law.

"What do we do?" Wilham asked, one hand upon the sword he wore at his hip.

"Nothin'," Blade replied, "unless they o'ertake us."

Despite his words to Wilham, he didn't intend to do nothing. He'd keep his eye fixed on Rose, studying her every gesture, watching her every step. He wouldn't let her out of his sight for one instant. Then, when they reached their next stop, he'd get her alone and question her until she gave him the truth.

Opportunity came along sooner than he expected. Drogo the cook, Fulk the butcher, and the two tanners decided they'd not eaten well enough in Hillend and insisted, albeit with little argument on Father Peter's part, on halting at the next inn along the road for a cup of ale and a bite of something more substantial than the barley gruel they'd had for breakfast.

To Blade's satisfaction, the inn was ill-lit and as tightly packed with travelers as a barrel of pickled herring, perfect for his purpose.

"Keep that Highland hen occupied," he muttered to Wilham, who—good man that he was—never questioned Blade's requests.

Wilham raised a brow. "I hope ye don't mean to finish what ye started yesterday."

Blade responded with a frosty glare. "Not if the king himself ordered it."

Wilham grinned, and Blade watched as his man approached the Highland woman, cleverly feigning to have something in his eye and begging her to come look at it in the light.

126

Meanwhile, Blade made his way through the crowd toward the lass. She'd just set her falcon to perch and was removing her glove when he snagged her by the waist, covered her mouth, and dragged her into the shadows beneath the stairs. She fought him, but had the good sense not to scream.

"What's the meanin' o' this?" she hissed when he moved his hand away. Despite the frightened quavering of her voice, she seemed relieved to see him, as if she'd expected someone else. "Unhand me, sirrah."

"Today, I'd speak with *ye*. Alone," he said, echoing her request of the day before. He did unhand her, but he also blocked her way so she couldn't escape.

She trembled and wrapped consoling arms about herself. "Haven't ye shamed me enough? Believe me, I'll not trouble ye again. Only let me go."

He cupped her chin, forcing her face up toward his, though she wouldn't look at him. "Who hunts ye?"

She started, and her eyes fluttered. "What do ye mean?"

"Who hunts ye?" he repeated.

"Hunts me? No one hunts me."

"Ye're a poor liar. Someone is followin' us. Ye heard them, too. Who is it?"

"How should I know?" She tried to tug her chin away, but he held it fast. "If ye don't unhand me this instant..."

"It may be I can protect ye from them," he told her, "but I must know who they are and why they pursue ye."

She hesitated, obviously considering his tempting offer. Ultimately, however, her fear of her pursuers outweighed her trust in his protection. Straightening her back, she looked him in the eye.

"I need no champion. No one is followin' me. No one has cause to follow me. I'm simply on pilgrimage to St. Andrews to become a nun." She pulled her chin out of his grasp. "And furthermore, my falcon will need no egg today. The mouse she ate yesterday will serve her well enough. So ye needn't trouble me again until the morrow."

Curse her stubbornness, the woman was lying through her teeth. But what was her secret? Who followed her? A cheated merchant? A robbed nobleman? A fellow assassin? If it took him the rest of the journey, he'd discover the answer. For now, however, he and the lass remained in check.

"I'll be watchin' ye," he warned, backing away with a mocking bow. In a dour mood, he sauntered toward Wilham, who sat by a sheepskin-paned window while the Highland woman's thick fingers prodded at his eye.

"Ah," Wilham crowed when he spotted Blade. "I think 'tis gone, goodwife," he said, rapidly blinking his eyes. "I can't thank ye enough." With that, he rose to meet Blade, leaving open-mouthed Tildy behind.

"Anythin'?" Wilham asked.

Blade shook his head.

"They should have ridden up by now," Wilham said. "Whoever 'tis, they're takin' great pains not to be seen."

Those great pains extended long into the afternoon. The riders remained at the edge of hearing and just beyond sight in the obliging shroud of fog, and though Rose's falcon continued to fret, the lass resisted the incriminating urge to turn her head, at least while Blade watched her.

He was true to his word. He never let Rose out of his sight. Even when they stopped at The King's Arms for cider. Even when Rose stole off in the direction of the orchard behind the tavern.

At last, Rose thought as she picked her way through the misty orchard, she'd escaped the condemning eye of that wretched brute. As if 'tweren't troubling enough to know that someone dogged them, Blade had to torment her by watching her every move. Hadn't he humiliated her enough already?

'Twas unforgivably wicked, what he'd done last night. Taking her hand and placing it...there. Just thinking about it made her blush.

Yet after she'd crept back to her bed like a whipped hound, the mortifying shame lessened to be replaced by a kind of curious wonder.

Had she made him swell like that? God's eyes, his man's part was as thick and solid as the grip of a lance. And yet there was a velvet heat to his flesh that had seared her palm.

Her cheeks warmed, and she cursed silently, shuddering off the dregs of her musings. She wrapped her rough cloak closer about her as she drank in the sweet scent of last year's rotting apples. She'd not be gone long. Tildy had gone to the privy, and Rose needed just a moment or two of peace. Between the dark felon's watch, Tildy's direful whispering, Wink's irascible mood, and the knowledge that the riders behind them might be Gawter's men, she was frayed with worry.

She'd hoped to find solitude. Instead, as she crept through the orchard, she heard a strange sound that halted her in her tracks. She thought at first 'twas an injured animal, crying in pain. But as her eyes filtered through the mist, she beheld a figure slumped beside an apple tree.

'Twas Ian Campbell the soldier. He knelt in the mud beneath the tree in his linen shirt, his head buried in his hands, his shoulders heaving with great sobs. Her heart went out to him at once, and she longed to lend the poor man comfort for the pain he suffered.

But she understood the pride of men well. She wouldn't shame him by intruding upon his moment of solitude. She'd half-turned to go when she saw him pick up the dagger lying beside him.

Her heart wrenched against her ribs.

What did he intend to do with the blade? Nothing good, she was certain. His grim, tear-stained face, his eyes, glazed with defeat, and the fingers clenching the haft of the dagger with white-knuckled force told her as much.

Her breath came shallow as she watched him slowly lift his shirt with one hand, exposing the pale flesh of his stomach. Dear God, nae!

She must stop him.

Somehow, she must stop him.

Her heart pounding, she began shuffling toward him as casually as possible, as if she'd only arrived, humming under her breath, creating noise to alert him to her presence and hopefully distract him from his dire purpose.

It partially worked. He wrenched the linen shirt down and swiftly wiped away the evidence of his tears with the back of his arm. But he didn't rise from where he knelt, and he didn't sheathe his dagger. Which meant he'd not changed his mind, only delayed his action.

"Oh, good day!" Rose called out with faux cheer, tromping forward. "'Tis a beautiful orchard, isn't it? Pears, apples, damsons... 'Tis no doubt lovely in summer, with blossoms thick on the branches. 'Tis Ian, aye? Do I have it right? My name is Lady Rosamund, and I..."

She prattled on like a squirrel until her chittering began to annoy him, jarring him from his gloom, arousing instead his ire.

"Cease!" he snarled.

She swallowed hard. At least the despair was gone from his eyes. If she could keep him engaged...

"Why, what a temper," she clucked, her felicity undimmed. "Anyway, I imagine the cider here is good. Have ye tasted it yet?"

He didn't reply. Instead, he looked at her in confusion, as if she'd said something completely unintelligible and absurd.

"Nay, neither have I," she said brightly, approaching with courage she did not feel. "We'll have to go in and have a cup."

She sincerely hoped he wasn't the kind of man to lash out at whatever stood in his way, for she meant to plant herself firmly in his way.

She drew close, and his shoulders began to heave with quick breaths like those of a desperate wolf cornered by a hunter.

"Here," she said, eyeing his dagger. "What's this? Ah, ye must be plannin' to shave." She hunkered down beside him. His eyes widened, rolling like those of a panicked mare. "Let me help ye, then, Sir Ian," she offered, her heart fluttering in her breast. "I always shaved my father's beard. Didn't nick him once." The smile on her face wavered only slightly as she held her hand out for the dagger.

He stared at the ground. "Go," he groaned. "Leave me."

His voice made her want to weep. But she knew tears wouldn't help him. "Nae," she said gently. "I won't leave ye."

"Ye..." he began, his chin trembling. "Go. Please. Go."

"I'm not leavin' ye," she repeated softly.

His will crumbled then, and his face dissolved into a grimace of sheer misery. The dagger dropped from his fingers, and his head sank into his hands. Though he tried to silence them, piteous sobs were wrenched from deep within his chest.

Her pulse still raced, but a relieved peace descended over Rose as she cast the dagger out of reach and rested a consoling hand upon the soldier's sleeve. For a long while she said nothing, and eventually his sobs diminished.

"Have ye ever seen the shrine at St. Andrews?" she ventured.

He made no reply.

"I grew up there," she told him. "The cathedral is a wondrous place, second only to heaven, I'm certain. God surely resides there. There, we shall all find peace...and hope...and redemption. Isn't that why ye've come on pilgrimage?"

He shook his head. "There's no redemption for me."

She frowned, then tightened her grip on his arm until he looked over at her, his eyes red with weeping, his face wet with tears. "Ye're wrong, Sir Ian. Even for those who killed Christ, there was redemption."

Blade shifted behind the wall of the tavern, loosening his grip on the dagger he'd been clenching since Rose had first started toward Campbell. It appeared she was out of danger now. But the fool lass had risked much, stealing up on the soldier like a hunter stalking a wild boar. What had possessed her?

Maybe 'twas her soft heart that led her to rescue this wounded animal, the same way she'd tamed her one-eyed falcon.

Whatever motivated her, her tenderness and compassion and strength was touching.

His throat had thickened at her words to Campbell. Did she truly believe that a soul as errant as the soldier's could be saved? If so, he wondered what she would say of *his* sin...

Before he could think too long on it, he allowed cynicism to seep in and strip the hope from him. He was nothing like the soldier, after all. Blade hadn't come on pilgrimage for redemption. He knew his crime as well as he knew his boots, and after two years, they were an equally comfortable fit.

Indeed, Campbell might be the only one of the company with a true pilgrim's calling. 'Twas unlikely he was part of any murder plot. The battle-weary man had no stomach left for bloodshed, other than his own.

At last assured of Rose's safety, Blade entered the tavern. He wouldn't speak of Campbell's torment, not even to Wilham. Which proved, he supposed, that there was a shred of decency left in him.

Wilham had managed to allay Tildy's worries somehow with one of his clever stories and a tankard of cider, so that by the time Rose returned, the Highland woman was soused enough not to notice her long absence.

When the travelers lit out from the tavern again, the riders behind them had vanished. Blade wondered if his suspicious mind had played games with him, casting doubt where it didn't belong. Perhaps he'd mistaken their proximity in the confusing echo of the mist. Whatever the circumstances, they no longer dogged the travelers, and the falcon, sensing his mistress's relief, now perched calmly upon her glove.

Cowdenbeath nestled in the lap of a lush glen, and as they began their descent, the sun peeked low from beneath the solid wall of gray clouds, taunting them with a departing wink. Their inn for the night was appreciably larger than the last accommodations, with four chambers reserved for the pilgrims and a bounteous feast of rich stuffed capons, mushroom pasties, herb fritters, and mulled wine set on the table.

Rose was pensive this eve as the pilgrims supped and chatted and belched around her. Blade wondered where her thoughts were.

Campbell, though quiet, seemed less somber. Guillot the apprentice, who sat beside the soldier with something akin to worship in his eyes, even coaxed a word from him when he whispered something in his ear.

Drogo the cook told the first tale of the evening, delivering it with enormous relish, waving his meaty hands about and playing the parts of all the characters, training his voice first to a low growl and then to a great bellow. He told of some kitchen misadventure wherein a Scots laird made the mistake of hiring a French cook. The story culminated in its last line, which was, "I said haggis, not gag us!"

The pilgrims laughed uproariously, and the phrase was oft repeated throughout the rest of the evening.

To everyone's amazement, shy Guillot volunteered to tell the next tale.

'Twas a magical story about a young maiden who found and tamed a wounded wolf. But to the maiden's distress, the wolf returned the favor by slaying her bridegroom. When 'twas revealed her bridegroom was truly a wolf in man's clothing who had intended to kill her, the maiden's gratitude broke the enchantment over the good wolf, and he was transformed into a man. The couple married and lived happily ever after.

After the tale, a collective feminine sigh filled the room. Blade, however, with his practical eye, had discounted the tale from its beginning. Obviously, none of the ladies sighing so blissfully had ever seen a wounded wolf. The maiden in the story was a fool to approach such a dangerous, defensive creature.

Then he remembered Campbell earlier. He'd been dangerous and defensive, yet Rose had marched brazenly up to him. And he couldn't deny that if Rose hadn't arrived to stop the soldier when she did, Blade would have stepped in as well.

He frowned, sipping thoughtfully at his spiced wine. Rose and he must both be fools.

As he set his cup down, he let his gaze rove to where Rose sat, wondering if she, too, wore the dreamy expression that graced all the other women's faces. But to his amazement, she stared bleakly at the table, tears pooling in her eyes.

His heart ached suddenly, as if he'd suffered the dull blow of a blunted lance. What troubled her? All the other women had enjoyed the lad's story. Why hadn't she? She should be content tonight. They had good lodging and plenty of food. And she should be doubly pleased in the knowledge that, because of her, Campbell lived to enjoy the tale.

Her tears brimmed, but didn't fall, and her gaze slid to his. For once, she hid none of her sorrow from him, and the naked despair in her eyes was so great and so real that it shook the very foundations of his soul.

Never had he seen so forlorn a face. Rose's melancholy roused feelings in him that had lain long dormant—strong and perilous urges to slay whatever dragon afflicted her.

He should ignore those impulses. Only a fool would touch a fire that had burned him before. Pursuing her demons was unthinkable. Imprudent. Unwise.

He finished off his mulled wine and sighed, aware with a sinking certainty that coming to her rescue was as inevitable as the rising of the sun. By the Saints, he was no better than that soft-witted maiden with her wounded wolf.

# Chapter 9

Rose sensed Blade coming toward her as the pilgrims retired from the dinner table, but she turned away from him. She didn't wish to speak to him. She didn't wish to speak to anyone.

Guillot's story had stung her, like salt in a deep cut. The love shared between the maiden and the wolf had seemed so moving and magical, and it pained Rose to face the reality that she'd never experience such love.

Why was she so cursed? she wondered bitterly. There was neither wounded wolf nor gallant hero in her future. Did she not deserve even a small measure of tenderness, of loyalty, of devotion? Even Campbell—sinner that he was—seemed to mellow this eve under the reverent affection of the storyteller.

But instead, Rose was condemned to a wretched choice between two undesirable fates.

She knew her tears were self-indulgent. She wasn't some free-spirited waif who might transcend the rules of her gender and the duties of her rank. Noblewomen most often married according to politics and not the dictates of their hearts. And if she chose not to marry, she was expected to exempt herself only by taking Christ to husband. She recognized that such was her obligation in life.

Still, it didn't keep her from desiring what she couldn't have. But tonight she'd rather not have to explain such callow desires to a seasoned knight who was well-versed in the duty required of nobility and would surely mock her selfishness.

So she hid her face and hurried off before he could call her back. And in the upstairs chamber, by the filtered glow of the rising moon, for the first time in her life, fearless, headstrong, spirited Rose cried herself silently to sleep.

The next morn dawned fair and bright. Rose, drained of tears and weary of despair, found herself in a reflective mood and determined she'd take inspiration from the promising sky. Perchance, by the light of day, she might examine her destiny more clearly. So as she walked along the grassy path touched by golden light, she tried on the garments of resigned peace. Her weeping and longings of the night past had been infantile, she realized. Today, she would grow up. Today, under the clarity of a cloudless heaven, she would fix upon her fate with a more rational eye.

After all, she decided, she had much to be thankful for. She was a titled lady. She didn't have to toil in a shop like Tildy. She wasn't so needy that she must seek a husband as desperately as Brigit. She had wealth enough for food and clothing and any trinkets that caught her eye. She'd been fostered by a generous and loving family—nurtured by Lady Anne, spoiled by Laird William—and she'd had many friends growing up. She'd owned a fine palfrey and painted dolls, gowns of velvet and silk, and even a pleasance garden full of flowers.

Indeed, when she thought of all she'd enjoyed through none of her own devices, she seemed rather an indulged child. She'd wanted for nothing. Perhaps 'twas time to pay for her pampered lot in life.

"Tildy," she solemnly announced as they ambled through a meadow jeweled with bluebells, "I've thought much these past few days, and I've decided..." She hoped her resolution was firmer than her voice. She cleared her throat. "I've decided," she repeated more deliberately, "I'm goin' to join the convent when we arrive in St. Andrews."

"What!" Tildy's squawk startled Wink, and the bird skittered up Rose's sleeve.

Tildy grabbed her arm and skewered her with a glare. "Ye're jestin' with me, aye? A bonnie young lass like ye who could have any lad in all the world?"

Rose smiled ruefully. While that was certainly flattering, 'twas hardly true. Politics played too great a part in the marriages of noblewomen.

"Ach!" Tildy spat, frowning toward the nuns walking before them and lowering her voice. "Ye canna want to waste your youth and that bonnie face, locked behind the walls of a nunnery."

Rose furrowed her brow. She wished Tildy wouldn't speak so bluntly. It cast doubt upon her decision. "I've heard, if one chooses wisely, that life in a convent can be pleasant and peaceful, rewardin' and—"

"And barren!" Tildy huffed, garnering the ears of the sisters, who turned their heads about in simultaneous askance.

Tildy screwed up her forehead and embellished for their benefit, "Barren...*Baron*...Walter. Ye wouldna know him. He's English."

Satisfied with the lie, the nuns resumed their silent journey, and Tildy continued in a whisper. "Dinna ye have a betrothed, lassie?"

"I...I won't marry him." Uttering the words aloud seemed to lift a weight from her spirit, and she realized to her relief that while she might be desperate, she wasn't willing to bargain with her heart.

Tildy considered that for a moment, then murmured in Rose's ear, "Are ye afeared o' the marriage bed?"

"Nae."

"Then what is it, lassie?"

"I can't explain it to ye."

Rose's admonition didn't keep crafty Tildy from guessing. "Are ye...have ye, that is...are ye no longer a maid?"

"Nae, 'tisn't that," Rose hissed, blushing.

The cogs of Tildy's brain continued to turn, and Rose suddenly wished she'd never confided in the merchant. "Yer betrothed, did ye do somethin' wicked to him? Did ye put frogs in his bed? Or mustard in his wine?"

Rose sighed. If only 'twere so simple. "Maybe I'm simply moved to become a nun," she suggested. "After all, this is a holy journey, and we're surrounded by inspirin' pilgrims o' great piety and devotion."

Unfortunately, just then, one of those pious pilgrims, a tanner, happened to stumble over a root on the trail, falling with a thud, a splash of spilled ale, and a rather loud and foul string of curses. Tildy raised a dubious brow.

"The pious pilgrims in this lot," Tildy revealed, "can be counted upon one hand. I'd be surprised if any o' this company came for holy purposes at all."

Rose nodded. 'Twas true. Most of them seemed to have ulterior reasons for going on pilgrimage. Guillot fled a cruel master. The scholars sought wives. Drogo and Fulk, Jacob and Lettie seemed to see the travel as a temporary reprieve from their spouses. Brigit looked for a husband. And Ivo and Odo appeared to have no other motive in mind but to sample to drunkenness the brews of every tavern between Stirling and St. Andrews. Even Rose herself couldn't claim redemption as the impetus behind her journey.

As they continued along on their counterfeit pilgrimage, Tildy, like a hound unwilling to surrender a bone, gnawed away at Rose's resolve.

"Well," the old woman said in a huff, "I ween 'tis God's will that a woman birth bairns." She sniffed. "I had three weans myself, but..." She wiped her sleeve across her nose. "All three were lost to me. So my husband bid me as he lay dyin', 'Tildy,' he said, 'find ye a guidman and make ye some more wee ones. They'll bring ye joy and take care o' ye in your wanin' years.'"

"So ye've come on pilgrimage to find a husband?"

"Oh, lass, nae!" Tildy replied with a giggle. "Nae, I've come to St. Andrews to see if there's a market for Highland wool there. My first man passed on a long while ago. I've been through four husbands since! And I gave each one a litter o' bairns." Pride shone in her eyes. "I've seven lads and five, nae, six lasses, and at last reckonin', an even score o' bairns from them."

Rose bit her lip. She'd known that going to a nunnery meant she'd never have children, but she'd relegated that fact to the back of her mind. Tildy's fond words were a stinging reminder.

They walked on mutely then, and the brilliance of the morning paled in Rose's dismal regard. Each footfall now seemed like a step closer to her doom.

The terrain began to reflect Rose's sense of impending gloom. The forest thickened almost imperceptibly as the stretches of sunlight dimmed and narrowed, and shadow widened to fill its place. Birches and willows and rowans crowded the path with darker and denser branches, leaning over the pilgrims with twisted limbs, like prying necromancers attempting to divine their secrets. Blossoms dwindled to an occasional clump of daisies lucky enough to find light, and even the sparrows deserted the deepening wood. A pervasive gravity weighed down the travelers, diminishing their chatter, for what few words they exchanged seemed swallowed up by the oppressive thicket. Eventually, the sun was almost entirely shut out by the trees, and Rose was thankful for the company of the pilgrims, pious or not. The path wound through the forest with almost calculated cunning, slithering and loitering and folding back upon itself until Rose was certain they would snake endlessly through the woods.

"There's a clearin' a wee bit ahead," Father Peter announced with sudden gaiety in the silence, startling more than a few of them. "We'll stop there."

True to the priest's word, a reprieve from the burdensome shadow at last appeared in the form of a large round depression in the break of trees where the ground was soft and grassy and flowers of every kind bloomed in profusion. The pilgrims laughed in relief as they stepped into the broad pool of light, and Rose's heart calmed as she welcomed the embrace of the comforting sun once again. Even Wink stretched her wings as if to say she was quite through with darkness for a while.

The pilgrims dispersed with renewed confidence, sprawling in the sunken meadow, picking flowers, clucking like flocks of chickens. Tildy, who had been mincing along the trail in discomfort for the last mile, set off with Lettie to find a bush not too far from the circle of light where she could ease her needs.

Rose tried not to look at the dark outlaw who passed behind her, but the soft clink of his chains conjured up his visage. 'Twas easier to displace him from her thoughts when they traveled well apart. Now, hearing his shackles, catching his scent, and, aye, *feeling* his presence, filled her senses and flooded her mind. She dared not lift her eyes to him.

Taking a fortifying breath, she marched to the midst of the meadow. The ground was spongy, almost like a living thing, and mushrooms made faerie circles throughout the glade. The place felt enchanted, yet the dark trees surrounding the lea appeared as if they might close over it at any moment, feasting upon the sunlight and the flowers and the pilgrims in one gulp. She shivered as she loosened Wink's jesses.

"Mind ye stay close," she murmured to the falcon, "for I've no wish to traipse through this eerie wood lookin' for ye."

The warning was hardly necessary. Wink never strayed far, and the tame creature always returned to Rose's arm.

She smiled as the bird caught the breeze and soared in lazy upward circles, cocking her head this way and that, instinctively seeking prey with her one good eye. For a long while, Wink played in the sky, dipping and turning, fluttering, then gliding, widening her range until Rose thought it best to call the falcon back.

But just as she lifted her wrist to summon Wink, the bird paused in mid-air, flapping furiously to hold her position. Rose frowned. 'Twas the bearing a falcon took just before it dove in for prey.

"Wink!" she shouted, but the bird ignored her.

Then, while Rose's jaw dropped, the falcon plummeted like a stone toward the dense trees.

Rose instantly picked up her skirts and ran clumsily across the wet sod toward the spot Wink had disappeared. She must hurry if she didn't wish to lose her pet. What the devil had possessed the bird? Wink had lost her eye when she was a fledgling. She couldn't possibly have learned how to hunt. What had she spied to make her dive like that?

Rose tried not to think about the ominous trees as she loped toward the border of the meadow, tried not to imagine how much like a wall of hostile soldiers they looked. She squeezed between two oaks where there was no path and followed a straight line into the tangled wood. The way was rough and overgrown, but 'twas the most direct path, and if she strayed from her course, she might lose her falcon. Branches slapped at her arms and caught at her hair. Gnarled roots rose to trip her. But she set her eye square ahead, silently cursing the willful bird who'd picked the most unfortunate time to plot rebellion.

To Rose's relief, the thicket thinned in a moment, revealing a small but lush clearing. Wink had likely plunged onto the carpet of grass here. She spied a flicker of movement through the branches and stepped gingerly forward.

Then she beheld a most curious sight. At the far edge of the clearing, Simon the palmer knelt upon the ground with his dagger out and a small pile of wood splinters at his feet. She was about to call out to him to ask if he'd seen Wink when she noticed the parchment-pale cast of his skin and the frozen terror in his face.

She heard them before she saw them. Low growls rumbled like distant thunder, surrounding the spot where the palmer sat shivering.

Wolves.

Three of them.

Shaggy, gray, snarling beasts.

They growled and snapped their jaws. Saliva dripped from their fangs, and their hackles stood stiff upon their muscular shoulders. Horrified, she watched them creep boldly on enormous paws toward the trembling palmer.

What should she do? she wondered. There wasn't time to fetch help, but the palmer could hardly hold off three hungry beasts with his single dagger, and Rose had no weapon with her to lend him aid.

'Twas useless to call out for help. Not only would her cry never pierce the thick foliage, but 'twould instantly alert the wolves to her presence.

She'd nearly decided to take that risk anyway, to burst loudly toward them out of the trees in the hopes that the commotion would startle them into fleeing.

But before she could move, she heard a familiar screech from a nearby elm. While Rose watched in astonishment and dread, Wink swooped down from the branches and dove directly toward the slavering beasts.

"Nae, Wink!" Rose cried, but 'twas too late.

The falcon latched onto the back of one of the wolves, gripping hard with her talons and flapping her wings, pecking furiously at the animal's skull.

The other two wolves, unnerved by this new enemy, retreated while their brother tossed his shaggy head, trying to loose the tenacious pest that plagued him. But Wink held fast, wildly beating the air, at last drawing blood with her curved beak.

At first, the wolf hunkered low to the ground and howled in misery, frightening his wary companions further into the deep wood. He whimpered piteously, pawing at his bedeviled head.

The falcon's moment of triumph, however, was brief.

Without warning, the exasperated wolf fiercely whipped his head around, catching his small tormenter between his sharp teeth. With brutal vengeance, he snapped his huge jaws together.

"Nae!" The scream ripped painfully from Rose's throat.

What happened next seemed to take an eternity, as if time slogged through thick treacle. Rose's ears filled with numbing silence, and her heart sank to the pit of her stomach. She could draw no breath, for it had been torn from her along with the scream. Her limbs felt leaden as she broke from the trees and strove forward on impossibly sluggish feet. Behind her, someone shouted, but she paid no heed. All her attention was focused on her poor bird.

The wolf turned his bloodied head and speared her with narrowed eyes the color of mustard. But desperation drove her as she lumbered relentlessly forward. She must save her bird. She must snatch Wink from the wolf's cruel maw.

She was almost there, almost. The wolf was but yards away. Just a dozen more dragging steps and...

She was suddenly yanked violently backward by her skirts. The impact bent her double, knocking the wind from her, jolting her from her strange lethargy.

"Stay!" came Blade's fierce command.

Rose fought against his restraining grip, trying to break free. He didn't understand. She had to get to her bird, had to rescue Wink.

But Blade thrust her aside, hurtling past her with a roar to face Wink's attacker himself.

Blade had noticed the willful falcon when it first chose to rebel, diving out of the sky and deserting its mistress at the most inopportune time in the most inopportune place. He'd watched Rose follow the wayward creature into the forest.

Shaking his head, Blade had pursued them, palming the pair of speckled eggs he'd found for the bird's supper. He had no choice but to go after Rose. After all, a falconer might wander for hours looking for a fugitive bird.

He'd arrived at the clearing just in time to hear Rose's piercing cry of distress, to witness her bolting out of the trees.

Her scream had sent an icy frisson of lightning along his spine. He'd yelled at her in warning, but she'd been deaf to his cry, recklessly rushing toward the wolf that gripped her pet between its teeth.

Cold dread froze the breath in his chest. He knew nothing would stop Rose. She loved that bird beyond reason, beyond sense. She'd do anything to save it.

He'd bit out an oath, clenching his hands, cracking the forgotten eggs in his fist. Jesu, he needed to get to her before she reached the wolf. With a bellow, he raced forward, cursing the chain that hampered his pumping arms. A branch whipped at his face, and he knocked it aside, leaping over a fallen log in his haste to intercept Rose.

She was but a half dozen yards from the beast when Blade finally reached her. Clutching a handful of her flying skirts, he hauled back hard enough to snap her neck, commanding her to stay.

Of course, she paid him no heed. She batted at him with desperate fists and cried in protest until he finally coiled his hand in her surcoat and hurled her backward.

He didn't stop to think. If he had, he would never have bolted forward in her stead to attack a pack of wild wolves. All he knew was that he had to save that damned falcon. The lass adored the crippled bird, and if she lost it...

With a snarl of rage, he lurched forward—unarmed except for the fury in his gaze and the vengeance in his heart.

Somehow, by God's grace, he wasn't killed.

His rampant savagery must have startled the wolves and taken the edge off of their appetites. For when Blade lunged to within a sword's length from the leader of the pack, the beast recoiled, dropping the troublesome morsel from its jaws. Dominated, it slunk off after its brothers—its ears flat, its tail drooping.

Blade's chest heaved like that of a warhorse primed for battle. His heart pummeled at his ribs, and unspent violence tingled along his arms.

He hastened toward the abandoned prey and felt Rose rush up behind him. He knelt before the creature that lay broken upon the grass. Its beak hung open in a soundless cry, and its breast pulsed rapidly. Its body bore the marks of the wolf's teeth, a mangled wing, flecks of blood. And yet there remained a valiant, defiant clarity in the falcon's eye that challenged death.

Still, as much as he prayed the bird might live, he feared 'twas too far damaged. With utmost care, he scooped the small thing onto one palm, then turned to look at Rose.

His grim expression must have revealed his doubt.

What he perceived in her face was terrifying. 'Twas far more than mere sorrow. Indeed, the despair in her eyes was so profound, it chilled him to the bone. For a long while she only stared at him—silent, hopeless. He couldn't draw breath, so inconsolable was her gaze. He'd encountered a woman's sadness before, but never had it pierced him so deeply, so utterly. While he returned her stare—unable to speak, unable to comfort her, unable to breathe—he watched her eyes fill with tears.

Rose felt numb. Time seemed to stop, and she saw the scene before her with the detachment of a dream. She knew she should look away, but her gaze was locked on the broken body speckled with blood, on the wing bent at an impossible angle, on the beak, parted in a silent scream. She sensed she should move forward, but her limbs felt weighted. She sensed she should weep, but her grief was too deep for tears.

This couldn't be happening. Wink couldn't be dying. 'Twas unthinkable. Only a moment ago, Rose was smoothing the feathers over her dear falcon's warm breast. Only a moment ago, her beloved bird soared high over the treetops.

She peered again at her wounded friend, and this time she swore the falcon looked back at her. She felt the burden of Wink's stare like a weight pressing upon her chest. And suddenly she realized the truth.

"'Tis my fault," she whispered bleakly. "If only I hadn't let her go. If only I'd waited till we were safely out o' the wood..."

"'Twasn't your doin'," Blade said firmly. But she ignored him.

145

"I should never have brought her on pilgrimage. I should never have taken her from Averlaigh. What does she know o' the wild?" Her brow crumpled. "Ah, God, 'tis all my fault."

"Nae," he insisted, "'tis no one's fault."

But she clung to her self-reproach, for it served to suffocate her mourning. "If only I'd kept her jesses tied. If only I hadn't let her fly free. 'Twas my hand that wounded her, as surely as if I stuffed her between that wolf's..." She broke off with a sob.

Blade felt her words like a dagger dragged across his soul. Of course, she couldn't know how they affected him. Nor how often he'd formed that same thought in the dark corners of his mind. Her lament dredged up his past, bringing it to the surface, filling him with the same regret she suffered.

Not a day went by when guilt didn't peck at him, when he didn't hear the endless echo of that other woman's scream, when he didn't imagine her blood staining his hands.

He knew how Rose felt. He knew *precisely* how she felt. He'd battled the same demons for two years.

"Listen to me," he said raggedly. "There's nothin' ye could have done to prevent this. Her fate was never in your hands."

How many times had he told himself the same thing? Yet he never heeded his own advice. Still he blamed himself for the deed. Still he didn't have the strength to face his past without smothering beneath a pall of remorse.

Guilt deafened her to his counsel as well. "I should have left her in the mews at Fernie. I should have—"

"Hist!" he said, his hand gripping her chin. "Ye bear no blame for this."

"But—"

"Did ye not feed her?"

"Aye."

"And keep her warm and dry?"

"Aye."

"And fly her when she needed to stretch her wings?"

She nodded miserably. "I wish to God I hadn't."

"Lass, ye cannot keep a bird from the skies. Ye saved the poor blind wretch when another falconer would have killed her ere she moulted her first feathers."

Her bronze eyes brimmed with a lake of tears as his words finally crumbled the last rampart guarding the keep of her grief. She began to cry softly, burrowing her face in her hands.

For Blade, empathy was as instinctive as chivalry. 'Twas unconscionable for him to stand by and do nothing while she suffered. He had to do something, *needed* to do something—anything—to ease her pain. No matter how impossible the task.

Wiping his free hand across his brow, he glanced down again at the falcon. Incredibly, its eye was still bright with life. But its mangled body reminded him of that other battered victim in his past, the victim he'd not been able to save. What if he failed again? What if he made another deadly mistake? What if he couldn't save the creature?

He bit at the inside of one cheek. What if he didn't try?

His heart pumping with renewed purpose, he turned toward the palmer, who had already recovered and was gathering his chips of dead wood. Blade scowled, for the knave doubtless intended to sell his harvest as relics, Splinters of the True Cross, in the next village.

"Simon!" he barked. "Bring me those sticks."

The palmer looked as though he might refuse, but Blade's stern glare convinced him to oblige. With a disgruntled frown, the man approached and deposited the sticks before him.

Blade set the falcon tenderly upon the grass, then sorted through the pieces, finding one of a suitable size for a splint.

"'T'won't work, ye know," Simon announced smugly.

Blade ignored him.

"A bird's wing can't be mended," Simon informed him, crouching nearby.

Blade tugged up the linen shirt he wore beneath his doublet and tore a strip of cloth from the bottom.

"The wretched creature can't possibly survive with a missin' eye *and* a broken wing," Simon decreed.

Blade snagged the palmer by the throat of his pilgrim's cloak. "This wretched creature saved your thankless life," he snarled. Then he shoved the man backward onto his bony backside, not because he disagreed with the man's predictions, but because the palmer's damning words distressed Rose.

Her eyes were wild and wide and anxious, and her bloodless knuckles clenched tightly at her skirts.

Simon, muttering under his breath, salvaged a few nearby splinters before he scurried off.

"'Tisn't true, is it?" Rose asked, her voice hoarse, her eyes demanding. "She'll live. She *has* to live. We're survivors, Wink and I." She tried to smile. "Stubborn lasses to the core." Then she bit her lip to still its trembling. "Ye won't let her die, will ye?"

Blade steeled his jaw against her piercing regard. What could he tell her? That Simon was probably right? That the bird was too badly hurt to recover? That a half-blind, lame bird wasn't worth saving? That he knew little to nothing of mending falcon's wings? That the last wounded creature he'd tried to save he'd killed?

"I won't let her die," he promised.

She seemed to draw strength from his words. Wiping the tears from her face, she crept forward to lend assistance.

"'Tis all right, Wink," she whispered. "The brave knight is goin' to help ye. Lie still."

Blade winced at her choice of words. He felt anything but brave. If he were brave, he'd tell her the truth—that her bird was doomed. If he were brave, he'd put the poor creature out of its misery with a twist of its neck.

Instead, he knelt in cowardice before the injured falcon and put his limited surgeon's skills to use. Gently, he positioned the broken bone of the bird's wing until 'twas straight. Then, while Rose held the wing in place, he wrapped it against the splint, weaving the cloth through the tattered feathers with painstaking care. All the while, the bird lay quiet, as if it understood that he meant it no harm.

The bird mustn't be allowed to try to fly, and so, once splinted, Blade folded the wing flat against the falcon's side. While Rose secured the bird, he loosely wrapped the remaining linen around its body to fix the wing in place. Still, though its eye was bright and its senses lively, the falcon made no protest, lying remarkably motionless in its mistress's hands.

'Twould be fortunate if it lived through the night, Blade knew. The palmer was right. For a healthy bird to recover from such injuries would take a miracle. For one already crippled...

Maybe he should tell Rose the truth. Maybe 'twas best not to give her false hope. Surely death's sting would be less if 'tweren't compounded by the ache of betrayal.

But Rose's tender words to the falcon melted something inside of him, and he lost all will to burst the bubble of her faith.

"Don't worry, Wink," she murmured. "Blade will take care o' ye. Despite his felon's chains and his dark looks, he's a good man, a gentle man." She traced a finger softly over the falcon's head. "Ye'll see. Your wounds will heal, and soon ye'll be wingin' across the skies again. Ye have my promise and a noble knight's word o' honor."

Blade nearly choked at that. His honor was questionable at best. But then she lifted her gaze to him, and the trust shining in her eyes—as clear and pure as a mountain stream—swelled his spirit. He didn't have the heart to withdraw his foolish promise.

Rose cradled the falcon in the crook of one arm, then reached out to clasp Blade's hand. Her fingers looked delicate against his scarred fist, but her grip was firm, as if 'twere now her task to lend *him* reassurance.

"She'll live." She seemed to speak to convince herself as well as him. "I know she will. We've weathered much, Wink and I. We both have wills of iron." The adoring gaze she cast upon the maimed creature wrested at his heart. "She'll survive. She *has* to survive."

Blade's throat thickened with emotion. He couldn't look at her anymore, lest his eyes betray his doubt. Instead, he withdrew his hand and rose to his feet, clapping the grass from his clothing.

She stood with his aid—the bird still nestled on her arm— holding to his hand longer than was necessary.

"I'll never forget your kindness," she whispered gravely, "no matter what happens."

He glanced sharply at her, but her gaze had already strayed to the forest beyond. She *did* understand then. She *did* realize her falcon might not survive. 'Twas not naivete after all that fed her optimism, but sheer determination. She simply refused to surrender.

A newfound respect was forged within him for this lass with a flower's name. She was no blushing pink rose whose frail petals wilted beneath the touch of the sun, but a rose of uncommon rich red, with a straight stem and a strong velvet blossom, and aye—he thought as they made their way back to the company of pilgrims—even a few prickly thorns.

# Chapter 10

Rose clasped her hands under the table so tightly she thought her knuckles would crack. Why she'd let Tildy talk her into attending supper this evening, she didn't know, for her thoughts were centered solely on Wink, who rested all by herself in the abandoned mews of Hawkhame in Kirkcaldy.

Ironically, despite their lodgings' name, for the last several years, the Lady of Hawkhame would allow no small animals in her demesne, for her daughter was deathly afraid of them. Thus, Rose was forbidden to bring Wink within the hall. And every moment spent away from her beloved pet added to Rose's anxiety.

As if Wink's absence weren't difficult enough to bear, Rose was forced to endure the well-intentioned pilgrims who made inept attempts to ease her worries. Indeed, the only relief she'd found tonight was in choosing a seat beside Blade at the table, who neither pried into her feelings nor gave her unwelcome advice. Unfortunately, he'd deserted her several moments ago, excusing himself to do God-knew-what.

Then, as an added insult, as if Wink's condition alone weren't enough to diminish Rose's appetite, the lady of the manor chanced to serve roast capon for supper. Rose, of course, had no stomach for the fowl, even less for the pointed tales this eve. Already, she'd endured Tildy's story of a magical healing bird lost by a greedy knight. Now Simon related a parable, and Rose swore if he breathed one more thinly disguised word about anyone's life or death being God's will, she'd strangle the palmer in his own sackcloth.

"...for who are we to ponder the mystery o' the Lord's ways..."

Rose clenched her teeth against a scream as Simon's patronizing tone grated on her ears and the nuns softly added their agreement. By the Saints, did they honestly believe that God might *mean* for her innocent pet to die? Did all religious zealots so blindly and helplessly rest fate in the Lord's hands? And if so, how would Rose ever endure being closeted with a bevy of spineless nuns for the rest of her life?

Wink's destiny did *not* rely solely upon the will of God, but the falcon's *own* will. Rose was sure of it. God had no reason to curse such a harmless creature, any more than He had caused Wink to swoop down upon the wolves. Nae, Rose was certain the animal had made a deliberate decision to risk her own life. Wink had been willing to sacrifice herself to protect her mistress.

Just as Rose had made the deliberate decision to take the veil. 'Twas not the will of God that she become a nun. 'Twas the will of Rose. Though 'twas a difficult, desperate sacrifice she made, 'twas hers and hers alone. Damn the nun's sermonizing, 'twas.

"...never questionin' God's will..."

Rose ground her teeth.

Suddenly a cool, steadying hand closed over her knotted fingers. She stiffened, shooting a furtive sidelong glance toward Blade, who had just returned. His face carefully betrayed nothing, but his hand remained secretly upon hers, dispelling her rage, his grip solid and reassuring. And quite possessive.

Her breath caught. Did the pilgrims notice his trespass? Her heart raced at his boldness. Yet she had no desire to withdraw her hand. She quickly scanned the faces around her. To her relief, even Tildy smiled obliviously on. Apparently, the linen draping the table concealed their perfidy. And so Rose, too, pretended nonchalance as she feigned to listen attentively to the storyteller.

She might as well have been deaf.

Blade's hand was a welcome comfort. Without breathing a word, he soothed her, the same way Rose was able to soothe

Wink by smoothing her rumpled feathers. Beneath his callused palm, her fingers unclenched, her burden seemed to lighten, her distress calmed.

"I've checked on your falcon," he breathed.

She swallowed, waiting for his news.

"As well as may be expected," he answered to her unasked question.

She nodded, letting out a shallow sigh. Amongst all these pilgrims, she realized, only the dark felon seemed to truly understand her.

Of course, everyone had shown her sympathy. Simon the palmer had relented to praise the bird's loyalty. The nuns had assured her that should her falcon die, the saintly bird would wing its way to heaven. The scholars had even offered to pool their coin to purchase her a new peregrine when they arrived in St. Andrews.

Yet no one but Blade grasped her desperate faith. No one but Blade made her believe there was hope.

And Rose needed to believe that, for deep within her, she knew 'twas more than her falcon's life at stake.

Wink was everything that Rose admired—freedom, bravery, independence, strength. The two of them had long shared a love of adventure and an affinity for the open sky. Rose had always felt that a part of her flew with the falcon, defying the envious pull of the earth, spreading her wings wide to encompass forest and glen and hill, soaring dauntlessly into the domain of angels.

If Wink died...

If Wink died, a part of Rose would die—her liberty, her fearlessness, her spirit.

Before, Rose had taken solace in the fact that, no matter which prison she chose—whether she must endure a loveless marriage or a monotonous convent—Wink would be with her as a winged symbol of her unbound soul. Every time the falcon sailed on high, a part of Rose would sail with her.

But while Wink hovered on the narrow brink between life and death, so, it seemed, hung the balance of Rose's own survival.

She didn't expect Blade to understand. Still, she sensed he somehow knew her distress. 'Twas as if his heart beat in tandem with hers, as if they shared some kindred suffering.

Blade's fingers curled under, gently stroking the tops of her hands, and 'twas all she could do to keep from dissolving into grateful tears beneath his compassionate caress. Slowly, she unlocked her fingers, turning her wrist, palm up, and they clasped hands.

There was far more solace than seduction in his clandestine touch, and yet her heart fluttered at what he dared. After all, Tildy sat hip to hip with her. Blade's man sat on his other side. One haphazard glance from either one would betray them. And yet Blade brazenly, fearlessly kept her hand in his, offering her comfort, lending her strength.

'Twas a reckless gesture. Nothing good could come of her growing affection for Blade. Their shared experiences, which connected them now as intimately as their entwined fingers, would only serve to confuse her heart.

Rose *had* a betrothed, a man she intended to thwart by taking the veil. She knew her two crossroads well and the direction in which she meant to go. Blade? He was like a wild and wayward path branching off into a forbidden landscape, tempting her from those clear avenues.

Still, for all the sin of it, she couldn't force her hand away, astonished by how natural his fingers felt surrounding hers, as if their two hands were halves of a broken vessel, now made whole. And if they only had this one bittersweet moment, while his fingers interlocked with hers...

Too soon, the palmer abruptly ended his tale. Everyone at the table applauded politely. Reluctantly, Rose withdrew her hand to join in the applause. Blade clapped as well, his chains rattling against his thigh, and she feared the moment of liaison was forever lost. But underneath the obscuring clatter as the pilgrims emptied the benches, he leaned near to speak the most dangerous words to her.

"Try to sleep," he whispered. "If ye need me in the night, come."

He meant Wink, if *Wink* needed him. Of course, he meant Wink. But later, as she lay awake upstairs among the slumbering females of the company, the echo of his words haunted her—*If ye need me, come.*

Across the room, one of the nuns was talking in her sleep again, her voice altered by dreams into a low purr, soft and playful. Rose sighed. She couldn't sleep. 'Twasn't that she wasn't tired. The strain of the day had left her exhausted. But she feared that if she ceased praying for one moment, if she let her heavy eyelids close in slumber, death might steal her falcon in the night.

She sat up, sweeping a tangle of hair back from her creased forehead. *Come*, he'd said, *if ye need me.* She shivered, pulling up the slipped shoulder of her linen underdress. Should she?

There was nothing more Blade could do for her falcon. 'Twas simply a matter of watching, waiting, and praying. Nae, she'd not trouble his sleep.

But neither would she lie tossing in her bed till dawn. Better she should sleep in the mews than lie awake all night on a feather pallet.

Shoving the coverlet back, she located her surcoat and slipped it over her head. With a stealth she'd learned from midnight forays into the locked chambers and forbidden passages of ancient Fernie House, she crept between the sleepers, down the stairs, and out into the dark courtyard toward the mews.

The first thing she noticed when she eased open the door of the outbuilding and stepped through was the soft clink of chains.

"Wink?" she whispered.

"M'lady."

"Holy sh—!" She nearly leaped from her slippers, despite the softness of his voice. "Blade?"

"Come in and close the door ere ye're seen."

She did as he asked, though the blinding darkness of the mews did little to ease her racing heart. The air was as dense and black as coal to her unaccustomed eyes, and though Rose was used to the close confines of a mews, the chamber was oddly devoid of the ubiquitous odors of moult and mutes.

"I thought ye might come." Blade's voice floated in the shadows.

"What are ye doin' here?" Rose swept out her arm in an arc, trying to get her bearings, and backhanded something. "Oh. Sorry. Was that your—"

"Forehead," he informed her.

"Oh."

"Here. Give me your hand."

More cautiously this time, she extended her arm. He caught her fingers, then tugged her forward.

"Ye couldn't sleep?"

She shook her head, then realized he couldn't see her. "Nae. Ye?"

She heard the shrug in his voice as he grunted. "My nights are oft troubled."

He guided her carefully toward the least dim place in the mews, a spot illuminated by a crack in the door, where Wink was tucked into a nest of straw. Blade whispered, "Your falcon, at least, is sleepin' peaceably."

"Wink." Just seeing her bird eased her fears. "Is she all right?"

"She's...breathin'."

So she was no worse, but no better. Rose swallowed hard. Of course, she couldn't expect Wink to wake up in the morn, shake out her feathers, and fly to the top of the manor wall. Such expectations were foolish. Still, she'd half hoped for some sort of miracle.

She turned to Blade, whose profile she could just begin to make out. "How long have ye been here?"

"Since supper."

She blinked. "Ye stayed with her all this time, watchin' o'er her?"

He snorted. 'Twas clear he thought it no great sacrifice, nor did he wish her to make much of it.

But for Rose, it meant the world. She tried to tell him so, but all she could manage was a broken, "Thank ye." The more eloquent words lodged in her throat.

He shifted beside her, rattling his iron chains again. She realized he hadn't let go of her hand. His fingers curved around hers as naturally as a vine clinging to a garden wall. She liked how it felt. She thought she might like to have him hold her hand forever. So she didn't speak, scarcely breathed, afraid that if she did, she might break the fragile thread binding them. The silence stretched and thinned before them like wool on a spinning wheel.

"Ye can't stay here," Blade murmured at long last.

She hoped that was regret she detected in his voice and that he couldn't sense the subtle desperation in hers. "'Tis safe for the moment. 'Tis hours yet before dawn."

"'Twill be here in the wink of an eye." He gave her hand a final squeeze and released it. "Go. Your bird will be fine. Ye need to sleep."

"I can't sleep in the hall."

"Ye needn't worry. I'll stay with your falcon," he promised.

"Then I'll stay as well," she said, jutting out her stubborn chin.

There was a long silence while he probably pondered how best to argue with her.

"Lass," he sighed, "if someone saw ye come hither—"

"No one saw me," she assured him.

"—and ye're discovered here with me..."

"No one saw me," she insisted. "I swear it." She was fairly sure she spoke the truth.

He let out a weighted breath. "Ye know what they'll think. A lady's virtue is—"

"I don't care what they think." 'Twas a reckless thing to say, and Lady Anne would have scolded her soundly for such irresponsibility, but at the moment, 'twas a heady feeling to speak the words. "My virtue is no one else's affair."

"'Tis *my* affair," he countered. "I'd rather not add seduction to my list o' crimes."

His comment caught her off guard. She hadn't realized her presence here was just as great a threat to him. But she didn't wish to leave. And she was so certain no one had seen her come this way.

"Please let me stay," she whispered, snagging his fingers again.

She saw the muscles around his mouth tense as he battled with the decision.

"I won't be any trouble," she swore. "I'll be as quiet as a shadow. And I'll steal back before sunrise. I promise."

Blade knew he was making a huge mistake.

No trouble? She was already trouble. And quiet? He'd never met a lass who didn't talk endlessly. Not that he minded. He liked the soothing discourse of women. But he doubted she'd stay awake to find her way back to her chamber.

By all accounts, he should send the wayward young lass off to bed. A lady of her rank never trafficked with a man who wasn't her betrothed, especially in a lowly mews at midnight, and most definitely not with a felon.

But the truth was he enjoyed her company. 'Twas lonely in the dark in an empty mews in the middle of the night, no matter how much he was accustomed to solitude. And the lass had a singular charm about her that intrigued and entertained him. So when she peered up at him with her vulnerable, shining eyes and her sweet promises, her fingers twining with his and her womanly scent clouding his senses, 'twas impossible to tell her nae.

He scowled. "I trust ye'll bring me a crust now and then when I'm rottin' away in your father's dungeon," he said dryly.

"We won't be caught," she insisted, catching his forearm. "And if we are, I'll defend ye."

She was audacious, this Lady Rose, far too reckless for her own good. But 'twas part of what he was beginning to admire in her, that untamed spirit and willful daring.

"'Tis crude lodgin's," he warned.

"I won't complain," she vowed.

"Come find yourself a seat in the straw then."

He guided her toward the nest he'd made of clean hay from the stables. He'd have to remember to pick every condemning piece of straw from her velvet surcoat before she returned to the hall.

When she was settled, he sat beside her, bracing his back against the wall and draping his arms over his bent knees. 'Twould be a trial, sitting so close to her warm, womanly body and not vividly imagining the crime he swore not to commit, particularly when seduction was an insignificant sin beside that which already damned him. But for a woman bound for convent, her virtue was paramount. So he'd clench his jaw, steel his resolve, and think of other things.

"Ye're very attached to your falcon."

"Aye. We're kindred spirits, Wink and I."

Was that her shoulder touching his? He cleared his throat. "How long have ye had her?"

"Six years." She was fidgeting now, trying to get comfortable. "She'd been abandoned in an eyrie on the ledge of a tower." She shuffled about in the straw, bumping against his hip. "Sorry. Her eye was missin' when I found her."

Despite her apology, Rose's hip remained planted firmly against his, and he wondered if she recalled the power of the beast she roused. His voice cracking, he attempted nonchalance. "Your falconer collected her for ye?"

"Nae. Our falconer thought I was a fool, that Wink was better left as carrion for the crows." She moved to mimic his posture then, drawing her legs up and catching them in the circle of her arms. 'Twas curiously endearing. "Nae, I climbed up myself and rescued her, kept her hidden in my chamber, and let another falcon hunt for her."

He sent a sharp glance her way. "Ye climbed up yourself? As a child?"

She shrugged. "I climbed everythin' when I was a child—trees, towers, walls. My foster mother told me 'twas terribly indecent. But I couldn't help myself. I've always been cursed with devilish curiosity." She tipped her head back against the wall, gazing upward into some happy, faraway space. "Once ye climb up, ye can see everythin'—distant crofters harvestin' their fields, knights tiltin' in the yards, milkmaids dozin' behind the stables." She giggled. 'Twas a delightful sound. Then she cocked her head at him. "Didn't ye ever climb trees?"

"Aye," he recalled. But for him, 'twas not a pleasant memory. 'Twas usually an escape from the constant tormenting of his older brother. He'd discovered that Morris was afraid of high places. So when his brother had a particularly violent day—swinging out at everything in sight, striking servant and beast and most especially his little brother Pierce—Pierce would seek refuge in one of the oaks surrounding Mirkhaugh until Morris's rage passed. The only thing Blade remembered seeing from the top of a tree was Morris's purpling face as he screamed up in frustrated fury.

Rose scratched at her knee. "I suppose 'tis why I love Wink so. Those wonderful places—they're her domain. She flies higher than I could ever climb." She sighed. "Did ye ever own a pet?"

He frowned at another unpleasant memory. "None o' my own. My brother kept hounds, vicious things."

"Vicious?"

Blade sniffed. "He kept them half-starved so they'd be more aggressive on the hunt."

He heard her quickly drawn breath. "'Tis cruel."

"He was a cruel man." Blade gained grim satisfaction from the fact he could say, "was." Shortly after Blade left Mirkhaugh, he received word that Morris had been murdered in a bloody fight at a tavern. Blade had been unable to summon any feelings of regret or sorrow. "A *very* cruel man."

Rose's voice touched him as softly as thistledown. "Then he's not much like his brother."

Blade stiffened. She had unwittingly stumbled upon his greatest fear, the fear he shared with no one, that he and Morris, born of the same father, might have similar natures.

He snorted. "Ye mean, his brother the mercenary? The felon? The one bound in chains o' disgrace?"

She lay her arm gently along his, weaving tender fingers between his clenched knuckles. 'Twas pacifying and terrifying all at once, for she tread perilously close to his heart.

"Ye're not a bad man," she murmured in earnest protest. "I won't believe it. Ye've been nothin' but gallant and generous and compassionate."

He wished 'twere so. But his soul had borne a burden of guilt too long. He knew well whose blood he shared and what sin he'd committed. "Ye hardly know me," he said hoarsely.

She looped her arm brazenly through his and rested her cheek against his shoulder. How long had it been, he wondered, since a woman had touched him with such familiarity, such trust?

"I know ye well enough," she whispered. "Ye can't hide your heart."

'Twas nonsense, some bit of a minstrel's verse. How could she know his heart? And yet a small part of him—the piece of Sir Pierce that Blade couldn't vanquish—seized onto her words like a drowning man clinging to an oar.

"Ye've the heart of a champion," she breathed, turning to peer over at him, bathing him in a gaze of adulation and tenderness.

To his chagrin, Pierce embraced that folly with the full force of his emotions.

Rose's face shone with feminine adoration, drawing his gaze to her with potent force, but something else flickered in her eyes, something intimate and secret and longing. Something dangerous. His breath stilled as she lowered her regard to settle upon his mouth, her lips parting infinitesimally.

By the Saints, 'twas clear what she wanted. Rose was too young, too unworldly, to hide her desires like the coy lasses who made a game of enticing men. Nae, she wore her yearning like a pennon flown from a high tower. And that longing mirrored his own.

Silently cursing his own madness, he granted Pierce his wish. He turned toward her, catching her chin in one shackled hand. He placed his lips lightly over hers, capturing her gasp within his mouth.

This time, their kiss was warm and soft and sweet, so unlike the fierce mating of their mouths before that it took him aback. Her body seemed to melt against him. Her limbs sunk under the weight of his tenderness. Her mouth sought his like a newborn seeking suckle.

This time, there was no savagery in their embrace. He neither forced her jaws apart nor scraped her with his rough beard nor invaded her mouth.

This time, he was moved to uncorrupted gentleness. And curiously, the light caress of her lips was far more powerful and intimate and compelling than that other kiss.

He tangled his fingers in her silken tresses, inhaling her sensual perfume. She leaned into him, filling his arms, pressing her yielding bosom to his unyielding chest until their embrace brought them heart to heart.

Faith, how long had it been since a woman had kissed him so? With such innocence, such affection, such trust? Again and again her lips blessed him with tender conviction, absolving him of his harsh past, promising him redemption, reminding him of the honorable man he once was—Sir Pierce of...

"Ivo!"

Rose drew back with a gasp.

Hell! That was Odo. Just outside the mews.

Blade's heart throbbed with unspent passion and a sudden urge to beat the tanner senseless. Instead, he sank back in surrender, wincing as he banged his head against the wall.

Odo stumbled past the mews, his voice thick with ale. "Ivo, where've ye got to?"

The tanner crashed into the door of the mews, nearly bursting it open, and Blade quickly pressed two fingers to Rose's lips to stop her from crying out.

"Here...good fellow!" Ivo replied from outside. His words were likewise slurred, and he let out an enormous belch they could hear from within the mews.

Odo shoved away from the door with a creak, and his voice receded. "Where's...where's...where's the lusty wench then?"

"Who, Brigit? Ah, shite. I thought *ye* were bringin' her."

The rest of their conversation trailed off into the night, and slowly Blade lowered his fingers from Rose's lips. His mouth felt afire, his blood coursed like a flooding river, his loins ached with need, and he both cursed and blessed the timely interruption that had saved him from himself.

Rose longed to strangle the drunken oafs.

She could still taste Blade, still felt the eager press of his mouth—warm, commanding, yet tender. Their kiss had been instinctive, each brush of their lips like the weightless winding of a single strand of cobweb, insidiously binding them together. And yet she'd felt no desire to escape, for his kisses made her forget time and honor and destiny.

In his arms, the world paused. Later she'd face what the future held. Later she'd confront her betrothed. Later she'd set aside earthly pleasures for the veil. But in that single precious moment, she'd welcomed oblivion, losing herself in Blade's kiss. And she wanted that moment back.

When she turned to Blade, however, 'twas obvious he didn't share her wish. He sat staring stonily ahead at his clasped hands. "I shouldn't have done that."

Her breath stopped. "Nae. 'Twas my fault."

"'Twas none o' your fault," he assured her, smiling ruefully at his shackles. "Ye're the virtuous noblewoman. Remember? I'm the outlaw."

"Nae." Sorrow and anger tumbled together through her thoughts. If those cursed tanners hadn't passed by...

"Ye should go back now." He added a dismissive sniff.

She stared at him. He was armored now in indifference. How quickly he put up his shield. How well he feigned nonchalance. Yet she knew the truth. There had been genuine warmth in his kiss, true passion in his embrace. He wasn't some unfeeling felon. Behind that cold iron and tough leather beat the heart of a man.

"I'm not afraid o' ye," she said.

He turned to her and scowled a long while, as if to distance her with his dire looks. But it didn't work. She kept remembering the bear in St. Andrews and the warm hide beneath the coarse fur.

At last Blade shook his head, heaving a sigh that seemed half exasperation, half amusement. "Intrepid Rose. Tell me, is there anythin' ye fear?"

She smiled. He was going to let her stay. She settled back against the wall, hugging her knees to her chest. "Ye tell me first. What do *ye* fear?"

He thought for a bit, then lifted one corner of his mouth in a sly smile. "Questions."

She had the feeling 'twas only part jest, that he preferred to keep his past well-guarded. "Then I'll make a bargain with ye. Ask me one question—anythin' ye like—and I'll answer truthfully. But then I'll ask ye any one question, and ye must likewise tell the truth."

His frown was dubious. "Only one question?"

"Aye," she assured him.

He scowled, rubbing his jaw pensively for several moments, tipped back against the wall to stare at the ceiling, then announced, "All right then. I've got it."

"Aye?" she asked, squirming. There were a hundred mortifying secrets he might coerce her to reveal.

His face grew very serious, and she swallowed uncomfortably. Maybe she shouldn't have asked him to play this game after all. What if he asked who was pursuing her?

"Tell me, Lady Rose, is it truly in your heart to become a nun?"

Rose started. 'Twas a question she hadn't expected, a question that shot to the center of her soul like an arrow sprung from an archer's bow, and something she didn't dare think about too deeply. For she knew the unfortunate answer all too well. She also knew that she had to lie to him.

"Aye," she said, unable to look him in the eye.

He made no reply, and at first, Rose imagined his silence meant he'd taken her at her word.

She was wrong.

"I think ye're cheatin' at this game, lass," he chided. "I think your lips belie your heart."

She blushed, for they both knew the truth. She felt no calling for the church. She deluded even herself about the destiny awaiting her. Yet what else could she do, knowing she must believe the lie or fall into despair?

She felt his gaze upon her a long while, and a part of her wished she could confess to him, blurt out everything that had transpired since that fateful day in Averlaigh. But some secrets were too dangerous to share.

"What question will ye ask o' me then?" he finally conceded.

But Rose no longer found the game fun. He was right. She'd cheated. Still, one question had piqued her curiosity for some time now.

"What was your crime?"

His jaw visibly tightened, and some dark memory shadowed his eyes. She almost wished she hadn't asked.

But as quickly as the silent storm appeared, it vanished, and Blade's sardonic smirk reappeared. He was going to lie, too.

"A lass once asked me too many questions, so I locked her in a coop to join the rest o' the cluckin' hens."

She cuffed his arm. "That's terrible. If ye're goin' to lie, at least do a good job of it. Somethin' like, I was a notorious reiver on the seas of Araby. Or I stole the jewels out o' the bishop's crozier. Or I seduced a dozen virgins in Edinburgh."

"I doubt there are a dozen virgins in Edinburgh."

"Well...not anymore."

He actually laughed at that. Actually, 'twas more of a bark than a laugh, but it served to lighten her spirits again. She rested her chin on the top of her knees, inexplicably content.

After a bit, she asked, "Do ye suppose Brigit was really meetin' the tanners?"

"That sounds suspiciously like another question," he accused.

"Hmm. Does it?"

"Aye," he answered carefully.

"Shall I stop askin' questions then?"

"Aye."

"Are ye sure?"

He growled. "No more. I surrender."

"Very well," she giggled. "Then tell me a story, a true story. Somethin' that happened to ye when ye were a lad. And in turn, I'll tell ye how I tamed the great bear o' St. Andrews."

Blade never got to hear about the St. Andrews bear. A quarter of the way through his story about the voyage he took to the Orient with his father, Rose yawned and leaned up against him.

Halfway through, she squirmed at his shoulder until he lifted his arm out of the way and made room for her against his chest.

When he reached the part of the tale where his father showed him the strange gray worms that spun silk, she lay fast asleep, sprawled across his lap in unabashed abandon.

He let his voice fade away and just watched her. Her face, mashed against his chest, was as innocent as a bairn's. Her hand curled upon his ribs, palm inward. She sighed in her sleep, and her breath warmed his flesh through the linen of his shirt. A stray lock of hair covered her brow, and he carefully brushed it back with his thumb.

A smile touched his lips. Gone was the perfectly composed beauty. In her place was a charmingly vulnerable young lass with disheveled tresses, a soft mouth contorted by a yawn, and now a childlike hand scrubbing at her eye. A curious warmth surrounded his heart at the sight. How 'twas possible, he didn't know, but he thought he liked this windblown blossom even better than the flawless flower.

A strange peace settled over him as he cradled her against his heart, as if he'd traveled a long way and had arrived home at last. Rose nestled against him like she belonged there, and he couldn't deny she felt perfect in his arms.

But even as he reveled in contentment, he knew 'twas a false pleasure, no more substantial than a dream. Rose and he were disparate souls from two different worlds, come together only briefly as a consequence of fate. Neither knew the other's past. They'd shared only brief conversation and two memorable kisses. In less than a week, they'd part ways, never to meet again. 'Twas folly to imagine it might be otherwise.

He stole one final kiss from her, a quick brush of his lips upon the crown of her head, before he eased her off of the chain of his shackles. She mewled in drowsy protest as he propped her upright, but never fully wakened, even when he stood her up on her wobbling legs.

He sighed. Sneaking her back into the hall wouldn't be easy. She obviously couldn't walk there on her own. He'd have to carry her then and pray no one prowled about the manor tonight.

She was lighter in his arms than his suit of armor, he thought, as he stole around the perimeter of the starlit courtyard. Her velvet skirts served to dampen the sound of his chains, but he was careful to keep to the shadows to avoid discovery.

He'd almost reached the door of the great hall when the icy point of a sword swept suddenly across his throat, freezing his blood, and a cloaked figure emerged from a dark corner of the wall, hissing.

"What the devil have ye done?"

# Chapter 11

For God's sake, Wil, put that away!" Blade hissed back.

"Not until I hear an explanation."

"Is that *my* sword?" he whispered in disbelief. "Ye're threatenin' me with my own sword?"

"Ye surrendered it, remember?"

Blade swore under his breath. "Will ye at least let me return her upstairs?"

"I want to know just what ye're returnin' her *from*."

Blade let out a long-suffering sigh and made an attempt to explain. "Nothin' happened."

Wilham smirked. "Nothin' happened."

"Nothin' happened."

"She looks awfully content," Wilham snipped.

"Maybe she's dreamin' that she's out o' the cold night air and warm in her bed," Blade said pointedly.

Wilham tensed, accidentally jabbing Blade with the tip of the sword. Blade winced, and Wilham winced in turn. Poor Wilham—he didn't have the mettle to kill a man in cold blood. Blade was half-tempted to simply back off and walk away, just to show Wilham how empty his threat was.

"Ye know, Wil, if ye slit my throat, she'll tumble to the ground."

"Damn it, Blade," he bit out, ignoring Blade's logic. "She's a titled lady. 'Tisn't like dallyin' with a tavern wench. Ye can't haul titled ladies off to the stables."

"Nothin'...happened," he repeated. "Now are we goin' to stand here till sunrise?"

"Ye're certain?" Wilham asked, squinting as if that made it easier to discern the truth. "Nothin' happened?"

Blade only looked at him.

"Would ye swear it on your mother's grave?"

"My mother's alive, Wil."

"Would ye swear it on *my* mother's grave?"

Blade sighed. "All right. I swear it on your mother's grave."

"Ye didn't swive her?"

"Your mother?" Blade said sardonically.

Wilham gestured pointedly with his brows at Rose.

"Nae," Blade answered. "I didn't swive her."

"Then what *did* ye do?"

Not for the first time since they'd started on the pilgrimage, Blade wished his sword were in his hands, for he longed to pommel Wilham with the flat of it all the way to St. Andrews.

"Can't this wait?" Blade muttered.

Wielding Blade's sword obviously made Wilham smug. "Nae," he said, jutting out his chin. "Just give me the brief version."

Blade's blood boiled, but he supposed Wilham was only looking after his best interests.

"I went to the mews to watch over her falcon."

"I know that."

Blade frowned.

"I watch your back, remember?" Wilham said.

"She was worried about her bird, so she came."

"I saw her."

Blade grimaced. "Well, if ye know so damned much, why are ye askin' me what happened?"

"Because ye were alone in there together for nearly two hours."

Two hours? It had seemed like far less. "We...talked, that's all."

"Talked."

"Aye."

"Talked about what?"

"I don't know. Climbin' trees. Flyin' her falcon. Sailin' to the Orient." A smile touched his mouth. "She told me she once tamed a bear." He would have liked to hear that tale.

Suddenly Wilham lowered the sword and stared at him incredulously. "Well, by all that's holy, I never would have believed it."

Blade frowned. "What?"

"My fine fellow," he said, an enormous grin pasted on his face, "ye're in love."

Blade swore.

Wilham chuckled.

"May I go now?" Blade growled.

"By all means," Wilham said, sketching a deep bow to let him pass. "Love. Now that's a different tale altogether." His knowing voice was as irritating as a knife on a grinding wheel. "Take your time."

The sun fired its first yellow shafts through the split shutters onto the plaster wall. When Rose awoke, she couldn't recall how she'd ended up back in the manor. The last thing she remembered was thinking how soothing Blade's voice was, particularly when she rested her ear against his broad, resonant chest. She must have fallen asleep while he was telling his tale of the Orient. How remarkable the night had been.

Wilham, Blade's friend, had slipped a missive to her through a servant, letting her know that Wink had made it through the night and was resting. Rose planned to visit the mews to see for herself, right after her bath. The Lady of Hawkhame had indulged her guests this morn by providing two chambers with great steaming tubs, one for the men and one for the women.

Flinging aside her linen shift, Rose sank blissfully into the clove-scented water. Never one to linger at her bath and well aware that others waited to bathe after her, she lathered the tallow soap into her hair and briskly scrubbed her skin till it tingled. She was eager to learn how Wink fared for herself and, she had to admit, even more eager to see Blade again.

Her heart staggered, just remembering his kiss. When she thought of his smoldering gaze, his seductive mouth, the way his hands seemed to claim her, a warm wave of yearning enveloped her, hinting at deeper pleasure, promising her...

Someone banged hard on the oak door. "Lads!"

Rose gasped. 'Twas Blade. Her eyes widened, and she clapped her arms across her breasts.

"Have ye drowned in there?" he bellowed.

She bit her lip, unsure what to do.

"Come, lads!" he called, pounding again. "The water'll be colder than a harlot's heart by the time ye—"

He pushed the door open before she could speak. He peered in. She watched, mortified, as his eyes flitted over her features, his glance fleeting yet perceptive enough to memorize every inch of her body.

Blade sucked a hard breath between his teeth. He would carry that image of Rose with him to his dying day. He tried to avert his gaze—truly he did—but it peeled away only reluctantly.

She was a vision in pearl and ebony and rose. Wet locks of hair framed her face and trailed over her creamy skin, past her eyes—round with shock, her flushed cheeks, and her open mouth. Lithe limbs enwrapped her, concealing her most private places, yet displaying the artful curve of her shoulder, the tender swell of her breasts. Her legs, doubled before her, were long and shapely, and—curse his unruly mind—he had no trouble at all imagining them locked around his waist.

It took all his will to train his eyes upon the plank floor after feasting on such a sight.

"Sorry," he managed to mutter. "I thought..."

Damn that conniving Wilham. The crafty varlet had told him the three scholars were bathing in this chamber. Now that he knew Blade didn't intend to seduce and discard Lady Rose, he must be planning to thrust the two of them together at every possible opportunity.

Blade quickly decided 'twas better to simply close the door than try to explain Wilham's misguided antics.

"Sorry," he repeated.

"Wait."

He froze.

Surely he'd heard wrong. He frowned, uncertain. Then, swallowing an overwhelming urge to graze her luscious contours with his eyes once more, dragged his gaze instead to her face.

She looked as if she'd forgotten what she wished to say, and though a part of him would have her continue to forget so he might continue to gaze upon her, another part of him—the noble part—suffered unspeakable torment.

Her eyes bound him as surely as the shackles binding his wrists, and he watched her lids lower subtly with longing. His heart bolted, and the breath lodged in his chest. This was no Siren's game she played. Nae, she was an innocent. The desire playing over her face was as raw and primal and genuine as the hardening in his braies. He continued to stare at her—past decency, past honor, past shame...

"Out o' my way, ye knave!"

Tildy came barreling down the passageway, trying to shove her way past Wilham, who was attempting to block her view and slow her progress.

"But, Goodwife," Wilham said, "certainly Lady Rose would like..."

Blade backed out of Rose's chamber and into the hall, scrabbling at the door latch to close it as discreetly as he could.

"An apple tart to go with that lovely..." Wilham continued.

Tildy stopped in her tracks when she saw Blade. She knew at once some mischief was afoot. "What the devil are ye doin' at the door o' the women's chamber?"

Blade scowled, unable to think of a good answer.

Fortunately, Wilham's quick wit stepped in. "Ah, Blade, well done," he said, clapping him on the shoulder. "Ye see, my good woman? I posted him here to guard Lady Rose's bath."

Her gaze narrowed dubiously. Tildy had mellowed in her disdain of Blade since he'd done Lady Rose the favor of splinting her falcon's wing, but there was still a good deal of vinegar in her voice and a great deal of mistrust in her eyes.

"Hmph," she snorted. "'Tis like settin' a fox to guard chickens." She elbowed them aside. "Away with ye now, the both o' ye. *Well* away."

Tildy continued along the passageway past Rose's door and out of sight while they slunk off in the opposite direction. Halfway down the corridor, Blade cuffed Wilham on the shoulder.

"What's that for?" Wilham cried.

"Ye knew very well who waited behind that door."

Wilham gave him an irritating grin. "I did. Was she as lovely as ye imagined?"

Blade cuffed him again, harder.

"God's eyes!" Wilham yelped. "I think ye'd be grateful. After all, I got her guardian out o' the way so ye could..."

"So I could what?" Blade snapped.

Wilham shrugged. "Feast your eyes? Fetch her the soap? Help her scrub the places she can't reach on her o—"

Blade shoved him. "Cease!"

Wilham shoved him back. "*Ye* cease!"

Blade hauled him up by the front of his doublet.

Then, down the passage, the door to Rose's chamber creaked opened. They turned their heads toward the sound. A pale face surrounded by a riot of wet black hair peered around the door. The sight of her—so angelic yet so earthy—stole the breath from Blade. She opened her mouth as if to say something, but just then Tildy bellowed at her from the far end of the hall, and Rose ducked back into the room.

Too late, Blade realized what a ridiculous picture he and Wilham made, like two lads brawling in church. Muttering a curse, he released Wilham.

"Well, ye lucky bastard," Wilham said in wonder, straightening his doublet.

Blade frowned. What was he yammering about?

"*She's* in love with *ye.*"

Blade rolled his eyes. Wilham was a dreamer and a fool. No woman cared for Blade. He was a mercenary, a wanderer, a felon. And if the sweet and innocent Lady Rose ever found out what else he was... "No one loves a murderer, Wilham."

He shambled off then toward the chamber where the men's bath awaited, but he wasn't quite out of hearing when Wilham grumbled, "*She* does, even if ye're too blind to see it."

Rose strolled through the pleasance garden at Hawkhame with Wink tucked in the crook of one arm, using the other to fluff her damp hair in the sunlight. She wished that she could order her thoughts as neatly as the surrounding beds of primrose, violets, and gillyflowers.

What she'd intended to say to Blade when she poked her head out of the door this morn, she didn't know. 'Twas impossible to put words to her mixed feelings. But the thoughts that came closest were a perilous combination of *leave me alone* and *take me away*.

She'd felt absolutely paralyzed when he walked in upon her bath—trapped there by the pure, raw, primal lust in his eyes. A fiery current had coursed through her veins and seared the breath from her lungs. And 'twas a heady thrill to think she could make him feel such things as well. The truth—that she'd spent the night in the massive arms of that imposing warrior, lay her head upon that broad chest, and placed kisses on that tempting mouth—made her long for him with a yearning past reason.

And though he said nothing to encourage her passions, the unguarded desire in his gaze was enough. 'Twas a seduction far more powerful than words.

Tildy had interrupted them this morn. But there were still many moments left before the journey's end, and Rose wondered if her heart didn't lead her in the right direction after all. The future looked to be a dull and gloomy place for her. Why not seize one moment of happiness before 'twas lost forever? Why not grasp what joy she could in the little time left?

She twined her finger idly through a lock of hair. She'd never felt so drawn to a man before. No man had called so clearly to her soul. She'd had admirers in St. Andrews, certainly—fair-faced lads with laughing eyes and sweet natures—but none of them had attracted her in the way this dark, menacing felon did.

What was it, she wondered, that drew her to him? Was it his striking face? His powerful physique? Those eyes that could pierce her like a lance? Aye, all of them weakened her knees. And yet 'twas more than just his body that hastened her heart.

Maybe 'twas his wit. He jested and jousted with words keen enough to cut, yet tender enough to charm.

Maybe 'twas his chivalry. He'd fed her falcon, rescued her from thieves, loaned her his cloak.

Yet hadn't Gawter, her betrothed, been just as gallant? Hadn't he made all the appropriate knightly gestures—bowing over her hand, praising her peregrine, smiling at her quips? He had. But with Gawter, the overtures seemed only polite but cursory obligations of his noble rank.

'Twas different with Blade. His chivalry stemmed from another source—a fount of kindness deep within his soul. She sensed—despite his chains of disgrace and his fierce scowl—there dwelt inside his felon's body an angel of compassion.

"Sir Ian believes the outlaw is in truth a great noble."

Rose whipped about, so startled by the young apprentice's abrupt remark that she nearly dropped Wink. Guillot blinked and offered her a small smile. Over the last few days, Rose noticed the lad had seemed to blossom under the tutelage of his new hero, Sir Ian Campbell. The boy had appointed himself as a sort of squire to the soldier. Today Guillot's eyes looked bright, his step light, his stature tall and proud.

"What did ye say?" Rose asked.

"Sir Ian believes your outlaw friend, the one you call Blade, might be a lord."

Rose lifted her brows. "Why?"

"He says he has seen his face before."

Flustered, Rose whirled about before the lad could witness the telling flush of her cheeks, and busied herself, stroking Wink's breast. A lord! Her pulse suddenly pounded in her chest at the thought there might be some truth to Guillot's words.

Guillot seated himself on a small raised bench of chamomile beneath an apple tree. "Sir Ian said he saw a man with the same dark features at a tournament last year," Guillot volunteered. "He said he fought valiantly, winning every contest of arms. Sir Ian remembered him, because he refused the champion's prize, insisting it be sent in tribute instead to his castle."

A prickling began along Rose's arms, and a thrilling thought formed in her head. What if the tale were true? What if Blade were not the mercenary outlaw he appeared, but a nobleman with lands and a title?

"Well," she said, strangely discomfited by the news, "he obviously doesn't want it known. So I suggest ye keep it to yourself."

The lad looked contrite, but added, "I only thought, my lady, since he rescued you from thieves, and he mended your bird, and...I mean, the way he looks at you and..."

Her gaze darted toward the apprentice. "Looks at me? He doesn't look at me."

"Oui, my lady," Guillot said, his observations growing more distressing, and more exciting, by the moment. "As if you were a precious flower. Or an angel. Or—"

"Faugh!" 'Twas the only thing she could think to say, to stop his gushing and her thoughts, which were tumbling over themselves, gathering speed like a snowball down a hill.

177

'Twas ridiculous. Surely Guillot was only flattering her—the French were notorious romantics.

Besides, Blade's nobility changed nothing. First of all, there was no assurance that Blade was the same man Campbell had seen. Second, Blade had earned those shackles somehow, and not by throwing a woman to the chickens. They were probably justly deserved. Third, just because he looked at her as if she were an angel...an *angel*...

Lord, did he truly look upon her like that?

A rush of warmth effused her.

"Maybe, my lady, if it is true," Guillot ventured, knotting his fingers nervously before him, "you might restore him."

"What?"

Guillot dipped his eyes. "Sir Ian told me...what you did."

"What I did?"

He nodded. "He is sure you must be an angel. Sir Ian said you saved him from himself." He looked away, his mouth working. "If not for you, my lady—" He broke off, choked by emotion.

Rose finished the thought for him. Sir Ian might be dead.

The lad continued when he'd recovered his composure. "The outlaw, Blade, did me a similar kindness," he said. "So it would seem you are both angels of mercy." He chewed at his lip. "Forgive my boldness, my lady, but I believe perhaps you are meant to help the fallen knight, that you may hold the key to his shackles."

Blade, done with his bath and dressed, held out his wrists while Wilham locked the shackles about them again.

Wilham shook his head, replacing the key chain around his neck. "Chains. Shackles. Ach! Ye should have cropped your hair like I did. 'Tis far less trouble."

Blade wandered toward the shuttered window, easing it open. An errant breeze sighed through the treetops and ruffled his freshly washed hair as he gazed down to the walled garden below. She was there, among the others—her black tresses gleaming in the sunlight, her scarlet dress like a velvety blossom blowing atop the green sward. The lingering image of the pearly skin that lay beneath quickened his pulse, and he bit back the urge to groan aloud as his loins responded to the memory.

He steeled his newly shaved jaw, trying to convince himself he merely perused the garden for suspects among the half dozen or so pilgrims gathered there. According to Wilham, he was failing miserably.

"Why don't ye just go down there and have a word with her?" Wilham said, drying what little hair he had left with a linen towel.

"Who?" Blade said stubbornly, his eyes fixed on the scholars milling about among the fruit trees.

Wilham chuckled wickedly. "The red rose in the garden," he taunted. "The one with the sweet perfume. The one with the lovely twin buds above, and the soft, ripe petals below."

As irritating as Wilham could be, his words summoned up a vision of Rose that shot a pang of lust streaking through Blade's groin.

"Save your breath," he managed to mutter. "Roses always have thorns."

"Ah, but they're still the queen o' the garden," Wilham continued, undaunted. "Behold, the proud and royal rose who wears a crown where'er she goes..."

Blade, at the end of his patience, turned on Wilham with a scowl. "We're supposed to be huntin' assassins, not composin' verse."

Wilham lifted a dubious brow and usurped Blade's place at the window, leaning over the ledge to study the occupants of the garden. "Let me guess. The scholars?"

"Maybe," Blade challenged.

"Oh, I suspected as much," Wilham said with lavish sarcasm. "That Bryan has murder in his eye. And if Daniel and Thomas were to ever cease arguin' for more than the wink of an eye, who can say what mischief they might wreak?"

Blade skewered Wilham with a quelling glare.

Wilham was not quelled. But his sardonic expression faded, and he leaned back against the stone sill, successfully obstructing Blade's view of the garden.

After a pensive moment, he spoke. "At least grant me this, Pierce," he said softly.

Blade glanced at him. Wilham never called him by his given name. And he seldom spoke without a mischievous grin skulking at the fringes of his face. He did both now.

"Think on it," he asked. "This is a lonely existence. We cannot be knights-errant for the rest of our lives."

Blade sniffed. "Ye should have gone home," he muttered.

"And abandon ye?" Wilham shook his head. "I couldn't. But ye're joustin' with ghosts, my friend. 'Tis time ye came back to the livin'."

Blade *had* felt dead for the last two years. He couldn't recall the towns he'd ridden into, couldn't remember the faces of those he'd defeated in tournament.

"Ye need this, Pierce," Wilham insisted, moving aside to reveal the garden. "Ye need her."

Blade gazed at the lady set amongst the drab pilgrims like a crimson rose upon the emerald ground—her black hair gleaming like polished jet, her delicate face turning up toward the midmorning sun.

He felt the need rise in him, felt it in that animal part of him that lusted for her flesh and felt it also deep within his heart.

But more powerful was his need to crush such frivolous dreams and return to the despair to which he'd grown accustomed.

"She's not for the takin'," he told Wilham.

Wilham blinked. "Why? She's not wed. She's young, beautiful, o' the proper lineage. For the love o' Mary, she even has all her teeth. And she gazes upon ye as if..." Blade's glance darted to Wilham's face. "...as if the sun rose and set upon your shoulder."

Surely Wilham was mistaken. Aye, Lady Rose might desire his body, as often unworldly maids did, for he wasn't uncomely.

He'd been told so more than once. But 'twas only a fleeting attraction. Rose didn't care for him. How could she? She scarcely knew him.

"A wife, a home, children. That's what ye need. 'Tis time ye opened your heart," Wilham prodded.

But Blade had opened his heart before, and he'd destroyed what he'd held most dear. "Open my heart?" he said, smirking. "Not to that one."

"Why?"

"Wil, my friend," Blade sighed, clapping him on the shoulder, "only ye would choose for me a wife who's bound for the nunnery."

"Nunnery?" Wilham's brows raised, then furrowed. "She's bound for the nunnery?"

"Aye."

"Ye're jestin."

"Nae."

Wilham lost but a moment in contemplation. "Then ye'll have to change her mind."

Blade would have argued, but his eye was caught suddenly by a bright flicker from the edge of the woods beyond the garden wall.

Wilham droned on, lost in his machinations. "I know. I'll let slip how ye single-handedly bested the de Ware twins in tournament. Better yet, I'll mention the cache o' gold and jewels ye've won o'er..." He trailed off, sobering at once when he saw Blade studying something in the distance. "What is it?"

"Not sure."

Wilham followed his line of sight.

"A flash," Blade said. "The sun caught on... There."

"I see it."

Another glint of light sparked briefly against the dark trees, then was gone.

"Men-at-arms?" Wilham asked, squinting toward the forest.

"Maybe."

Two thick stone walls separated the woods from the pleasance garden, and guards were posted at close intervals along the outer curtain.  But Blade's heart still pounded as his gaze drifted over Rose—fragile and innocent and helpless among the flowers—while possible menace threatened only a few dozen yards away.

'Twas absurd.  What he'd seen could have been anything—a lady's mirror, a gardener's spade, the pale flash of a bird's wing—and yet some sense filled him with dread.

Wilham felt it as well.  "Ye want your sword?"

Blade snorted.  Of course he wanted his sword.  His fingers itched to hold the familiar weight, so much a part of him for the last two years.  But he'd taken a vow, and thus far he'd never broken his word.  'Twould take much more than *wanting* to convince him to break an oath.  "Nae."

"We'll be leavin' soon," Wilham urged.  "We won't have the protection o' the castle or the guards."

For several moments more, they kept vigil.  Finally, Wilham counted the pilgrims milling below.

"Blade."

"Mm?"

"Who's missin'?"

No sooner had he asked the question than another flash came from the trees.  'Twas the glint off of Fulk's axe, and Fulk and Drogo emerged.  They appeared to be quarreling.

"What the devil were *they* up to?" Wilham wondered.

Blade didn't care.  He was just relieved they weren't Rose's pursuers.  And that relief caught him off guard.  First, that he felt so protective of a woman who might, in fact, be a fugitive.  And second, because in his mercenary work, Blade always pursued his quarry with single-minded purpose until 'twas run to ground.  'Twas foolish—in some instances lethal—to let emotion interfere.

"A couple of assassins," Wilham guessed, "firmin' up their plans?"

"Maybe.  But what's their motive?"

"Revenge?" Wilham suggested.

Blade shook his head. "Unlikely, unless young Archibald o' Laichloan has killed one o' their kin."

"Coin?"

"Possibly."

"A butcher and a cook as hired assassins," Wilham mused, shuddering. "'Tis a chillin' way to dispose of a body."

Blade nodded. It had seemed altogether too convenient from the beginning that the two men, close companions, unbeknownst to one another, should by fate happen to join the same pilgrimage.

Still, there were others of the company who were just as suspect. The palmer, with his cache of fabricated holy relics, possessed the lack of scruples to commit such a crime for a handful of silver. The tanners, too, were a crude pair who might stoop to a felony to add to their purses. There was still the adulterous couple, Jacob the goldsmith and his paramour, Lettie.

And as long as he was doubting them, he might as well add to the list the Highland woman, the widow, the soldier, the apprentice, the nuns, the priest, and the three scholars, for none could be completely eliminated from the list of suspects.

Nae, the only pilgrims he could be fairly sure about were Wilham and himself...and of course, Rose.

Blade sighed. The pilgrimage was halfway through, and he was no closer to discovering the culprits.

"We should separate today," Wilham said, running his fingers through his chopped hair, trying to make some order of it. "We'll hear twice as much that way."

Blade grunted his agreement.

Of course, Wilham had set him up again. While Wilham went to bring up the rear of the company, he suggested Blade move to the fore, which was how Blade wound up just one Highlander away from Rose.

Not that he minded being close to Rose. He wasn't completely convinced that Fulk and Drogo were the only ones lurking in the wood. And while that unease possessed him, he'd just as soon place himself between Rose and danger.

He tried to pay heed to the nuances of the forest as they traveled, alert to discrepant sounds or sights. But 'twas difficult to focus while Rose distracted him with blushing glances.

*As if the sun rose and set upon his shoulder,* Wilham had said. Certainly the wench didn't worship him so fervently. And yet 'twas difficult not to wish 'twere true.

Her face was, in Wilham's words, as beautiful as her namesake. What Wilham didn't know, what Blade had glimpsed this morn, was that her body was no less perfect than her face. For that treasure alone, any man would feel blessed to claim her as his own.

But for Blade, her beauty ran even deeper. She had clung to him last night, as if he weren't a felon, as if he weren't a murderer. In her presence, by her grace, for one fleeting moment, his sins had been erased. She didn't judge him by his past, nor did she plague him about his future. She simply granted him the gift of the precious time they shared.

'Twas wrong, he supposed. Life couldn't be lived as if there were no consequences. One couldn't careen blindly down a path without knowing where it led. And therein lay the great battle waged between heart and mind, between desire and wisdom, a war too painfully familiar.

# Chapter 12

Curiosity had tormented Rose ever since Guillot had revealed that Blade might be a fallen noble. So when the pilgrims stopped at a tavern along the Standing Stane road, she decided she had to find out the truth.

Of course, 'twasn't a question she could ask outright. She'd have to be subtle. Prying secrets from a man who preferred to be mysterious was an art.

She never imagined 'twould be so difficult to speak with him. But as they stood together beneath the overhanging thatched roof of the tavern, a flood of sensual memories from the night before assailed her. Her heart fluttered, a flush warmed her cheeks, and her tongue all but failed her.

"I wished to...to thank ye," she murmured, her voice cracking, "for last night."

He gave her a hesitant nod. His chin was shaved clean today, and she couldn't help wondering how it might feel against her cheek, smooth like that, what 'twould be like to kiss him now.

"I...I'm sorry I fell asleep," she continued. Lord, she could smell the soap-scrubbed fragrance of his skin. "I would have liked to hear the rest o' your story."

"'Twas no great adventure," he murmured. "Not as heroic a tale as tamin' a bear."

"Oh, nae, 'twas quite a..." she countered, placing her hand on his sleeve, which stirred a memory of how well-muscled his arm had felt beneath that thin linen shirt last night. "A rivetin' story. But I was weary, and your voice was soothin'." She swallowed. "With your arms around me, I—"

"Lass," he growled. "I'd advise ye watch your tongue. We're not alone."

Before common sense could prevent her, she sighed, "I wish we were."

The only indication he'd heard her was a slight flaring of his nostrils, followed by a long silence. Rose blushed, withdrawing her hand. She'd been too forthright. But she'd spoken the truth. And with so few days left to pursue her heart's pleasure, there was little time for coy flirtation.

Blade eased the tension by changing the subject. "Your falcon will need to feed soon."

Rose nodded. She hoped her poor bird had the strength to eat. She'd left Wink in the tavern with Guillot, who was glad to watch over her. "Fulk and Drogo went huntin' for eggs in the forest this morn—"

"Huntin' for eggs?" He arched a brow. "Ah."

"To no avail."

He grunted. "I'll see what I can find."

"Thank ye. I'm...I'm truly beholden to ye."

"Faugh." He stared into his ale, slightly embarrassed. "Ye're always thankin' me for things knights are supposed to do for ladies." He took a drink.

"Knights?" she asked. Ah, here was her chance. She licked her lips. Then she added pointedly, "Or lairds?"

He choked on his ale.

Mayhap she hadn't been as artful as she thought.

When he was done coughing, he wiped his sleeve across his mouth. "What are ye talkin' about?"

She couldn't conceal the excitement in her voice. "Is it true?"

"Is what true?"

"Are ye a laird?"

His jaw tensed. "I told ye I'm a mercenary."

She couldn't leave it alone. "But were ye always a mercenary?"

"Nae." He took another swig of ale and stared into the woods. "Before that, I was a child."

She sighed. Blade had a tougher hide than the bear. "Ye know what I mean."

"Besides, I thought we agreed to no more questions."

"That was last night. 'Tis a new day. Come, sir," she coaxed. "Will ye not indulge me? A question for a question."

"Ye played me falsely last night," he reminded her.

"Very well." She bravely lifted her chin. "Today I'll answer ye truthfully, whatever ye ask. I swear it upon my honor."

"On your honor?"

She nodded.

He smirked, shaking his head. "All right." He took another sip of ale, then ran his thumb over the lip of the cup. "Then I'll ask ye again, is it truly in your heart to become a nun?"

She didn't figure he'd ask her the same question. At the painful reminder of her destiny, her heart thumped woodenly, and she lowered her head to stare at the ground before her. For a long while, she gave no answer, for it seemed that voicing her frustration would only increase it. But she couldn't run from fate forever. And she'd sworn upon her honor to tell him the truth. At last she whispered, "Nae."

From the corner of her eye, she saw him nod.

"'Tis simply that I have little choice," she confided. She battled the urge to crumble like an earthen dam in a flood, spilling all her secrets in one great torrent. "I..." she struggled. "I fear I'm not free to go where my heart—" She broke off, mortified to find a sob choking her.

Blade had never been able to resist a lady in distress. He'd spent too many years as a knight in shining armor. So he pushed away from the wall, took her cup from her, and set both of their half-finished ales upon the ground. Then, ignoring propriety, he clasped her by the elbow to guide her away from the others so she might weep in peace.

"Come," he said gently. "There's a watermill behind the tavern."

He hadn't meant to make her cry. He'd only wanted her to face the truth—'twas not in her heart to be a nun. He'd known that the first time he'd asked her. He'd known it the first time they'd kissed. And the second. And he knew it from the way she'd nestled against him in the dark last night—her soft, womanly curves cleaving to his body as if she were made for coupling.

The prideful part of him wanted to hear from her own lips that she wanted no part of the dismal, barren, passionless life of the convent.

Never had he meant to hurt her.

"Sorry," she said, a hitch in her voice, dabbing at her eyes as they traversed the grassy mound toward the mill. "I don't know what ails me. I don't often... I never cry. I'm usually...quite strong."

Her weeping wrenched at his gut. "I'm sure ye are," he said. Then he added, in hopes of cheering her, "Any woman who can tame a bear..."

She made a sound that was half-laughter, half-sob, and it made him feel even guiltier.

As they drew near, he began to hear the water from the mill pond as it gurgled and sluiced and tumbled noisily over the slatted buckets of the wheel. The stones beside the stream were wet and slick, so he held onto Rose as they approached the millhouse. Passing by the churning wheel, they ducked through the low doorway of the small building and into the dry interior, where the large round grinding stone sat unused at the moment.

Inside, the complaining squeak of wooden cogs and gears and the aroma of ground grain were oddly comforting.

Amber sunbeams spilled through the door, pooling on the plank floor and bathing the whole interior in warm light. Rose stood just inside the door, looking glorious against the tawny wood beams, like a brooch of ruby and onyx and pearl set in gold. Blade thought he could look at her forever. He wondered if he hadn't had another motive in bringing her here, one far more ignoble—a selfish desire to recreate the intimacy they'd shared last night.

Then she wiped the last tears from her cheek—tears he'd caused—and remorse filled him.

"I shouldn't have asked ye that," he apologized.

"'Tisn't your fault." She sniffed. "'Tis what I've been askin' myself all along."

He ran his hand over the rough surface of the grinding wheel. "And now ye have your answer."

"Aye." She closed her eyes.

"So will ye not follow your heart then?" He tried to make the question sound casual. He wondered if he succeeded.

She chewed at her lip. "Would ye?" She gazed up at him with moist eyes as if the world balanced on the edge of her question. "Have ye always followed your heart?"

He swallowed hard, wishing he could say aye and then prove it by crushing her in his arms, kissing her with all the dark passion and burning thirst he felt.

He lied instead. "A mercenary has no heart," he told her. "I follow my instincts."

Her eyes, bright with tears, softened as if she didn't believe him. Her voice was husky when she spoke, and he found that curiously alluring. "And what do your instincts tell ye?"

His instincts told him to thrust the bewitching wench up against the wall of the mill and plunge his aching lance deep into her yielding softness.

He clenched his teeth till they creaked like the mill cogs. Finally he let out a shuddering sigh. "My instincts tell me ye're a great deal o' trouble."

"So I've been told."

He gazed at her bowed head, at the shimmering river of ebony flowing over her shoulders to her waist. He couldn't imagine her chopping her tresses off in favor of a nun's veil, any more than he could envision her taming her impulsive nature to suit a convent.

After a time, she lifted her gaze and murmured, "I haven't had *my* question yet."

He braced himself. She was going to ask him again if he was a laird. What would he tell her? She'd sworn on her honor to speak the truth, and she had. He owed her as much. And yet his anonymity was the one piece of armor he couldn't afford to surrender.

"Tell me," she said so low he could barely hear her, her eyes trained on the sun-drenched planks of the floor. "Have ye...that is, do ye feel..." She clasped her hands tightly before her, took a deep breath, and started over. "Do ye feel any...desire for me at all?"

Blade's jaw dropped, all the strength draining from him. 'Twasn't the question he expected. The question he expected would have been far easier to answer. Desire for her? Satan's ballocks, she must be jesting.

Just gazing at her delicate hands, he remembered their light touch upon his arm. Focusing upon her lips, he instantly recalled the taste of her kiss. *Desire* for her? Holy Saints, aye, he felt desire for her.

She still stared at the floor, and he could see she held her breath, waiting for his answer.

What could he tell her? That her kisses filled him with molten need? That her touch set his pulse racing? That he could hardly bear to be alone here with her for want of seizing her, ravishing her...

"'Tis fine if ye don't." Her voice was thin and pained, but she spoke with dignity.

"Sweet Saints, woman," he breathed, "who wouldn't desire ye?" He spoke hoarsely, raking a hand back through his hair. "Ye're beautiful. Enchantin'." For a man of few words, suddenly he could not stop. "Magnificent. Intoxicatin'." He lowered his gaze to her lovely lips, parted in wonder. "Irresistible."

With a light gasp, Rose took a dangerous step toward him and placed a tentative hand upon his chest. Suddenly he could well imagine the intrepid damsel taming a wild beast. He closed his eyes, inhaling the clean fragrance of her hair.

And then, as he knew she would—as they both must have intended all along—she pressed soft lips to his.

Rose knew 'twas impetuous and wicked and greedy, but she couldn't help but steal a kiss. Especially when his clean-shaven cheek was so intriguing...his sensual mouth parted in invitation...and his eyes smoky and willing.

'Twas an innocent brush at first, gossamer light and tenuous, inquisitive and shy. She whispered wordless secrets into his mouth. He exhaled on a ragged sigh. And like the east wind, beckoning with its mysterious spices, his breath called to her, sending a warm shiver along her spine.

"We mustn't," he whispered against her lips.

"Aye," she agreed, deepening the kiss. Now that there was no stubble peppering his jaw, she could feel the yielding warmth of his flesh. She nuzzled his chin, reveling in the sensation.

He broke away, holding her at arm's length. His eyes were glazed with passion. "'Tis unwise," he gasped.

She wiped the back of one fluttering hand across her tingling lips. "Aye." Sweet Mary, he was right. She was bound for convent. In a few more days, they'd never see one another again. 'Twas foolish to think...

He caught the back of her neck and pulled her forward again, growling as his mouth closed over hers. She could taste his impatience, and 'twas intoxicating. Every inch of her skin felt alive, sensitized, shamelessly eager for his touch.

Again and again he kissed her, his hands winding through her hair and cupping her chin. She angled into his embrace, savoring the heat of his body and the flavor of his kiss. Her fingers dragged at his shoulders, bidding him come closer, and she willingly crushed her breasts against his doublet. A singing began within her ears, like angels' voices summoning her to heavenly realms, and those rich harmonies of yearning seemed to circle about her head.

She gasped against his cheek. Still she wasn't close enough.

He broke away for a moment, lifting the heavy chain that hung between them over her head, and capturing her again in his arms. Now she leaned fully against him, her velvet upon his leather, their bodies meeting as zealously as the palms of a Saint. Nudging her belly was the hard evidence of his longing, as keen and consuming as her own, and his conspicuous desire fueled hers. A bolt of scorching need shot through her, leaving a tingling in her breasts and a demanding fire between her legs.

He splayed his hands across her back, and everywhere the pads of his fingers touched her, she felt him leave his mark. His lips consumed her, his tongue swirled hungrily inside her mouth, and her own tongue answered with a kindred craving. His arms sank lower until he cupped her buttocks, pulling her against his thigh. She sucked in a shallow breath, pressing her woman's parts wantonly against his leg in an attempt to quench the burning there.

And still 'twasn't enough.

Her breath came in quick gulps, and her heart pounded as if it might burst from her ribs. His mouth trailed across her jaw, and when he nuzzled at her ear, his breath sent a hot shiver through her.

"Have I answered ye, lass?" he whispered.

She quivered, overwhelmed by the hushed intensity of his voice, of his kisses, of his seduction. Oh, aye, he'd answered her.

His teeth gently caught the lobe of her ear, and she moaned as her control slipped swiftly away. Her frenzied hands stroked and slid and clutched at whatever she could find of him.

His mouth moved lower then, nibbling along her neck, taking the chain of her pendant between his teeth, nuzzling the neckline of her surcoat aside so he could feast upon the crest of her shoulder.

He made sounds low in his throat—primal sounds that called to her as surely as a buck summoning a roe—and her heart thrilled with the impulse to answer.

She felt his hands climb up her back toward the laces of her surcoat, and she made no protest, for she likewise clawed at the ties of his doublet to gain access of her own. Her lips sought the pliant muscle of his chest, and she eagerly sampled the savory flesh there.

Her gown slipped slowly from her shoulders. Blade's breath, labored and heavy, seared her skin as he kissed his way downward. She gasped, abandoning her own exploration as she grew overwhelmed by his. Her head tipped back in ecstasy as he traversed her throat, then her collarbone, then the upper curve of her bosom.

A surge of yearning flooded her breasts, stiffening her nipples until they almost stung. She flushed hotly, mortified to discover that she wanted to feel his mouth upon her there as well. His thumbs tugged gently but insistently at her clothing, and she arched back, straining to free her breasts from their velvet prison.

Almost painfully aware of the craving between her thighs, wondering if he suffered the same intense hunger, she slid her palms down the front of his open doublet, then lower, seeking the root of his desire.

He was swollen and solid as rock, and he groaned loudly when she touched him, as if her fingers penetrated his chausses to brand his flesh. Still, he pressed back against her hand, like an ascetic welcoming the bite of the lash, and she stroked along his rigid length, soothing and stirring him all at once.

But when she compressed her hand about him, he hissed against her bosom as if in pain, withdrawing to sink upon his knees before her.

Her shoulders were entirely revealed now. Her crimson pendant was her only adornment, and her surcoat barely caught on the peaks of her breasts.

She supposed she should feel shame. But when she gazed into Blade's passion-veiled eyes—dark and smoky and wild and desperate—she felt only an inescapable longing to yield.

She closed her eyes and caught her lip between her teeth. 'Twas madness, this wanton surrender. Yet she desired nothing less. With trembling hands, she caught the front of her surcoat and pulled it steadily down for him, shivering as she exposed her breasts fully to the balmy air and his lusty gaze.

He sighed in fervent approval, leaning forward to kiss the spot below her pendant and between her breasts, tickling her with the soft brush of his hair. His fingers swept along her ribs to circle beneath her breast, and he cupped her gently in his hand. She held her breath as he lifted her for his pleasure, and the agonizing anticipation of his touch sent gushing warmth through her loins.

His thumb brushed across her taut nipple an instant before his lips claimed her. She gasped at the incredible liquid heat as his tongue bathed her and his mouth took suckle. She clasped handfuls of his soft, clean, thick hair, moaning low in her throat at the sweetness as he drew tenderly at her nipple, again and again.

Then he withdrew, and as his sated sigh chilled her moist flesh, stiffening her again, she made a mew of dissent. But he only meant to shift to her other breast, and as his hand enveloped and caressed and hefted her, she felt again the sensual magic of his touch.

And still...still 'twas not all she desired. The arousal of her breasts only served to fuel the flames raging below. She thrust her hips forward, seeking in vain to find some satisfaction, but her only reward was a deep and rueful chuckle from her tormenter.

"Ah, lass," he lamented, "ye desire what I dare not give."

"Please," she entreated, unaware of what she asked, only that she needed...more. "Please, Blade."

He seemed to struggle with some great quandary. His chest, half bared from her meager advances, rose and fell heavily, his jaw tensed, and his brow furrowed as if he played an unwinnable game of chess.

"Please," she whispered.

Finally, he nodded. Still kneeling, he widened the laces of her surcoat even more, allowing it to fall from her arms and slide to the curve of her hip. He pulled her close, resting his cheek against her bosom, then slipped his other palm along her belly, beneath her garments, toward the source of her distress. His shackle was cold and rough upon her skin, but his supple fingers made apology for that, stealing her breath away with their tenderness. She braced her hands upon his shoulders, afraid she might collapse beneath his torturous onslaught.

"Is this what ye desire?" he whispered.

She nodded, her eyes squeezed tightly shut.

His fingers moved lower, delving into her damp nest of curls, and she bit her lip to keep from crying out—whether in protest or gratitude, she didn't know.

"Show me where," he murmured, though she could tell by his sure hand that he knew his destination well.

Her breath caught once, twice, thrice as the tip of his finger found the core of her arousal. She sobbed as he moved his fingers slowly across and over and around her flesh, tugging and sliding with sensual precision. She dug her fingers into his shoulders as he stroked her burning nubbin, amazed that his touch only made her crave more. She writhed wildly against his hand, gasping when the shackle pinched at her flesh.

"Easy," he bade her, withdrawing his hand momentarily to slide the shackle back. "Easy, lass. 'Twill come soon enough."

She didn't know what he meant, but she trusted him. As she watched in curious amazement, he lifted his hand to his mouth, moistening his fingers with his tongue. His nostrils flared as if he savored the taste of her, and the gesture sent a heady thrill through her.

Then he slipped his hand beneath her garments again. This time, his fingers, made slick, fluttered across her with compelling haste, bringing her ache to a more and more finely focused point, beckoning her to higher and higher planes of sensation.

Soon the pleasure and agony and longing escalated even further, reaching such intense heights that for an instant, she couldn't breathe. The dizzying silence seemed to stretch into eternity, and she felt as if a delicate rain of warm sparks showered her.

Then, as suddenly as thunder, she was wrenched with a violence that thrust her hard against him. Her hips strained. Her fingers clawed at the muscle of his shoulders. She groaned a wordless cry of release, and her knees buckled in final surrender.

She bowed her head over his, weak with wonder and relief, and he carefully slipped his hand from her, embracing her about the waist.

She gasped, wrapping grateful arms about his head, glowing with contentment. "Oh, Blade. Blade."

"Blade!" a voice called from outside. "Where are ye?"

Wilham!

Blade cursed.

Rose panicked.

Her heart pounding and her legs wobbling like a milkmaid's stool, she struggled to find the sleeves of her surcoat.

Blade stormed to his feet. His face was black and full of fury, yet he managed to keep his wits about him.

"Arm," he hissed, thrusting out his hand.

She gave him her arm, and he helped her stuff it into her sleeve.

"Blade!" Wilham was getting closer.

"Shite!" she exclaimed, her eyes widening.

"Other arm," Blade directed.

She shoved her other arm violently into the sleeve, making the rip bigger in the process. Then she wiggled the surcoat up over her shoulders, fighting frantically to get the underdress to cooperate.

"Blade!" Wilham said. "Where the devil—"

"If ye value your life, Wilham," Blade yelled out grimly, "ye'll give me another moment!"

"But what are ye—"

"Not now!" he bellowed.

Blade spun Rose around, placed a knee against her backside, and wrenched hard at the laces of her surcoat.

"Too tight," she gasped.

He released them a bit, then knotted the top. Satisfied, he wheeled her back around and gave her a curt, reassuring nod.

"Blade? Are ye in..."

The man was just outside the millhouse. And now that her common sense was returning, Rose realized what a compromising position they were in. Aye, her garments were in place again, at least fairly well in place, but there was no disguising the telltale disarray of her tresses and the flush of passion in her cheeks. Thank God 'twas only Wilham and not Tildy or the nuns.

She glanced at Blade, who raised a questioning brow. She took a breath and nodded, then furrowed her brow. Blade's doublet was askew. She straightened it for him, then steeled herself for the encounter.

Blade ducked under the doorway, half in, half out of the millhouse.

"I should chop your head from your shoulders," she heard Blade mutter.

"Ah, so this is the thanks I get for comin' to your rescue," Wilham complained.

"My rescue."

"They're lookin' for her, ye know."

Blade cursed.

Rose gasped. What if they found her? What if they knew what she'd done? What if they banished her from the pilgrimage? What if they sent her back to Averlaigh?

"I told Father Peter I'd check inside the millhouse," Wilham said.

Blade's response sounded like the warning growl of a wolf.

Wilham continued, undaunted. "Come, Blade, out o' my way. I won't lie to a priest."

With an oath of protest, Blade let him pass. Though she was dressed, Rose still clasped a self-conscious hand to her bosom as Wilham stuck his head inside the door. He smiled smugly, perusing all the gears and cogs and beams inside the mill, then winked at her, and exited.

"There," she heard him declare. "I've checked it. Now hurry along, Blade. The pilgrims are restless." There was a short pause. "And fix her laces before ye return, my friend. Looks to me like ye've grown a wee bit rusty."

An observer would have assumed 'twas the copious ale or the bounty of food or the tanners' merry tales that warmed Blade to his marrow this evening as the pilgrims supped at The Green Dragon. Only he knew otherwise.

His pleasure was due to the blushing Rose beside him, who—unbeknownst to everyone at supper—rested a plundering hand upon his thigh under the table.

Tonight, whenever their eyes met, hers softened with secret knowledge, and a smile played about her lips. Though once quenched, apparently her thirst for him persisted.

As for Blade, he'd never hoped for requiting. When she'd pleaded with him in the millhouse, when she'd begged for release, he'd made the decision to appease her wishes. But despite his own roaring lust, he refused to gratify it at an innocent's expense. So now, though he ached for her, he expected nothing in return, not even so much as that delicate hand resting in taunting proximity to his lap. In short, he harbored no regrets.

How could he? She gazed upon him tonight as if he'd given her the world. 'Twas a magnificent feeling. He'd never experienced such intoxicating pride, even when he'd bested the de Ware twins. And that feeling of triumph made him want to give her even more.

But what more could he give her? He couldn't offer her marriage. By choice, he'd been stripped of his noble rank. He laid claim to no property, no title. Despite his illustrious family history, Blade had nothing to offer a bride.

Rose giggled at Odo's amusing story, and Blade couldn't help but smile at her charming gaiety.

Maybe he should live as audaciously as Rose. She seemed to embrace every experience as if neither the future nor the past mattered, but only the moment. She lived to revel in what befell her today. If only he could be so free...

A spate of raucous laughter brought Blade back to the pilgrims' stories. Ivo was recounting a jest he'd once played upon Odo.

"So I'm waitin', ye see, till Odo is deep in his cups."

"Which I rarely ever am," Odo said drunkenly.

Everyone laughed.

"And I drag him over to the tannin' vat."

"He tells me 'tis a bathhouse," Odo protested.

"There I deposit him." Ivo giggled helplessly. "And there the fool soaks all night!"

"I kept wonderin' when the women were comin'," Odo said.

"When I come back in the morn, he's pickled like a herrin'!"

The pilgrims roared. Even Blade had to grin.

"But that's not half as amusin'," said Odo, "as the time I brought ye the rats."

Ivo groaned. "Faugh, the rats!"

Odo rubbed his leathery hands together, warming to his tale. "I borrowed the miller's cat once to clean rats from the tannery. That cat must have killed two dozen o' the beasties, left 'em at the door, as cats are wont to do."

Ivo snickered and wiped his nose with his sleeve.

"Well, says I," Odo continued, "What am I to do with all o' these dead rats?" He thoughtfully stroked his chin.

"He comes to me..." Ivo put in.

"I come to Ivo, and I says, 'Ivo, I've got a special order from the sheriff.'"

Ivo nodded enthusiastically.

"I dump out this bag o' rats," Odo continued, "and I says, 'The sheriff wants these skinned and tanned.'"

Ivo shook his head. "Says he's goin' to have little purses made out of 'em for his daughters."

Odo turned to his friend. "How many did ye skin and throw in the vat?"

"God's hooks," Ivo said with a chortle. "A good dozen ere ye let me in on the jest."

Rose laughed beside Blade, and the clear, carefree sound warmed him to his boots. He felt a fierce longing to be alone with her again, to weave his fingers through her hair, to breathe the wondrous scent of her body, to trace her womanly curves with his palms, to bring her passions to fruition once more.

The tanners continued, each besting the other with tales of good-natured knavery. But Blade's thoughts centered on Rose. And because the inn was raucous and noisy, and because he was drunk on ale and desire, and because a rebellious part of him decided he might as well live as recklessly as Rose, he leaned toward her and whispered in her ear.

"Do ye know how I hunger for ye, Rose?"

He witnessed her quick intake of breath. Then her lids dipped in response, and she parted her lips. Still, she dared not look at him. Her fingers tensed on his thigh, and a streak of hot lust raced through his loins.

"Do ye want me as well?" he breathed.

Her eyelids fluttered and she nodded infinitesimally.

Then, without his bidding, the brazen wench allowed her fingers to wend their way toward the part of him that desired her the most.

He sucked a slow, silent breath between his teeth, the thrill of her touch heightened by the fact that he mustn't let anyone at the table know what mischief she worked upon him.

The little witch took her time, torturing him, giving him a sweet smile as she worked her cruelty upon his thigh. Then her fingertips grazed lightly over the bulge in his chausses, and he clenched his hands atop the table.

She stroked along his length, and even though two layers of cloth separated them, he felt the heat of her fingers like the glowing blade of a new-forged sword. A groan escaped him, and Wilham, seated on his other side, turned in askance.

"Are ye all right?" he murmured, frowning. "Ye look ill."

Blade tried to take a steady breath, but 'twas difficult, so difficult, with the woman caressing him like that.

"Fine," he managed, giving Wilham what he knew was an unconvincing smile.

Wilham arched a dubious brow.

"Is somethin' wrong, Blade?" Rose asked, her face as guileless as an angel's.

Blade clamped his teeth as a wave of sweet agony washed over him. The wicked wench tormented him deliberately.

Wilham leaned close and whispered across Blade to Rose. "Does he look ill to ye?"

She furrowed her brow in faux concern and whispered back. "He does look a bit...flushed." She slipped her hand deviously along his inner thigh then, delving between his legs to carefully caress his ballocks. It took all Blade's strength not to moan in pleasure. "Are ye sure ye're feelin' well, Blade?"

"Fine," he choked. Then he turned to her with a lusty glare that would have singed any other woman's eyelashes.

But Rose was undaunted, amused by his struggle to remain composed as she worked her wiles upon him. And to his utter surprise, he found her devilish ploys strangely tantalizing. She challenged him, he realized. And no knight could refuse a challenge. Despite the sweat beading his lip, he gave her a grim smile and turned back to Wilham. Never mind that Rose worked seduction on him mere inches away. He'd focus on Wilham's words.

"Any news?" he murmured under another clamorous tanner's tale. He picked up his cup and sipped casually, bent on ignoring Rose entirely.

"There's still pursuit," Wilham replied.

"Pursuit?" Blade repeated, though at first the word held no meaning for him. Forsooth, no words held meaning when Rose touched him like that, running the back of her knuckles along the swell of his...

"Aye," Wilham said, scowling. "Are you certain ye're..."

"Aye!" Blade answered, too sharply. "Aye," he amended.

Wilham looked impatient. "How many o' those did ye drink, Blade?" he asked, nodding at the ale. "I said, there's still someone followin' us."

Blade managed an instant of clarity. Danger. There was danger nearby. "Who?"

Wilham shook his head. "Three, maybe four, is my guess. Mounted."

Then Rose enveloped him completely in her hand, making his hips jerk and his thoughts scatter.

"Mounted?" he aped, though the word came out on a squeak.

Wilham's brows drew together sharply. "Maybe we'll talk when ye're not half-drunk," he muttered.

"Nae!" Blade said with a shudder of new resolve. "Nae." Very well. The lass had won. 'Twasn't so bad, he decided, to surrender to so formidable a foe. Nor to one so beautiful. "A moment," he told Wilham.

Then he turned and surreptitiously reached beneath the table to clasp Rose's errant wrist. When she wheeled about, her cheeks were flushed, her mouth parted. So, he thought, she was not as unaffected or aloof as she pretended to be. The idea pleased him immensely. He grinned.

"I yield," he conceded under his breath.

"But..." she began, attempting to stroke him again.

He placed her hand firmly away from him, upon her own lap. "Lass, if ye keep this up," he whispered, "I'll start bellowin' like a wild boar and swell to such enormous size I'll knock o'er the table."

She stifled a giggle, and he longed to swallow the delicious sound in his own mouth. The emotions in her eyes were like the rapidly shifting canopy of a June sky. Desire clouded the clear, innocent heaven, and amusement sprinkled down like rain. He realized with a powerful surge of joy that he adored her.

'Twas amazing. He hardly knew her. And yet an intimacy had formed between them, as strong and swift as a spider web spun overnight. He felt like the willing fly caught in that web.

Her gaze lowered to his mouth, and though a part of him yearned to accept her unspoken invitation—to knock the platters from the table, throw her down amidst the startled pilgrims, and consummate their mutual desire—he wisely refrained. There would be ample opportunity for them to be alone in the next few days. He'd make sure of it.

"Later," he promised, giving her hand a parting squeeze.

Her eyes smoldered, and he took a deep breath to still his skipping heart. Then Wilham loudly invited Blade to come inspect the tavern's collection of steins from Germany, and they excused themselves from the table.

"Mark ye," Wilham groused once they were away from the others, "we only have a few more days to find the culprits."

Bladed nodded.

"Mounted men travelin' at a slug's pace," Wilham said, shaking his head. "I'm thinkin' they may have an ally among the pilgrims."

Blade frowned. 'Twas possible the conspirators had split up—that one of them rode behind while the other traveled with the pilgrims. He blew out a frustrated breath. If 'twas true, then they'd made no progress. "The assassin could be anyone."

Wilham shrugged. "Maybe. Maybe not." He studied the row of lidded steins lined up on the shelf.

Blade studied his friend. "What do ye know?"

With an air of distance, Wilham picked up a stein and opened the hinged lid. "Well, if ye hadn't been so...distracted this afternoon..."

Blade clamped the lid shut with his palm, lifting a questioning brow.

Wilham immediately abandoned his aloofness, placed the stein back on the shelf, and leaned close to whisper, "Father Peter."

Blade waited.

"He has the perfect cover," Wilham said. "He's leadin' the pilgrims. He knows the road. No one would ever suspect a priest. And," he added significantly, "I heard him tell the palmer 'twas his last pilgrimage. His *last* pilgrimage." Wilham rocked back smugly on his heels, awaiting Blade's response.

Blade wasn't sure what to think. Wilham might be right, but what he offered was hardly proof. Too many others had come alone on the pilgrimage. Any one of them might be the culprit.

"What about the palmer?" he suggested. Ever since he'd caught Simon gathering splinters for relics, just thinking about the man left a nasty taste in his mouth. "Or the widow? Or the apprentice?"

Wilham scratched thoughtfully at his chin. "The palmer *is* a disagreeable sort," he agreed. "The widow? She's too intent on slippin' into the trews of every man on this journey. If she knew about the men followin' us, she'd have bedded down with them long ago."

A huge guffaw rolled across the tavern. 'Twas Fulk, slapping Drogo on the back after yet another story from Odo.

Wilham arched a brow. "Fulk? Drogo? They went off in the forest this morn."

Blade shook his head. "They were lookin' for eggs for Rose's falcon."

"Ye're sure?"

Blade nodded.

Wilham lifted his chin toward the falcon, who perched in a quiet corner of the inn. "They didn't find any. The bird hasn't eaten yet."

"Nae."

"But she's survivin'." He shook his head. "'Tis impressive. Ye might have made a fine surgeon."

Blade snorted, but he was pleased. Just as Rose had said, she and her falcon were both survivors. Still, the bird would have to eat soon, or its strength would wane.

The tanners finished their tales, to the protest of the pilgrims. Apparently, their knavish antics had been thus far the most entertaining of all the company.

Just before everyone retired upstairs, Rose sent Blade a clandestine glance of such heat and promise that it served to warm him half the night.

Unfortunately, that warmth kept him sleeping only fitfully, and thinking about Rose did nothing but aggravate what was already aroused. He needed a lungful of bracing air. So, when the moon hung past midnight, he pulled on his boots, taking care not to wake Wilham, and crept down the stairs, out into the night.

The air was chill, and his breath curled out in a tendril of fog. A low mist covered the ground, but overhead, the stars glittered like sparks. As he gazed up at them, he wondered if what the astrologers said was true, that a man's fate could be read in the heavens. What did the stars say about him? And was there a way for a man to change his destiny?

A low clucking just beyond the corner of the inn caught his ear. The innkeeper's chickens. Blade ambled toward the sound. Maybe one of the charitable hens had laid an egg. As long as he was awake, he might as well try to get Rose's falcon to eat. Aye, 'twas a miracle she'd survived the wolf, but 'twould be a tragedy if the bird died of starvation. Rose would be inconsolable.

He ducked into the chickens' roost. The hen made a soft cackle of protest when he snatched an egg from beneath her, then settled amicably enough over the remaining one in her clutch. When he'd finished, Blade let himself back into the inn.

The falcon perched in a corner of the main room, near the banked fire. He approached cautiously, wary of startling her. But to his surprise, the bird was awake, as if it had known he was coming. He cracked the egg and offered it to the falcon on his palm.

"Come on," he whispered. "Eat. Ye have to eat if ye want to survive."

Wink's head perked up, but the bird only shuddered on its perch.

He brought his hand closer. "Take it," he encouraged. "'Tis fresh and warm. Come on, ye stubborn lass." The falcon only eyed it suspiciously.

"Come on, Wink," he breathed. "Do it for your mistress. Do it for Rose."

Blade would have sworn the bird cocked its eye at him. Then it tentatively dipped forward and pecked at the warm liquid. It shook its head vigorously, ruffling its neck feathers, but tipped down for another bite.

Blade smiled. Rose would be relieved.

He continued to hold the egg until the falcon ate her fill, then wiped the remainder from his hand with straw from the floor. 'Twasn't much food, but 'twas enough to keep her alive another day.

"That's a good lass," he murmured, stroking the feathers of her breast till she sleepily closed her eye.

He glanced over at the stairs. He'd promised Rose he'd come to her later. He wondered if he could steal into her chamber. Making as little noise as possible, he crept up the stairs.

Just as quietly, Wilham was descending.

They nearly collided. Blade cursed under his breath and fell back against the wall, his heart pounding. "What in hell are ye doing?" he hissed.

"Is she with ye?" Wilham asked.

"Who?"

"Rose."

"Nae," he said smugly. Obviously, Wilham wished to catch him in some compromising position with Rose. "Not this time."

Wilham looked more serious than Blade had seen him in a long time. "Then where is she?"

# Chapter 13

Rose stole out of the inn into the crisp night, clutching Blade's missive tightly in her hand. He waited for her. *Your love*, the note read. She smiled, and the crescent moon smiled back at her as she followed the stone path toward the well where Blade told her he'd be waiting.

Her heart quickened—partly in excitement, partly in relief—when she saw the silhouette moving beside the well.

"Blade," she breathed, hurrying her steps. Already she could imagine his arms around her, his mouth claiming hers...

The exact moment she realized 'twasn't him, she couldn't say, but in that moment she slowed her steps, and misgiving sent a shiver up her spine.

She was an instant away from turning to scurry back to the inn when another dark shape lunged at her from the shadows. Her breath caught on a gasp. But the sound was smothered by a sack of rough cloth rasping down over her head, shutting out the stars.

Brutal hands wrenched her off her feet. She tried to scream. But the breath was jarred from her as a stout arm hefted her up. She twisted in her captor's punishing grasp, punching out at whatever she could hit. He swore as her fist made contact with something soft. But her victory was brief. The sack was yanked further down, pinning her arms and hampering her struggles.

Again she tried to cry out. A huge hand closed over her face, blocking the sound and her air. Desperate for breath, she opened her mouth wide, then clamped down hard with her teeth. Her attacker emitted a foul curse, reflexively snatching his hand back, then stuffed the fabric into her mouth to stifle her cries.

This couldn't be happening, she thought wildly. An inn full of pilgrims stood only a dozen paces away. Surely someone would hear the disturbance.

There were more of them now. One attacker squeezed her mercilessly about the waist. Another seized her legs, upending her. Nae! She'd not let them take her away. Her heart pounding frantically, she kicked out in a last savage bid for freedom. She was rewarded by a dull blow to the back of her head.

For a stunned instant, she thought they'd removed the sack from her, for her vision filled with bright stars. But the dots of light faded like cooling sparks, leaving only a coal black oblivion.

"What do ye mean, 'where is she'?" Blade asked, his heart lurching violently. "She's not upstairs?"

Wilham shook his head.

Blade refused to panic, despite the knifing pain in his chest that told him he already had. There had to be a good reason for her absence.

"I'll check the privy," Wilham offered.

Blade nodded. Of course. She was likely there. Why had he been worried? After all, Rose's falcon was still downstairs. She wouldn't leave without her precious pet.

But his assurances were dashed when Wilham returned, empty-handed. Agonizing moments later, they stood in the stable after searching every corner of the inn and the outbuildings without finding a trace of Rose. Blade's mind began filtering through the unpleasant possibilities.

"The horsemen followin' us," Wilham suggested, lifting a candle to shed a pool of light over the straw of the stable. "Any o' these mounts theirs?"

Blade scrutinized the three horses. Two of them looked well past their prime, scarcely fit to travel. They likely belonged to the innkeeper. The third was a fine steed, but he remembered its owner from the inn, and that man was traveling in the opposite direction. "Nae."

So their mounted pursuers weren't staying at the inn. They likely still lagged behind. Maybe they were camped in the woods. Unless...

Unless they'd already found what they'd come for and left.

The thought chilled him.

Snatching the candle from Wilham, Blade strode out of the stable, across the grass toward the main road. There were hoofprints in the mud, but 'twas no surprise. Horses traveled past every day. Still, there was fresh horse dung along the road, and there seemed to be a grouping of recent prints that led to and from the inn without going past.

"What's this?" Wilham asked, coming up behind him with a crumpled piece of parchment. "I found it by the well." Blade held it up to the candle. They read it silently together.

*Dearest Rose, I can wait no longer. Come to me before midnight at the well. Your love.*

There had to be some mistake. It couldn't be *his* Rose. He perused it again.

Nae. He'd read the letter correctly. Rose had gone to the well to meet..."your love."

Her love. The words felt like a punch to the gut. For a moment he couldn't breathe.

Rose had played him for a fool, he realized. She'd toyed with his affections and led him a merry chase, all the while fully aware that her love wasn't far behind. He ground his teeth against the pain, letting anger rush in to fill the hollow in his heart.

But though he trembled with rage, in his heart's place throbbed a dull ache. A familiar, cruel voice told him he should have known better than to trust a woman.

He crushed the note in his fist. It fell, fluttering, from his fingers.

She'd betrayed him. Rose had betrayed him.

The woman he'd lent a cloak in the rain, brought supper when she was half-starved, rescued from thieves. The woman for whom he'd lost two nights of sleep nursing a falcon back to health. The woman with whom he'd shared kisses and desire and, God pity him, begun to fall in love.

He should have been accustomed to the acrid taste of treachery. 'Twasn't the first time he'd supped on that empty dish. But this time, it had come when he'd allowed his soul to become vulnerable. This time it tasted as bitter as rue.

Then an even more grim possibility occurred to him.

Was the one who'd written the letter merely Rose's lover, or was he her accomplice? Could Rose be the one scheming to murder Laird John's son? Had her beloved co-conspirator trailed her all the way from Stirling? Was he holding her in his arms even now, kissing her lips and murmuring assassination plots in her ear?

Wilham bent to pick up the note. "Wait."

But Blade didn't want to wait. He was weary and sick at heart. He wanted to bandage his wounds. And he wanted to forget he'd ever met the deceitful wench with the breathtaking face and delicious mouth and adoring eyes.

"Who wrote this?" Wilham asked.

Blade turned his back and began marching back to the inn. "I don't know. And I don't care."

Wilham grabbed his arm, halting him. "Somethin' isn't right."

Blade clenched his jaw. Of course, something wasn't right. The woman he'd trusted—the woman who'd given him a glimpse of redemption, the woman who'd almost convinced him he was a man worthy of affection—had betrayed him. "What's not right, Wilham?" he said bitterly. "The fact that I was gulled by her false heart? That ye were gulled by her innocent eyes? Or that Archibald of Laichloan is goin' to be killed by a sweet-faced maid?"

"What?" Wilham let go of him and stepped back in shock. "Ye think Rose is the assassin?" He narrowed his eyes almost viciously. "God's bones! The maid *is* innocent." Wilham seized his arm again. "Listen to me. Ye have it all wrong."

Blade wrenched his arm away. "I was a fool," he growled, "and so are ye if ye believe her innocent."

God, he should have known. If he hadn't let his lust get in the way of his logic, he would have seen. The signs were there from the beginning—her lack of baggage, her ridiculous story about becoming a nun, her watchfulness of the pursuers.

"Damn your eyes, Blade, she *is* innocent!" Wilham hissed. "Ye, of all people, should know that. By the Cross o' my sword, man! What kind of assassin rescues half-blind falcons and shows kindness to felons in chains?"

Blade didn't want to listen to him. Wilham's reasoning only served to widen the cracks in his heart. He turned and strode off again.

Wilham followed at his heels. "Do ye honestly believe the lass is capable o' murder?"

"Maybe." 'Twas a lie. He couldn't even imagine it. Aye, he'd seen her knock thieves about and charge a pack of wild wolves, but murdering a defenseless lad? 'Twas unthinkable.

Still, though she might not do the deed herself, for the right reward, she might be party to the crime.

Wilham spat out a curse. "Can't ye see what this is?" he said, flapping the missive under Blade's nose.

Blade had had enough. He snarled into Wilham's face. "Damn ye, Wilham! Must ye pour salt in my wounds?"

"'Tis a trap, Blade. Listen." Blade tried to ignore the harsh syllables as Wilham read the letter aloud once again, but they rang like death knells in the frosty night. "Blade, they lured her out here. She thought she was comin' to meet *ye*."

Blade's laugh was full of pain. He would have liked to believe that, and he instantly regretted his impatience with Wilham, who was a loyal friend to try to persuade him of such nonsense. But the truth was far more believable. Rose had been waiting for this assignation since the beginning. The pilgrimage was simply a convenient way for a single woman to travel. Now her lover, her fellow assassin, had met up with her, and they'd carry out the rest of their plan.

And Blade? He supposed he'd been no more than a pleasant diversion for her. The thought soured his desolate mood, slowly curdling his anger. But 'twas better that way. With his heart full of vengeance and rage, there was less room for pain.

"She was comin' to meet me?" Blade echoed grimly. "Then I mustn't disappoint her, must I?"

"Nae," Wilham replied, ignoring his sarcasm. "The poor lass must be terrified. We've got to rescue her."

Blade shook his head. Sometimes Wilham only heard what he wanted to hear. He had no intention of rescuing the treacherous woman. Rose and her lover were assassins. He intended to seize them. 'Twas as simple as that.

As they made their way back to the inn, Wilham stopped suddenly. "Why Rose?" he asked, screwing up his forehead. "Why would anyone take her?"

Blade sighed. He didn't have time to engage in Wilham's labyrinth of theories. He had outlaws to hunt.

"Unless they want us to nibble at their bait," Wilham said. Then he snapped his fingers. "That's it, Blade! If ye were the killer, and ye wanted to get rid o' two pryin' fellows who were about to stumble upon your plot, how would ye do it?"

Blade scowled. He didn't like Wilham's riddles.

Wilham answered himself. "Ye'd lure them away with an even more intriguin' crime to solve." Wilham nodded, well pleased. "Blade, my friend, the real co-conspirator is still lyin' in his bed at the inn. And whoever 'tis, he's waitin' for us to fall into that trap, to ride off after Rose." He rubbed his hands together. "But he doesn't know who he's dealin' with. We won't fall for his trickery, will we? We'll stay right here and..."

Blade stared soberly at his friend.

Wilham squirmed under his regard. "Naturally, we'll go after Rose anyway, even if 'tis a trap," he said. "After all, we can't just leave the lass to—"

"I'm goin' alone."

"What? Nae. There could be a dozen o' them."

Blade didn't think so. So large a retinue would attract too much attention. He shook his head. "Three, four at the most."

"I'm goin' with ye."

"Nae." Blade didn't believe Wilham's story of subterfuge, but 'twas a good excuse to get him to stay behind. Blade wasn't sure he wanted Wilham to witness how he handled the betraying Rose. "If ye're right, if 'tis a trap, someone should stay with the pilgrims."

He saw the conflict in his friend's eyes. Blade never rode anywhere without Wilham, especially not into danger. But if Wilham honestly believed that Rose had no part in the plot, that the real assassin still traveled with the pilgrims, then someone had to stay behind and stand guard over the culprit.

Wilham drew himself up. "Ye stay. I'll go after Rose."

Blade arched a brow. They both knew that while Wilham possessed lightning wit and keen senses, Blade was far superior with a sword. And whether they believed 'twas a mission of rescue or retribution, a deadly sword arm was required.

Wilham read the message in his eyes. But he crossed his arms over his chest in challenge. "What good are ye against a pack o' kidnappers with your sword arm in shackles?"

Blade scowled, dreading the gloating that was bound to follow. "I won't be shackled."

"Indeed?" asked Wilham, lifting a scornful brow. "But what about your penance? What about your redemption?"

Blade shouldered him aside, pushing his way through the inn door.

Wilham argued with him the entire time he prepared for the journey. 'Twas clear he disapproved of Blade's plan. Nonetheless—faithful companion that he was—once outside, he saddled the best steed for Blade, setting aside enough coin to recompense the horse's owner threefold.

When it came time to unlock his shackles, Wilham hesitated.

"If I do this," he said, gripping the key in one hand and Blade's sword in the other, "I want your promise that ye'll do Rose no harm. No matter what ye believe." He raised a hand to stop Blade's protest. "Nae, I won't listen to your slander. I know she's innocent, even if ye're too stubborn to open your eyes to the truth. She's not Julian, Pierce. She's nothin' like Julian."

Wilham was right. She wasn't like Julian. His brother's wife had been a victim, moved to betrayal by a misplaced need to protect the very man who tormented her.

Rose had no excuse. She'd used Blade for her own amusement. And now she'd pay.

"I won't touch her," he lied.

Wilham unlocked the shackles, and Blade, freed, spread his arms wide, flexing his shoulders. Wilham pressed the sword into Blade's hands, and Blade sheathed the weapon, mounting up with Wilham's assistance.

"Ride fast," Wilham said, "and rejoin the pilgrimage as soon as ye're able."

The men clasped arms in farewell, and before the sun lightened the sky, Blade set out along the west road. The weight of both his broadsword and his cold heart were comfortably familiar. That he didn't intend to keep his promise to Wilham was no great burden upon him. His spirit was already as heavy as lead.

He'd been a fool to ever think there might be penance enough for him.

He was well past redemption.

Rose had feigned sleep for hours. Like a new-captured falcon, she found that the cloth covering her head—at first a source of panic—now became a refuge.

She knew who her captors were. And she knew 'twas best not to engage them. So she remained silent, riding mile after mile, as limp as a fresh-slain deer across her abductor's lap, listening, waiting. Thirsting.

Why they hadn't killed her at once, she didn't know. After all, 'twas what Gawter had threatened. Perhaps the men wished to torment her before they murdered her. Or, more likely, perhaps Gawter intended to keep her alive long enough to bear him an heir, then see to her demise. For the moment at least, she still lived and breathed, though the latter was arguable. With the rough cloth sack wound tightly about her head, her breathing was labored, each inhalation more stale and hot than the last.

She felt the sun, glimpsed light through the coarse weave of the cloth. Exactly how long they'd been traveling, she didn't know, but 'twas past midday, and by the sun's position, they were indeed headed west, back toward Averlaigh.

It had been a trap, she realized. And now that she recollected the language of the note, she was appalled by what a blockhead she'd been. *Your lover*, the missive had read. Those words could have been written by anyone. 'Twas obviously a trick, penned by one of the men who'd seen her with Blade. And, lovesick fool that she was, she'd fallen into the snare completely.

She wondered what Blade would do when he found her gone. If he realized she'd been abducted, he'd come after her. But she half hoped he wouldn't. After all, he was only one man against many, a shackled mercenary without a sword against four of Gawter's best knights. And while Gawter may have issued instructions that Rose be brought back alive, there would be no such allowances for Blade.

Tears welled in her eyes as she thought about never seeing him again, but she bit them back. Better Blade should remain safe and well than embroiled in her thorny affairs. Nae, she prayed he'd remain with the pilgrims and ultimately find the redemption he sought at St. Andrews. And she hoped with all her heart that he'd take care of her precious Wink.

The men had stopped twice already to water their horses, and the sound of the gurgling stream had made her throat ache with thirst. But she dared not let the men know she was awake, lest they inflict worse torment upon her. So she allowed herself to be hoisted down and laid out along the stream's edge, nearly weeping with frustration while the others refreshed themselves.

She couldn't go forever without water, but she knew at some point she'd make a stand, and surprise was her best weapon. She had no intentions of going willingly with the men all the way to Averlaigh, for she harbored no illusions about Gawter's temper. He meant to kill her, sooner or later. Of that she was certain. If she'd returned to him of her own volition, he might have been forced to show her mercy. But now he held her life in his hands. Nae, she had to escape. Or die trying.

They traveled on until the sun finally sank in the sky, stopping at last to make camp. Thus far, the men had spoken little, their chatter mostly trivial. But now their conversation centered around her.

"Ballocks! How hard did ye hit her?" her captor demanded, slipping her from his lap into another man's arms. "She hasn't moved so much as an eyelash all day."

"If ye've killed her..."

"God's hooks! Didn't ye check to see if she was still breathin'?"

"Ach, so it's my fault now, is it?"

"Lay her down then. We'll take off the sack, see what we've got."

This was her chance. They half expected her to be dead. Like a falcon swooping down upon prey, she might catch them unawares.

She forced her body to remain slack while they wriggled the bag upward, resisting the overwhelming urge to yank her surcoat down when it rose up with the cloth.

"Come on, wench. Ye can't be dead now."

"I don't care if she's dead or not," one of them guffawed. "I'd like a turn between her bonnie legs."

"Quiet!"

The bag pulled free of her head.

"Is she?"

Rose didn't move. She took a long, invisible breath of fresh air to revive her spirits and counted slowly to three. She felt their presence as they leaned near.

At three, she yelled, exploding outward with her arms and legs, cuffing and kicking and flailing as violently as she could. She caught one man on the chin with her foot, another with an elbow to his shin. Her knee lodged between one man's legs, and she placed a well-aimed punch at a leering eye. While they recovered, she managed to scramble to her feet. She swung hard about with her fist, clipping a man on the jaw, bruising her knuckles. With her other arm, she shoved one man into another, knocking their heads together with a loud crack.

Then she tore away toward the horses. If she could just reach that first mount...

She took three great steps, then vaulted up, seizing the reins with one hand, the saddle with the other.

She almost made it.

But these were seasoned soldiers.

Before she could swing her leg up over the saddle, she was dragged down by the back of her skirts. She tried to kick her assailant, but he yanked her hard, and she lost her grip on the saddle. Even then, she would have fled afoot, but he tripped her, and she fell headlong to the ground. Behind her, she heard three swords unsheathe. And knew she was doomed.

She shuddered as cold steel pressed at the back of her neck, and prayed for quick death.

"Argh! My ballocks!" one man whimpered. "The she-devil's ruined me."

Her captor planted a knee in her back and wrenched her head back by the hair. She winced in pain.

"I could snap your neck," he spat, "ye daughter o' Satan."

He hauled her up instead by her hair, making her eyes sting with tears, and stood her up before him, her neck gripped in his hand. His eye was already beginning to blacken from her fist, and she took some satisfaction in that. But there was no mercy in his dire gaze.

"Know this, wench," he growled. "Sir Gawter's not a patient man. He'll likely reward us for tamin' ye. And we'd gladly break ye just for the sport of it."

His words sent a chill through her bones, but she refused to cower. He shook her once by the throat, then let her go.

The man who was bent double in agony lumbered up then, a watery-eyed sneer marking his pallid face. So quickly that she couldn't dodge it, he swung around with his mailed hand and split open her cheek. Pain burst across her face as she was knocked back against the horse, dazed.

"Ye stupid fool!" the first man shouted. "Not where it'll show!" Then he drew back his fist and gave her a brutal punch in the stomach.

She caved forward, wheezing for breath, shaking in shock, hurting so much she prayed for sweet unconsciousness.

Blade fell back into his mercenary habits with the ease of a knight donning a well-worn gauntlet. Though the distraction of going on a pilgrimage had been an interesting break, his mood at present was more suited to the solitude of the hunt.

His quarry wasn't difficult to track. The riders took no special care to hide their passage. One of their mounts had a worn shoe and thus, a distinctive print. But they'd left hours before him and likely traveled in haste. They might be difficult to catch.

Why they fled west, he didn't know. The assassins had said they were going east to St. Andrews. The further he pursued the horsemen, the more he wondered if Wilham might have been right about Rose's disappearance being diversionary.

Still, it didn't deter him from his course. He had a crime to uncover. There was wrong to be righted.

In a secret corner of his mind, he recognized the assassination was the least of his reasons for coming after Rose. She'd betrayed him, and if there was anything he stood for, anything for which he'd scour the ends of the earth, 'twas justice.

It took all of one day and most of another, hard riding and with nothing but stale bread and cheese for sustenance. But when he finally caught up with the riders at twilight of the second day, creeping up on their camp with the stealth of a seasoned hunter, all his plans for righteous retribution took an unplanned turn.

From his vantage point in the shadows of the trees, he spied them—four men in matching red cote-hardies, cooking their supper over a blazing fire.

He was surprised to discover they were not miscreants, but noble knights. Usually, men who wore the colors of a lordly house carried themselves with a lofty bearing. Rarely did they sleep on the ground when there was an inn nearby, and only during a siege did they move about so secretly.

But what amazed him more was that Rose wasn't among them.

His first thought was that she hadn't gone with them after all, that she might have refused to leave with her lover, that she'd bid the man adieu at the well and chosen to remain with the pilgrims...with Blade. But he cast that sentimental thought aside like an over-sugared sweetmeat.

The other possibility shook him to his foundations. Maybe they'd...done something...to Rose and disposed of her. Maybe she was...

He dared not even utter the word in his mind. For all of his vengeful thoughts, there was a part of him—a weak, vulnerable piece of his heart—that still clung tenaciously to the hope that he was wrong about Rose. And that part of him would languish forever if anything had happened to her.

Thus, with a conflict so twisted it confounded his brain, he prayed that Rose was still alive...so that he might wring her treasonous neck.

The men laughed as they turned a brace of spitted rabbits over the fire. One of them left to piss against a tree, and in that dark gap left by his absence, Blade spotted Rose.

She sat beyond the fire, tethered to a fat oak. Her arms were bound before her, and she was gagged. Her hair was snarled, her torn surcoat hung off one shoulder, and her cheek bore a bloody bruise.

Wilham had been right. Rose *was* innocent. These brutes had abducted her. And they'd...hurt her.

Shame, then fury, rose so quickly in him that his blood surged through his veins like molten steel. Without thought, without stealth, purely on warrior instincts, he drew his sword, crashing forward through the trees with a mighty roar in his throat and fire behind his eyes, wielding death.

Rose saw the men scatter, and her mind flashed back to that time long ago—to that other roar, when all the other children had been afraid, and Rose had held her ground.

Whatever wild animal approached, it couldn't be as vicious as her captors. They'd already bloodied her cheek, bruised her ribs, and half-starved her. So while Gawter's men dispersed in a spate of panicked oaths, she waited numbly for death to come.

When she saw who 'twas, when she beheld Blade charging into the clearing like an enraged beast, all of the pent-up fear she thought she'd subdued, all the despair locked deep within her breast escaped on a great sob of relief.

He'd come for her. Blade had come to her rescue.

His hands were free of his chains now, and he brandished a sword as if 'twere an extension of his arm. He planted his feet wide before the fire. His chest was heaving, and his firelit face was a flickering mask of grim, controlled fury. 'Twas a face to set even her courageous heart racing in terror. No wonder the men had fled.

"Come face me, ye cowards!" he bellowed.

'Twas only when they came for him that she remembered he was one man against four. Her heart lurched. Sweet Mary! He was going to get himself killed.

She had to help him. Squirming violently against her bonds, she screamed behind the gag, hoping to garner his attention, hoping to get him to cut her free. But all that came out was a weak squeal.

He paid her no heed. Instead, he strode forward, swinging his broadsword in one hand with almost insolent grace.

"Come pay for your dishonor," he snarled toward the men.

She thrashed again, trying to convince Blade to loose her, but he didn't seem to understand.

"Turn away, lass," he called to her. "'Twill not be a bonnie sight."

Of course, nothing would convince her to look away now. 'Twas like asking her not to think of purple thistles. Her gaze was drawn to him with almost magnetic force.

And then the battle began.

She'd trusted the men to fight honorably. After all, though they'd been rough with her, they were still noble knights. Surely they battled under some code of chivalry.

Her expectations were dashed when all four attacked Blade at once.

But to her amazement, in a single smooth movement, Blade knocked aside one weapon with his own, skewered a second man in the shoulder, then spun to kick the third blade away and swung his sword around to engage the last assailant.

Never had she seen such dexterity, such daring, such strength. Sir Ian Campbell had been right. Blade *was* a peerless fighter.

Sparks flew from the flashing blades as the two knights clashed once, twice, thrice. The wounded man was slow to recover, but the other two regained their stances and thrust toward Blade again. One weapon he deflected. The second swipe he ducked beneath. The third man returned with a slash that sliced into Blade's doublet at the ribs, but went no deeper.

The wounded man rushed at him, and before Rose could even finish gasping, Blade dove for his legs, bowling him over. Blade instantly rolled to his feet to face the others.

They circled nervously, and Blade, impatient for their attack, stepped upon the back of the groaning knight, then over him, lunging toward the man on the right. Steel met steel, and the grating seemed to echo the tense discord of Rose's nerves.

Blade kicked out again to deflect the swipe of the man on the left, but the man in the middle used the opportunity to stab forward. Rose gasped as the blade appeared to pierce Blade's body. But he'd dodged the blow. The sword had slipped under his arm.

Blade arced his free hand over his opponent's sword arm, and jerked his arm back, pulling the man forward by his captive hand until he collided into Blade's shoulder.

The impact forced the man to drop his sword, and Rose— itching to rush forward and retrieve the weapon—struggled in vain against her bonds.

Blade then used the man as a shield. Just as the attacker with the injured shoulder thrust his sword forward, Blade shoved his captive into its path. The man moaned as his fellow's blade sank into his belly. His assailant spat out a string of oaths at his unfortunate mistake.

Rose watched in horror as the blade was pulled free. The man clutched at his stomach, blood seeping between his fingers, his face limned with astonishment and pain just before he fell senseless to the ground. She shuddered.

But Blade was already engrossed in another battle, caught between two of the remaining attackers. They prepared to swing around simultaneously from opposite sides, and Rose squeezed her eyes shut, sure they would cut him in half.

When she dared peek an instant later, Blade had dropped his sword and leapt up, clinging to an oak branch overhead. He pulled up his legs just as the swords whistled past beneath him.

Rose buckled in relief until she realized that Blade had just disarmed himself. He hung like a haunch of beef, waiting to be butchered. What would he do now? Damn his eyes! If only he'd freed her...

The three remaining knights surrounded their quarry, their eyes gleaming with vengeful glee. Rose couldn't bear to watch. But she couldn't bear not to. So she squinted her eyes, hoping to filter out the worst of what was to come through her eyelashes.

One attacker, the one who'd killed his fellow, couldn't wait for his revenge. He slashed toward Blade. Blade swayed back out of the way. While the man recovered, Blade swung forward again, hoisting his body up and over till he crouched atop the branch, out of their reach.

Rose wanted to shout for joy.

But the tree proved more prison than haven. He had no way down and no weapon. What acrobatics could he possibly employ now? Gawter's men had only to wait for him to descend.

They'd obviously come to the same conclusion, for they began to chuckle at his predicament. Even Blade's expression of righteous wrath took on a doubtful cast.

Then an ominous creak sounded, and the limb began to sag. Rose held her breath while Blade sank closer and closer to the threatening swords. With a sudden crack, the branch gave way, and Blade tumbled to the ground with a great crash and a deep thud.

To his good fortune, the limb felled the men below as well. In the confusion, Blade managed to move out of their range. But he was also out of reach of his sword.

Rose sobbed in frustration. She didn't know how much more of this anxiety she could endure, violently rocked between hope and despair.

Within moments, Gawter's men tossed aside the broken limb, staggered to their feet, and lumbered toward him again.

Blade looked about urgently, seeking a weapon—anything— to defend himself. He picked up a long branch, testing its strength by striking it against his palm, but the thing broke off.

The attackers drew closer, their faces smug, and Blade retreated toward the fire, scanning the ground.

When he'd backed as far as he could go, when flames appeared to lick at the back of his legs, the men lunged at him as one, and Rose winced, sure Blade would fall into the fire and be consumed.

But he turned and dove over the leaping flames, rolling in the dirt on the other side. When he came up, he was wielding a flaming brand.

Armed now, Blade thrust the log before him, driving his assailants back. They deflected him as best they could with their swords, but fire was a daunting enemy. Finally, one of the men, losing patience, grabbed the brand in his mailed hand, planning to disarm Blade by tossing the thing aside before it could do damage. But as he flung it away, the flames leaped onto his cote-hardie faster than a beggar falling on a dropped coin. He slapped at the fire, cursing as he tried to extinguish it, but it only intensified with his flapping.

To Rose's horror, the man closest to him, the one who had punched her so mercilessly in the stomach, began to laugh as if he thought his fellow's suffering a fitting end for his poor judgment.

Soon the man was shrieking in panic, squirming as the hungry fire fed on his garments and then his flesh. But his companions did nothing to ease his agony, and soon the wretch was beyond help. Sickened by the sight, Rose shut her eyes tightly. When the man began to scream, she wished she could close her ears as well.

Abruptly, the screaming stopped, and she opened her eyes again. But 'twasn't Gawter's knights who had put an end to the man's suffering. 'Twas Blade. He'd seized the man's fallen sword and delivered the blow of mercy. The fire consumed what remained of the man's dead body while his head burned a few yards away.

And now Blade was armed. He advanced on the two remaining knights, his mouth twisted in revulsion. He swept the bloody sword down twice, tracing a violent X in the air.

"Ye whoresons aren't worthy of your armor," he sneered.

Then he engaged both men at once in a clash of furious steel. Rose had never beheld such speed, such power. He spun and slashed and thrust with the unpredictability of a summer squall. Unlike the gallant combat of tournaments, his fighting had a rough, crude character. He fought, not for style, but for efficiency. Lacking a shield, he elbowed his opponents away, backhanded them, even shoved them across the clearing with the sole of his boot.

One man fell backward, and Blade would have run him through had the other knight not swung around with a sword he was forced to dodge. The fallen man found Blade's lost sword behind him and swept it up, gloating as he faced Blade armed with two weapons.

But Blade remained undaunted. He joined his hands on the hilt of his sword, and the increased strength of his blows sparked off the man's weapons, jarring them until the blades shivered. He drove his opponent back with a vengeance until the man, cornered against a tree, gasping and grimacing in fear, dropped the weapons. Blade's sword flashed in the firelight as it circled for the killing thrust.

But Blade's chivalry prevented him from slaying the unarmed knight. Instead, he plowed his gauntlet into the man's face. The clout made a sickening crunch on contact, and the force knocked the man's head back against the tree. His eyes rolling and his nose dripping blood, he slid slowly down the trunk into a heap at the foot of the tree.

Rose wished she could have cheered, but while Blade had been preoccupied, the last remaining knight—the cruel one who had driven his fist into her belly, the one who had abandoned his companion to die an agonizing death—had decided to try another tactic. The sharp edge of his sword pressed against the rapidly pulsing vein in her throat.

# Chapter 14

Blade turned, and the sight before him—the woman with the battered face and her tormenter standing beside her, leering in smug contentedness, threatening her—brought so many memories crashing down around him that he staggered under their weight.

Not again, he thought.

Visions of the past swam before him with palpable clarity. Bruises on the woman's cheek. Her torn gown. Tangled hair. Blood. And then the sounds. The nauseating smack of her abuser's fist. Gasps. Weeping. And over it all, the fearful hush of the crowd. Then the incredible, unfathomable chuckle of satisfaction, clashing with the woman's piteous sobs. The same chuckle Blade heard now as the demon before him—not his brother this time, but a monster of the same ilk—gloated over his victim.

For a moment, Blade couldn't move. The memories unmanned him. His arms trembled, and his knees grew weak. Apprehension loosened his grip upon the sword.

Not again.

"Put away your sword, sirrah!" the man jeered. "I've won the day."

But something in the man's voice tweaked Blade's ear, awakening him from haunting memories. 'Twas not the same at all. And suddenly he was wrenched back to the present.

This was not his brother.

This was not Mirkhaugh.

And when he glanced into Rose's eyes—shining with courage and determination and rage—he realized this was not his brother's wife.

His grip tightened again upon the hilt, and hot blood flooded his veins.

"Come fight me like a knight!" Blade roared.

The man's eye ticked in displeasure, but he managed to bite out a reply. "Brash words from a felon."

"At least I don't hide behind a woman."

The man's mouth twitched as Blade's insult found its mark. But 'twas a dangerous game. One slip of the sword...

"She's not *my* woman," the man replied. "'Tis no matter to me whether she lives or dies. But ye... Drop your sword now, or her next breath will be her last."

Blade studied the man's face. The man's eyes glittered with the same coldhearted malignance as his brother's. He was sincere. He'd kill Rose. Without remorse. And without blinking an eye.

Blade cast a quick glance toward Rose. She frowned, staring intently at his hip. She'd noticed his dagger, the weapon he wore at his hip for close combat, and she wanted him to use it. But she didn't understand. He was several yards away. By the time he reached the villain...

She met his eyes, sending him an unspoken message of childlike trust.

"Drop it!" the villain bellowed.

Blade muttered an oath. He had no choice. Rose had suffered enough. He couldn't let more harm come to her. His shoulders lowering in resignation, he let the sword fall from his fingers.

"There. 'Twasn't so difficult, was it?" the man crowed, though he wiped the back of his hand across a brow beaded with sweat.

Then, with a cocky salute, the knave started to lower his sword.

An instant later, Blade's dagger whirled through the air. By the grace of God and Blade's steady hand, the knife sheathed itself deep in the villain's chest. Blade whispered a prayer of thanks.

He wasted no time with the incredulous brute who choked in pain and surprise, staggering and gasping for air. The man would eventually die. His only concern was for Rose. He picked up his sword, rushed forward, shoved the wheezing man out of reach of her, and bent to slice her bonds.

By the time he loosed her gag, the man had shuddered out his last breath and lay silent in the leaves.

"Blade," Rose croaked, lifting trembling arms around his neck. There was such relief, such faith, such tenderness in that one syllable that it swelled his heart and illuminated his soul.

Overcome with compassion and self-reproach, he swallowed a lump of shame. How could he have ever suspected such a good-hearted woman of betrayal? Wilham was right. She was as innocent as a flower—sweet, pure, delicate...

"Damn your hide," she whispered against his cheek, jarring him from his remorse. "Why the devil didn't ye loose me earlier?"

He grinned, relieved. Her body might be bruised, but her spirit was unbroken. He lifted her carefully in his arms, carrying her toward the flickering firelight so he might tend to her hurts.

"Would ye have run to safety as I commanded?" he asked, hunkering down by the fire and settling her upon one knee.

Her mouth quavered on the verge of a smile. "Maybe."

"Maybe?"

"After I lent ye assistance."

"I feared as much," he told her, brushing a stray lock of hair back from her bloodied cheek.

She was too weary to argue. She was almost too weary to drink the watered wine he offered her from his flask. But she managed a few swallows, finally lowering her eyes in exhaustion. Then she relaxed against his chest with a trust that warmed him to his core and began, miraculously, to heal his damaged spirit.

He thought she'd fallen asleep. While she lay quiet, he perused her injuries. Her jaw sported a dark bruise, her cheek was split, and there were scrapes along her neck. But her bones, at least, seemed whole. He wondered if she was fit to travel.

Her eyes still closed, she said faintly, "Let's go. This place reeks o' death."

Blade was only too happy to oblige. After he kicked dirt over the fire and set the knights' horses free, he mounted his own steed with Rose before him. 'Twas a long ride back, but Rose was as light as thistledown in his arms. He hastened the horse along the road until, several hours later, he happened upon a crumbling cottage purporting to be an inn.

'Twas near midnight, but a few pieces of silver persuaded the innkeeper to let the last remaining chamber to a traveler and his wife. After seeing that the horse was safely stabled, Blade carried Rose upstairs to their room, a shabby place with a straw pallet and chinks in the plaster. But 'twas warm enough, reasonably clean, and safe.

She stirred as he laid her out atop the bed.

"'Tis all right," he murmured. "No one will hurt ye now, I swear."

As a noble knight, he was obligated to protect and defend the helpless. But for the first time in his life, when he made that pledge, he meant it with all his heart.

Blade ran the back of his hand over Rose's precious locks. She made a soft sound of relief, then curled on her side, falling asleep again almost instantly. He swore that as long as he breathed, he'd not let harm come to a single hair on her head.

He lifted the coverlet over her, secured the shutters, and, bunching his satchel to bolster his head, stretched out at the foot of her pallet, his sword at the ready beside him.

Though he was exhausted, he didn't fall asleep immediately. Something picked at the back of his brain. Who were the men in the red cote-hardies? And why had they taken Rose? They'd made no demands, and they could see she had no possessions with her. Yet, of all the pilgrims, they'd purposely selected her. They'd been sent by someone, whoever belonged to that red crest. 'Twas not one Blade recognized, but in the last two years, the king had granted land to several nobles. It could be anyone. And though the thought caused a foreboding twinge in his chest, he realized it was probably someone Rose knew.

He wouldn't wake her again tonight, but on the morrow, he'd make Rose tell him everything. After all, he couldn't protect her from an enemy he didn't know.

Some time later, when he'd slept a few hours, but the world was yet dark, he heard someone creeping close. His fist had already instinctively coiled about the hilt of his sword, but he soon realized the interloper was Rose. Dragging the coverlet with her, she eased down beside him.

"Move o'er," she said, her voice soft and demanding at the same time.

He released his sword and opened his arms. She nestled easily into the curve of his embrace, as if she'd belonged there all her life, wriggling herself into a comfortable and intimate position that roused his blood and taxed his restraint.

"Ah, witch, ye don't know how sorely ye tempt me," he breathed against her hair.

But his silk-voiced temptress was already asleep.

When Blade awoke the next morn, Rose was still slumbering on the warped wood planks, cradled in his arms. 'Twas absurd, but he couldn't remember sleeping so peacefully, not even in his feather bed at Mirkhaugh. 'Twas heaven lying with Rose, her soft hair tickling his chin, her skin smelling of womanly slumber, her body warm and soft where it clung to his. He hated to disturb her.

But the day grew late. And now that Rose was safe, they had to intercept the other pilgrims. After all, Rose still planned to journey to St. Andrews, and Blade had an assassination to prevent.

So as gently as he could, he urged her awake.

"Rose? Rose."

When she turned drooping eyes to him, he winced at the cut on her face, made all the more vivid by the light of day.

"Is it time to go?" she murmured.

"Aye."

He reluctantly extricated himself from their pleasant entanglement, rose to fetch a linen cloth and water from the pitcher beside the bed, then returned to crouch beside her.

"Tell me," she ventured, rubbing at her eye. "How is Wink?"

He smiled. Here the lady sat, her face bruised, her garments torn, snatched from the jaws of death, and all she cared about was that crippled falcon of hers.

"Better." He dipped the cloth in the water. "She ate an egg."

He pressed the wet linen to her cheek. She winced once, but managed to remain brave for his ministrations.

"Who's carin' for her now?"

He wiped away a spot of blood from Rose's ear. "Wilham. Though your Highland nurse is likely fightin' him for the privilege."

"We'll join them soon?"

"Aye."

She grabbed his wrist. "How soon?"

He swiped at the tip of her nose. "So many questions."

She relinquished his arm with a sigh.

He relented. "We'll leave after I've seen to your injuries."

"God's teeth," she pouted, ducking away. "I'm well enough. Let's leave now."

He frowned, catching her head by the chin to more closely inspect the bruise along her cheekbone. "I have a few questions for ye first."

She bit at her lower lip, obviously disconcerted.

He swabbed at a scratch beneath her ear. "Who were those men?"

She shrugged. "I don't know."

He didn't believe her, but neither did he think she'd feed him a blatant lie. She may not know them by name, but...

"Whose knights were they?"

"Their...their crest looked familiar," she admitted. She screwed up her forehead as if trying to remember, but wouldn't look him in the eye. "I believe...Greymoor?"

The name sounded vaguely familiar, but he didn't know the man. "And what would Greymoor want with ye?"

She opened her mouth to say something, then closed it and shrugged. "They...didn't say."

He could see by the guilty dip of her eyes that she *did* know Greymoor.

He caught her chin again and forced her to look at him. "Lass, I just slaughtered the man's knights at great peril to my own body. If ye know anythin' o' this nobleman and his demands, I would learn it."

A shadow crossed her eyes then, and he glimpsed the battle ensuing within her. Her indecision filled him with sudden misgiving. Jesu, had he killed guiltless men?

Nae, he decided. Guiltless men, knights worthy of their armor, did not beat women. For that alone, they deserved to die.

"Please," she implored. "Don't ask me that. I don't dare answer."

What was the lass hiding? "I told ye I'd protect ye," Blade murmured. "Do ye not trust me?"

Rose rested a placating hand upon his chest. "'Tisn't that," she assured him.

"Then what?"

She bit her lip again, reluctant to say.

He whispered an oath. "Lass, if ye intend to betray me..."

She gasped. Betray him? Was that what he thought? Betray the man who had ridden to her rescue? Who'd risked his life to save her from Gawter's minions? The man whom she wished with all her heart she could possess?

"Nae!" she cried. "Ne'er."

But neither could she divulge the truth of her capture. Gawter *would* come after Blade. The man Blade had left alive would insure that. 'Twas clear Gawter had spared no expense when it came to claiming what he deemed was his, even if, once he'd won Rose, he might well kill her. And when he came for the man who'd slain his knights and delayed Rose's capture, he'd come with an army. Blade, for all his amazing prowess with a sword, was no match for an entire company of knights.

The dark mistrust clouding his eyes chilled her. He was right. He deserved an answer. But she refused to tell her handsome champion anything that would get him killed.

"I can't tell ye," she said. "I'm sworn to silence." In a way, 'twas true. Gawter *had* threatened to kill her if she spoke of his perfidy.

Her answer didn't satisfy him, and she wished she could tell him more.

"Please, ye must believe me," she beseeched him. "I would ne'er play ye false."

The ice in his gaze thawed marginally, but doubt yet shadowed his eyes. She gulped. Dared she bare her heart to him? Dared she reveal her soul?

"I'd ne'er betray ye." She licked her lip and took a steadying breath. "I love ye."

Surprise flickered in his eyes, and for a breathless moment, she thought he was going to respond in kind. But uncertainty prevented him. He obviously needed convincing.

So with the impetuous nature she was born to, she grasped his linen shirt, leaned forward, and placed a gentle kiss upon his mouth.

He was unmoved at first, cautious, cool. But as her mouth lingered, she felt his resolve soften. Slowly he yielded to the affectionate brush of her lips, finally answering her with tender kisses of his own.

Her pulse hastened as his fingers cupped her face. She experienced again the blissful abandon of his embrace. The future, the past had no meaning. She existed in the moment, kissing the man she loved with all her heart and wishing that moment could last forever.

She threaded her fingers through his hair and circled her thumb around his ear. His shudder sent a vibration of desire through her as well. The hot current sang up through her belly, tightening her breasts, and down to awaken the place between her thighs. Her body responded with lightning haste, as if it recalled quite well the pleasure this man had offered before—pleasure that, once remembered, she hungered for with undeniable greed.

His breath steamed against her skin, and she shivered lustily as he kissed his way down her throat. His fingers couldn't unlace her surcoat fast enough, and once the garment dropped over her shoulders, once her breasts lay bare, he wasted no time in sampling their bounty.

Rose gasped as his mouth opened to take in one straining nipple. She swooned as his tongue swirled about her flesh, bathing, sucking, leaving a trail of fiery sparks wherever it roamed.

And then—God forgive her—she wondered what his lips would feel like...down there.

'Twas as if he spied upon her thoughts. No sooner had she blushed to imagine such a thing than he swept her up from the floor, depositing her on the bed, and, lifting her skirts and parting her legs, proceeded to kiss his way up along the inside of her thigh.

Her fingers tangled in the linens, and her face felt afire. Surely he didn't intend to do such a thing. And yet he proceeded inexorably toward that spot of her innermost craving. She writhed in protest even while her moans urged him on. She grasped his shoulders with hands that simultaneously pushed him away and held on desperately. And still he advanced.

His hair brushed with tantalizing softness between her legs as he grew closer and closer to her most secret place, and she tensed, fighting the guilty desire to hide herself from him.

He paused. "Ye don't desire this?" he murmured huskily.

She could not look at him. "Aye, but..."

"'Tis my desire as well," he assured her, running the back of his hand delicately over her woman's curls.

She quivered and made no more protest, though her mind fought against the idea like a fledgling resisting flight. But like the bird, when she felt Blade's breath upon her woman's parts, when he parted her nether lips and lay his warm, wet tongue upon her flesh, she leaped to soar with all the natural grace with which her sex was endowed.

Like the fledgling's first flight, 'twas brief. His lips and tongue, devouring her in expert mouthfuls, led her to such heights so quickly she could scarcely catch her breath. He suckled her, drawing her up and up until she reached the top of her ascent, suspended high above the world.

She felt delirious, the way she had when she was twelve summers old, climbing the crumbling tower of the old Fernie keep to teeter on the high parapet wall, a gust of wind away from toppling to the stones below, wavering breathlessly between flying and falling. She clutched the linens ferociously.

And then she crested the heavens and dove toward the earth. She cried out with the glory of the sensation, her head thrashing across the pallet. Her nails dug into the straw mattress, and her legs... She had no idea what her legs did, but she feared she'd crush Blade with her convulsions.

After her descent, after her lungs filled with air again and her pulse began to slow, she could finally face her delectable assailant.

To her relief, he didn't appear in the least reviled. Instead, his eyes were smokier than before, riddled with lust so transparent that her heart tripped, and her passions began, impossibly, to rise again.

She wanted him. But this time she wished to give him pleasure. She wished to witness him ride the wind and kiss the stars. She wished to see his brow furrow in ecstasy. To hear his groans of passion and to feel the shudders rack his body. Aye, she wanted him now.

He moved upwards over her, smoothing her hair back from her sweaty forehead with his thumb. His nostrils flared, and she could see a vein pulsing heavily in his throat.

"Ye're like ambrosia on my tongue," he murmured.

She closed her eyes and swallowed hard. His words ignited her desire. She grabbed the edges of his shirt and rolled over, hauling him with her until he lay flat on his back and she sat atop him.

He raised his hands in mute surrender, as if he wasn't certain what she might do to him. And something about that uncertainty excited her. He was hers now. She could do whatever she wanted with him. If only she knew what to do.

Kissing. He liked kissing. She bent toward him, and her hair tumbled into his face. Withdrawing, she tucked her tresses behind her ear and tried again. His lips met hers, and this time they tasted of musk. Ambrosia, he'd said. Perhaps not, but 'twas not unpleasant. She wondered if he tasted the same...down there. She wondered if she had the courage to find out.

Almost as if he heard her pondering, that part of him swelled against her where she straddled him, a blatant invitation. She remembered how it had felt that night Blade had placed her palm there. Still kissing him, she moved one hand over his shoulder and down along his ribs, turning it to cross his belly and capture the beast rising within his chausses.

He gasped against her mouth, and she felt a heady surge at what she'd wrought. Intoxicated by power, she stroked his iron length to watch him suck the breath hard between his teeth. She pressed him firmly through his taut braies, and his eyes squeezed shut as if she tortured him. But she had no fear of hurting him.

He'd stop her if she did. And after all, it had been the same for her—an agony of pleasure.

But she yearned to bring him succor. And so she broke off her kisses and sat back upon his thighs, plucking at the points of his braies.

He raised his head and caught her wrist. "Ye need not," he rasped.

She smiled slyly down. "Ah, but I do," she breathed.

He let go of her then and collapsed back on the pallet. When she'd untied the points, she unfolded his braies, and his proud staff jutted free. For a moment, only a moment, she hesitated. 'Twas an imposing thing and unfamiliar. How a woman's frail body could encompass such a thing, she couldn't fathom.

But Rose of Averlaigh had never been afraid of anything. And so she dauntlessly laced her fingers through the intriguing nest of black curls at the base and slowly worked her way along the thick pillar of muscle that pulsed when she touched it. 'Twas amazingly soft, like velvet.

She embraced him with her palm, and he groaned. Glancing up, she saw he'd cast his arm over his face while his other fist gripped the bedclothes with white-knuckled force.

"Nae," she bid him. "Don't hide away. I want to see your pleasure."

He complied, and the sweet suffering she glimpsed in his face almost convinced her to forsake her maidenhood, mate with him, and be done with it. But the road to her fulfillment had been fraught with such pained pleasure, and so it must be for him.

She longed to take him to the wondrous place he'd shown her. But she knew so little. Their bodies were so different. She didn't know where to begin.

He must have sensed her uncertainty.

"Give me your hand," he directed.

She did so, and he bathed her palm thoroughly with his tongue, then guided her hand downward again. He sucked in sharply as he folded her palm about his staff. Encompassing her hand in his own, he slowly slid her hand up and down along his length in a smooth, sensual rhythm.

"Aye," he breathed, and she watched his face as it beamed in a sort of blissful wonder. "Aye."

His grip grew firmer by degrees and more rapid, his breathing harsher, his expression more intense. Rose felt a wave of empathic exhilaration, reveling in what the mere touch of her hand could wreak.

And then a great shudder rocked him, and with a mighty roar, he arched deep into her hand, exploding with milky nectar. 'Twas miraculous and empowering and bonding, and Rose was left speechless by the intimacy of what they'd shared.

Afterward, Blade gathered her against his chest. His heart pounded like an armorer's hammer, and he covered her face with so many grateful kisses that she was moved to laughter.

"Ah, Rose," he sighed, a weary smile of pleasure lighting his face. "I wish this moment would never end."

And in a small, reckless corner of her spinning mind, Rose wondered if it might not be so.

"Why not?" she asked rashly. "Why don't we run away together, ye and me, right this moment? Ye've said ye have no ties. What difference will it make if we ne'er go to St. Andrews?"

He chuckled and squeezed her tighter. "No one would miss *me*. But I fear someone may notice ye gone, lass."

They might notice, she decided, but they'd hardly care. Sir Gawter wished her dead. To his mind, she *would* be. Her mother wouldn't grieve her absence. And as for her fostering family, she'd send word to them that she was safe and content.

She *would* be content. She didn't care who Blade was, what he'd done. Together, they could fight the demons of his past and face a lifetime of happiness.

"We could say I was killed by my abductors," she suggested.

He smiled, obviously not taking her seriously. "What about your falcon?" Blade murmured.

Rose frowned.

"And my Wil?" he added.

She sighed and snuggled against Blade's comforting shoulder. She'd realized 'twas only a childish wish. Rose was a grown woman now with obligations and loyalties. She knew that. She couldn't run away from duty. Nae, as heavenly as 'twas to reside here in a landscape of dreams, Rose and Blade lived in a world of honor.

And so, after they floated awhile in a haze of drowsy euphoria, they made preparations to leave.

'Twas a hard ride for the steed, for it had to carry the both of them a long distance to catch up with the rest of the pilgrims. But the sturdy creature managed, and by late afternoon, they loped up behind a familiar group of motley travelers, at their aft a crop-haired knight bearing a falcon.

# Chapter 15

Blade thought Wilham would never stop yammering, demanding to know every detail of Blade's adventures. But at least it kept his thoughts off of Rose, who was busy fussing over her bright-eyed bird and endlessly assuring Tildy that she was, on the whole, unharmed.

In Blade's absence, it seemed Wilham had done more than his share of investigation into possible suspects for the impending crime. As they continued along the road to Cameron, Wilham whipped a scrap of parchment from his pouch upon which he'd scribbled in charcoal the initials of all the pilgrims. Beside each were notes only he could decipher, so he enlightened Blade as to what he'd uncovered.

"First, Father Peter," he confided. "As ye know, the priest talked o' retirin' from pilgrimage after this trip to St. Andrews."

At Blade's blank stare, Wilham leaned in conspiratorially. "What better way to insure he lives well the rest o' his days than to commit one highly lucrative sin, a sin o' which no one would ever suspect him?"

"Ye think the priest is bein' paid to kill the lad?" Blade asked in disbelief.

"Maybe."

"'Tis possible." He frowned. "Who else is on your list?"

Wilham cleared his throat and scanned the page. "Simon the palmer. I don't have to tell ye about his exploits. Splinters o' the True Cross. Holy Water. The man makes a fortune sellin' relics. He'd pass off his own mother's bones as a saint's if 'twould earn him sixpence." Wilham rattled the parchment importantly. "I heard him tell the goldsmith that he was lookin' forward to collectin' a sizable sum for a certain valuable skeleton in St. Andrews."

"And?"

"Valuable skeleton? Archibald o' Laichloan's perhaps?"

'Twas a grim possibility, but it didn't make sense to Blade. "Why would Simon bother with the skeleton of a laird's son when he could just as easily collect the bones of a vagrant?"

"He may have his reasons," Wilham said. "Let's see, where were we? Ah, Jacob the goldsmith. It seems his dalliance with Lettie has worn on him. Brigit the widow confided in me that—"

"She confided in ye?"

Wilham shrugged. "Women trust me. I have an honest face. Anyway, Brigit said she was considerin' takin' up with Jacob if she could get Lettie out o' the way. But Lettie would have none of it. She insisted Jacob would never leave her, because—in her words—their bond went deeper than anyone could guess." He repeated pointedly, "Deeper than anyone could guess."

Murder made strange bedfellows and deep bonds. Blade had wondered all along if the guilty plotters might be the goldsmith and his mistress. They obviously had a history together, and despite the lack of a clear motive, 'twasn't hard to imagine the stealthy pair skulking about on murderous business.

"Unfortunately," Wilham said with a sigh, "all that went awry when Jacob indeed took up with Brigit."

Blade arched a brow in surprise.

"Aye," Wilham asserted, "since yesterday. Lettie is all forlorn now, weepin' and moanin', and Brigit's fawnin' on the rich old dotard like he's offered her her weight in gold."

So vanished that theory.

"Now here's somethin' very interestin'," Wilham continued, tapping a finger on the parchment. "Mary and Ivy—"

"Mary and Ivy?"

"The nuns. They've been seen by the scholars to engage in rather questionable whisperin's."

"Wilham, they're nuns. Nuns always...whisper."

"Ah, but do they quarrel so with one another? And when their quarrel's ended, do they repair it with a kiss?"

"A kiss?"

"A kiss."

"They *are* sisters."

"Are they? Did anyone ask?"

"They have to be sisters." But Blade didn't know it to be true. 'Twas only that they looked so much alike.

"And if they're not sisters, then what?"

Blade grimaced. "Good friends?"

"*Very* good friends, by the look of that kiss." Wilham wiggled his eyebrows suggestively. "They may be brides o' Christ, but it looks like they may be dallyin' with Sappho."

That didn't surprise Blade. He suspected that nuns, pledged to a life of chastity, found affection where they could.

"Another interestin' point," Wilham said. "They mentioned bathin' in Loch Walton."

"Walton's not far from Laichloan."

"Aye, which means they may know Archibald."

Blade glanced ahead at the line of pilgrims. The nuns walked in worshipful obedience behind the priest.

"What if the lad discovered their secret?" Wilham suggested. "What if Archibald saw them...bathin' together? What if he threatened to reveal their sin to his father?"

"Laird John?" Blade scoffed. "I doubt he has much interest in condemnin' a pair of errant nuns. He has a manor full of errant daughters."

"True." But Wilham wasn't discouraged. He apparently had ample suspects left on his list. "Very well, let's consider the scholars and the chinks in their particular armor. Thomas has a penchant for fabricatin' tales. Ye missed his story last night, by the way, a fascinatin' account of a pair o' willin' virgins he met on his travels to the Orient."

Blade shook his head. "Thomas? The lad is scarcely old enough to have traveled to the Orient, and the last thing he'd be likely to find there is a willin' virgin."

"Agreed, but that's my point. Ye see, accordin' to Bryan, Thomas considers it a matter o' pride that he can concoct a convincin' lie on the spot."

"Accordin' to Bryan."

"Accordin' to Bryan, whom..." Wilham scanned his notes. "Thomas says is unnaturally infatuated with women."

"Unnaturally?"

"He speaks o' swivin', mornin', noon, and night—who has slept with whom, what he saw the stable lad perform upon the milkmaid, whom he'd like to bed. Daniel concurs, though he hastens to add that Bryan rarely deigns to engage in such sport himself."

"Daniel concurs." 'Twas beginning to sound like rumor upon rumor, none of them grounded in fact.

"As for Daniel, Bryan speaks o' his gamblin' habits with great disdain. Apparently, he cannot resist the lure of a wager. He even has five shillin's ridin' on which o' the three o' them will first find an honest woman for wife."

Blade lifted a skeptical brow.

"I know," Wilham interjected. "'Tis a hopeless wager."

"So what leads ye to believe the scholars might be plannin' Archibald's murder?"

Wilham smugly tapped his head. "Ah, 'tis about a woman." He drew himself up proudly over what he deemed the clever workings of his mind. "What if Bryan loves Archibald's betrothed, but cannot have her? Daniel has wagered that Thomas cannot win the wench for Bryan, and Thomas, an expert at deception, plans to do away with Archibald, lie about it, gain Bryan his beloved, and collect his winnin's."

Blade could only stare at Wilham. 'Twas the most ridiculous, convoluted scheme he'd ever heard. He told him so.

"Listen, Blade," Wilham hissed, nettled. "While ye were off rescuin' your damsel in distress, I was here gatherin' important information. If ye're goin' to—"

"Fine." 'Twas obvious Wilham had gone to a great deal of trouble. But without the balance of Blade's practical nature, Blade feared that perhaps Wilham's imagination had been given too free rein. "Go on."

Wilham sniffed. "Fulk the butcher and Drogo the cook—the ideal recipe for murder." He smirked at his own jest. "Well, I said it before. The butcher makes the perfect axe man when it comes to disposin' of a body, and the cook... Well, suffice it to say one should never ask exactly what goes into haggis."

"Their motive?"

"I'm still workin' on that." Wilham consulted his list again. "On to the tanners," he decided. "Ivo and Odo, ever brewin' trouble, ever lurkin' about. Well, I got them drunk last night and—"

"Got them drunk? They're *always* drunk."

"Be that as it may, when I questioned them about their tannin' trade, they loosened their tongues quickly enough to boast about the great noblemen who'd commissioned their work."

"Laichloan?" Blade guessed.

"The same. And," he said, glancing about to insure no one overheard him, "they grumbled that he had yet to pay them."

Blade nodded. Indeed, the pair of brutes might scheme to hold Archibald hostage for payment. But murder?

"Then there's the Highland woman," Wilham announced. "What is she doin' so far from her home?"

"She's a merchant." He shrugged. "Merchants travel."

But Wilham intervened. "I'll tell ye what I think. I think she may be travelin' under an assumed name. Laird John was at the Borders fightin' last year. Remember his boasts of oustin' the

Kerrs from their stronghold?" Wilham nodded smugly. "I think this Tildy may be a Kerr, and she may be hot for revenge."

The concept was plausible, though 'twas nigh impossible to imagine the stout old woman murdering a young lad. She'd more likely whip his backside with a willow branch and send him to bed without supper.

"Anyone else?" Blade asked. Thus far, no one was without suspicion.

"We know 'tisn't Rose." 'Twas a statement, but he looked askance at Blade.

"'Tisn't Rose."

"And we know 'tisn't either of us." He referred again to his parchment. "That leaves Campbell and Guillot."

"And what have ye discovered about them?"

Wilham frowned. "God's hooks, Blade. I've only had two days. I can't work miracles."

Blade smiled and clapped his friend on the shoulder. "Ye've done well."

Secretly, however, Blade worried. They were too close to the target and too far from finding any real suspects. From Wilham's calculations, any of them might be guilty. And from Blade's point of view, none of them seemed capable.

On the morrow, they'd arrive at St. Andrews. Blade wished he had more time. More time to solve the mystery. And more time to sort out his feelings for Rose.

She'd be lost to him once they reached St. Andrews. She'd continue on to the convent, take the veil, and he'd never see her again.

He told himself she was only a lass like any other, a woman whose charms he could replace. But he didn't believe the lie. And reiterating it in his mind only left a bitter taste in his mouth.

They had only one night left, and he was torn between gently extricating his affections from her in their remaining hours or letting himself be consumed in a great blaze of final reckless passion.

'Twas that indecision that compelled him to drink himself senseless when the pilgrims finally repaired to Cameron House for the night.

The lady of the house was evidently renown for her bounteous supply of Greek wine, for it flowed as freely as water. Everyone imbibed with abandon, and soon the great hall rang with the clamor of drunken fools.

Even Rose's straight back seemed to wobble as Blade lifted drowsy eyes to her, and she burst forth with a giggle over nothing at all.

Wink surveyed her mistress and the other loud revelers with stern disapproval, ruffling her feathers and hunkering in displeasure atop her perch at the back of the hall.

Father Peter's sweating face was as ruddy as his wine, and his belly jiggled every few moments with a hearty laugh.

Simon the palmer kept dozing off, his head bobbing, his mouth hanging open.

Fulk and Drogo sat arm-in-arm, commiserating about their long absence from their women, weeping and repenting of all the unkind things they'd ever said about them.

The scholars made sport of guzzling down their drinks and challenging each other to feats of coordination none of them could accomplish.

Lettie sniveled about her lost love, trying to garner the sympathy of Campbell the soldier, who sank lower and lower toward oblivion with each cup of wine.

Guillot the apprentice couldn't stop hiccoughing.

Brigit and her new paramour, Jacob the goldsmith, fawned over one another with embarrassing display.

The two nuns, likewise, seemed to have cast off their inhibitions, their eyes meeting lasciviously, their hands joined atop the table with more than sisterly fondness.

Tildy snored loudly, her chin perched impossibly atop the hand she'd clapped over the top of her cup.

Wilham, trying to remain solemn so he might discuss the forthcoming crime, managed to twist his tongue around every other syllable so that he wound up snorting at the end of each sentence, which then sent him into gales of laughter.

Only the tanners seemed unaffected by the wine, just their usual drunken selves.

But 'twas Rose, sitting across from Blade, who amused him most. She was so full of languid pleasure that it manifested in a constant smile. Everything appeared to enchant her, from the stumbling feats of the scholars to the lame jests of the priest, from her Highland guardian, dozing atop her wine, to the soldier sliding beneath the table.

Blade watched her take another drink, and their eyes met over the rim of the flagon. She lowered the cup, grinning at him with open delight. Then she hiccoughed, and they shared a chuckle.

God, but she was lovely. He'd never find another woman of such beauty, such grace, a woman of such heart and spirit. His eyes began to well up, and he tore his gaze away, cursing the wine that was turning him into a weeping sot.

"Tales!" Father Peter cried suddenly.

"Tails, gentlemen!" Bryan slurred. The scholars, as one, staggered to their feet, turned about, and bent forward to tug down their breeches, exposing their buttocks and eliciting great laughs from the pilgrims.

"Lady Rose!" the priest shouted.

"Jesu!" Rose's startled eyes widened. "Jesu," she amended, "bless the lady of this house and all her progen-, progen-, all her children."

"'Tis your turn for a story," Father Peter said.

"But I have no..." she began.

Blade nodded at her. "What about the St. Andrews bear?"

Everyone began to chant, "St. Andrews bear" so loudly they woke Tildy, and soon Rose had no choice but to accommodate them.

Blade listened as Rose related the story of a courageous, impetuous, obstinate young lass. As the tale wound around his ears, he couldn't help but fall more deeply in love with the woman that young lass had become. She was compassionate and curious and intrepid. She possessed a heart as tender as a blossom, yet as strong as iron.

And the bear? Blade was like that bear, he realized. He was the savage creature she'd tamed—rough-hewn and surly and wretched. She'd braved his fierce roar and penetrated his tough hide. And now she held his heart in her hands.

How would he ever endure the pain of her leaving?

The story ended, and, despite his melancholy, Blade smiled at her. Rose—her eyes dipping in besotted pleasure—grinned coyly back.

"Ye, sir! Wilham!" the priest commanded. "Ye've interrogated the rest of us mercilessly on this journey. Come bend our ears now with a tale o' your own makin'."

Wilham screwed up his forehead, thinking, but all that came out was a loud burp. Giggles filled the hall. Then he thumped upon the table.

"I have it!" he announced, floundering to his feet to deliver the story. "I shall recount the tragedy," he said dramatically, "o' two brother knights and the woman who came between them."

Blade stiffened. Wilham could not mean to tell that tale. 'Twas his own, for the love of God. If anyone discovered who Blade was...

He prodded Wilham's knee hard beneath the table, to no avail. Maybe his friend was too besotted to feel the jab. But Wilham turned to him then, placing a hand upon his shoulder, and Blade could see in the soft shine of his eyes that he wasn't quite as drunk as he pretended. Wilham knew very well what he was doing, and he didn't intend to stop.

He released Blade then and gestured grandly for the others.

"Not long ago, at Mirkhaugh, not far from where our journey began," he said, "dwelled a laird and a lady of honor, wealth, godliness, and charity. They were loved by their vassals, knight and peasant alike, for they were benevolent and fair to all. And because the laird and lady were well contented with one another, the lady soon grew large with child."

Blade stared at his wine. He wondered if Wilham knew the torture to which he was subjecting him.

"But upon the night o' the child's birth, the stars hung in such disarray that the heir born to the laird possessed a corrupt heart and an evil soul. And though he was coddled and adored and dressed in the finest o' garments, the lad grew to be ungracious and cruel."

Blade tapped his finger upon his cup. The room was silent, as 'twas whenever Wilham related a story, for he was a gifted teller of tales. At Mirkhaugh, all the children gathered about him to hear his lofty adventures.

"But when the lad was five winters old, the lady was blessed with another son, and this one was everythin' her first was not. He was kind and forthright, generous and humble, wise and loyal, courageous and true, just and— "

"Who was this paragon o' virtue?" Blade blurted sardonically, unable to endure so much praise. "Galahad?"

Everyone laughed, but Wilham held his gaze and said solemnly, "He was everythin' a knight should be, even ere he won his spurs."

Wilham's words moved Blade, for he spoke from his heart. And Blade knew that no truer friend walked the earth. If ever they returned to Mirkhaugh...

But Blade couldn't return. And soon he'd be reminded painfully of the reason for that.

"The oldest brother was rightful heir," Wilham continued, "and thus the younger obeyed him in all things, though at times 'twas to his own peril and shame. He endured the ridicule that his jealous siblin' heaped upon him and turned his cheek when his brother's angry fist clouted him. Even when the wicked lad became a malevolent man, rainin' hard blows upon him, still the younger son brooked his brother's punishment in silence.

"But when the villain began to practice his ruthlessness upon others, the young brother could abide no more."

Blade stared at his clasped hands. He sat mutely while Wilham recounted his past attempts to remedy his brother's damage—slipping meat to Morris's starved hounds, mercifully killing a pair of kittens Morris had tortured half to death, freeing a terrified peasant locked in Morris's oak chest.

As Wilham droned on, Blade began to relax. His secret was surely safe, for no one would believe 'twas true—all those small acts of mercy he'd performed nor the unfathomable wickedness of his brother.

Then he caught Rose's eye.

She knew.

He could tell by the grim awe in her face that she knew.

He supposed it should come as no surprise. He'd told her about his brother already, about Morris's cruelty.

But she didn't know the entire story. If Wilham finished the telling, if she heard about his own terrible crime...

He ground his teeth, lowering his eyes to his clenched hands once again. 'Twas better this way, he decided. 'Twould make their parting simpler. She'd be horrified. He'd be ashamed. And they could separate, while the brief moment of happiness they'd shared faded into insignificance.

"When the laird o' the castle died," Wilham continued, "and the time came for the oldest son to take a wife, he wed a young, frail wisp of a lass who bowed her head and trembled when she met him. For a fortnight, he jealously kept her in his bedchamber, and long into the hours of evenin', her plaints and shrieks and weepin' could be heard."

Blade shut his eyes. He could still recall those piteous cries, even years later.

"But none dared cross the man who was now laird. And so the denizens o' the keep kept to the shadows and spoke in fearful whispers, but not a soul braved his chamber door. Until..." Wilham paused for dramatic effect, taking a sip of his wine. "The younger son, one morn, while his brother was out huntin', stole into the room. What he beheld there was too horrifyin' to recount."

Blade could remember every detail with perfect clarity. Julian's naked body, spread and trussed to the bedposts like a hide for tanning, riddled with black and purple and yellow bruises. One eye swollen shut. Her lip split. Her hair matted with blood. Wrists and ankles chafed raw from the ropes. Her mouth bloody, one tooth dangling from its socket. Her breasts scored with the marks of Morris's teeth. The bedclothes stained with blood.

"She was yet alive," Wilham said, "but like everythin' the brute owned, she was maltreated and mutilated almost beyond recognition. The younger son cast his gaze away in shame that his own blood kin had wrought such cruelty upon his bride, and he swore—though God might curse him for the deed—he'd make the devil pay for what he'd done.

"He loosed the gentle lady from the ties that bound her to the bed and clothed her and gave her what succor he could, though he dared not tarry in his brother's chamber for what further shame his presence might bring upon her. Then, armed with his sword and his honor, he left at once to seek vengeance upon her abuser.

"They met in the courtyard, by the full light o' day and before the good folk o' the castle. First they had words, and all who heard were amazed at the power o' the younger son's speech, for never had they heard a man dare to raise his voice against their villainous liege.

"The older brother clouted him across the face for his insolence and drew his sword. The younger son pulled forth his own blade, declarin' that he fought for the honor o' his brother's dishonored wife.

"'Twas a brave deed, for he knew at any moment his cowardly brother might command his knights to slay him outright. But the older brother had hated the younger far too long to give another the pleasure o' killin' him. So they engaged blades, and while a crowd gathered, they battled, nickin' and slashin' and dolin' out minor injury, each to the other, until both knights were covered in blood.

"At last, the younger knight found an advantage and dealt his brother a severe wound, grievous but not mortal, along his flank.

The man fell back, screamin' in outrage and pain, and the youngest son smiled in grim satisfaction. But soon, as he was a knight o' great honor, the pleasure o' revenge was soured by the sight o' his kinsman's blood on his sword, and the younger man, sickened by his own savage violence, turned away to withdraw."

Blade tasted bitterness at the back of his throat, the taste that always came to him when he relived what happened next. Almost as if he were there again, his face flushed with the heat of shame and horror. His breath came in shallow sips, and though he clenched them tightly together, his hands trembled. He couldn't bear to look at Rose.

"But as he turned aside," Wilham said softly, "the crowd gave a great gasp, and he felt of a sudden a deep thrust o' steel in his back. His reflexes like lightnin', he instinctively whipped about and plunged forward in answer with his blade."

Blade's eyes watered, blurring the table before him. Why Wilham had put him through this, he didn't know. 'Twas an anguish beyond endurance.

"His sword found its mark, sinkin' straight and true into his attacker. But, alas, this once, he found 'twas not his brother who'd dealt the treacherous blow. 'Twas not his brother who'd stabbed him in the back. His avengin' blade had pierced and slain..." He paused, and not a whisper broke the stillness. "His brother's ungrateful *wife*."

Wilham waited for the gasps to subside before he continued. "When the young man saw what he had done, he was filled with such self-loathin' and remorse that he fled the castle and his home in disgrace."

The ensuing silence was so complete that Blade could hear his own thudding heartbeat.

"What happened to him?" 'Twas Campbell the soldier.

The hall was as still as death for a long while.

Blade could stand no more of the grim tragedy. "Accordin' to Dante, he's in the seventh circle of Hell," he grumbled.

Some of the pilgrims chuckled, not in amusement, but to lighten the dark mood. Wilham, however, didn't so much as smile, and Rose...Rose looked as if she might weep.

Rose bit back an anguished sob. Her heart ached for the tormented man before her. To have endured such a tragedy...

She longed to rush to Blade's side, take him in her arms, hold his troubled head upon her breast and soothe his damaged spirit. Blade wasn't a felon. 'Twas *he* who'd been wronged. God's eyes! If his sword hadn't slain the woman, Rose would have enjoyed finishing off the thankless wench herself.

Of course, 'twas probably the wine speaking for her—Rose wouldn't kill a spider. Still, a surge of righteous outrage flooded her veins, and she yearned to come to his defense.

As soon as the company adjourned, she did just that. The world spun as she stood up, the wine dizzying her. But she hurried to his side before he could leave, tripping at the last moment to collide with him. He managed to keep them both upright, though he, too, reeled slightly from the drink.

"Oh, Blade," she gushed, peering up into his sad, beautiful eyes, unmindful of the pilgrims around her. "'Twasn't your fault. Ye couldn't know—"

His sharp look quelled her. What had she said? Why was he frowning?

He sighed, then took her by the elbow and ushered her nonchalantly outside to the pleasance garden, where the cool air sobered her somewhat. By the faint light of the crescent moon, she could make out the silhouettes of the fruit trees and rosebushes and beds of flowers. She breathed in a deep breath of night, and he turned her toward him.

"Ye must tell no one," he bid her.

"Tell no one what?" Her lids felt heavy, but she managed to raise them enough to stare at his delectable mouth.

"Who I am."

"The young brother in the story."

"Aye, but I beg ye, say nothin'."

"Why?"

He cast his gaze upon the stepping stones and said tightly, "'Tis my shame to bear, and I'd bear it in secret."

She leaned forward then, grasping his doublet and gazing into his eyes, willing him to understand. He staggered back a step, against the stone wall of the garden.

"Nae," she said, "'tisn't your shame at all. Ye're not to blame."

His voice was as bitter as rue. "'Twas my blade that killed her."

Overwhelmed with compassion, she tried to lend him comfort, encircling his neck with her arms. "No one could blame ye for that. 'Twas an honest mistake."

She saw his mouth working, saw anger flash across his face.

"I'm a seasoned knight," he growled. "I should have seen her. I should never have thrust..."

She felt his tension, sensed his self-hate, and she yearned to bind his wounds, to give him back his honor. Pity didn't move him. Perhaps rage would.

"Listen to me," she commanded fiercely. "'Twas that bloody mewlin' milksop's fault."

He blinked, startled by her oath. But she was angry, and when she was angry as well as drunk, her tongue wagged with a will of its own.

"What kind o' woman would lash out at the man who saved her from such a beast?"

"'Twasn't her fault," he argued. "She was little more than a child. She couldn't have known—"

"Satan's ballocks! Even a hound doesn't bite the hand that feeds it."

"She was only shieldin' her husband," he insisted angrily, "the man she swore to honor."

"Then she was a bloody halfwit!" Rose charged. "And not worthy o' your saving her."

"Ye weren't there!" he hissed, his temper flaring. "Ye wouldn't know."

"Nae, but I know *ye*!" she cried, grasping the back of his head and commanding his gaze. "And I know ye have more honor in your thumbnail than that woman had in her entire wretched body."

Something altered in him then, an infinitesimal surrender in his eyes, as if he wanted to believe her.

"Aye," she whispered. "Aye." Her eyes were drawn to his mouth, and she moved her hands forward until she cupped his face.

Their kiss was as natural as the gentle sweep of the night wind. Their mouths—hot with ire, soft with liquor—met and mingled and mended all their harsh words. Rose felt the need in his kiss, not just lust this time, but something more profound, the need for redemption, the need to purify himself in her soul.

Maybe 'twas the fresh breeze or the haze of drink or the desperation she felt, knowing 'twas their last night before St. Andrews, but she suddenly longed to give herself to him completely, to make this eve momentous and memorable and eternal. On the morrow she could repent. On the morrow she could yield to the church. But tonight she wished to render unto Blade the one thing that was hers alone to give, to grant him absolution.

She broke from the kiss long enough to murmur against his lips, "Lie with me."

He stilled.

"Lie with me, Blade." She circled a finger around his ear. "Please."

His voice was gruff, ragged. "Ye're besotted."

"That may be, but I have enough o' my wits about me."

"Not if ye wish to bed a felon."

"Ye're not a felon. Ye're a gentleman. And a hero. And a knight who's the very model o' chivalry." She swallowed. "And ye're the man I love with all my heart."

He cradled her face in one hand and brushed his thumb across her lips. "What o' the convent? What o'—"

"I don't want to think about the convent. I don't want to think about the morrow, and the next day, and the years to come, and the rest o' my life. I want to savor this moment."

She tried to kiss him again, but he held her away, wavering uncertainly, searching her face as if he sought some important truth there.

Then at last, to her great relief, he made his decision. He pulled her into his arms and swooped down upon her mouth with all the desperation of a condemned man. He kissed her till she was breathless, till her heart thrummed like a timbrel, till the air no longer chilled her skin.

The taste of his lips was more intoxicating than the wine, and she tilted her head to delve her tongue further into the warm recesses of his mouth.

Soon she found her body straining toward him of its own volition. Her arms entwined about his neck, her breasts swelled against his broad chest, and she pressed her hips wantonly against his muscular thigh. She wove eager fingers through his hair, moaning softly as she strove to get closer.

She plucked at his doublet, trying to access the warm flesh beneath, but her untrained fingers were frustrated by the garment. He had no such difficulty. He removed the thing with ease, leaving only linen beneath. She reached under his shirt to run the flat of her palm across his bare chest, savoring the supple curve of muscle there. He gasped and clasped her roving hand against his breast.

But she wanted more of his flesh, more of his warmth. She sank before him, letting her fingers slide over his waist to the top of his braies. Kneeling, she brushed her hand over the hard bulge that throbbed at her touch, then pressed her cheek against him, relishing the groan of desire coming from deep within his throat.

Suddenly he hauled her back up, then swept her off of her feet into his arms. He carried her to a bed of clover among the flowers and, spreading out his discarded doublet, lay her down atop it, among the sweet-scented grass and blossoms.

257

For a moment, he only looked at her, his eyes drifting over every feature of her body. Then his hands repeated the course, tracing the line of her brow, sweeping over her lips, rounding her shoulder, cupping her breast, caressing her waist, dragging across her hip and along her thigh, brushing her knee and ankle.

"Ye're certain?" he murmured.

God, aye! she wanted to shout, but—floating beyond words—she nodded instead.

Slowly, carefully, as if she were some fragile treasure of carved ivory wrapped in silk, he stripped her clothing from her, piece by piece. She shivered more from his adoring perusal than the night air, but he soon remedied the chill by removing his own garments and stretching out atop her.

She gasped. Everywhere their flesh touched melted together like copper and iron in a crucible. The heat of his body multiplied hers. 'Twas heaven to be surrounded by so much warm skin, and she moved restlessly beneath him, still aching to be closer.

"Ah, Rose," he sighed. "Ye're so sweet, lass. So temptin'."

He kissed her again, and she could feel his trembling restraint as his muscular lance swelled against her, prodding, needing.

"Closer," she breathed.

Her nipples grazed his chest, and her hips ground up against that questing part of him. She slid her hands across the vast expanse of his back, over a rough scar that made him spasm momentarily. It must be the place where the woman had stabbed him, she decided. She wished she could smooth it away, erase all traces of it from his body and his memory.

He separated briefly from her to place his hand between their bodies, running his fingers through the damp patch of her woman's hair until he found the tender flesh within. She bucked upward against his palm, her craving for his touch compelling her to lose control.

Her breath came in gulps, and her blood rushed in her ears.

"Please, now!" she cried.

He shuddered, and his voice was rough. "'Twill prick ye sorely."

She wanted no warnings. No regret. No hesitation. She wanted only him.

"I don't care. Take me now," she pleaded.

"Ye're certain?"

"Aye."

"Forgive me," he whispered, then slowly pushed a finger into her, easing the way for his entry.

Rose knew a moment of doubt. Already her flesh was taut about his finger, and though the intrusion felt so right, so perfect, what she begged for was far larger. Surely 'twould split her in two.

But she'd come thus far. And every mother on earth, save the Virgin Mary, had survived the ordeal. She didn't wish to die with her maidenhead untried. And, Lord, she wanted to go to that place again, where time hung silent and the sky exploded in a burst of stars.

"Take me," she entreated again.

What nudged at her was softer than his finger, and when he pressed into her the first bit, sucking a hard breath between his clenched teeth, 'twas far from painful.

"Forgive me," he breathed again.

Then he strove forward, and she felt her flesh tear. God forgive her, she cried out with the pain and tried to squirm away, for the sting was like the cut of a knife. But he was patient. He held her still, whispering soothing words against her hair, and slowly, gradually, her body stretched to receive him. Her eyes watered, but when he withdrew, it didn't hurt as much. He plunged slowly into her once more, and this time the burn decreased to a dull ache. Soon there was no pain at all, only a deep, intriguing sense of fullness as he engaged her completely.

He kissed away the moisture along her lashes and smoothed the furrow from her brow. Far sooner than she expected, she was enveloped in a haze of desire again, for their joining seemed the perfect culmination of passion.

"Ah, God," he gasped, his body shivering against her. "I can't..."

He seemed overwhelmed by sensation, which pitched her own lust even higher. And still, as impossible as 'twas, she yearned to be closer, to encompass him and be encompassed. She enfolded his broad shoulders in her arms and wrapped her legs about his thrusting hips, reveling in the complete penetration.

"Ah, Blade," she sighed.

"So sweet..." he panted. "So warm...ah, God...not yet..."

She sensed him holding himself back while the caress of his flesh against her coaxed her to new heights. Her body glowed, sated yet unsated, with a frenzy that continued to climb until her control utterly dissolved and at last she soared wildly up like a rogue falcon. On the brink of a dive, she hovered—still, silent— her breath a slow inhalation that swelled her lungs till she thought they would burst. And then she plummeted earthward with shuddering speed, fearlessly plunging into the soul- shattering depths of release.

An instant later, he followed where she led, groaning and arching as spasms rocked him along the long descent. Then he sheathed himself one final time within her, clasping her close to his chest as if he'd never let her go. Their gasps and ragged whispers swirled together across the silent night as their tremors subsided.

"Hold me," she breathed. "Hold me fore'er."

He kissed her forehead, then each eye, and enfolded his arms beneath her, lifting her into his embrace. They stayed like that for a long while, their breath slowing, the air cooling about them, and Rose knew she'd never been happier. Never *be* happier.

"Fore'er," he agreed.

And they both pretended to believe the lie.

# Chapter 16

Blade's head throbbed when he awoke the next morn in the men's chamber to an eye-stabbing knife of brilliant sunlight. Apparently, by the grumbling around him, he wasn't the only one paying the price of overindulgence in Greek wine. The mood was surly amongst all the pilgrims as they bestirred themselves from sleep, smacking wine-sour mouths and wandering toward the great hall in search of something to ease their dry throats.

But everything changed when he spotted Rose. Groggily descending the steps, he caught a glimpse of her across the hall. With her falcon on her arm, she came in from the outdoors, smiling and flushed and breathless from her morning adventures. Her skirts were dirtied at the hem, but she'd tucked a red rose behind one ear, and he would have sworn she was haloed in sunshine.

Suddenly Blade didn't care about his aching head. Just looking at her set his heart to pounding, for he knew what resided beneath her lush gown of red velvet. And his body remembered well their coupling. Even now his loins stirred at the memory of her silken tresses, her supple breasts, her yielding flesh. She truly was a lovely woman. She'd make a beautiful bride.

For someone else.

Someone deserving. Someone decent. Someone whose hands weren't bound by shackles, whose heart wasn't bound by shame.

His chest was wrenched with pain as she caught his eye, flashing him a smile of pure adoration. At least, he consoled himself, she had no regrets about what they'd done. But then maybe she expected him to sue for her hand now, to save her from the convent by offering her marriage.

That he couldn't do. He wouldn't ask her to live as he did— homeless, nameless, a wandering sword-for-hire. 'Twas no life for a titled lady.

She wouldn't understand. Her heart would be broken. But one day she'd come to realize that he'd done what was best. One day she'd find a handsome nobleman to carry her off on his white steed, to a castle with a mews the size of the king's stable. And maybe...maybe she'd remember him.

He shrugged off his melancholy mood and descended the last step. Today was their final day together. He'd be damned if he'd spoil it for her.

'Twas Wilham who reminded him that they had another mission today. 'Twas the day of reckoning, and they were no closer to discovering Archibald's assassins. And so he vowed, reluctantly, to intensify his efforts on that score.

It occurred to him, as they trod the final steps toward St. Andrews, that nine days together were long enough to make enemies of most any men, and the pilgrims were no exception. Despite the joy that should have heralded their approach to the celebrated city, the travelers bickered amongst themselves. The earliness of the hour and the dank mist that lurked over the landscape served to hang a pall over the entire company.

The scholars moaned about their aching heads. The tanners groused over the lack of ale in holy shrines. Lettie and Brigit pecked like hens at one another, and Jacob rolled his eyes in weary disgust. Campbell grew sullen and withdrawn, confounding Guillot, who moped beside him. Drogo and Fulk argued over some insult one had given the other at supper. The two nuns walked in frosty silence, and Blade swore he saw one of them clout the other. Simon was his usual morose self, and Tildy, normally animated, only muttered about her weary old bones and the damp weather. Even Father Peter looked worn about the fringe, and 'twas easy to believe that 'twould indeed be his last pilgrimage.

Rose seemed the only stream of sunshine on the gloomy day, and though it frayed Blade's composure, he finally screwed up enough courage to speak with her.

He caught up with her and asked conversationally, "Ye know well the shrine at St. Andrews?"

She brightened at his appearance. "Aye."

Suddenly her beauty, her adoring eyes, the memory of the intimacy they had shared, left him at a loss for words, like a peasant meeting the king. "'Tis...wondrous."

She let her hand drop beside his and, with clandestine grace, ran a finger along his palm. "'Tis impressive, I suppose." Her eyes were trained on the path ahead, but her eyelids dipped sensuously as she told him, "Last night...was wondrous."

He swallowed. Aye, 'twas. More wondrous than a dozen St. Andrews. Last night would haunt him the rest of his days.

"Ye know," she murmured low, "I meant what I said." She glanced up at him, whispering, "I love ye, Blade, with all my heart."

Her tender words were like a welcome dagger in his chest, akin to the bittersweet, savage thrust he'd dealt her last night. But, God forgive him, he couldn't answer in kind. To do so would be careless, irresponsible, foolish. Yet words spilled from his lips unwilled. "I'll never forget ye."

"Nor I ye."

He furrowed his brow, weighted with guilt. "What I said last night...about fore'er..."

"I know," she said, and he could discern clearly now the hint of melancholy at the back of her eyes, the sadness that had likely been there all along, the sorrow she'd buried under sunny smiles and gay laughter. "I know. But we have today. And I've no regrets."

Her brave face made him feel all the worse, as if his own heart might break. 'Twas absurd. His heart had been shattered years ago. Surely there was nothing left to wound.

"There 'tis!" someone shouted suddenly, and the rest of the pilgrims joined in, their spirits revived.

A few miles hence, rising above the mist, stood the great twin spires of St. Andrews. For some, like Father Peter and Simon the palmer, 'twould mean another badge on their cloak or another coin in their purse. For some, like Campbell and Guillot, the cathedral represented penance and forgiveness. For many, 'twas simply the end of a colorful journey. For Rose, it meant a turn in her life's path. And for Blade? What he'd almost believed might be his last chance for redemption he now looked upon with dread. Looming above the city ahead was the end of hope.

As planned, they'd arrived on the Sabbath, and they now entered the city as the bells began tolling the call to Mass. The streets soon flooded with worshippers—citizens and pilgrims, nobles and servants, merchants in robes of brocade and polished gems, beggars in grimy tatters, penitents in sackcloth—all swarming toward the cathedral.

Even Rose, clutching tightly to her falcon, appeared to be carried along by the throng at a whim, like a blossom on a swirling stream. But she seemed excited, not frightened, and she must have read his concern, for as they drifted apart, she laughed and sent him a merry promise across the crowd. "After Mass!"

Blade cast a backward glance toward Wilham, who shrugged as he tried to keep an eye on the members of their company. As much as Blade wanted to stay with Rose, he had a murder to prevent.

At the summit of the grand cathedral, as the horde pressed into the sanctuary, Blade struggled to keep sight of everyone in the teeming chaos of velvet and broadcloth, perfume and sweat, laughter and scolding.

The St. Andrews residents swept forward with rude haste past the vast arches of the cathedral, seeking the spots closest to God, while visitors paused in hushed reverence at the door. Blade and Wilham hovered over their flock like anxious shepherds. But the pilgrims, tired of one another's company, were more than willing to sever ties, and Blade and Wilham were forced to separate to maintain surveillance.

Candles filled the sanctuary with golden light, and Blade remembered when he'd first seen the cathedral as a lad. St. Andrews, with its vaulting arches and stained glass windows gleaming like jewels, its gilded altar and the sweet smoke drifting like celestial spirits past the pillars, had seemed like heaven. Now, he realized, something had been missing. An angel.

He glanced over his shoulder. There she was now, standing with her falcon near to the door, her reverent face illuminated by candlelight, as beautiful as a saint.

Spiced incense wafted through the air, quieting the worshippers, and Blade directed his attention forward again. The altar seemed a mile away. The figures at the fore in rich-colored copes looked as small as finches. And between Blade and those figures swam a sea of people—two of whom, despite the sanctity of their surroundings, plotted murder. He scowled, scanning the crowd, wondering if he faced an impossible task.

He spotted Ivo and Odo behind a pillar. They'd smuggled in a wineskin and were passing it back and forth.

Fulk was easy to find, for he towered over the congregation. Drogo stood beside him, and they both looked awestruck by their surroundings.

The sister nuns, despite the hushed reverence of St. Andrews, were bickering again at the back wall of the cathedral.

The Highland woman had planted herself in the midst of some well-dressed nobles and was scrutinizing them from head to toe, almost like a cutpurse sizing up victims. Blade narrowed his gaze as she surreptitiously fondled the fabric of first one lady's surcoat, then a gentleman's cloak, and concluded she was only examining the quality of their garments.

Father Peter had cheerfully bullied his way to the front of the sanctuary, and Simon had used the priest's considerable girth to clear the way.

He couldn't locate the others. Where were Jacob and his two quarreling mistresses, Lettie and Brigit? Campbell and Guillot? The three scholars?

Were any of them brazen enough to commit murder in a sanctuary during Mass? Blade eyed the arch above him, wishing he could survey the congregation from that superior vantage point.

Mass began, and Blade shot one last uneasy glance toward Wilham, who was stationed at the opposing arch. Then he frowned. Wilham was gesturing emphatically, stabbing a finger toward the back of the cathedral. Blade cast a wary look over his shoulder. There was nothing he hadn't seen before. Rose was near the door, and the two nuns were still speaking in furious whispers.

He shrugged at Wilham.

Wilham gestured again, more forcefully, toward the nuns.

Why Wilham was fascinated with the squabbling pair, Blade didn't know, but he obliged him, turning to watch them again.

Ivy's arms were crossed over her bosom, and she turned her back on Mary. Mary kicked Ivy in the shin, making the sister hop in silent pain. Then, for good measure, Mary elbowed her in the ribs.

Blade sighed in impatience and glowered at Wilham. Now was not the time to indulge in juvenile spectacles, no matter how entertaining.

Wilham frowned back and began making his way toward Blade. Meanwhile, Blade caught sight of Guillot. The lad stood beside one of the pillars, with tears in his eyes and his hand on the shoulder of Campbell, who knelt on the stones beside him. Neither seemed of a mind to commit murder.

"Did ye see?" Wilham whispered urgently, coming up beside him and seizing his arm.

"See what?"

"The nuns."

"Wilham, we're not here to—"

"Look!"

He glared down at his arm until Wilham released it, then turned to observe the nuns again.

Ivy bit out some invective to Mary. Mary's mouth opened to a shocked "O." Then Mary landed a healthy smack across Ivy's face, skewing the nun's wimple sideways.

Blade shook his head.

"Keep watchin'," Wilham urged.

Ivy grimaced and ducked from the blows as Mary continued to slap at her, then snagged Ivy's wimple with a vengeance.

"Wilham," Blade said under his breath, "while ye're watchin' the wrestlin' match, the murderers are—"

Mary suddenly tore Ivy's wimple off and dropped it on the floor.

Blade couldn't have been more astonished if a cart had run him over. It couldn't be. And yet... Unless he was mistaken, there—limping in pain, wincing in humiliation, and scrambling to retrieve the wimple—stood young Archibald of Laichloan.

Blade glanced back at Wilham, baffled. But Wilham was already grinning like a smug halfwit.

"'Tis him, isn't it?" Wilham whispered.

"What in the name o'...?"

"I thought that face looked familiar."

"But why would he...? How...?"

"Let's go find out," Wilham suggested.

Blade agreed. Whatever was going on, the victim was now in sight. They might not know who planned to kill him, but they could keep him from being killed.

By the time they made their way to the imposters, Mary, done with her mayhem, stood in icy silence, while Archibald was still trying to repair his wimple.

Blade snagged the lad by his elbow, while Wilham offered his arm to Mary, and the four of them retreated to a dark corner of the cathedral.

Archibald might have suffered Mary's attack, but he was having none of Blade's authority.

"What's the meanin' o' this?" the lad hissed, pulling his arm out of Blade's grip.

"We know who ye are, Archie," Blade confided.

The lad pouted, then turned to sneer at Mary. "Ye've ruined everythin'."

"Ye're in danger, lad," Blade confided. "We're here to keep ye safe."

"Danger?" Panic widened his eyes. "What kind o' danger? Is my father here?"

Blade intended to tell the lad there were assassins after him, but he didn't know if he could trust Mary. "Who is she?" he said, nodding to the lass.

Archibald threw her a withering glare. "Nobody."

Mary took offense at that and punched his shoulder.

Blade had to make Archibald understand. "Heed me well, lad. Someone's plottin' against ye. I heard them at The Black Hound the night before we left."

The lad stuck out his lower lip. "Everyone's plottin' against me." Then he narrowed his eyes at Blade. "I know ye, don't I? Ye're him—the one that killed his brother's wife."

Blade stiffened, and Wilham took over, seizing the lad by the front of his habit.

"Look, Archie, we have reason to believe there are assassins after ye."

Wilham's whisper proved too loud, and the people in front of him hissed at him to be quiet.

"Assassins?" Archibald squeaked. "But he can't be that angry."

"Who?" Blade asked, his hand going to the pommel of his sword.

"My father."

Blade and Wilham exchanged glances.

Wilham spoke. "Why would your father be angry with ye?"

Blade took a guess. "Ye ran away from home."

"What?" Wilham exploded.

The crowd scowled and hushed Wilham again.

"Didn't ye?" Blade asked.

"Maybe," the lad conceded.

"Why?"

Mary answered for him, glaring scornfully at Archibald. "He said we was goin' to get married. He said he loved me. He said everythin' would be rosy when we got to St. Andrews. But 'tisn't rosy, is it, Archie?"

The hair stiffened at the back of Blade's neck as he recalled the exact words he'd overheard at The Black Hound. "Ye promised her that when ye got to St. Andrews, Archibald o' Laichloan would be *dead* and *forgotten*."

"Aye," Mary replied with a sniff.

Blade sighed heavily, then grimaced and rubbed at the furrow between his brows.

Wilham threw up his hands. "God's eyes." As the crowd turned on him again with scowls of disapproval, he crossed himself, adding, "Are upon us all."

Blade arched a brow at the runaway lad. "Let me see if I understand. Ye ran away with..." He gestured to Mary, who straightened proudly.

"I'm the miller's daughter."

"The miller's daughter," Blade repeated.

Archibald thrust out his chin. "I won't be a pawn in my father's game o' chess. No one can tell me who I can and cannot wed."

Blade's jaw tightened as his patience wore thin. "So ye ran away together. And now?"

The lad shrugged. "I've had a change o' heart."

Mary sobbed once and punched him again in the shoulder.

Wilham shook his head. "So there are no assassins?" he asked.

"Apparently not," Blade replied, "unless you count the miller, who will likely want to kill him."

The lad scowled. "I won't go back. Ye can't make me—"

"Oh, ye'll go back," Wilham assured him, "at the point o' my sword, if need be."

Blade felt like a dolt. He'd been gulled by a child. There'd never been an assassination plot. Dead and forgotten indeed. The upstart lad had simply run away from home.

'Twould doubtless prove an entertaining tale for supper. Rose would especially appreciate how a pair of nuns had fooled two seasoned knights.

Where was Rose anyway? He skimmed over the landscape of faces again, searching for her familiar countenance. Some movement at the door caught his eye—something flitting along the stones amongst the cripples and blind beggars—and all at once the world seemed to tilt on its axis.

Wink.

And she was alone.

Rose should have known.

Of course, Gawter would realize she'd gone to St. Andrews. 'Twas practically her home. But since she hadn't intended to return to Fernie House straightaway, she'd believed herself safe from him.

Her mistake was in forgetting the four men-at-arms he'd sent to follow the pilgrims, waiting for an opportunity to abduct her. There was only one place such a pilgrimage could end up. All Gawter had to do was ride swiftly to St. Andrews and wait.

Which he had.

And now he dragged her forcibly along the deserted streets, his face a mask of victorious fury. He'd snatched her so quickly, so unexpectedly within the sanctuary that she'd had no time to cry out. Once outside, when she'd recognized his sneering grin, she'd tried to shriek, but he'd muted her cries with a suffocating glove. Even then, she kicked and fought him, biting into his hand hard enough to pinch the flesh. But he was strong, and he lugged her down the lane with no more trouble than a falcon carrying off a struggling mouse.

The few indigent souls hobbling along the streets might have glanced briefly at the spectacle, but they knew better than to interfere with a nobleman. They cringed in reverence and scurried off like beetles.

"I warned ye, my bride," Gawter snarled as he jerked her along. "I warned ye what would happen."

Where he was taking her, she didn't know. But she sensed that spot would mark her grave. They turned down lane after lane, each passageway becoming narrower than the last, the shops leaning closer and closer above like gathering crows watching their every move. The fog curled along the damp streets, disguising their passage, deadening their footfalls, and her one frail hope—that Blade would come for her—gradually evaporated like mist in sunlight.

Finally Gawter found what he desired—a dark, dismal corner between two slumping shops that looked to be abandoned. He hurled her forward toward a pile of moldering refuse. She stumbled to her hands and knees, gagging on the stench, and a pair of startled mice scuttled off along the wall.

The mice reminded her all at once of Wink. For one horrible moment, panic gripped her. What would become of her falcon? The bird was half-blind and crippled and lost among all those people within the sanctuary, people who might trample her in their carelessness.

Then she forced her racing pulse to calm. Wink would elude the crowd. Just as she'd eluded the wolves. Just as she'd eluded death. What had Rose told Blade? That she and Wink were survivors.

Her heart fortified, Rose staggered to her feet and faced her foe bravely. She wouldn't beg for her life. She wouldn't give him the satisfaction. But neither would she make it easy for him.

"My foster parents will find ye," she told him. "And when they do, your life will be forfeit."

"Hardly. Ye're my betrothed, my...chattel. I may do with ye as I like." He leered, adjusting his gloves. He studied her for a moment, then arched a brow and chuckled low in surprise. "Oh, dear. Did ye think I meant to kill ye?"

Rose swallowed. If he didn't mean to kill her, why had he dragged her to this deserted corner?

"Oh, nae, my darlin' Rose," he told her, his silky voice at odds with his sinister bearing. "'Tis not so dire as that. Ye see, Averlaigh still lacks an heir, which ye'll kindly provide." He surveyed the rotting shops, the pile of offal, the dank ground, taking a deep breath as if he relished the odor. "What do ye think? 'Tis an idyllic spot to spawn."

Rose shuddered. Never. Never would she let him sully the beautiful memory she had of Blade. Never would she let him pollute the perfection of their union. "Ne'er."

"I thought ye might play the blushin' virgin," he sighed. "But I suspect 'tis a farce. My spies kept a close watch on ye and your lover."

"Your spies lie rottin' in the woods."

She saw the rage simmer behind his eyes, but he clenched his teeth against the urge to bite at her bait.

"Your champion was careless. He left a survivor who confirmed where ye were headed," he sneered, "and on whose arm."

"Then ye know I'll ne'er submit to ye."

"Oh, but ye will," he assured her. "Didn't your mother tell ye? I'm a master o' seduction."

He tightened the glove on his hand, flexed his fingers, and before she could grasp his intent, drove his fist forward into the tender flesh of her cheek.

She fell backward, cutting her hand and bruising her hip. Splinters of pain radiated from her cheek as the cut reopened, and her vision swam in a watery blur.

No one was going to save her, she realized. No one would witness his crime. No one would hear her screams.

But she vowed she'd die before he could infect her with his seed.

The beggar lifted a scabbed finger toward the dingy lane, and Blade tossed him a coin. Blade—his chest heaving with the exertion of his harried search—had to use stealth now. He was close to his quarry.

Like a slinking wolf, he slipped along the passage, his pulse throbbing, his ears straining. Then he heard voices from around the next bend.

Cautiously easing around the shop on the corner and peering down the lane, he saw the flash of a blood-red tabard a moment before he heard the dull thud of fist hitting flesh. For an instant, the sound paralyzed him. How many nights at Mirkhaugh had he slept with his hands pressed to his ears, trying in vain to shut out that grotesque sound?

But then the memory of Rose—young and innocent and sweet—assailed him. The vision brought him to his senses like a sobering slap, freeing his frozen limbs.

Rage outweighed caution. He charged forward with a roar, unsheathing as he came, his blood seething.

"To me, sirrah!" he shouted.

The man wheeled about lazily, and his voice dripped with sarcasm. "Ah, your hero has arrived, my darlin'."

"Draw your steel!" Blade commanded, advancing.

He couldn't bear to look at his fallen Rose for fear that what he saw might unman him. But from the corner of his eye, he saw her move. Thank God, she was still alive.

"I don't think so," the man said with mocking calm.

Blade continued his charge anyway, halting only when the point of his sword met the man's pale throat. The villain—curly-locked and fair, dimpled and rosy-cheeked—had the sweet face of a lad. But his eyes gleamed with debauchery, the same corruption that had infested his brother's gaze.

"Draw your sword," Blade warned him, "or I'll kill ye where ye stand."

The man's brows lifted in faux innocence. "And for what offense would ye murder me?"

He narrowed his eyes. "Maybe I'll murder ye simply for the pleasure of it."

"Why, then they'll hang ye, good sir, from Gallow's Hill. Ye cannot kill a woman's husband just for the sport..." He halted mid-sentence with a gasp of feigned shock.

Blade froze. His shock was not feigned. Husband. Had the villain said husband? His thoughts roiled wildly while his heart careened in his chest.

The churl clucked his tongue and spoke over his shoulder. "Why, darlin', didn't ye tell him? 'Tis half the thrill, ye know, tellin' your lover about your jealous husband."

Blade tried to ignore the storm of emotions coursing through him—pain, betrayal, fury, sorrow—but 'twas too late. The armor around his heart had already been pierced by Rose's love. And now it weakened with each traitorous word.

Rose's silence condemned her and crushed him.

"Well, I'm sure ye'll find another sweet thing to warm your bed," the man said, fluttering his fingers in farewell. "Run along now. 'Tis none o' your affair."

Numb, Blade lowered his sword, and the man bent to haul Rose to her feet. Blade glanced at her only briefly, long enough to glimpse the blood on her cheek and the regret in her eyes.

"I'm sorry," she whispered. "I couldn't tell ye."

Blade tensed his jaw, wanting to believe her. But he couldn't afford to trust her. He'd made that mistake before—coming between husband and wife.

He'd been wrong about Rose. She was a weak woman, just like Julian. Just like Julian, she'd weep and wail that her husband was cruel, and just like Julian, she'd betray the man willing to champion her against him.

No more, he decided. Chivalry had taught him to defend the helpless, but experience had taught him the price of meddling.

Yet when he turned in defeat to leave, something troubled him, compelling him to stay.

Rose had been a virgin. This knave might be her husband, but if he was, 'twas in name only, for he'd never consummated the marriage. And Rose had insisted all along the pilgrimage that she traveled to St. Andrews to take the veil. So she'd obviously fled this man to seek sanctuary in a convent. Her avowed husband had sent his guard after her, giving them free reign to use her as they willed. The man clearly bore her no love, and she surely despised him.

And though Blade might prove as witless as a lad thrice burnt by fire, he grasped at those thin slivers of truth.

Maybe Rose wasn't like Julian after all. Maybe she wouldn't shield her abuser. Maybe she wouldn't betray Blade.

His back still turned, he closed his eyes. "I would hear it from your own lips, Rose. I would hear that ye're willin' to return to your husband, to share his bed, to bear his heirs."

He waited for her "aye," but it never came. Instead, while he languished in uncertainty, she bit out slowly and distinctly, "I'd rather burn in Hell."

No words had ever gladdened his heart so fully. No words had ever inspired him to battle so quickly. With a determined flourish of his sword, Blade spun around to face his enemy and defend his love.

Before Rose could take another breath, Gawter cursed, pushing her aside to draw his weapon. Having learned from her encounter with the thieves, she quickly scurried out of sword's reach.

At first the men circled, each judging the other's skill. Gawter thrust forward. Blade deflected his sword and jabbed back. Gawter knocked the blade aside.

Then Gawter made a quick advance forward, pushing Blade back with rapid slashes. Blade whirled and came around with a broad sweep of his sword, forcing Gawter to leap back. Then Blade drove forward, hacking mercilessly. Gawter retreated, dancing along the wet stones.

Blade had a clear advantage until his foot slipped on a patch of damp moss and he nearly lost his balance. Gawter used the opportunity to aim a long thrust forward. Blade was forced to use his arm to toss aside the blow, and in the absence of proper armor, his doublet was slashed through to his skin.

Rose winced, but Blade was hardly hampered by the injury. He answered with a vengeance, sparks showering as his sword rasped along Gawter's blade. Gawter skittered back again, and Blade followed him, forcing him to engage his weapon.

The swords clashed and clanged with a clamor to rival the bells of St. Andrews. Blade sliced through Gawter's cote-hardie at the waist, drawing blood. But Gawter was no untried swordsman, and when Blade's shoulder dipped as his next thrust fell short, he advanced, nicking Blade's throat.

Rose gasped as Blade fell back, raising a thumb to his neck that came back bloody. Then, snarling like a wolf, Blade circled his quarry, watching for a weakness.

Gawter wiped the moisture from his brow with his sleeve, attempting to cover his anxiety by cockily tossing his sword from one hand to the other.

But Blade wasn't intimidated. Indeed, he must have thought Gawter a fool, for he simply waited until the weapon was in midair, then, with a flick of his sword, sent it sailing across the lane to clatter against a crumbling wall.

Relieved of his sword, Gawter swore and reached for his dagger.

To Rose's utter amazement, Blade chivalrously tossed aside his sword and drew his own dagger. This was no mercenary, not at all. No matter how much he denied his honor, it burned there within him, a luminous gallantry that no single foul deed nor years of exile could extinguish. Her heart warmed with pride.

The combat was just as fierce with lesser weapons. They nicked and slashed and jabbed each other until their fighting hands were slick with blood. Gawter's combat became desperate, frenzied. But Blade had the advantage of having engaged in brutal warfare outside of the lists. He threatened and cuffed and distracted Gawter with taunts of his dagger until Gawter began to dodge blows that Blade never struck and thrust his knife through empty air.

Blade finally cornered his frustrated foe against the mound of refuse and kicked the knife from his hand so that it skidded across the lane. Then he planted his boot in the middle of Gawter's belly and shoved him backward. Gawter stumbled, tripped, and went sprawling on his hindquarters atop a heap of broken pottery and rotten vegetables.

Rose sighed in relief. Gawter was disarmed. He was harmless now.

She didn't worry that he might speak to the authorities, that he'd have Blade arrested. He had too much pride for that. He'd not breathe a word of his defeat at the hands of a felon. And now, all she wanted was to go to Blade, to her champion.

Blade sheathed his knife and started to turn to her, but behind him, Rose saw a glimmer of life from Gawter. The brute wasn't as defeated as he appeared. As she screamed in warning, Gawter lunged up, a shard of pottery in one fist, and stabbed forward.

Blade was uncertain at first whether 'twas fresh pain or the haunting sting of old wounds as his back twinged. Rose's shriek seemed part of the slash, slicing through the air as sleekly as the point sinking into his flesh.

It hurt like the devil, but didn't go deep. His padded doublet and his scar, thick and knotted, prevented that.

Still, time froze, and his mind spiraled back again, back to the events of that fateful day. His body yearned to repeat what it had practiced over and over in his nightmares—turn and thrust, turn and thrust—but he'd tossed aside his sword, and he'd sheathed his dagger. The pain began to spread like numbing poison across his back. Stunned, he swayed on his feet and gazed down helplessly at his empty hands.

Then, behind him, the man screamed. Like the breaking of an enchantment, the sound severed Blade's tie with the past, hauling him out of his shock and bringing him to his senses.

His eyes burned as he reached behind him and plucked the shard from his back, then turned with clenched fists to face the churl who'd stabbed him.

But the breath escaped him when he saw the man staggering backward into the pile of garbage, his face a rictus of horror and disbelief, his fingers scrabbling at the sword protruding from his belly.

Rose stood over the brute like a beautiful avenging angel. Her eyes were alight with righteous fire, her cheeks were flushed, and her chest was heaving.

Blade stared at her in wonder. Sweet Saints, she'd come to his defense. She'd managed to sweep up his sword to deliver a killing thrust to his attacker. His heart swelled with gratitude and admiration.

Then she turned a shocked gaze to him, and he realized the impact of what she'd done. Rose wasn't a battle-seasoned knight accustomed to killing. She was a gentle lady. Her deed would scar her for the rest of her life.

As if to insure her suffering, the man whimpered, "Rose, ye killed me."

Her brows furrowed, and Blade spit out an oath, cursing the man for his cruelty. Then he stepped forward and seized the haft of his sword.

"Nay, *I* killed ye," he said, wrenching the blade from his belly and thrusting it again into the man's black heart.

Rose sat on a broken barrel, trembling with the shock of all that had passed. Never had she imagined herself capable of such bloodlust. Blade had been kind to make the killing blow, to take the sin of murder upon himself. But that didn't change the fact that she'd wished Gawter dead with all her heart. And her own savagery frightened her.

Blade gave him a hasty burial beneath the mound of refuse— a fitting grave, Rose thought, for the brutish swine. When he was done, he came to crouch at her feet, took her quivering hands between his own, and began to question her.

She answered woodenly, hardly knowing what she said, telling him that nae, Gawter had neither kin nor keep, that he'd wanted to marry Rose for her holdings. Nae, she didn't know where Greymoor was. Aye, they'd planned to live at Averlaigh. Nae, her foster parents didn't know she was here.

After his interrogation, they fled the scene like two bloody soldiers traveling home from war, winding their way back to the cathedral in pensive silence.

But now that her shock had passed, now that she began to think about the consequences of her actions, she felt as if a yoke had suddenly been lifted from her. Her betrothed was dead. No longer did the decision of wedding or taking the veil hang over her head. She was free to follow her heart.

Now she could run away with Blade. They could find a place far from Averlaigh and Mirkhaugh and St. Andrews, far from the ghosts of their past. They could make a new beginning...follow a new dream...together.

They reached the door of the sanctuary, and Rose stopped Blade, gazing up into his somber eyes with hope. But before she could share her dream, Blade spoke.

"Father Peter can see ye safely to the convent."

Her heart caught. "The convent?"

"Mass will be o'er shortly, and—"

"But I..." She flushed, ashamed of having deceived him. "I never wanted to go to the convent." She twisted her fingers together. How could she explain? "'Twas for sanctuary." She averted her eyes, mortified by the appalling truth. "Ye see, my betrothed was...he was beddin' my mother. He only wanted heirs o' me because my mother is barren." She shook her head. "I couldn't tell ye before."

His answer, long in coming and strangely solemn, made her wary. "Ye deserve better."

She gave him a shaky, uncertain smile. "I've found better."

When he didn't respond, her heart flopped over. She nervously licked her lips, and tears stung at the back of her eyes. Did he not mean to ask for her hand? She was free now. And they were in love. She knew they were. Could he possibly mean to leave her?

His voice was gruff, and he wouldn't meet her eyes. "Nae. Ye deserve a man with a home, with a name."

She swallowed, silently cursing the waver in her voice. "Your home is Scotland. Your name is Blade. 'Tis enough for me."

He sniffed. "Ye're young. Ye don't know what 'tis like to wander endlessly, to wonder when your next meal will be, to subsist on what ye can carry on your back. 'Tis no way for a lady to live."

The tears welled thickly now, and Rose felt her chest collapse so that she could hardly draw breath. "I told ye. I'm...a survivor."

Blade's heart felt like it was being squeezed through an apple press. Speaking about his life—the struggle for subsistence, the unpredictability, the loneliness of the road—made him realize how miserable he was. And looking upon Rose's tearful face, her imploring eyes, her trembling lips, made him aware of all he intended to sacrifice for that life.

Was it worth it? Was it worth avoiding the pain of returning to Mirkhaugh to continue living as a felon if it meant he could never have the one thing in his life that was good and beautiful and pure? And what if Mirkhaugh denied him? What if he was stripped of his title in earnest, banished from his home forever, executed for his felony?

Nae, 'twas too great a risk. Better that he should always wonder if his kin still despised him than return to the site of his crime and remove all doubt.

And better that Rose should find another—a worthy man who could give her all the happiness and stability she deserved, who could assure her of a long and comfortable life. He'd tell her so...gently.

But before he could breathe a word, she shoved at his chest, snarling viciously at him. "Damn ye to Hell, Blade!"

He cast a wary eye up toward the spires of St. Andrews. It took an intrepid soul to curse on the steps of the holy cathedral.

She stabbed an angry finger at his doublet. "I know ye care for me. Are ye so bloody fond o' your fugitive ways that ye'd not abandon them for my sake?"

A tiny voice deep inside him was bellowing the very same thing. A tiny voice that sounded curiously like Wilham. Maybe he *was* addled. Maybe he was a bloody, raving madman. Maybe his redemption *was* to be found in St. Andrews. Not within the holy sanctuary, but in the absolving angel before him.

For now he walked along a dagger's edge, knowing he must leap one way or the other. On one side of the knife was Rose—beautiful, precious Rose, with eyes the color of a quenching stream, lips that tasted of spring, arms that comforted and aroused and tamed him. And on the other side was...

Slow, agonizing death.

There was no choice. The answer stood before him, frowning in wounded frustration, trying to conceal her pain behind a mask of rage. Curse his soul, he'd hurt her enough.

"Rosamund," he decided, taking her gently by the shoulders, "go to the nunnery." She bit her lip and was on the verge of furious tears when he cupped her face in one hand and said, "Wait for me there. If I'm able, I'll come for ye by Lammastide."

The wind abruptly went out of the sails of her anger, leaving her blinking in confusion. She searched his eyes. "Ye will?"

"If I'm able," he repeated. The odds were against him. He knew that. But if he didn't try...

"Lammastide?" she croaked. Three months probably sounded like an eternity to Rose.

"If I don't return..."

"Ye will," she said, smiling now through her tears. "I *know* ye will."

He swallowed hard. Her innocent faith was hard to endure. "If I'm not back by Lammas...then take a husband or take the veil."

For Rose, three months passed on the back of a snail. One day was much the same as the next at the convent—nuns in drab habits murmuring along the passageways, gathering for the sumptuous Sabbath meal of ubiquitous bread and broth, prostrating themselves before the altar, not so much to worship, Rose suspected, but to sleep after rising at such an unholy hour.

The only interruption in the dull routine was when her foster parents visited. They brought news of her stepfather's death and her betrothed's mysterious disappearance, which had thrown Rose's mother into a rage. Rose was relieved that Gawter's body hadn't been found, and apparently, a neighboring nobleman had made an offer on Averlaigh, so Rose's mother, deeply in debt and furious with Rose's decision to join a religious order, had sold her property and moved herself into a modest home in Stirling.

But none of that concerned Rose. What consumed her was the fact that today was the first of Lammastide, and Blade hadn't yet appeared.

Visitors had stopped by the nunnery all day long, bringing Lammas offerings of bread and coin for the poor. Rose had stationed herself at the convent gate to watch them come and go, biting her thumbnail and searching their ranks for the face she dreamt about each night. Still he hadn't appeared.

Now she paced back and forth through the nunnery's herb garden with Wink on her arm, unable to resist glancing frequently toward the western road, where the sun continued, against her wishes, to sink lower and lower in the sky.

"Ye'll see, Wink," she said with forced cheer, smoothing the feathers over the falcon's breast with nervous fingers. "He'll come."

Wink ruffled her feathers, which had grown back nicely, all but a tiny patch over her blind eye. The bird no longer wore the bandage around her wing. Thanks to the healing skills of one of the nuns, the bone had fused. But Wink couldn't fly.

As for Rose, the nuns had welcomed her, though 'twas clear from the start they didn't approve of her intrepid ways. In their minds, 'twas reckless to hoist oneself onto the lower limb of the apple tree to pick fruit. Rose wondered what the nuns would think if they knew she'd scaled towers and battled thieves.

As always, Rose bobbed her arm for Wink, encouraging her to flap. She might not be able to fly, but the bird needed to stretch her wings, for she would founder without exercise.

Rose's gaze drifted inexorably back to the west. The sun was but an inch from the top of the hills now. She let out a quivery sigh.

"'Tisn't so bad here, is it, Wink?" Her voice cracked. "'Tis...peaceful. Ye have a place in the mews with Sister Mildred's kestrels, and I have a warm bed. Sister Beatrice keeps hens, so there are plenty of eggs for ye. And I can do just fine on barley broth and oatcakes."

Three-quarters of an inch.

She gulped. "I won't have to pray *all* the time. Sister Margaret says even when I'm no longer a novice, I'll still have an hour or two free in the afternoons. We can stroll through the garden or go down to the sea. Does that sound good to ye?"

Half an inch.

Tears burned in her eyes. She'd been so certain he'd come. So sure that he'd keep his promise.

Now she could see she'd been a fool. He'd never meant to return. He'd only made that vow so she wouldn't make a fuss about his leaving.

Lady Rosamund of Averlaigh was going to become a nun. She'd already decided against taking a husband. She couldn't possibly love another the way she had Blade.

She clamped her jaw to still its trembling. Tomorrow she'd take the veil. And from that day forth, she'd be a bride of the church. Thereafter, the days would be woven together like threads on a loom, one into the next, their pattern never changing, until the cloth of her life was complete. Aye, she'd be a nun...a whispering, wan, withered old nun to the end of her days.

Wink's talons flexed suddenly on Rose's glove, and she frowned at the bird. But before Rose could prevent the wayward beast, Wink coiled and sprang off of her arm, flapping her wings furiously.

Rose cried out in dismay. She should have leashed the poor falcon. Wink couldn't fly. Not properly. The reckless bird would get herself killed.

Then Rose looked aloft and slowly lowered her arm in disbelief. Wink wasn't falling. She wasn't even faltering. Indeed, she was flying as well as she ever had, high into the heavens, far from the mundane world, wild and joyful and free.

"Wink!" A tear spilled from Rose's eye as she smiled up at her precious pet. "Oh, Wink!"

Wink circled the old chapel closely at first, cocking her head this way and that, gradually widening the spheres until her flight encompassed the walls of the nunnery. Then, while Rose watched with mixed emotions, she soared off, away from Rose, away from St. Andrews, toward the setting sun.

'Twas best this way, she supposed. If Rose couldn't be free, at least Wink deserved to be. Still, her eyes flooded with tears as she watched her precious falcon diminish in the western sky.

Rose's eyes were so blurred by tears that at first she didn't see the horsemen descending the far west hillock. Even after she noticed them, she forced her racing heart to calm, bracing herself against false hope.

'Twasn't Blade, she chided herself. There were dozens of them. 'Twas hardly a man coming to claim his bride. Two score, nae, three score knights crested the rise, a veritable army. They were likely a contingent of soldiers stopping in St. Andrews on their march to Edinburgh, then on to the Borders to fight the English.

Still her foolish heart pounded, and she wiped her eyes to better see who approached with such royal bearing.

Yet more soldiers poured over the rise, and she shielded her eyes, squinting against the setting sun to catch a glimpse of the noble knight who rode at their fore.

The lead rider stopped all at once, and Rose's breath caught. High above him, her wayward bird wheeled and soared in her own heaven, oblivious to the army of dangerous knights below. Then the great knight suddenly raised his gloved hand, and to Rose's amazement, Wink dove and fluttered down, landing neatly atop the man's wrist.

"Blade." Her lips moved, but no sound came out. Her throat was too thick with tears.

Mother Ellen would have scolded her soundly for picking up her skirts, clambering over the garden wall, and tearing off across the countryside like a heathen. But Rose didn't care.

Her beloved felon had arrived as he'd promised—his honor restored, his heart healed, and his arms wide open—and Rose felt as free as a falcon.

# Epilogue

No pilgrim's tale could be complete without a final accounting of the personages who shared the journey.

Because 'twas his last pilgrimage, Father Peter set in his own hand the account of what befell the company afterward. Since the beloved priest, God rest him, was long of wind and short on truth, I have taken the liberty of making brief what was once unwieldy, and—may the Lord pardon me—strained what truth I could from his elaborate history.

The Father settled peacefully within the walls of a monastery near St. Andrews, where he spent as many hours regaling wide-eyed novices with his adventures as he did in prayer.

Simon the palmer continued to make a lucrative, if brief, business of traveling on pilgrimage and selling relics. Within a year, the old palmer contracted a wasting sickness and died. As a matter of note, his bones were later exhumed and sold by another enterprising palmer as those of Saint Swithin.

Drogo the cook and Fulk the butcher, having learned something of the value of a good wife, made their amends at St. Andrews and returned to their respective homes, where they were showered with greetings from their pining women, who had learned the value of a good husband. They eventually ended up in the employ of the same laird, where the resplendent feast they prepared for visiting royalty in 1406 became the stuff of legend.

Jacob the goldsmith returned home to discover that his wife had run off with his apprentice. Hoping for consolation, he sent Brigit the widow a costly jeweled girdle, inquiring if she might consider renewing their acquaintance.

Brigit, in a pique of ire over Jacob's philandering ways, and having successfully caught the eye of a brawny cooper with nine children, no wife, and an appetite for good beer, thought it a grand jest to send the thing to Lettie.

Lettie, meanwhile, greatly influenced by her visit to the holy cathedral at St. Andrews, had repented of her lustful ways and her wandering eye. When she returned home, 'twas to renew her vows to her husband and become a dutiful wife. Thus, upon receipt of the goldsmith's trinket, she had it melted down and made into a belt of gold links for her husband.

The tanners, Ivo and Odo, continued much as they had since they were young lads, drinking and making merry till they grew old and their hides were as tough as their wares.

Ian Campbell the soldier found at long last the redemption he sought at St. Andrews, just as Rose foretold. Standing before the holy shrine, he received a vision that told him to go forth unto all the lands where he'd slaughtered the innocent and make repair. So, buckling on his armor, and with the lad Guillot as his squire, he became a knight-errant, rescuing damsels, aiding the poor, and righting wrong wherever he could. Eventually he became known as Ian the Good.

Tildy, intimidated by the variety and quality of woven goods available at St. Andrews, reported to her Highland kinsmen instead that the Lowland woolens there were far inferior, and they'd do well to make their purchases on northern soil.

While in St. Andrews, the three scholars, Thomas, Bryan, and Daniel, made the acquaintance of a trio of sisters, daughters of a Master of Logic who was hoping to help form the first university in Scotland. The lads and lasses fell hopelessly in love, if one may consider a lifelong passionate debate between six persons of fiercely independent opinion, love.

Mary, the miller's daughter who disguised herself as a nun, decided, after a sound thrashing by her father and a stern lecture from her mother, 'twas best to avoid entanglements with the nobility. She took over the inn when her parents grew feeble with age, feeding and lodging and cleaning up after the nobles who passed by, but never again did she let her heart become ensnared by their ilk.

Ivy—Archibald of Laichloan—was accompanied home by Wilham, who afforded the boy no comfort along the way. Indeed, he threatened to make the lad wear his nun's habit all the way to the gates of Laichloan and only spared him when the boy burst into tears at the thought. Laird John was suitably relieved at his heir's return, Wilham was handsomely rewarded, and once Archibald laid eyes on his breathtakingly lovely fifteen-year-old betrothed, he wondered what madness had driven him to take up with the miller's daughter.

Wilham's reward was the property of Averlaigh, which he'd purchased from Rose's mother with the coin he'd earned for the return of Archibald. True to Blade's predictions, a bevy of willing lasses awaited Wilham's return, and 'twasn't long before he chose from among them a flower of uncommon grace and kindness who believed the sun rose and set upon his shoulder and laughed in delight at his every jest.

And as for Pierce and Rosamund of Mirkhaugh, they lived a long and happy life filled with adventure and romance. Their mews became renowned for its fine strain of kestrels, many of them the progeny of Wink, and the hills surrounding Mirkhaugh were never without some stray child with black locks and skinned elbows, climbing trees, flying falcons, and getting into mischief. Somehow the precious whelps all managed to make it home at day's end whenever their father's friend Wilham came to visit, for he never tired of regaling them with lusty tales of adventure. They listened eagerly as he recounted the tournament where their father had jousted with the de Wares and told the story about their mother taming a bear in St. Andrews.

But their favorite tale, the one he never tired of telling, was always the legend of how their mother and father met, battled thieves, survived a kidnapping, prevented a murder, and fell in love—the romance of Blade and his Rose.

**Excerpt from NATIVE GOLD by Glynnis Campbell**
*Book 1 of the Native West Trilogy*

California, 1850

$S$akote had to return to the waterfall. As much as he wanted to put the white woman out of his thoughts, along with the place where she'd stolen his senses, he had to go back. The hunting pouch was a gift from his father, and the tools in it—the snares, the knives, the mountain hemp line—would take days to replace.

So with a pouch of dried deer meat and a promise to his mother that he'd bring back woodpecker feathers for her husband's wahiete—his crown, Sakote set off for the waterfall.

The pouch was where he'd left it, beside the great boulder. But still his eyes searched the wet banks of the pool, looking for some sign of the woman who'd come here. There was nothing. She'd left behind no scrap of cloth, no scent, not even a footprint.

But that didn't mean her spirit was gone. She lived here still, in the rush of water over the stones, so like her laughter, in the green depth of the pool, like her eyes, and in the heat of the sun upon his shoulder, reminding him of the warmth of her arms around him.

"Damn!" There were no words of anger in Sakote's language, so he borrowed the curse from the white man.

It didn't matter what the elders said, what the dream tried to tell him. He must follow the old ways, the ways of the Konkow, or they would be lost. The white woman showed him another path, a dangerous path, a path he must not take.

The sun continued to blaze upon his back, and he knew a quick swim in the pond would cool his blood and his anger. He took off his moccasins, freed his hair, and loosened the thong around his breechcloth, letting it fall to the ground. Climbing to the crest of the boulder, he took a full breath and dove into the shimmering midst of the pool.

The bracing water sizzled over his skin as he plunged deep through the waves. The cool current swept past his body, swirling his hair like the long underwater moss, washing away his thoughts.

He broke the surface and shook his hair back, then swam for the waterfall. It pounded the black rock like the *kilemi,* the great sycamore log drum the Konkow danced to, and made a mist that hid the small cave behind the fall. He climbed out onto the slippery ledge and stood up, easing forward into the path of the fall to let it pummel him with punishing force, driving white spears into his bent back and shoulders. But it also awakened his body and challenged him. He slowly raised his head, braced his feet, reached toward the sky with outstretched arms, and withstood the heavy fall of water with a triumphant smile.

Unfortunately, the loud thunder of the fall prevented him from hearing that he was no longer alone at the pool.

Mattie's jaw dropped. Her breath caught.

She'd memorized the way to the waterfall, and after sketching miners all morning, decided to make a few drawings of the pool. If she'd hoped that the Indian might return there, she knew it was a foolish hope. The fact that he had indeed come back, and in such bold display, couldn't have amazed her more.

What in God's name was he doing? The Indian stood at the foot of the waterfall, as naked as the day he was born, letting the water beat him within an inch of his life and grinning all the while.

She thought to yell out to him, to reprimand him for such indecent behavior, such outrageous liberties, such flagrant...but then the artist came out in her. She realized that what she beheld was beautiful, that *he* was beautiful. It was as if she witnessed the birth of a god.

Stealthily, she perched on a rock wedged between two trees, hoping the lush foliage and her drab plaid dress helped to conceal her. She found an empty page and set to work sketching.

He couldn't remain there long, she knew, or else he'd be pounded into the rock. She had to work quickly, penciling in the bare bones and trusting the rest to memory.

Sure enough, just as she finished the roughest of renderings, he brought his arms down through the fall like great white wings and dove into the middle of the pool.

His naked body slicing through the water sent a rush of delicious fire through her. Her pencil hovered over the page. It was wrong, what she did, making pictures of him in his altogether without his knowledge. And yet, she thought, patting a cheek grown hot with impropriety, it felt so right.

He bobbed up and flung his hair back, spraying droplets of water across the rippling surface.

Mattie pressed her pencil against her lower lip.

He swam forward, sluicing through the water as smoothly as a trout. Then he wheeled over onto his back and floated on the surface, boldly facing the midday sun like some pagan sacrifice.

Mattie's teeth sank into the pencil.

She could see everything—the naked sprawl of his limbs, the corona of his long ebony hair, the dark patch at the juncture of his thighs, and its manly treasure, set like a jewel on black velvet.

He was Adam. Or Adonis. He was Icarus fallen from the sky. Hera cast into the sea. As innocent as an angel. As darkly beautiful as Lucifer.

Mattie blushed to the tips of her toes. She most definitely should not be witness to this...this...she had no word for his wanton display, but she was sure it was completely indecent. Still she couldn't tear her eyes away. He was utterly, irrefutably perfect. And looking at him left her faint with a mixture of emotions as dizzying as whiskey and as unstable as gunpowder.

With trembling fingers, Mattie slid the pencil from between her lips, flipped to a new page, and began to draw. Despite her rattled nerves, her hand seemed steady, for she captured every nuance of shade, every subtle contour, each flash of translucence, as if the water lived and moved upon the paper. And the man... He was so true to life that she half expected the figure to lazily pitch over and swim off the page.

A fern tickled her nose, and she brushed it back, then leaned forward to put the finishing touches on the portrait—a few more branches dabbling in the waves, a leaf floating by his head. She decided on the title, scribbling it at the bottom beside her signature.

Just in time. The Indian knifed under, a flash of strong tan buttocks and long legs, disappearing beneath the surface and into the green depths.

Sakote saw the movement of branches from the corner of his eye, but gave no indication. If it was a deer, he didn't want to frighten it from its drinking place. If it was a bear, his splashing would scare it soon enough. If it was a white man, he would have to be clever. He floated a moment more, letting the waves carry him gently toward the deepest part of the pool, watching for sudden movements through the dark lashes of his eyes. Then he gulped in a great breath and dove to the bottom, where the water was cold and shadowy.

He came up silently, on the concealed side of the big granite boulder, and eased his way out of the water and around the rock until he could see what hid in the brush.

Mati.

She wore another ugly brown dress with lines of other colors running through it like mistakes, and her hair was captured into a tight knot at the back of her head. She bit at her lower lip and leaned out dangerously far between two dogwood saplings, shielding her eyes with one hand, searching the pool.

Sakote didn't know what he felt. Joy. Or anger. Relief. Dread. Or desire.

She leaned forward even further, worry wrinkling her brow, and Sakote bit back a shout of warning as the saplings bent almost to the breaking point.

"Oh, no," she murmured.

The words were only a breath of a whisper on the breeze, but they carried to his ears like sad music. Mati edged between the two trees and took three slippery steps down the slope. Meanwhile, Sakote used the mask of noise to move in the opposite direction, up the rise. While she scanned the water, he crept behind her, stopping when he found the sketchbook on the ground, frowning when he saw the figure floating on the page.

Now he knew what he felt. Fury. He glanced down at his naked body, at his man's pride, shrunken with cold to the size of an acorn, then at its perfect duplicate drawn on the paper. And he felt as if he would explode with rage.

He must have made a sound, some strangled snarl of anger, for Mati turned. And screamed.

## About The Author

Born in Paradise, California, **Glynnis Campbell** has embraced her inner Gemini by leading an eclectic life. As a teen, she danced with the Sacramento Ballet, worked in her father's graphic arts studio, and composed music for award-winning science films. She sang arias in college, graduating with a degree in Music, then toured with The Pinups, an all-girl rock band on CBS Records. She once played drums for a Tom Jones video and is currently a voice-over actress with credits including "Star Wars" audio adventures, JumpStart educational CDs, Diablo and Starcraft video games, and the MTV animated series, "The Maxx." She now indulges her lifelong love of towering castles, trusty swords, and knights (and damsels) in shining armor by writing historical romances featuring kick-arse heroines. She is married to a rock star, is the proud mom of two grown-up nerds, and lives in a part of L.A. where nobody thinks she's weird.

Follow Glynnis on Facebook:
**https://www.facebook.com/glynnis.campbell**

Visit her website for all the latest news, and to sign up for Glynnis's newsletters and sweepstakes:
**http://www.glynnis.net**